A Boy on the Farm

A Boy On The Farm

A Nostalgic Novel

M. Wayne Clark

ISBN 978-1-938796-78-4 paperback
ISBN 978-938796-83-8 ebook

Library of Congress Control Number: 2020924626
Edited by Michele Chynoweth
Graphic Design by Candy Abbott
Cover Shutterstock 507237520

Published by Fruitbearer Publishing, LLC
P.O. Box 777 • Georgetown, DE 19947
302.856.6649 • FAX 302.856.7742
www.fruitbearer.com • info@fruitbearer.com

The characters in this story are all fictional and created by the author. Any resemblance to individuals living or deceased is purely coincidental.

Printed in the United States of America

Dedication

To my sisters and brothers and to the memory of our mother, whose love knitted us together as a family, thank you for your support and encouragement in life and in my writing.

I am also very grateful for my dear friend David Wendel's early readings of the manuscript. The suggestions he gave me were invaluable.

I also want to express my gratitude to Michele Chynoweth, my editor, who helped move *A Boy On The Farm* in the right direction.

This manuscript would have never become a book if it weren't for my publisher, Candy Abbott, whose faith in me and belief that what lies between these two covers is worth a read.

To all of you, I will say again, Thank you!

Introduction

Emily Dickenson wrote a poem that began, "Tell all the truth but tell it slant," and I recall her saying if you do this when writing narrative, "the results will dazzle you." Her words became for me the foundation for what follows in *A Boy On The Farm*.

As far back as I can remember, I wanted to write stories of a farm family and the relationships they had. Mother, father, brothers, sisters, and community are all connected in obvious and not-so-obvious ways. In farming communities today, this is less obvious than it was in the pre-1980s. If you have read my two previous books, you would know many of my stories are influenced by an agrarian way of life and the characters' faith-walks that come alive.

A Boy On The Farm invites you to tag along with a young farm boy as he tells his life stories through the eyes of his heart. I hope that the journey you take with your young guide will make you want to linger longer in his company when life moved at a simpler pace.

M. Wayne Clark

Contents

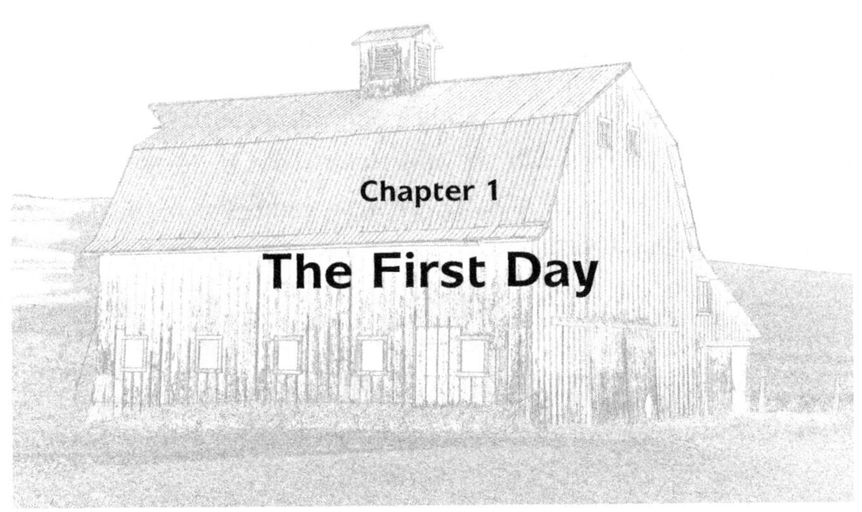

Chapter 1

The First Day

I wonder if Mrs. Maxine Kates, my Sunday School teacher at Spring Creek Methodist Episcopal Country Church on the gravel road two miles south of our farm, really understood that she didn't have it quite right. Maybe it was because the minister always came on Sunday, or because those who should know Luke and Matthew said Jesus walked out of the tomb on the day after the Jewish Sabbath, also a Sunday.

I'm not sure why they all had it wrong, but they did. I know for a fact that the first day of the week is not Sunday, but actually Monday! "How do you know that?" you ask. Monday is the first day of the week because on the third Monday in the month of August, from the beginning of Creation, school started. On that first Monday morning of the school year, a booming voice came from the bottom of the stairway, saying, "Victoria, Theodore, Ruby, it's time to get up! The bus is coming soon!"

I found out in later years that "soon" was a relative term; however, when you are eight years old, you heard the voice as a commanding one—the kind of voice I now imagine a drill sergeant uses on the recruits their first day in the Army, or a football coach uses in the locker room at half time when the team is six points behind. It was truly a no-nonsense voice.

At my age, I had no idea how a drill sergeant or football coach might sound, but I knew the voice I heard on Monday morning. It was a voice of authority, and I knew I had better respond to the call—or else.

The voice belonged to my mother. She was a short, slender, brown-haired, blue-eyed woman who all of my cub scout buddies would have thought was "hot" if the word had been in an eight-year-old's vocabulary in those days to describe one of their pal's mothers. As it was, they said with eyes wide open, "Your mom is sure pretty!" Well, that was okay for them to say, and it made me proud, but at seven a.m. on Monday morning, that voice coming up those stairs to our bedrooms was anything but pretty. It was the voice of business. I was almost always the first one down the stairs.

On early fall mornings, when Mother Nature started to lay her frost blanket down over the sprawling hillside that was our front yard, the living room stove was crackling with fresh firewood. While it was actually never a race between my sisters and me, I always tried my best to be the first one down the stairs. Slipping out of my pajamas, I quickly put on clean BVDs, jumped into my jeans, grabbed a shirt, socks, and shoes, and dashed down the stairs. My reserved spot behind the wood stove was where I carefully finished dressing. Fortunately, I was never burned. I will say more about this stove and its warmth on another day. For now, it is enough just to know when there was a red glow on the stove's backside, a person would feel pretty toasty standing behind it. The basic rule was to not linger longer than necessary, and that is one rule I did follow.

While I raced down the stairs, my younger sister, Ruby, dawdled. I guess at six years of age and just beginning school, a person has a reason to dawdle. In those early years during the winter months, Ruby and I slept in the same room, so I know from firsthand experience that she dawdled. While I was out of the room in a flash, Ruby would slowly rise out of bed, giggling, and then, clothed in her PJs and socks that she slept in all night to keep her feet warm, would thump down the stairs on her bottom.

Having been served a bowl of corn flakes or Cheerios covered in cow's milk, Ruby would leisurely munch away while our mother went upstairs to select Ruby's outfit for the day and then dress her after breakfast to make sure everything was put on right side out and her shoes were on the correct feet.

I would regret it if I didn't bother to tell you about my older sister, Victoria. Both Victoria and Ruby had our mother's good looks. At eleven going on twelve, Victoria, like most girls her age, primped. Even in sixth grade, Victoria was allowed to wear cancan slips to school. It wasn't until I became older and wiser about older sisters that I came to understand cancan slips and primping in the fifties and early sixties were part of a thing called a "rite of passage." I'll tell you more about cancans and primping later. What you need to know for now is that while Victoria was doing whatever sixth-grade girls do to get ready for school and Ruby was under our mother's watchful eye, I was tolerating a breakfast of Cheerios and cow's milk, poured directly from a mason jar, and Wonder Bread toast.

Neither my mom nor my father ever said it, but I think Cindy was a surprise. I am glad she is in our family. Cindy has blond hair like Ruby does. When I am playing with her and Ruby, they both like horseback rides and the tickle game. I think the first family name Cindy could say was Teddy!

I must tell you, pouring cow's milk out of a mason jar is a feat to be accomplished. Any third-grade farm boy will let you know that left to sit undisturbed in the icebox overnight, a jar of unseparated milk will separate, and the cream will rise to the top, and you will have skim milk below it. Unless you really like cream on cereal, you need to be a stirrer. "Stirrers" are people who take tablespoons and use them to vigorously stir the cream back into the milk so that when you chew up the Cheerios and milk, you don't get a thick whitewash of cream on the roof of your mouth. Ugh! Once in a while, I would accidentally drop the spoon into the jar, and it would sink into the abyss. I wouldn't tell anyone, but I would definitely hear about it after school. Of course, my reaction would be, "I didn't do it, Mom. I think it was Victoria." The only problem with that line of defense was that Victoria rarely ate cereal on Monday morning. She was primping. She barely had time to chew and swallow down a piece of toast. Somehow, Mom always knew. To this day, I wonder, *how did Mom know that it was my slippery fingers?*

After breakfast, hair combed, and schoolbooks collected, we had to take turns watching for the bus. I should say Victoria and I had to take turns. Ruby was not able to see the bus that far away. Taking turns meant that you sat on a chair and stared out the kitchen window waiting for the yellow school bus to peak over the hill across the way. When you saw the bus, you yelled, "There's the bus!" Then you grabbed your books and homework, and if needed, put on your coat and cap or scarf and ran out the door, down the hill, climbed up the bus stairs, found a seat, and then waited. Even after the driver greeted you as he looked up into his mirror to make sure you really were sitting down, we all still waited. We weren't waiting for Ruby because when the bus came, she forgot to dawdle and kept up with me as we trotted toward the bus. The waiting was for my older sister. Sometimes the driver would honk his horn. It didn't matter. My older sister had style. Victoria never ran. The bus driver never left without her. I think he liked her.

When you are eight years old, you don't pay much attention to the rhythm or patterns of life. You are too busy exploring, collecting, tattling, choring, and playing with friends or your brothers and sisters or your dog. But I guess when you think about it, there is a rhythm and pattern to the Mondays of the school year.

Monday was the day you received your new spelling list. Usually, my teacher, Mrs. Jefferson, would write the list on the board, and we would take our number two pencils and write them out on a piece of paper from our tablets. Mrs. Jefferson would say, "Now class, this week, you will be learning more words that have prefixes or suffixes, and you will also learn more compound words." Then she would write words like: working, playing, disappear, granddaughter, and peanuts. After she wrote the list out and scanned the class to make certain we were writing them down ourselves, she would continue. "Your assignment for spelling tomorrow is to write out sentences using all of these words." I never remembered anyone ever raising his or her hand to ask Mrs. Jefferson what the words "prefixes" or "suffixes" meant.

And so, our school day on Monday would begin. As long as the weather permitted, recesses were outside on the playground. My friends and I would often play tag, cowboys, double dares on the jungle gyms, and when the teacher who had recess duty wasn't watching, we would run through the jump rope, causing the girls to scream.

I liked Mrs. Jefferson. In third grade, we still had Show and Tell, or I should say, we had to write and tell. Mrs. Jefferson made us write one to three sentences on what we wanted to say AND we could talk only on that subject or subjects. Mrs. Jefferson said that was a good way to teach us not to ramble. If we started to ramble, Mrs. Jefferson would tell us to sit down. Whenever I took a turn at "write and tell," she seemed interested in what I said, and then she would ask questions like: "How many miles is it to your grandmother's?" or "Where does your cousin live?" It didn't matter that she asked everyone else questions. I thought she was paying attention to what I wrote and said, and that made me feel special. When we were all done, Mrs. Jefferson collected our papers. Even if you did not have a turn that day to tell, you still had to write.

Monday lunch was pretty good. We never had goulash on Monday, which was something to be happy about. Goulash always looked like maggots crawling around after a great battle, and all of them were severely wounded and there were no Band-Aids. Well, I think you get the picture. We usually had chicken fried steak and mashed potatoes with gravy on Mondays. I always asked for no gravy, and the cook would say, "A farm boy that doesn't eat gravy! Well, I never." Then she would smile and scoop my mash potatoes on the plate.

For two cents, you could buy extra milk. Most of my friends bought extra milk. I liked the town milk that came in the cartons we had with our lunch, but I never liked it enough to dish out an extra two cents. Besides, if I had asked for extra milk money, my mom would have said, "You can have all the milk you want before and after school. You don't need extra money to be buying more milk. I don't have the money to give it to you anyway." I never asked.

Monday afternoon classes were more fun, or maybe I should say they were interesting. In the morning, we had spelling, math, and geography. In the afternoon, we had reading, writing and penmanship, and sometimes social studies. I think I was best at reading and writing. As I would admit in later years, reading and writing were also my greatest challenges.

I was a "finger reader." Do you know what a finger reader is? I do. It's when you put your finger beneath a word and move it along to the right as you read word for word. Finger reading helped me keep my place. I think Mrs. Jefferson put me in the middle reading group, the Sparrows, because I was a finger reader and I would mispronounce words that I could spell from memory. Every day, from the very first day of school until the last school day in May, Mrs. Jefferson would say, "Okay class, when it is your turn to read, sit up straight, feet flat on the floor, and remember fingers are used to hold your book not to be inside your book!" She said that to everyone, but I knew she was especially addressing me and Jeffrey Thomas. He was a finger reader, too.

After our second recess on Monday, we had writing. I think every student, until you were a sophomore in high school, had the same first-day assignment: share what you did the past summer. The way Mrs. Jefferson announced it brought a mixture of groans, giggles, handclaps, and yawns.

In first and second grade, the teacher used Show and Tell. Susie Sneade was at the top of the heap, and she always brought something great to show and brag about. Her parents took her to places most of us only saw on the National Geographic television specials, so she would bring in things like a peacock feather her dad bought her at the Chicago Zoo. Once for Show and Tell, Susie brought what she claimed to be a buffalo horn. She said she had saved her allowance, and when her parents took her to South Dakota, she bought it at a genuine Calvary fort. I don't know. Her horn looked just like it came from one of my Uncle James' cows, and my Uncle James lives in Illinois. Susie would give us a long commentary on whatever she brought to show us. The teacher would always have to interrupt her and say, "Okay, Susie, it's time for someone else to talk now." Susie usually smiled and went on talking. Our second-grade teacher finally had to come up to the front of the class and, with a firmer voice, look Susie right in the face and say, "Susan, I said it is time for someone else to share. Go sit down." Susie pouted a little, but the teacher just called on one of my other hand-waving classmates.

In the third grade, things were different. On the first day of school, Mrs. Jefferson calmly smiled and said, "I want you to write a one-page description on What I Did on My Summer Vacation." When it came time to write, Mrs. Jefferson instructed us further. Remember, you will be graded on how you write a sentence, your penmanship, and your spelling. Okay, class, get out your pencils and one sheet of paper." Desk lids went up immediately, causing several pencils to roll onto the floor and their owners scrambling to retrieve them, then you could hear paper being ripped out of twenty-seven tablets in unison, accompanied by a bit of chatter floating back and forth between students. "Quiet down!" Mrs. Jefferson said loudly, and order was restored. "You can start—now."

Throughout the year, Mrs. Jefferson had other subjects for us to write about, but in the beginning, it was this summer vacation stuff.

As soon as Mrs. Jefferson said "now," you could hear Susie and a couple other kids' pencils racing across the paper as if the letters and words coming out of those pencils were pigs racing to the feed trough.

My pencil was stuck in neutral, full of lead, but no words. What to write was lost in a wilderness called my brain quietly murmuring to itself, *Why bother?* Finally, something started to stir up there, so I started to write.

What I Did on Summer Vacation

I worked and then I did nothing. The End.

I wanted to hand my paper in, but I knew better. Mrs. Jefferson would only tell me, "You did more than that! My goodness! Go back to your seat and think harder. You only have about thirty minutes, so you better not daydream." I had already daydreamed as much as I could under the circumstances. I was devastated. Being a tenacious fellow, I started again.

What I Did on Summer Vacation

This summer, I started to do real outside chores. It wasn't much fun, but I wasn't given a say in the matter. My mom made me gather the eggs. Once, I cracked an egg because the hen pecked at my hand and it scared me. I dropped the egg. I scraped some crushed corn cobs over it, but the rooster came over and began to peck at the cobs and the egg. I think he ate the egg. My mom said eating raw eggs might make you sick, so I left the chicken house without gathering the rest of the eggs. I didn't want to be blamed for a dead rooster. It must not have killed him because later, he was outside the chicken house strutting around.

After gathering the eggs, I had to go out in the pasture and bring the cows home for milking. In the summer, the milk cows and the bull are out in the timber. It's not really a timber. It's just a bunch of trees and a lot of ravines. I play sheriff and rustler in the ravines, but not with real cows, just imaginary ones. Most of the time, the real cows are up on the grassy slopes of the pasture. I try to call them by yelling, "Come, boss. Come, boss!" But they never come home when I call them. Sometimes they just start walking the other way, still munching grass. I don't like the cows.

One of the other chores I have to do every day is throw hay down for the cows and the bull and put feed out in front of the stanchions. I have to do some other stuff, but I am almost out of paper, so I get to quit. Oh, I almost forgot, I always have to feed my dog, Pal. We feed him scraps from the table. He doesn't get leftovers or dog food from the store. He just gets scraps. I wish I didn't have to do chores. I will probably have to do them forever. The End.

By the time I started to write about Pal, I had to write really small and crowd my letters because I had written everything else in big cursive letters to take up more space. I think Mrs. Jefferson will still be able to read what I wrote. I hope so. If she can't, she will make me write it again.

The rest of Monday afternoon went by rather quickly, and when the bell rang at three-thirty, I think everyone was ready to go home, including Mrs. Jefferson.

Riding the school bus home is different than riding it to school. Usually, everyone is dismissed at the same time, and on the first day, the country kids are all led out to the bus by their teacher who makes certain they get on the right bus unless they have an excuse that says their mother or father or someone who has permission will be coming to pick them up. Junior and Senior High School kids don't count because a lot of them don't ride the bus in the afternoon. They have sports or other activities that take place after school. I guess once you are in junior or senior high school, the teachers must think you can find your own bus if you're not staying for activities because I never saw a teacher bring one of them out to the bus line or make sure they weren't outside goofing off and would miss their bus.

I had new jeans to wear on the first day of school. My mom must have thought that I would grow taller by the end of third grade so she never trimmed off the bottoms. I had to roll my jeans legs up three or four times into cuffs that came to a point at the toe of my shoes. A lot of mothers must have thought their sons were going to grow taller because most of the guys wore their jeans with the pants legs rolled up. Even some of the high school boys wore their jeans that way, but I think they were done growing. They just did it because they thought it was cool. I didn't think about it much except wishing that I only had to roll my jeans legs up twice. I mention wearing new jeans because I had to change into my farm clothes as soon as I got home.

One of my chores I forgot to mention earlier was my sour milk chore. Outside of the barn was the milk shed. After milking the cows, my dad would pour the raw milk into a big separator bowl. Before he ran the milk through the separator, he would fill the mason jar I brought down to the barn full of milk to take to the house after chores. The separator made a lot of noise when it was running. There were two spouts on the bowl—one for cream that ran into a cream can and the other for skim milk that ran into a five-gallon bucket. Skim milk is what milk is called after the cream is separated out. Usually, there would be two-and-a-half five-gallon buckets full of skim milk after each milking.

My job was to take the skim milk from the morning's milking and carry it out to feed to the pigs or chickens. I think that was the worst chore I had.

Feeding the chickens wasn't too bad, except the trip was all uphill. I usually tried to carry the milk in the five-gallon buckets instead of putting some in smaller buckets and making more trips. I wanted to watch television or go play, so I tried to get through my chores as fast as I could. This is one chore with which I probably should have taken the time and made more trips. I would start out okay, but the bucket was heavy, so the milk would swoosh from side to side, making big waves of milk pour out. It wasn't long before milk was hitting dry land and splashing up onto my pants legs. Of course, the bucket was always lighter by the time I reached the chicken house than it was when I started, but I have to admit I didn't do a very good job with the carrying business. I just wanted to be done with my chores.

I used two buckets when I fed the pigs. By the time I climbed the fence and lifted the buckets over, the pigs were all over me like flies going after watermelon rinds on a hot August afternoon. Making the journey from the fence to the pig trough was a walk through a barnyard minefield. I had to dodge snorting pigs, steady myself while sliding through pig manure, and try to dump two buckets of milk at the same time into the trough. It might have been easier if I just carried one bucket, but then I would have had to take the trip through the minefield twice. I tried to take that trip as infrequently as I could. One thing you could be sure of, I never had to call the pigs to come and eat. They were always waiting for me, snorting and grunting as if to say to one another, "Hey, the food truck arrived! Let's ambush the guy and take the load fresh from the tank!"

By the time I finished my chores, I smelled like sour milk, chicken feathers, and barnyard stew. My mom always made me take my chore jeans off in the back room and put on a spare she kept for me to wear in the house. After chores, there was only a little time to play or watch TV before supper, and right after supper, I would have to do my homework. I had homework from day one. I remember that first day, at least my assignments weren't so hard, but I knew my mom would not let me do anything else until they were done and she checked everything over.

My mother always made supper. When I was eight, there wasn't a lot on TV or in the newspaper about healthy or nutritious food except advertisements about eating bread with twelve different vitamins and drinking the kind of milk that came in cardboard cartons and not out of a mason jar.

There were a lot of advertisements about smoking cigarettes. My dad smoked cigarettes. When I was eight years old, I didn't know that smoking was bad for your health, and I guess a lot of other people didn't know that either. There were a lot of people smoking cigarettes on TV. The same could be said about unhealthy eating, if there ever was such a thing. We just had regular farm food.

As far back as I can remember, my mom always fried pork chops for supper on the first day of school. She made mashed potatoes from potatoes; she had my sister, Victoria, peel when she came home from school. Mom also made gravy from pork chop grease, milk, and flour, *ugh*. I never ate gravy. I used butter. We also had sweet corn. I usually ate my sweet corn with a big swab of butter, lots of salt, pepper, and more salt. There was a freezer in our back room, and it was filled with batches of sweet corn my mom and aunt put up in the summer. My dad was the only one who ate bread and butter with supper. It was town bread. I didn't like it much except to use for sandwiches.

Sometimes we would have dessert, and sometimes we didn't, but that first school night, we had peaches from the freezer. My mom and aunt put up a mess of peaches in freezer bags earlier in the month. The peaches tasted really good and reminded me of peach popsicles my aunt would buy me. Our peaches were sweeter though and tasted like they just came off the tree, and you ate them with a spoon, not from a stick.

After supper, I took the scraps my sister scraped from the supper plates into a saucepan out to feed my dog Pal. As soon as I left the house, I yelled, "Here, Pal, Here, Pal!" and then I whistled. I taught myself how to whistle when I was five. By the time I was whistling for Pal, he was right by my side, waiting to eat. I remember the only thing Pal never ate was tomatoes. Otherwise, he ate pretty much anything that I put into his dog dish. I think he liked the bones and gravy the best, so it worked out that I didn't like gravy. Pal always licked his bowl clean.

When I came back into the house from feeding Pal, my older sister Victoria would have already started to wash dishes. My younger sister Ruby wouldn't have to do them for years until she was old enough. It was my job to dry. Drying dishes was my last chore for the day.

When I finished with the dishes, I sat down at the table and did my homework. My father was still at the table. He spent about a half an hour every evening drinking coffee, reading the *Omaha World Herald,* and smoking unfiltered cigarettes. I didn't like cigarette smoke, but of course, I didn't say anything.

I never remember my father asking me, "How was your first day of school?" "You have homework to do?" "Do you have any new kids in your class?" And he never ever asked me, "Do you need any help?" He usually just sat there reading his paper, smoking his nonfilter cigarettes, and drinking his black coffee.

Spelling was always my first piece of homework to tackle. I would write out my list of spelling words on a piece of paper and then use them in a sentence. After I was done with spelling, my mom sat at the table with me and listened while I read aloud. She never questioned my finger-reading. She just listened and helped me pronounce words I was stammering over.

At the time, I didn't realize how easy it was to slip back into an after-school routine that was started the previous year and would last all the way through the sixth grade. The only thing that would change was the homework, which would become more difficult.

On this particular evening, when my third-grade homework was done, I sat at the table for a few more minutes. I stared at the front page of the *World Herald,* imagining a conversation with my father that would go something like this:

"So you have Mrs. Jefferson this year?" my father would ask.

"Yes, I do. I think I like her," I would answer.

"Oh good. Her husband farms on the other side of town, but his mother and father still live on the farm, so he and Mrs. Jefferson live in town." In that short imaginary conversation, my father would have told me more about Mrs. Jefferson than I ever knew before.

"Live in town? Wow!" I would say in a high pitched, excited voice. *"Can I have a horse?"* I would ask out of the blue but with the same enthusiasm.

In my imaginary conversation, my father didn't answer me.

Someday many years later, I will come back to this present time. It will be a memory, and in that space, I will reenact the language and conversation, or lack thereof, my father and I had. I will sit in the silence of a pain that is not visible from the surface, but a pain nevertheless—one that lives inside thoughts and is embedded in emotions that young boys have when fathers, unaware of their own hurt, distance themselves from positive emotional bonding with sons.

In my silence, I am left with creative thinking and self-doubt. *There must be something wrong with me,* I think. *I am not good enough,* I decide. Then I try to forget, but the pain remains and what terrifies me is the doubting of my own thoughts and emotions drawn from this memory. *What if I am wrong? What if we actually had had joyous and lively conversations and I am remembering an imaginative episode with fictitious characters to ease my own desiring? What if . . .?*

I find myself wishing that I was back at school, and it was time for recess. I leave the table. Homework done, I go into the living room and lay down on the floor to watch TV before bedtime.

As I said before, it is easy to slip into a routine. Someone once told my mother that it takes forty days to create a habit. We had a lot of rituals that mostly grew out of habits when I was growing up. One of those rituals was preparing for bed. About eight p.m., my mother or older sister would put the tea kettle full of water on the stove and turn on the gas burner. When the water was hot, my mother helped my six-year-old sister wash up and put on her pajamas. Next, it was my turn. My mother didn't help me. I washed myself. Then my older sister Victoria washed. I think. Maybe she took a bath because she was in the bathroom for a really long time.

Bedtime was nine p.m. for me and Victoria. My baby sister, Cindy, and little sister, Ruby, were already sleeping. Without fail, when the television credits were running after an eight-thirty show, my mother would announce, "It's nine o'clock. It's time for bed."

I always responded, "Aw, Mom, can't I stay up a little longer?"

And she would always reply, "Up to bed, young man. You have school tomorrow."

My father didn't really take part in the washing up or bedtime ritual. He usually was either asleep in his chair or still at the kitchen table drinking coffee, reading the paper or a farm magazine, and of course, smoking a non-filter cigarette. If he wasn't sleeping, I would usually put my arm on his shoulders and kiss him goodnight on the cheek. He replied with silence.

My mother always kissed me back when I kissed her goodnight. Turning to the upstairs stairway, I would begin the journey with uncertainty and almost always be afraid of what monsters and nightmares waited for me as I entered my room and crawled into bed. When my imagination was exceptionally active, I would wait until I was lying perfectly still in bed before saying my prayers.

I said my prayers in bed for two reasons. First, in the winter, it was way too cold to be kneeling on the floor and praying. Second, and probably most important, I didn't want to be kneeling at my bedside with eyes closed and have a robber easily konk me on the head. When I finally thought everything was okay, I said my prayers:

"Now I lay me down to sleep, I pray the Lord, my soul to keep. If I should die before I wake, I pray the Lord my soul to take. God bless Mommy and Daddy (Yes, I said it that way), my sisters (and since I didn't have a brother, I couldn't ask God to bless him), my Grandma and Grandpa, my aunts and uncles, and everyone else. Please help me not to have bad dreams; don't let any robbers come into our house; don't let me wet the bed; help all the poor people and help me be good. Amen."

If I was still afraid, I would sing, "Jesus Loves Me," but not out loud, only in my mind. Somewhere between the third "Jesus loves me," and "Yes, I know," sleep came.

Chapter 2

Tuesday Night Dance

In the olden days, we had Wednesday and Friday off for Thanksgiving, which meant the Tuesday night before Thanksgiving, we could stay up later. I think that is why the junior high principal decided the Holiday Dance would be on Tuesday night. He probably figured since junior high kids were hard to get up on any school morning, having the dance Tuesday night before Thanksgiving would save a lot of parents' breath and time trying to make sure they were up for school the next morning.

Since my older sister was in seventh grade, she was going to the dance tonight. This was the first school dance she ever attended. She had been practicing in the living room with *American Bandstand* on TV. When I would come in from doing chores, I wanted to watch Mickey Mouse or cartoons, but there she was with the ironing board out in the middle of the room, ironing clothes and dancing around. My dad said she had ants in her pants. What he says might be true, but I have seen my parents square dance, and his comments made me wonder . . . *If she had ants in her pants when she rock and rolled, what did my father and mom have in their pants when they square danced?*

My folks decided my father would take Victoria to the dance, and my mother would pick her up; that way, my father would be able to be in bed right after the weather report at ten because he had to get up at five-thirty a.m. to milk.

When we sat down to supper, my mom said, "Victoria, after supper, you can go on upstairs and get dressed. I will do the dishes for you tonight." Victoria was always a small portion eater, but she ate slowly. This evening she might as well have not sat at the table at all. After grace was said, there she was, and then she wasn't, her feet already racing up the stairs to get ready.

"Can I go with you, Dad?" I asked, thinking if I could go, once we got into town maybe my father would buy me a pop. My father was reading the paper, so he didn't have to answer me. I waited. Finally, after drinking all of my water and having nothing else to do, I asked again, "Can we go with you, Dad?" This time I said "we" instead of "I" thinking if I included my younger sister Ruby, my mother would hear me and think I was being kind. She would then encourage my father to take us with him.

You had to listen very carefully to hear him as he turned the page of the paper, "I guess," he said.

"Can I go too?" Ruby shyly asked, not realizing that my going meant she was also going. Then she saw me out of the corner of her eye, shaking my head "yes."

Still, being little, I guess she had to press the issue. "Does that mean I get to go, too, Mom?"

"Yes, dear, you can go too, but not until you finish drinking all of your milk." By the way my mother was starting to look, I could imagine she was probably saying to herself, *This isn't going to work. Victoria, all dressed up, Ruby and Teddy and their father with his non-filter cigarette hitching a ride in his mouth, all of them in that broken down, cold red pickup.* "Sam, why don't you use the car?" Mom suddenly asked. "I think it would be more comfortable for everyone." What I think she really meant was Victoria's nice dress wouldn't get wrinkled and her hair wouldn't smell like cigarette smoke. I also think she probably wanted to say more about my father acting at least a little more excited about his oldest daughter's first school dance. My mother knew that a dance and time with your friends was something really special for a young girl, especially when you live out on a farm, miles from town, and seldom see your friends outside of school hours.

My father put the paper down and took another sip of black, unsugared coffee, his look telling my mother that he would let it be and would take us with him in the family car, a '55 Chevrolet that he had to work on just about as much as he worked on the pickup. His expression quickly changed as Victoria walked into the kitchen. "You aren't going out of this house looking like a tramp, young lady!" he barked.

Victoria stood really still and tried to explain, "But, Dad, all the girls—"

He interrupted her. "All the girls or not, you march right up those stairs and take those, those can-cans, or whatever they are, off!"

"They are can-can slips, Dad. Mom wears them when you guys go square dancing," Victoria boldly said.

"Well, that's different." You could tell he was pondering what to say next. I think she almost had him beat, but he quickly recovered and used his never-worn-out ace. "Don't you talk back to me, young lady!" I think he must have thought he owed her some kind of an explanation, so he added, "Your mother isn't twelve. She's . . ."

At that point, my mom made some sort of gurgling sound she often makes when she and my father are arguing in front of us and she becomes aware of the fact that maybe we are listening just a little more than she would like us to. She gurgles as a sign to my father that they need to put a pin in it for the moment. The gurgling is also a way for her to say without words, "Sam, you aren't going to win this one. You'll be digging a hole that you might regret. I'll handle this from here." I must say it is a powerful gurgle. The only other person I know who can make that sound is my grandmother. I've heard her make it to my grandfather. They are Romanian, and they speak Romanian a lot in front of us kids and my father. The gurgling must be the leftovers of a Romanian word, I guess. It has stopped a lot of disagreements, at least for the moment.

After the gurgling, my mom, with Cindy fast asleep in her arms, turned slowly to my older sister. "Victoria, hurry upstairs and take off two of your can-cans. You can wear one and only one!"

"No one understands me," Victoria whispered, a few tears streaming down her twelve-year-old cheeks, but then ran upstairs and did exactly as she was told. I guess one can-can and a ride to the dance in a '55 Chevy is a whole lot better than sitting at home.

So now we were driving down the road toward town. My mother made Ruby and me wear jackets. I didn't want to, but I wasn't going to jeopardize losing my trip to town, so I was wearing a jacket. Victoria was in the back seat with Ruby. I have to say she looked really nice. She looked more than nice. She looked hot! Remember, I told you that brothers don't think that way about their sisters, so to me, I guess she just looked pretty. I imagined her dancing with all the good-looking guys that you can see on *American Bandstand* and maybe one of them buying her a coke. Then it dawned on me, I better start talking to my father about buying Ruby and me a pop before we had to go home.

"Dad," I said, as we were on the bridge crossing the Nishnabotna River, "Can we have a pop when we get to town?" There was that expected silence. *Why do grown-ups do that to kids? Especially fathers? There's a question, but where is the answer?* Pressing my luck, I started again, "Dad . . ."

I couldn't get the rest of my thoughts into words because Victoria screamed from the back seat, "Dad! A deer!" The deer must have heard Victoria because it stared right at her and then we heard "Bam! Crumble! Chink! Chunk! Chink!" My father said some words I only hear him say when a cow kicks him or the pigs root under the fence and get out, or when he hits his finger with a hammer. I can't write the words down. If I did, my mom would put red pepper on my tongue. My sister Victoria screamed again. I just sat there thinking, *There goes our pop.*

The car stopped. It sounded really dead. I looked out the window and then asked, "Where did the deer go, Dad?"

He didn't answer. I guess it was because he was already halfway out of the car. I wasn't going to miss anything, so I got out also and looked under the car just like my father did. We both saw the same thing. The deer's hind legs were spread out behind his crunched tail, and his front legs made it look like he was trying to climb up next to the engine. His antlers were almost touching the inside of the car's hood. Still saying some really bad words, my father got up and opened the car's hood. He looked inside, and I did too. "Gee, Dad, those are big antlers," I said with amazement.

"We aren't going anywhere soon," my father said in between those same words I can't repeat.

"What's that?" I asked him, pointing at the long pieces of rubber he held in his hand.

"It was the water pump belt," he said to me, answering my question.

"Oh." I still didn't really have a clue what the rubber pieces he held in his hand actually were, but I pretended I did.

"How am I going to the dance?" Victoria began to cry, being somewhat disconnected from the predicament the car, the deer, and the rest of us were in.

"Don't cry, Victoria." Ruby hugged her big sister, then started crying herself. "I'm scared," she said, holding Victoria tight.

So here we are, I thought, *right down the road from the Miners' and down the road the other way from the Maxwell's. Hmmm . . . I sure hope my father doesn't make me walk to the Maxwell's for help. They have a German shepherd. He is big, and he is a really mean dog!* But knowing my father, I knew we weren't going to be motionless very long. Taking a second look under the car, Dad grabbed the front legs of the deer and yelled, "Teddy, look under the hood and push the antlers down while I pull on the legs."

I could hear him really good, but I think he yelled because he was still mad at the deer. I climbed up on the bumper and grabbed the antlers and pushed just as my father was tugging. In a short time, we had the deer lying alongside the road. "It's a big deer, Dad." I was amazed once again by the size of the antlers and how long the deer was.

"Can I see, Dad?" Ruby ventured forward by herself. I could see that Victoria just thought the whole ordeal was disgusting and ruining her plans for the evening. There was no way she was going to stare down at the run-over dead deer with car tracks across his rear end. No way at all! Just about the time Ruby had a second look at the deer and asked, "Can we take him to the doctor, Daddy?" a car came over the hill and slowed down. It was Mr. and Mrs. Miner and their son Bruce.

Joe Miner rolled down his window, stuck his head out, puckered his lips, and gave a whistle. "That's some deer, Sam. Bet it did a mess on your engine."

"No," my dad said in a much more calm voice than he had used earlier. I think he didn't swear because Mrs. Miner was in the car, and she was an Adventist just like my grandmother. I suppose my father wasn't quite sure what would happen to you on Judgment Day if you swore in front of an Adventist. "He just ripped up my water pump belt. Do you mind asking Harry at the Deep Rock to bring a new belt out to me, Joe?"

"No problem. I would be glad to do it, or would you prefer to ride in with us?" Mr. Miner eyed Victoria, who had already returned to the back seat of our car and was sitting there pouting in her dress and can-can.

"No, I'll wait here," my father replied, "I think I can get the other part of the fan belt pulled loose."

"Sam, I think Victoria is dressed for the dance. Do you mind if she goes with us?" Ruth Miner asked as she leaned over toward the open window. Before my father could answer, she went on to inform us, "Bruce is going to the dance, also." She then smiled in Victoria's direction. I am sure Mrs. Miner did not hear it, but in spite of the invitation offered, I heard a slight groan from the back seat. It is the kind of groan a first-grade guy would make when he finds out that he gets to be first in line for ice cream on the last day of school, but he has to hold hands and walk to the lunchroom with a girl who thinks he is kind of cute. Only now the groan is coming from a girl, my sister, who is imagining the gossip in the girl's bathroom if she shows up at the dance in the same car with Bruce Miner.

"Sam, I am sure Harry will come quickly, but why don't we take Ruby and Teddy with us too?" Joe Miner offered. "Ruth and I were going to the Chatterbox for coffee, and we'd love to treat them."

"Can I go? Can we go? Daddy, please," Ruby asked, looking up at our father with big brown adorable eyes.

"We'll behave," I added, knowing that was the least thing my father was thinking about at the moment. I offered the "behave" part because it was the mature thing to say, but truth is, I didn't want to jeopardize any chance of possibly being so near to having a bottle of pop.

When my father finally spoke, he simply said, "Thank you, Joe. I appreciate it. Do you mind driving the kids home? I am not sure how long all of this will take." My dad dug into his pocket and brought out a quarter and tried to hand it to Mr. Miner.

"Yes, we will be happy to take them home, and please keep your quarter. I wouldn't think of taking it. We are neighbors. You have helped me plenty of times. It is our treat. This is what friends and neighbors do for each other." Mr. Miner shook my dad's hand as Mrs. Miner opened the door and called out to my little sister, "Ruby, you can sit in the front seat with me."

Without hesitating, Ruby jumped into the front seat while I was waiting for Victoria to get in the back seat. I looked at Bruce. I could tell he was hoping Victoria would sit by him and who was I to inhibit a possible budding romance? Victoria, however, had other ideas. She politely but firmly guided me into the car first so that I was sitting between Bruce and her. I saw Bruce's look go from wild delight and great expectation to steep disappointment and defeat as I slid over toward the middle of the back seat, but if he had half an imagination like I did, tomorrow he could be telling all his friends that Victoria and he rode in the back seat of their car to the dance; that she came with him, but they made an agreement they would dance with other people because it was their first school dance and they didn't want to act like snobs! He could leave the rest of the story to be played out in his friends' imaginations, of course. He could have imagined all of that and said whatever he wanted, but I have to say, sadly, I don't think Bruce is a very imaginative person, so I don't think Victoria had much to fear.

In a short while, Victoria and Bruce were dumped off at the dance. So here we are, Ruby and me, at the Chatterbox with Joe and Ruth Miner. Ruby could only drink half of her grape pop. I asked Mrs. Miner if she wanted it but she said, "Oh, heavens no! I am too full of coffee. I guess you will have to drink it, Teddy." So along with my full bottle of root beer and all the French fries and ketchup I wanted to eat, I also drank half of Ruby's grape pop! I sure was lucky. I liked the Miners and was also glad that I didn't have to go to bed early that night. I drank a lot of pop!

When I finally did go to bed that evening, I thought about the deer crossing the road just at the same time we were driving by. *Why would he do that? Why didn't he wait?* He was a beautiful creature. I never give it a second thought when I see a dead raccoon or a stinky skunk along the side of the road, but a deer with such big antlers, it seemed to be such a waste. *Why didn't he wait? Why wasn't my father driving slower?* I was still thinking about the deer when I said my prayers, so I asked Jesus to bless the deer even though he was dead. I think it's okay to ask Jesus to bless dead animals. I don't know. I might ask our Sunday School teacher, Mrs. Kate, someday what she thinks about it all. I don't think it would be a good idea to ask my school teacher, Mrs. Jefferson, this kind of question. Jesus blessing dead animals or not is probably a Sunday question, not a Monday question.

I was almost done with my prayers when my thoughts were interrupted with a root beer burp. My burp reminded me of earlier in the evening when I was sitting in the booth at the Chatterbox with Ruby and Mr. and Mrs. Miner. I hadn't been in the Chatterbox very often. It's a fun place. They have a jukebox, and you can buy malts, burgers, fries, just about anything you want to eat while you are listening to your favorite rock and roll song. When we were with the Miners, there weren't any kids our age hanging out. I guess kids our age don't hang out like teenagers do. "You're too young to be hanging out downtown by yourself," my mom used to tell me when I asked her why I couldn't stay downtown awhile after school. I guess that's what mothers say to kids my age.

I really didn't want to tell you much more about the Chatterbox. After the burp came, I just kept lying here thinking hard again about that deer and the Miners. We were stranded on the road, and along came the Miners. They could have just honked and passed us by like Mrs. Carver would probably do, but they didn't. They stopped to help, and they took my sister and me to town with them for a treat. They could have just taken Victoria to the dance. Why did they take us, too? Why did they do that? I think it's more than being an Adventist. My mom says they are really kind, and my father says that they are nice neighbors.

I remember when Mrs. Kate told us a story about a lady whose husband died. I think she said he didn't have something called a "Will" so the debt collector at the bank took all their money. She was kicked off their farm and had to live in a small shack in town on the other side of the railroad tracks. The only money she had was from what she earned sewing clothes for people. One day when she went to church, Jesus was there. He saw her empty her whole coin purse into the collection plate. Jesus said, "This woman gave more out of her heart than most people gave out of their wallets." As soon as Mrs. Kate was done with the story, I remember someone asked, "How did she pay for her electricity?" All Mrs. Kate said was, "She didn't." Then my friend Johnny asked," How did she buy her groceries?" Again, all Mrs. Kate said was, "I don't know." No one asked Mrs. Kate any more questions. We were all quiet until the bell rang for Sunday School to be over.

Now, I know the Miners aren't poor. At least, my father says that they aren't, but they sure don't live high on the hog either. So when I think about what they did, I have to say they were very generous toward our family. When it comes to money, Mom says Mrs. Miner is thrifty, and my father says she is tight with her money. I think my parents are the same way, so I know what they are talking about, but I am thinking different about the Miners.

They didn't offer a ride or a treat just because we are neighbors, and they play cards with my parents. (Yes, some Adventists do play cards!) I think they acted the way they did because, in their generosity, they are kind people. I know about the words *generous* and *generosity* because I had to memorize them for the weekly spelling test. I think the Miners' generosity is something more. We aren't their children. The sheriff wouldn't arrest them if they didn't take us to the Chatterbox and treat us, and my parents certainly wouldn't stop playing cards with them. They just did what they did because that is the way they are with everyone. The way Mrs. Miner looked at Victoria told me that she wasn't looking for a girlfriend for Bruce; she was feeling compassion for Victoria.

Generosity, kindness, compassion, those are big words and long thoughts for a guy my age. I'll have to look them up in my mom's dictionary and ask Mrs. Kate about them when we go to Sunday School again. I will have to try and practice what they mean. I guess that's all I have been thinking about, so I better finish my prayer and go to sleep.

Early the next morning I had to help my father sort some pigs before the truck came to take them to the stockyards in Omaha. We had to have them all sorted before eight a.m.

I don't like sorting pigs. It's really cold outside, and this morning I had a hole in the bottom of my right shoe. Even though I had two pairs of socks on, just as soon as I stepped into the pigpen I knew that the squish underneath my feet meant that my socks would soon be wet, and my right foot would get really, really cold.

This morning, the pigs weren't herding very well. My dog, Pal, jumped over the fence and started to bark and chase the pigs just about the time we had them cornered to crowd them into the loading pen. Pal really likes it when we load pigs. I think she believes she is Rin Tin Tin or Lassie and she is corralling bad guys or robbers. Without paying any attention to my father or me yelling at her, Pal jumped at a pig and bit hard down on its left ear. The pig squealed and ran right toward me. I was holding the wooden gate that I was using to herd the pigs toward the loading pen while my father was using another gate.

"Watch out, Teddy! Don't let those pigs get out! Pal, get out of there!" my father ordered a bushel of demands and instructions before he started using the words I can't use.

"I am trying, Dad. This gate is heavy!" I yelled back. About that time, the pig with the bite on his ear hit my gate hard, knocking me over right into the slop. His buddies all saw their opportunity to take a run for freedom, and they did!

"I told you to hold that gate!" my father hollered, running toward me.

"I did," I said defiantly while tears welled in my eyes; I fought hard so they wouldn't fall down my face in front of my father. "I couldn't help it," I added, trying to defend myself.

"Go tell your mother we need her help," My father demanded as he picked up my gate and turned away.

A few seconds later, I stuck my head inside the back porch door and called, "Mom, Mom, Dad told me to come and get you. We need your help." My mom took one look at me and, without a word, put on her jean jacket, headscarf, and boots. By the time we were back in the hog lot, my father had tied the two gates together to make a lane narrowing into the loading pen.

I wondered to myself, *Why didn't we do this before?* I couldn't wonder very long on the thought, though, because my father was giving my mom and me orders. "Your mom and I will go out and bring the pigs up the lane, Teddy. You start closing this gate when the last pig comes by." My father seemed to be calmer in my mom's presence, and Pal found a rabbit to chase, so in just a few minutes, the pigs were corralled in the loading pen. All that was left was to wait for the truck and for me to sneak back to the house and thaw out my right foot.

An hour later, the truck came, and I was back outside doing some chores my father had lined up for me to do. I was happy to see the truck, because that meant I could stop pretending to be working hard and go help drive the pigs up the chute. Just like trying to drive pigs into a narrow wooden gate lane, unless there is a ton of food at the top, pigs don't drive very well uphill, and loading chutes travel uphill. When the truck was loaded and was being driven out the barnyard gate onto the gravel road, I could hear the pigs squealing their goodbyes. I imagined some of their conversations as they began their very first and final trip:

"Goodbye, Charlie! Goodbye, Francine! I wonder where we are going," Marvin the dog-bit-ear pig might say.

"I think we are going to pig school," Junior offers.

"I doubt it," Butch, the bully of the bunch, would respond. "There's no such thing as pig school. I've seen this truck before. My friend, Thomas, went away in this very same truck three months ago. He never came back."

"Oh, never!" Clara squeals.

"Never," Butch repeats. Then there aren't any more squeals because they all come to realize their ride only carries a one-way ticket.

Chapter 3

Going Into Town

This morning, after chores, I was at the kitchen table, putting on a fresh pair of socks when my father came in from the back room. As he sat down and lit a cigarette, my mom poured him a cup of black coffee. Then without asking, she poured me a cup of hot chocolate from the saucepan she had been heating on the stove's back burner. I like my mom's hot chocolate. I think she is very generous with the cocoa, and sometimes I see her add vanilla flavoring to the chocolate like she did this morning. *She's telling me I did okay this morning with my chores,* I thought to myself.

"Your dad's going to Shelby," my mother said, looking at me. "He said you can go with him, so put on your school shoes, wash up, and comb your hair."

"Thanks, Dad!" I said, looking at him, not expecting a return glance. Finishing my hot chocolate, I did exactly as my mom said, so I would be ready to go when my father finished his cigarette and coffee.

We are going in our red pickup. The pickup rattles a lot, and if you pull the floor mat on the passenger's side back, you can see the road through a hole in the floor. It takes a long time for the pickup to warm up, but I don't care. I'm going to town, and I even have a dime in my pocket I want to spend.

"What are we going to do, Dad?" I asked as we began our trip. The pickup doesn't have a radio, so I am thinking just maybe my father and I can have a talk about my having a horse or maybe a couple of runt pigs to raise.

"We have to go to the elevator to buy some pig chow and calf feed," he answered matter-of-factly as he pulled a cigarette from the pack in his overalls and let go of the steering wheel to light it with a match he struck on the match cover with two fingers.

How did he do that? I wondered. The pickup never wavered. He used one hand to put the cigarette in his mouth and the other hand to hold and strike the match. *My father is really talented.*

"Are we going anywhere else?" I asked, really hoping now that he would say, 'Sure, we are going to stop at the Main Street Café to have coffee.' If my father is having a coffee, just maybe I would have a pop. I would probably have an orange because I haven't had orange pop for a long time.

My father didn't answer, so I knew we were going to the elevator and then back home. I didn't see my mom give him a grocery list, so I know we aren't going to the store, but I am still going to hope that maybe, *just maybe . . .* It takes about twenty minutes to travel to Shelby. Part of the way is gravel, and the rest of the way is by County Road D. My father isn't talking, so I ask, "Do you know all of these people on this road, Dad?"

"I suppose so," he says with some effort.

"Who lives there?" I ask, pointing ahead to a really nice two-story farmhouse with a garage connected to it, just like houses in town.

"The Calhouns," my father answers.

"Do I know them?" I quiz him, thinking maybe I know some Calhouns from Sunday School, but since we don't go to the Lutheran Church in Shelby very often, I cannot be sure.

"I don't know," my father replies.

So, I am guessing, unless my father is really mad at me, the pigs, the cows, or my dog, Pal, he isn't very interested in conversing or using up too many words. It's not much fun riding with all of this quiet and rattling, so I pretend to have a conversation with the farmhouses we pass until we arrive in Shelby.

Shelby is a thriving little town. It has a bank, an elevator and feed mill, a grocery store, a lumberyard, a café, two beer joints, and three churches. Oh, I almost forgot, it also has a funeral home. The elevator is right across the street from the bank. Next to the elevator and across the alley is the Murphy Memorial Methodist Episcopal Church. Murphy's church has the same last name as our country church does, Methodist Episcopal.

All of my father's family, at least the ones who go to church, say they are Lutheran, so every now and then, we come to Shelby and go to the Lutheran Church. I think we do so because two of my aunts have told my father that he was in the wrong church, and they were praying for him to remember his Confirmation and get back right with the Lord. I heard them tell him those very words when we were at the family reunion last year in Council Bluffs. I didn't dare ask them how they learned what was right with the Lord because I was afraid they would make me go to Confirmation like they made my mother take my sister Victoria. She is still going, and she has homework every week!

Instead of heading right into the elevator office, my father walked across the street to the bank, and I followed him. He pointed me to a chair, and he went into a room with a man in a black suit, you know, the kind of suit that funeral directors wear. Through the office window, I saw my father reach into his bib overalls and pull out the check that came in the mail last week for the pigs. The banker's face didn't look very happy. Maybe he was sad that all of those pigs had to go to market. I don't know, and I don't think my father will tell me.

After what seemed to be a very long time, my father came out of the office, followed by the man in the black suit. They both went up to the bank window, and the man wrote something on a slip of paper that my father signed and handed to the bank teller. The bank teller then counted out some money and put it in an envelope for my father. When my father headed for the door, he didn't even look my way so I knew I better get up and follow him. I don't really know what they said or what made the banker and my father look so unhappy, but I just have a hunch if the banker had offered my father a cup of coffee and a cookie, he would have probably said, "No, thank you."

Seconds later, we entered the elevator and feed mill front door. "Hi Sam, how are you doing?" The man behind the counter reached over to shake my father's hand. A slight change seemed to come over my father as I saw him become more relaxed than he had been at the bank.

"I just came from the bank, "my father revealed, "and I need some pig chow—about ten bags and two bags of calf feed."

"The bank. Hmmm . . . you look like you could use a drink. How 'bout a coffee?" Before my father could say anything, the man turned his head slightly and yelled, "Hey, Matt! Sam's here! Bring up ten bags of pig chow and two bags of calf feed for him on the loader."

"Okay," a voice somewhere in the back shouted out.

"It'll take a few minutes, Sam. Come on in my office, and we will have a cup. Got some fresh homemade Christmas cookies." Without waiting for an answer, the man turned toward the office and then immediately turned back, "Teddy, here's a nickel. Buy yourself a pop and come into my office."

Without hesitation, the man immediately flipped me a nickel that I missed catching but had no trouble retrieving. *A nickel, cookies, and pop! I sure hope they have orange in the machine,* I say to myself. *And I still have my dime!*

It's important for you to know, the man is Don Taylor. I think he has known my father and some of his family for a long time. He goes to the same Lutheran church that my aunts attend. You know, I told you that they want my father to be reconfirmed in the Lutheran church. Mr. Taylor and my father must be really good friends because my father has been here this long and hasn't pulled out a cigarette. When I saw my father relax more, I was glad that I came with him and that I met Mr. Taylor. I think I like him. Mr. Taylor must not smoke because he doesn't offer my father a cigarette. Looking around, I see a sign on the wall that reads, "I don't smoke. I don't mind if you smoke. I just don't have ashtrays and the broom's at home." The sign makes me laugh. My father must have read the sign too because he doesn't reach for a cigarette all the time we are here.

My father and Mr. Taylor talk a long time and drink a lot of coffee. It's okay by me because I have more than one cookie. Maybe I had two, no three. It was a long talk. When my father finally says that we need to be going for the third time, he gets up, which means I need to do the same.

"Thank you, Mr. Taylor, for the pop. I was hoping your machine had orange pop, and it did!" I said as my father and I were heading out the door.

"Oh," Mr. Taylor said after giving me a smile, "Just a minute, there's something more." Reaching from behind the counter in the outer office, he brought out two calendars, a pen with the elevator's name on it, and five suckers. "Here's a calendar for your mom and one for you, Teddy, and a pen and suckers for you and your sisters. I think there is an extra sucker for you."

"Gee, thank you!" my voice cracked with excitement as I clutched the loot that he handed to me and purposely did not look at my father for fear he would make me give it all back.

We were almost out the front door when someone from behind the counter called out, "Sam, your wife wants you on the phone!"

My father quickly turned around and walked back to the phone. I was surprised that my mom called him. It's a long-distance call. No one in our family is allowed to call long distance except, I guess, my mom and dad. I think that's why my father moved so fast. He always says, "The phone bill is too high. We need to stop using it so much." My mom still calls my grandmother. She lives out in Nebraska so I know that costs a lot more. I have never heard my father say anything when my mother calls Grandma. He never talks to my grandmother over the phone. It's probably because she speaks broken English, and it's even difficult to understand her when you are talking face to face. I have to listen really hard. The best language my grandmother can talk is Romanian. She lived there before she came to the United States. My mom can talk Romanian. She usually talks Romanian when she is speaking to my grandmother over the phone.

"Okay, anything else?" I hear my father ask my mother before he hangs up the phone.

"What did Mom want, Dad?" I'm anxious to hear what he has to say.

"We need some bread," my father answers.

Great! I say quietly to myself. The new grocery store is on the edge of town. I forgot to mention it when I was telling you about Shelby, but it's there. As we drive into the parking lot, I ask, "Can I come with you, Dad?" Most of the time I have to wait in the car or pickup, but after visiting Mr. Taylor, my father seems a little more relaxed than he was when we came out of the bank. I am sure the cold wind has something to do with what he says next.

"I guess so," he responds, and we both hurry inside.

My father heads right toward the bread while I scan the candy aisle next to the cash register. There are a lot of choices in this aisle. There is everything from penny bubble gum and taffy squares to nickel and dime candy bars. I quickly spy the Stark wafers. One package holds a lot of wafers with chocolate, mint, strawberry, lemon, and all other sort of flavors, but the wafers are really, really thin. *I can buy two,* I reason, *but they still go fast.* Almost up against the register, I see the cough drops. They are a dime—one whole dime. Covering my mouth, I try out my cough. *Yep, I think I have one. It's not as good as my older sister's cough she had this morning, but I'm sure if I don't have some cough drops, it* will *get worse.* My mother would probably make me gargle hot saltwater if my cough gets any worse. My mom says, "You can't be too careful. Sore throats almost always come with winter colds." A quick glance behind me tells me that my father is coming so I have to make up my mind really fast. "I want some Luther Brothers Black Licorice cough drops, please," I hear myself say as I lay my dime and cough drops down on the counter.

"Hmm . . . I heard that cough, Teddy," the store clerk says loud enough for my father to hear as he steps up behind me. In my thoughts, I am hearing her say, "You really are spending your money wisely." I like what my brain is telling me, but I also know that I like licorice, and when you suck on cough drops really slow, they last longer than Stark wafers!

"Where did you get that dime?" my father asks me suspiciously as he watches the transaction.

"I saved it from the money Mr. Godfrey gave me when I helped him with his hay this summer." I had been prepared with an answer because I knew my father would be surprised I had a dime, and probably even more amazed I could save it as long as I have.

After my father paid for the bread, we left the store and drove away.

Nothing was said until we were almost home, and then my father told me, "After you change your clothes, I want you to go out to the calf pen and chip the ice out of their water trough and take them some water." Even though the water trough for the calves was frozen, the cow tank wasn't. My father had put some kind of stove in the tank and filled it up with corncobs and poured a little kerosene on the cobs. When he lit the cobs, you could smell the kerosene, but the water tank did not freeze overnight. I have never drunk water out of the cow tank. Have you ever seen our cows drink? They slobber right in the water but still go on drinking. Yuck! You'll never catch me drinking from the same tank they do.

I didn't answer my father because of all of the thinking I was doing about the cow tank, so I was taken off guard when he said, "Did you hear what I said?"

"Sorry, I was just thinking. Yes, I heard."

He didn't ask me what I had been thinking about, but after I spoke, I started to wonder and imagine the conversation he and my mom would be having about his visit to the bank. It didn't take too much imagination as I have heard similar bank conversations between the two of them before.

My mother would usually say something like, "Maybe I can save enough for us to buy more chicks this spring."

My father would probably answer, "A few more dollars from egg money won't help much. The landlord will be visiting this summer. I'm sure they'll want to raise the rent. I've asked them to put in some terraces in the east pasture so we could plant crops there, but they keep telling me that they don't have the money. They don't have the money. They . . ." I think that is where my father grows quiet again.

I am realizing more that he must believe all of the money problems and family finances are his fault. I also believe he sees it as a man's problem because that was the short and easy view put to him when he was growing up. Maybe that is why he doesn't talk to my mom about it very often.

After a few more moments of quiet, my father says something to my mom that I've heard him talk about when he lets me go into Mr. Franklin's office with him. "I guess I'll need to start milking more cows, that's all. We have to wait to see if the bank will loan us the money for the cows. It's not too promising. Mr. Franklin reminded me again this morning that our December payment on our present loan is overdue and . . ."

Insightfully, my mother hears the despondency in my father's voice and, with a slight smile full of effort, says, "Maybe selling another can full of cream a week and extra eggs will see us through until the next harvest." Then she leans over my father's right side while pouring him more coffee and touches his shoulder ever so lightly. I'm also wondering throughout this dialogue, *Who is touching her shoulder? Where do comforting words for her come from?*

Before my imagination shuts down, I hear my father say, "Maybe," while taking a long draw from his non-filter cigarette, then unconsciously blowing smoke in my mother's face causing her to react by quickly moving away while coughing.

After arriving home, I changed into my chore clothes, only this time I put on two pairs of socks and stuck a piece of cardboard on top of the hole in my right shoe. My mother artistically traced my foot on a piece of cardboard and cut it out for me. She did a good job because it fits nice and tight inside my shoe.

"I guess we will have to wait and see if this time they agree to loan us the money for the new milk cows," I hear my father say as he pulls his coveralls back on. His words make me think that I wasn't too far off in imagining the conversation I thought he and my mom might have.

"It'll work out. Somehow it always does." My mother softly offers him some comforting words.

"Maybe," my father says over his shoulder as he walks out the back porch door.

Hearing the wind slam the door shut, I take the kettle of hot water from my mother that she suggested I pour over the ice in the calf trough before I start chipping away. Prepared to face the cold, I soon follow my father out the door, but I'm not walking in my father's footsteps. I take a different path. Snow starts to fall.

Chapter 4

Christmas

Christmas came on Thursday the year I was nine. I am not sure why, but we only had a half-day of school on Monday so our full Christmas vacation really started on Tuesday. Before we hop into Tuesday though, I have to help get you ready. It has been really cold this past week. In fact, it has been so cold, I can't convince my younger sister, Ruby, to go outside and play Sergeant Preston of the Yukon with me, even when I promise her I will be the dog when we are using the sled, and she can be Sergeant Preston. She said, "No! It's too cold!"

I ask my older sister to come outside and have a snowball fight with me or help me build a snow fort, and she rolls her eyes looking down her nose at me and says, "Are you nuts?"

So, I am happy that I received a train set for Christmas to play with. *I can't believe it! I actually got a train set!* And, I also received a package of plastic army men and a package of plastic cowboys and horses. I will admit the plastic horses were not what I asked for. I know by now you don't have to guess what I asked for and wanted more than anything in the whole wide world—yup, you guessed it, a horse! I am not complaining because a train set was somewhere high up on my list, certainly before pajamas and new underwear.

You'll never imagine what happened when I started to play with my train set on Tuesday after Christmas, but I am not ready to hop into that just yet. I have to tell you some other things first and second.

Remember, I told you that Christmas came on Thursday this year? We opened our presents on Christmas Eve, and on Christmas Day, after all of our morning chores were finished, we went to Nebraska to see my grandparents and some of my aunts and uncles. My grandmother made Romanian chicken stew with mush. My mom made three pies and Christmas cookies. My Aunt Mary roasted a duck and brought vegetables, mostly the ones I don't like—peas, corn from the can, and canned Brussel sprouts. Oh, yes, my Uncle Woodie brought beer for my father, Uncle Charlie and, of course, for himself. My Aunt says Uncle Woodie likes his beer, and my mom agrees.

We always receive clothes and money from my grandparents for Christmas. Most of the time, my mom has to take my older sister's clothes back because Victoria doesn't like the color. Victoria says, "I would rather have a brown sweater. It will go better with my skirt," or, "Mom, you know this blouse is too old fashioned. I would rather have one like the girls wear on *American Bandstand*."

I really think Victoria just wants to go to the city with my mom and pick out her own clothes because I heard some of my friends say their older sisters say the same thing about any of the clothes they get at Christmas time, even if they came from Santa Claus! It doesn't seem to cause any problems between my mother and my sister, though. Sometimes my sister gets her way, and sometimes she doesn't. I think it depends on my mother's mood and all the other stuff she may have to do in the city. It might also depend on the trip my mom takes my grandmother on before Christmas to pick all of this stuff out and pay for it. My mom has always taken my grandmother Christmas shopping because neither she nor my grandpa drives a car. My grandpa drives a tractor and a team of mules or horses that he has, but he hasn't driven a car since he moved to Nebraska.

A week or two before Christmas, my mother usually drives all by herself to my grandparents' farm to take grandma shopping. My grandmother doesn't actually ever go shopping by herself anymore. I can hear the conversation they would have in my head. My mother would say to my grandma in Romanian, "Mama, we will go downtown to Brandies. They have nice boys' and girls' clothing. It'll be crowded, Mama, but you can take your time, and I will look around while you shop." My grandmother wouldn't say anything until they reach the Brandies parking ramp. After receiving her parking ticket from a man in the booth, my mother would go around and around, up and up until she's on a floor where she thinks she can find a place as close to the department store door as she can. All the while, my grandma would be saying under her breath, "Yoi, yoi, yoi! Domdi!, domdi!, domdi!" I have heard my grandmother say that a lot more than my grandpa. I have thought before that maybe it was a prayer my grandma was saying when something bad was going to happen. My mother told me once all she was really saying is, "Oh my! Oh my! Oh my!" Knowing how religious my grandma and grandpa are because they read the Bible out loud every night, I still think grandma is saying a prayer and my mother has forgotten what it means in English.

In my really neat imaginative story, my mom finds a parking space that is just right, and the two of them are off for some shopping and looking around. Grandma's eyes become very large as she looks around and says to my mother, "Margareta, too much, too much!"

In Romanian, my mother answers, "Lotsa ma paucha, Mama!" I've come to know a rough translation of this means, "That's what you think!"

My grandmother has been and still tries to be a very independent lady. Even as young as I am, I know a lot about my grandmother and grandfather. In the old country, both of my grandparents had been married to someone else. I don't know what happened to grandpa's first wife, but grandma's husband was killed in some kind of war. Before that, he and my grandmother were farmers. When he went to war, my grandmother continued to work the fields with horses, did cooking and home care, raised a crop of vegetables that she took to market, and bartered for what she needed, all the while raising her two children. When her husband died, Grandma had the grit and courage to escape the post-World War One turmoil of Eastern Europe and find her way to Indianapolis, which is somewhere east of Nebraska.

Grandma met my grandfather in Indianapolis. I'm not quite sure how she did it. I'll have to ask my mother someday. I know my grandfather worked on the railroad before he came to Nebraska to be a farmer. Maybe they met on the train when my grandma was traveling to Indianapolis. My grandpa might have been a conductor or a ticket man. He probably was a ticket man. He might have been walking down the aisle, saying, "Tickets please, tickets please." When he came to my grandmother, he looked at her and said, "Tickets please."

Grandma handed him her ticket and then started to fumble through her purse looking for her children's tickets. I bet if she had had her apron on, she would have found them right away in her apron pocket, but I don't think you were allowed to wear aprons on trains in those days. "I know they are in my purse somewhere," Grandma says in Romanian sounding fearfully uncertain.

"You speak Romanian," Grandpa says, looking surprised.

"You speak Romanian," Grandma says back at him, just as surprised while she is looking into his big brown eyes and stops searching for the tickets.

"Where are you going?" Grandpa asks, still speaking Romanian.

"I'm going with my children to Indianapolis," she answers.

"Oh! I live in Indianapolis." Grandpa tells her. I'm sure he is looking kindly toward Grandma's children, and then, glancing back at Grandma, he offers, "I have a son in Indianapolis. He stays with my sister while I am on the train. My sister is Romanian, too. *How silly to say that,* my grandfather thinks. *Of course, if I am Romanian, she is Romanian too.*

"That's nice," my grandmother comments, not knowing what else to say to the man with big captivating eyes and a handsome mustache.

I'm thinking next comes the silence filled with an abundance of opportunity, a "now or never" pause before the journey moves ahead or is lost into nowhere.

Grandpa musters courage to break the silence. "Do you want to get married?" he asks.

"Sure," Grandma answers.

Sometime after they arrive in Indianapolis, they get married, and Grandpa moves everyone to Nebraska. He and Grandma start farming, have more children, and go to the Adventist church. One of their children is my mother.

So years later, my mom and grandmother are at Brandies looking at clothes Grandma might buy us for Christmas.

"May I help you?" a young sales clerk asks my mother, ignoring my grandmother.

"You can help *her,*" my mother says, glancing quickly from the young lady to my grandmother.

"Oh," the clerk says. Then she repeats the offer only this time to my grandmother.

My grandmother smiles and, turning to my mother, asks in Romanian, "What did she say?" I really believe my grandmother knew what the clerk said, but she just wanted the clerk to know that she was visible.

"She wants to help you, Mama," my mother answers and almost says something about my grandmother being coy, but decides it is best not to prolong the conversation.

"I would like to see boy's jeans," Grandma says in broken English.

"I'm sorry. I don't understand," the clerk speaks to my grandmother slowly and loudly, enunciating every word.

Grandmother's next comment is in her native tongue and probably not something that she would dare repeat at an Adventist Church Service. My mother smiles softly at my grandmother and then comes to the rescue. "Please, show us your boy's husky jean sizes," she says with the same smile holding its own on her otherwise stressed-out face. The clerk accommodates them as quickly as possible and says very few words until a purchase is made.

"Please come again," she speaks to the pair passing her by and heading for the elevator.

"Maybe," my mother responds, not wanting to leave the floor with the clerk having the upper hand.

It was probably a long day for my mother. She arrived home still having her chicken chores to do, supper to make, and just needing to be available for any assistance any one of her four children might need before bedtime. Looking at her that evening, you would have seen a mother who had a sense of calm and a peaceful look quite unlike the face she wore only a few hours earlier as she left the department store. If you were to ask her, "What changed?" she would simply say, "My Christmas shopping is done, and now I can do the things I enjoy doing at Christmas." No one ever seemed to ask her what it was she really enjoyed doing. I think it was, and probably still is, something we all took for granted—fulfilling our wants and needs is what gave her joy.

Friday, we all went back to our grandparents for the holiday celebration. I am sure our family is like any other when they gather for the holiday. There was a lot of eating, seconds on dessert, opening presents followed by a gush of "ah's" as each person took a turn showing off what they received, and for some of us, a rush to the bathroom or bedroom to try on our gift of clothing to make sure it fit. Of course, we were the first to leave because we had chores and milking to do.

Since I really want to get back to Tuesday, I am going to skip Saturday and Sunday. Well, I guess I did want to tell you that we went to church on Sunday. We probably went to church because it was still pretty close to Christmas, and my parents must have thought baby Jesus would stay around a little longer if we all showed up and gave thanks for the presents we received. All the other neighbors must have thought the same thing because pews were full and their relatives, hanging on for leftovers, came with them.

I also have to tell you that Monday wasn't fun at all. My father made me clean out the hog house. Have you ever cleaned out a pig house in the wintertime? Straw and manure are trampled down under the feet of swine until they are good and matted. On top of this, the cold air freezes the mess. Let me tell you, this stuff is hard to pry loose and when you do a steamy aroma rises into the air that finds its way right up your nostrils! It doesn't smell like baked bread, that's for sure. I wish my father had shipped more pigs to market!

Tuesday morning, as soon as I was done with my chores, I changed into my inside clothes and went straight to the parlor. My parents had set up my train tracks on a large piece of plywood held up by two sawhorses. I had saved boxes that Christmas presents came in and made buildings to set along the tracks. I also used my sister Ruby's blocks and old Lincoln logs to make a fort. In a short while, my train was traveling from Cheyenne to Ft. Laramie carrying soldiers, who now were cavalrymen, and their horses to their new frontier fort.

"There's something blocking the track up a ways," the engineer shouted to the captain riding in the locomotive with him and his crew.

"I see it!" the captain shouted back. "Do you think it's a trap?"

"It might be," the engineer answered. "There have been several skirmishes, and two Sioux were killed by deserters from your fort." The engineer grimly slowed the train to a stop and looked suspiciously at the pile of rocks that was up ahead on the tracks. When the engineer pointed toward the pile, the captain barked to the sergeant, who was coming up to see why the train had stopped, giving him a quick command to bring up some soldiers and clear the tracks.

"They better make it quick!" the engineer said.

Soldiers marching double-time passed the engine and were soon on the tracks pushing, throwing, and heaving rocks. The tracks were partially cleared when the soldier standing guard over the detail shouted out, "Captain! Indians!"

"Get your men aboard, Captain!" the engineer commanded much in the tone of a general seeking to have his soldiers under cover and not directly in harm's way. "I'll have to plow through the rest of the rocks! Hurry!" the engineer added as an arrow whizzed through his cab window, narrowly missing his shoulder.

"I'm ready to go!" I said to myself as I put the soldiers in the boxcars and the open coal car. Then without hesitation, I turned the train switch to full power expecting the engine to speed ahead, crashing through the rocks I made out of crushed up pages of yesterday's newspaper. In a few seconds, all aboard would be safe and sound.

To my surprise, confusion, and dismay, the train did not move. Not willing to see my soldiers slaughtered, I shut the switch down and then turned it to full throttle once again—not even a sputter came out of the engine. The train was dead on the tracks, and I did not have a white flag or handkerchief to tie on the outside of the cab. "My guys will never make it to Ft. Laramie. I have to act quickly," I said to myself. "Blow your whistle! Blow your whistle! Keep blowing! Blow out an SOS! Maybe the guard on duty at the fort will hear the whistle or see the smoke from the smokestack!"

While I imagined the whistle blowing out a distress call of SOS, I rushed to the kitchen where my mom was making bread and hollered, "Mom! Mom! My train is stuck! It won't move! What's wrong?"

My mom did not have the same sense of urgency that I had. She calmly stopped kneading her bread and, after wiping her hands on her apron, suggested, "Why don't we have a look at it?"

When we arrived back into the parlor, my mom checked to make sure the transformer was plugged in and that the train was on the tracks before she turned the switch on expecting, as I had, to put the train in motion. There was nothing except a very dull murmuring noise coming from the transformer; the engine remained motionless. "Hmmm . . ." my mother said after turning everything off and then repeating the earlier steps she had taken, still receiving the same results.

"What's wrong, Mom?" I asked, expecting a very good answer.

"I don't know," she responded quietly. Then she went into her bedroom and returned shortly with a book of instructions. After reading a couple of pages to herself, she continued to read, only this time she was reading out loud for me to hear, "if the train doesn't move and you hear a low humming sound, the transformer circuit has burned out. This is caused by overuse or leaving the transformer on for more than three hours at a time." Then she put the book down and said, "I know the problem."

"What, Mom, what?" I asked anxiously.

"Well . . ." my mom started out very slowly as if she wasn't quite sure how to tell me what happened. "Your father and I set your train up on Christmas Eve after you went to bed. Your father commented that he never had a train set and seemed really happy we bought you this one. Anyway, he played with it for a couple of hours. Starting, stopping, backing it up, going forward, fast and slow . . . and then doing it all over again. I went to bed. Your dad was having so much fun; he said he wanted to play with your train just a while longer. Honestly, Theodore, I have never seen your father so excited over anything, let alone a train set. If I had only known. I woke up early Christmas morning, and your dad wasn't in bed. I went to the parlor, and there he was lying on the floor, sound asleep. Teddy, I think your dad, unintentionally, left the transformer on all night."

"Did he really play with my train?" I asked, not questioning my mother but astounded that he would actually do such a thing. He never said anything to me about it, nor did he come into the parlor to play with the train while I was playing.

"Yes, he did," my mother answered.

"Why doesn't he want to play with me, Mom?" I must have sounded disappointed when I asked because my mother took some time before answering.

"Teddy, I think your dad was embarrassed that he played with your train so long, and when he left the transformer on, I guess he found it really hard having to explain how it all happened."

"But why, Mom?" I asked, growing more puzzled, and then added, "Dad hasn't ever played anything with me. Michael's dad plays checkers with him, and when I stayed over at his house, his dad popped popcorn and played Monopoly with us. Robert says that his dad plays catch with him and that they go bowling, hunting, and fishing together. Dad hasn't ever done anything like that with me, so I guess he hasn't ever played with me."

"I'm not sure your dad really knows how to play, especially with his children, Teddy," my mom offered reflectively as a tear slid down her cheek. "We'll go into town this afternoon and have the transformer repaired. I'm sure your father will approve."

When Mom left the parlor, I just sat on the floor, staring at my train and having a conversation in my head. Now that I am wondering why my father doesn't play, I guess I do remember once when he played hide and seek with Ruby and me. Last September, Mom sent Ruby and me down to the barn with a pint jar to have my father save her some cream when he separated. We were having company that night.

"Will you play with us, Daddy?" Ruby asked shyly, not aware at all that he was just about ready to start milking.

"I guess so," he said to my surprise and continued, "We'll play hide and seek. I'll hide in the cornfield. Theodore, you count to fifty, and then you both can try to find me. Theodore, you hang onto Ruby," my father calmly instructed me.

"Sure, Dad!" I answered with anticipation while closing my eyes. I hung tightly onto Ruby's hand and counted slowly . . . "one . . . two . . . three . . . fifty." When I opened my eyes, my father was gone. Without any prompting, Ruby pointed toward the outside barn door, "Daddy went that way!" She tugged on my hand as she pointed with her free hand toward the opened door. From where we stood, we could see the green corn stalks talking to one another through the early evening breeze.

Have you ever walked in a late summer cornfield when there has been plenty of good rain and sunshine? Corn stalks are unbelievably tall. The husk on the ears of corn have turned from a greenish-yellow peach fuzz to a dark brown just like a guy's beard might mature, only much faster. With the leaves on the stalk spread out, stretching for room, you can't see too far across from row to row, and you can't see too far ahead. With all that green, cornfields are a good place to hide at least until time and weather dry them out. Our father was hidden deep. Every so often, Ruby would call out, "Where are you, Daddy?" The first few times she called, we heard our father respond, "Over here, over here," but that was all. In a little while, Ruby called out again, only this time with a touch of fright. "Where are you, Daddy?" No answer. Ruby clutched my hand a little tighter, and looking up at me, said, "I'm tired of playing, Teddy. I want to go see Mommy."

"Okay, Ruby," I said, disappointed in myself for not being able to find my father. I am a Cub Scout. I already have a merit badge for tracking animals, but my father isn't an animal. He is much smarter.

When we came close to the barn door, we heard my father whistling the same tune he always whistles when he is milking.

Ruby broke loose of my hand and went running into the barn. "Daddy, Daddy, we couldn't find you. Where were you, Daddy?"

"I was here milking, Ruby," my father answered.

When you sneak back to home base and aren't caught, you are supposed to yell out. My father never did. He just went back to milking. I suppose my father wasn't really playing with us. I guess he was just tricking us. I wish my merit badge would have been about tracking fathers. Maybe if I had found him, he would have counted to fifty and let me go hide. I know I would have left some clues for him so he could find me, but that never happened. This is the only time I remember my father playing or even trying to play with us. I guess I'm still asking myself, *Does this count? When fathers hunt, bowl, or fish with their sons, are they playing with them or just tricking them, or are they just doing something to pass the time?* Sometimes I suppose I have more conversations in my head than I do with someone else.

After my mother made what sounded to me like a promise to get my train fixed, I lay down behind the living room wood stove and very soon was deeply engrossed in reading one of the books my parents bought at a farm sale. I was reading a story about how Roy Rogers and Trigger together rounded up a band of horse rustlers. It must have been a couple of hours before I stopped and went into the kitchen. To my surprise, a new transformer was sitting on the kitchen table.

"Your father went into town after milking and was able to make a deal at the hardware store. They had a spare transformer just like the one we bought you. Your father bought it for you, Teddy," my mother explained as I held tightly onto the transformer.

"Wow! Can I go hook it up, mom?" I asked, not really needing any more information.

"Of course you can," she said.

Before long, my train was crashing through the remaining rocks on the tracks. My soldiers were saved and on their way safely back to Ft. Laramie while the Indians and their tired horses went back home. Then without any explanation, the scenery around the track changed, and Roy Rogers with good ole Trigger were relaxing and singing in the coal car while the imaginary stolen horses and rope-wbound horse thieves were secured in the boxcar. We were taking horses back to their owner and thieves to jail. I believe Trigger was happy to be riding on the inside of the train instead of galloping along beside it. He and Roy had done a good day's work rounding up rustlers. My soldiers were safe and probably eating supper in the mess hall by now while their horses were munching away on hay in their stalls. I have to say my father did a pretty good day's work himself.

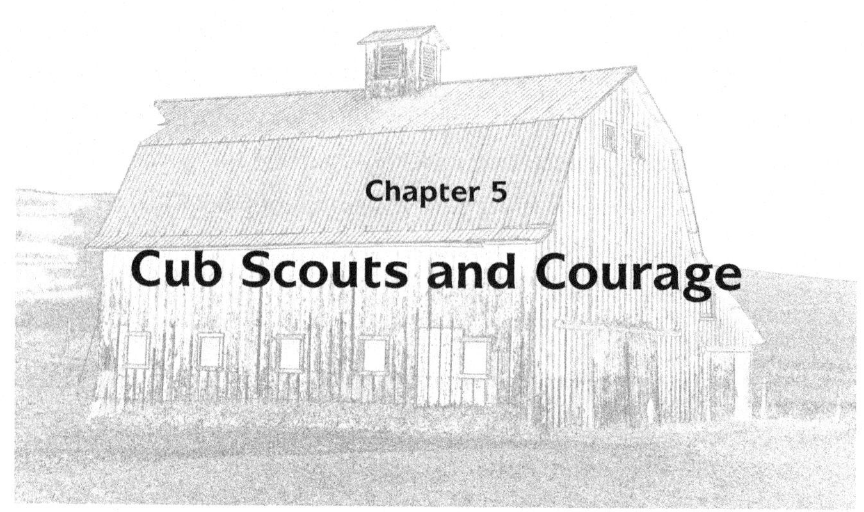

Chapter 5

Cub Scouts and Courage

It's raining when Ruby and I are running down the lane to catch the school bus, and Victoria is walking slowly, hoping just by chance the boys staring out the window at her will see her new hairdo comfortably sitting beneath the umbrella she bought with her babysitting money. Even though it is spring, this Tuesday morning is chilly. I don't care. I am wearing my blue Cub Scout shirt and yellow scout tie with blue trim. My kerchief is held together by a genuine Indian arrowhead fastened to a leather loop my tie goes through. I received my arrowhead from my scout leader, Mrs. Kristen, for earning more arrows under my Wolf badge than anyone in our den. She said her husband found the arrowhead when they were hunting for blackberries in their timber. Can you imagine it? I sure can. There was probably a grandmother picking berries a hundred or two hundred years ago at the very spot.

"Running Water, what are you doing here?" the grandmother says, looking up startled to see the young man who has not yet gone through the ceremony to be a warrior coming toward her.

"I've come to take you home, Grandmother," the young man speaks quietly as he looks around the area where his grandmother is picking berries.

"But I am not finished, Running Water. I need to collect the berries before my friends, the blue jays, take them all," Grandmother insists.

"Grandmother," Running Water says politely as he picks up her basket, "You are to come now. There is a wild dog out here. Iron Face said he saw him earlier this morning in this very area. Iron Face said the mad dog took down a fawn and dragged it off into the brush near the river. He is certain to be a very strong dog. We must go back, Grandmother. The birds aren't singing here. Listen. The dog is near. The berries will be here tomorrow. If not, the birds need them more than we do."

"You are right, Running Water, "Grandmother says, impressed by the steadiness and confidence Running Water's voice carries.

"I'll protect you, Grandmother," Running Water assures her as they turn toward the village.

"All will be well, Grandson. All will be well," Grandmother repeats as they start to walk.

The two have walked only a short distance when, from the corner of his eye, Running Water catches the brush, starting to sway against the gentle breeze. Then, in protest, the brush breaks into a thrashing noise as if it is trying to hold something or someone back but is not strong enough to do so. Within seconds, Wild Dog jumps out into the path by which Running Water and Grandmother travel. Wild Dog's growl is ferocious. The dog seems to have no bark. Its only sound is the savage growl ripping through the space between itself and its prey.

Grandmother stands motionless even though her insides are shaken by the dog's presence. Her years serve her well as she remains silent and stone-like while quite aware of the danger she and Running Water face.

For a second, Running Water's thoughts slip into the stories he has heard from his brothers and grandfathers as they sat around many evening fires. "The true test of a warrior's courage," they all seemed to agree, "is not in the action taken when confronting danger, but in the calling forth of the Spirit from the marrow of one's being to bring out the strength that gives him wisdom to see the danger's vulnerability in order to act accordingly."

For Running Water, there was only a brief moment of terse emotional pain that he soon recognized coming from his fear. In those seconds, he realized fear had not fogged his brain and he saw clearly what he must do. His decision gave him a keen sense of peace.

Running Water went through the steps he had first learned and then practiced from childhood on taking down prey. Now, his response was one of courage, respecting his own fear and acknowledging the power of Wild Dog. His eyes did not flinch as he accepted Wild Dog's challenge. His bow and arrow seemed to become part of him as he commanded their obedience.

With swift, deliberate action, he aimed. Wild Dog also sensed the challenge and as he had done so many times before, positioned his body to leap upon this intruder who smelled like an enemy and now was his prey. Wild Dog vaulted into the air. At the right moment, Running Water let loose the arrow he had held tightly on the bowstring. "Die well, my enemy." Running Water's words wrapped themselves around the arrowhead and traveled with it through Wild Dog's massive fur and tender skin, coming to rest uninvited into Wild Dog's heart. Instantly, with only a shriek of pain, Wild Dog fell dead at Running Water's feet. Running Water took his knife and cut through several strands of Wild Dog's Hair. Thanking Wild Dog, he lifted his hand and let the strands of hair run free with the wind.

"Running Water, I'll finish picking my berries now." Grandmother says with a presence of calm revisited. "There will be a new story to share tonight," she adds. Once again, Running Water gives his grandmother a smile as he leaves her to resume her picking.

Somewhere in those few seconds, the story of survival, bravery, and courage slipped into the pointed arrowhead's DNA and, like a time capsule, opened up at just the right moment into my brain.

I think when I wear my scout shirt and wash my ears out really well, I'm smarter.

On Wednesdays, we have our first spelling test of the week. It's called a practice test, but we are graded, so I study the words on Tuesday evening. I don't have to pronounce them correctly; I just have to memorize them and use them in a sentence. This Wednesday, I spelled every word correctly, and my teacher wrote a note on my paper: "Very creative sentences, Theodore." I wrote sentences like: "Scouts must always choose the right way to act. Courage takes thinking as much as action. Bravery begins with facing your own fears." I underlined all of the spelling words I used in the sentences just in case my teacher couldn't see them.

I wish we could have had spelling before recess. If we had, maybe I would have listened to my conscience and my own sentences. Maybe I would have chosen a better way to behave than I did. You should really know what happened to me on the bus earlier this morning before I tell you what I did at recess.

When my sisters and I got on the bus, the seat I usually sit in was taken. Marsha Goodie, a girl in Ruby's class, had her cousins stay overnight with her. The three of them were sitting in my seat. I had to go back toward the middle of the bus to find a seat.

My mom and the bus driver told me earlier this school year, "Theodore, sit in the front seat; that way, the bigger boys won't tease you." They both called me Theodore, so I know they were serious.

About the time the bus driver quit looking in the mirror to make sure we were in our seats, Gary Badman knuckled me really hard on the back of the head. It hurt, and tears came to my eyes, but I didn't say a word or turn around. He likes it when I turn around and yell, "Gary, stop that!" He likes to see if I am crying.

The bus driver had told me once, "If you don't make such a big deal about it, he'll leave you alone."

The bus driver has never said a word to Gary. He just yells, "Sit down, Theodore!" I don't know why he always yells, "Sit down, Theodore!" Half of the time, I have already turned back around in my seat. I never really stand up. I just think the bus driver sees what he wants to see sometimes. When the bus driver tells me to sit down, I think it's my fault Gary knuckled me and doesn't like me. This morning, when knuckled the second time, a couple of junior high girls laugh. Gary must have thought he was getting the attention he wanted because he started to call me names and pull on the back of my scout tie. Just about the time he was going to knuckle me again, I stood up, turned toward him, and said in a squeaky voice, "Leave me alone, Gary! You think you're funny, but you're not!"

Once again, I hear the thundering voice, "Sit down, Theodore, or I'll stop the bus!" It's the bus driver. Just like always, I believe I think he is blaming me for all of this. I stood up when I was reacting to Gary. I was hurt, mad, and embarrassed, all at the same time.

Gary wasn't any of those things. He just looked satisfied. He got the reaction from me he wanted. With a familiar smirk on his face, Gary mimicked the bus driver, "Sit down, Theodore!" The junior high girls giggled and then as if on cue, chanted, "Sit down, Theodore. Sit down, Theodore."

In a humiliating posture, I turned around. My eyes looked up to see the bus driver glaring back at me through the mirror above his head. Retreating into my own confusion and self-blame, I sat quietly for the rest of the journey while trying hard to disappear into the green vinyl bus seat. In the few minutes left on the route to school, Gary and some of the other high school boys started to talk about the football game they would be playing Friday night and how they would squash their opponents.

The junior high girls chattered about how cool Sal Mineo was on *American Bandstand* last night. "Isn't he just gorgeous?" Mary Lou sighed as she glanced at Gary.

"He has the dreamiest eyes," Clair added.

"And his voice . . . I wish I could be on *American Bandstand* when he sings. I think I would just die. I would simply die," Annie chimed in, not to be left out of Sal's fan club.

They were talking about Sal Mineo, but like Mary Lou, the rest of them also had their eyes glued to the back of Gary's head with his black, greasy hair staring back at them.

The damage had been done. No one was actually physically hurt, but there were hurts all the same that day, and they were not just mine.

I survived another bus ride, but my self-confidence was bruised. Confusion over why I was targeted by Gary lingered in my mind. I felt hurt, lonely, and scared. Sometimes some feelings come so frequently and are so familiar, a body just begins to expect them and starts to make room for the actions that come before them—like putting yourself into a cocoon, pretending that you are the only one riding the bus, and being ready to run if you think another attack is coming. At least I had my Cub Scout shirt with my genuine arrowhead kerchief holder on, and that mattered to me. I could make it because what I had to hold onto was just enough.

Later that morning, before our spelling test, we had recess. On Wednesday, several of us guys play Calvary because we wear our Cub Scouts shirts. Usually, we chase imaginary Indians that always seem to elude us or rescue damsels in distress who are really girls in our class playing jump rope or just hanging out but have no interest in being rescued.

This Wednesday, one member of our gang, Mike, decided we should seek out rustlers who stole Calvary horses, and once found, we would take them to the guardhouse. Everyone agreed.

Darrell was sitting on the teeter-totter by himself, looking lost in his own dreams. Darrell is often alone. I think it's maybe because his ears are dirty and he doesn't always wash very well before coming to school. I don't know. Darrell is a bit slower in spelling and English than most of us, but WOW! you should see some of the pictures he has drawn, and he always gets hundreds in math tests. Darrell is in our Cub Scout den, but he doesn't have a scout shirt. I'm not sure why he doesn't. I never asked him. I like Darrell some and we have played checkers and worked on some stuff at our scout meetings, but I didn't really consider him a buddy and hadn't given his friendship much thought, at least not until this particular recess.

Mike saw Darrell on the teeter-totter and shouted, "Hey, troop, there's one of the rustlers! Let's go get 'em."

"That's just Darrell," Tommy said unenthusiastically.

"Well, he's a rustler now. Let's get him before he escapes," Mike demanded as he raced toward Darrell with the rest of us following after him. In seconds, the four of us had Darrell surrounded.

"What do you want?" Darrell suspiciously asked Mike, who just happened to put his foot on the teeter-totter inches from where Darrell was sitting.

"We're taking you to jail, mister. We know you rustled those cavalry horses. Try anything funny, and we'll make trouble for you." Mike was talking just like the crooked sheriff did on Roy Roger's Roundup last Saturday morning.

"Leave me alone," Darrell demanded as he stood up and tried to step away from Mike.

Mike wouldn't let Darrell go. He grabbed him by the shirt and quickly yelled, "Help me, Tommy! This guy needs to know that we mean business! Come on, Roger, hit him. I got him tight."

Without hesitating, Roger punched Darrell right in the stomach. Darrell's face revealed the pain he must have felt, but he didn't say anything.

"It's your turn, Teddy. Show this rustler who's the boss!" Mike yelled.

"Let him go, Mike. He's not a rustler. It's just Darrell. He's not hurting us. Let him go." I heard myself trying to argue for Darrell's release, and I resisted hitting him, but I really did nothing to physically challenge Mike or Roger, who was assisting in holding Darrell down. I only used words that sounded very weak.

"Hit him—or are you yellow?" Mike's tone was taunting, sounding just like Gary's taunting I had experienced that morning.

I was filled with rage. I wanted to strike out not so much at Darrell but at Mike. Darrell only became an easy and defenseless target for my anger and frustration. Wham! My fist connected with Darrell's stomach, but my eyes were held captive by Darrell's expression when I hit him. I did not see the same look of pain that came when Roger hit him; instead, I saw a look of disappointment and betrayal.

Before any of us could say anything or make our next move, the bell rang. Roger and Mike started to run up the hill toward the school. When he was a few feet away, Mike turned and yelled back a warning, "Don't be a tattletale, Darrell, or we'll get even." Darrell stood there in silence. I was nearby but didn't say anything. As he started toward the school, Darrell passed me and quietly said, "I thought we were friends."

I was almost tardy getting back into the classroom. The rest of the afternoon went by in slow motion. I didn't dare look at Darrell, who sat only two desks from me on my right, and I certainly didn't turn to see if Mike or Roger would be looking like they were sorry for our actions. When I wrote out my spelling sentences, it was like I was trying to hide my guilt or something. I wanted to pretend that I did nothing wrong. The truth is, I did a really stupid thing when I didn't stand up for Darrell, and especially when I hit him. I was really dumb. *Why did I do such a thing?*

Of all the people in our class, I probably knew more than any student, other than Darrell, what it felt like to be picked on. As far as I know, Darrell didn't tell anyone about what happened.

I think Mrs. Kate would say that I sinned, that is if I told her what I had done. I am not quite sure I will ever tell her. I mean, if I won't tell my mom and definitely won't tell my father, I probably won't tell her. If I did tell her, she would probably ask me, "Theodore, what did Jesus do?" I would scratch my head and say, "I dunno." Rather than correct my English, she would go right ahead and tell me what the good Lord did.

No, before I ever tell anyone about what I did, I have to figure myself out first, at least as much as I can for a guy my age. All I know right now is that I did something wrong, and I don't like it very much. I know I have to be different. If I want things to change between Gary and me, I have to start changing the way I treat the Darrells I meet and start treating the Darrell I know as a person of worth.

We have Scouts in the community room above the fire station. After school, I walked alone to the station. When we were all there, our troop leader, Mrs. Kristen, had us all form a circle. Looking straight at me, she said, "Theodore, will you please lead us in the Scout pledge." I really didn't feel like saying the Scout pledge at the moment, let alone leading it, but I didn't know how to say "no" to Mrs. Kristen or even if I could say "no."

I slowly raised my hand and started: "I pledge to do my duty to God and my country, to be square, and to obey the law of the pack." I had the words memorized, so it was easier than I thought it would be. *Funny, isn't it, how you can say something and not think much about it?* For the moment, I didn't want to give the pledge much thought. After we were through, Mrs. Kristen talked to us about badges we could earn and projects that we had to do to earn gold or silver arrows under the badge. Mrs. Kristen said if we saw a fellow scout do something out of the ordinary that was helpful and good, we could put their name in for a special patch.

When we were working on our projects, Mike, Roger, and Tommy were distracted by the ambulance that was leaving the station downstairs on a call. They all ran to the window to see what direction it was going. Darrell had remained at the table and continued to work on a picture that he was drawing.

I took the opportunity to talk to Mrs. Kristen. Somehow, I found the courage to tell her about my part in bullying and mistreating Darrell. She is our scout den leader, so I didn't think she would really call me a sinner or whip me or make me go stand in the corner. I didn't mention anyone's name, but I had a sense that she knew. Then I told her that Darrell should receive a patch for courage because of the way he faced us that afternoon and came to Cub Scouts acting as if nothing had happened. Mrs. Kristen said she thought it was a good idea and would recommend the idea to the District Scout Director. Then she asked me some questions that I was not able to answer at the moment: "And what are you going to do about this mess, Theodore? Have you given any thought to how you want to work things out between you and Darrell or how you'll stand up for what is right the next time you are dared to join a group of bullies or their cheerleaders?" She didn't say anything else. My brain weighed a ton with all the words inside it.

After we were done and had all the tables and chairs put away, I went downstairs to wait for my mother or father. Mrs. Kristen patted my shoulder as she walked by and simply said in a whisper, "I know you'll do the right thing, Teddy."

Darrell was just a few feet behind her. I knew I had to do something sooner rather than later. When he was just about to pass me by, I said, "Darrell, wait a minute." He turned and, without a word, stood there looking at me. "I am sorry, Darrell. I was wrong. I'd like us to be better friends. There's this guy on our bus, Gary. He always picks on me all the time, and it hurts. He gives me knuckle sandwiches, and the junior high girls laugh. He's a bully. I realize now, this afternoon at recess, I was the one being a bully."

"Thank you, Teddy," Darrell said quietly before he continued to walk.

"Wait, Darrell," I reached out and took a hold of his shoulder. "Here! This is to let you know that I really mean what I said." I slipped off my prized arrowhead in its leather loop and handed it to him.

"I can't take that, Teddy," Darrell said, pushing it away.

"Yes, you can, Darrell. It's a giveaway. Just like warriors do when they come back from a good hunt or have a victory. They give away gifts and possessions to people in the village. It's an honorable act, and it's an honorable act to accept the gifts."

"But . . ." Darrell seemed stunned that I would offer him my arrowhead.

"I don't have any ponies to give you. They might be a lot harder to let go," I said grinning. About that time, my mom drove up, and I quickly said, "I'll see you tomorrow. We'll figure out how to deal with Mike together."

"See you tomorrow," Darrell called out as I was opening the car door.

As we were driving down the street, my mother looked my way and asked, "Where's your arrowhead?"

"Uh . . . uh . . . I gave it to Darrell," I calmly answered.

"What? I thought that was something you really treasured," she said with a surprised look.

"Yeah, but it looks better on Darrell," I answered.

There wasn't anything else said about my arrowhead. When we got out of the car, and before we went into the house, my mom gave me a big hug, whispering in my ear, "You're a good son, Theodore."

Did you know that Gary Badman and Darrell were cousins? I didn't know. The next morning when I sat down in my seat on the bus, Gary came up and sat beside me. I wasn't scared. I was surprised. He didn't say anything until we reached the school grounds. Just before he stood up, he turned to me and said, "You did a nice thing yesterday, Teddy. I'm going to be watching you from now on." He actually said this with a grin, so I'm guessing he meant it in a good way. Then he finished with, "just don't tell the girls on the bus. It'll ruin my cool."

"I won't. I promise." I said, returning the grin.

Wednesday afternoon recess is always different. It comes right after the first spelling test of the week. Our fifth-grade teacher, Miss Adamson, always tell us before we leave school on Tuesday, "Class, remember tomorrow is your first spelling test for the week. Take your spelling book home and study hard. Say each word out loud, pronounce it correctly, and write the word down. Remember, your score will count as a grade."

Miss Adamson always says exactly the same thing every week. I guess she wants us to be sure we study our spelling words. Most of us guys know it's just a practice test because we have the same words on Friday. I think that is when the score on the test really counts. All the girls in our class I have talked to really listen to every word Miss Adamson says as if she was saying the words for the very first time. I am not sure why they listen so hard. I just know all the guys in my class are Cub Scouts, and after school on Wednesday, we have our Scout meeting upstairs at the fire station. So just before the last recess, we aren't concentrating so much on spelling words correctly as we are eagerly anticipating the bell to ring so we can be cool and walk past the girls who are already outside in their own little groups.

We are still playing cavalry, but we don't say *playing* anymore; we say that we are *re-enacting western dramas.* After all, we have to have something to do at recess time. I know most of us feel a lot better when we think that way because we aren't little kids anymore. We usually pretend we are searching for renegades and avoiding ambushes. We practice stuff we have learned in scouts like tracking, even though there are no tracks on the tar-covered playground. I have my Bobcat, Tiger, and Wolf patches and two silver arrows and three gold arrows on my scout shirt now, so I am a sergeant in the cavalry. Our officers are all make-believe because there aren't any Boy Scouts in our grade. We think real officers should be Boy Scouts. I guess it would be funny if there were Boy Scouts since that would mean they were held back awhile, and they probably wouldn't want to be playing cavalry with us.

Being a sergeant means that I am one of the guys that give orders, and for a very short time, I actually have a few guys do what I tell them to do. It's fun. On this particular Wednesday, there weren't any renegades and no outlaws the sheriff asked us to track down, so our imaginary lieutenant, who just happened to be riding with us on this day, gave me a command to take three privates with me and go round up the stray horses that were lost when they were being brought to our fort from Fort Lincoln. After a few runs up and down the playground hill and around the merry-go-round, Joey, one of the privates, spotted the strays.

"Let's go get 'em, men," I commanded, and off we went right through Allyson and Sheryl's jump rope. The girls waiting to jump all screamed, and Sheryl dropped her end of the rope and stamped off only to turn back around and yell, "I'm going to tell Miss Adamson. You guys are in real trouble. Miss Adamson is going to call your parents, and you might be put in jail!" With her head to the ground, Sheryl was yelling so loud and stomping so hard she hadn't noticed Mrs. Adamson was standing right behind her nor was she watching where she was stomping, and she stomped right on Miss Adamson's foot! We scattered as fast as we could while trying to blend in with the other kids on the playground. From behind us, we could hear Miss Adamson's voice, cloaked in pain, call out, "Sh—errr—yl!"

"Oh, I'm sorry, Miss Adamson!" Sheryl exclaimed as she turned, surprised to see our teacher. Both Sheryl and Miss Adamson's faces were bright red. One was from the pain she was experiencing and the other out of embarrassment for the predicament she created. As Sheryl composed herself, she went on to explain, "It's all Teddy and those other boys' fault! They ruined our jump rope count and ran right through our rope! They should be spanked by the principal with a paddle in the office and . . ."

Having gracefully recovered, Miss Adamson put her finger up to her mouth, "Shh, shhh, Sheryl, calm down a bit. I think the boys learned their lesson. I am certain they won't interfere with you jumping rope in the future. Now let's go inside; recess is over." With those words, Miss Adamson blew her whistle, put her hand on Sheryl's shoulder, pointing her toward the south entrance of the school, gave her a slight push, and started to limp forward.

Sheryl's face looked disgusted, disappointed, and defeated all at the same time, but she didn't say anything else. We won! There would be no court-martial, no guardhouse, no hanging. And you know what? We were able to successfully drive all of the strays into the post corral and into their stalls, that is, if you allow your imagination to be stretched to see our classroom and rows of desks in such a way.

The fire hall is about six blocks from the school. As soon as the dismissal bell rang, we were on our way to more scout adventures and treats.

My mom is our den mother, and last night she made chocolate chip cookies. She said, "It's cheaper for me to make cookies at home than to buy store cookies." I agree with my mom not because of her arithmetic, but because my mom's cookies taste so much better than store cookies.

We always have treats after we race up the stairs to the large spacious room where we have our meetings. My mom gives us all a smile as she instructs us, "Sit down, boys, and you can have your snack. Tommy, you can pass out the cookies. Are your hands clean? Let me see. Okay, Tommy, everyone gets two cookies." I really have to let you come right into our meeting with me to hear the rest of the story because everyone else says it much better in their own voice than I can describe to you.

"Can I pour the Kool-Aid, Mrs. Hall?" Jimmy asks enthusiastically while waving his hand in my Mom's face.

"No! I want to do it!" George Adams yells at the top of his voice.

"Boys! Quiet down now, please. I'll pour the drinks this afternoon, but not until you all sit down." Mrs. Hall (that's my mother) uses her command voice a lot at the Cub Scout meetings, and everyone does exactly what she says—most of the time. My mom seems to receive a lot of respect from her boys. It doesn't seem to be because of her cookies, though they are homemade, and a few of my fellow troopers probably don't have homemade cookies at their house—but more because she shows a genuine interest in each of them and seems to draw out the best in their talents. When everyone is quiet, my mom gives a nod to Tommy, and he passes out two cookies to each of his fellow Cub Scouters.

All are watching Tommy to see how many cookies are left, but we would do the same thing regardless of who was passing them out, even if it was the Apostle Paul, or the President of the United States, or an Eagle Scout. No matter, we always sigh with relief because we also know my good ole Mom makes sure there is just enough for all of us to have second helpings. I don't know how she does it. It's like a magic trick I saw on the *Mickey Mouse Club* one time. A magician asked a Mouseketeer to hold an empty plate in front of him. After putting a hankie over the plate, tapping it, and saying some magic words, he made three balls appear out of thin air. With the Mouseketeer still holding the plate containing the balls, the magician placed a hankie over it again and said a few more magic words. Next, he had another Mouseketeer come up and remove the hankie. And there it was, another ball appeared on the plate. My mom can do one better than any ole magician. Instead of balls appearing on a plate, she makes chocolate chip cookies appear! And regardless of the number of boys, she is always able to make enough cookies appear from her Tupperware bowl for all us to have a second helping. Someday, I'll have to ask her how she does it, but not now because I'm too busy eating my cookies.

After examining our Scout books and the progress we have made working on our next badge or arrow, Mom talks to each one of us. She always says, "You are doing very well! Do you need any help? Are you willing to work just a little harder for your wolf badge or your gold or your silver arrow?" My mom encourages a lot. I don't think any of my Scout buddies want to disappoint my mom. We might not get any more cookies, so all of us say, "Yes, Mrs. Hall, I'll work harder." Or "I need help with this." I don't call her Mrs. Hall. I say, "Yes, Mom, I want to become a Boy Scout. I will work harder."

We planned our campout for the second Saturday in May. It really isn't a campout. We will go along a trail by the Nishnabotna River. When we arrive at a big sandy beach, we will build a fire and cook our lunch.

Last fall, we went on a cookout at the same place. I was paired with Eugene. I brought two matches kept dry in a baby food jar. Our Scout book says, "A scout should learn how to start a fire with just two matches," so that is all that I took. The day we went was very windy. I did everything the book said to do in order to start a fire. Everything! First, I found some dry grass and dead twigs. I built the twigs up like a teepee and put the dry grass on the inside.

Eugene watched me while I worked. As I carefully built my teepee and laid the dry grass inside, Eugene had a grin that wasn't going anywhere on his face. When I was done, I produced one of the matches from the jar and huddled over it as I struck it and tried to coax it inside the teepee. The wind blew it out. I wasn't giving up. I drew the second match and repeated my efforts, but the wind hadn't gone south and did the very same thing with this match. Remember, I only brought two matches. I looked at Eugene, who still had that grin stuck on his face. I was upset. Eugene didn't say a word. He just looked around to see if anyone was watching. No one was. They were all too busy trying to light their fires. Eugene gave me a smile, then took out his dad's cigarette lighter, clicked it like a pro, and in no time, we had a fire going.

Eugene and I fried potatoes and cooked pork chops! We ate pretty well, and the way we started our fire did not affect the taste of our food one bit. I didn't say a word on scout's honor, but I saw my mom glancing our way several times. She never came over to our campfire. She was too busy helping some of the other guys. Then she paired up with George to cook a meal because no one else did. I remember her asking, "George, would you please be my partner? I need someone to build a fire. Will you help me?"

"It's windy, Mrs. Hall. We'll never get a fire going," George expressed nervously, revealing his doubt.

"I'll show you how, George, but you must build up the kindling first and stay calm. Okay?" My mom spoke quietly, so George had to really concentrate to hear her. When everything was ready, my mom pulled a candle out of her pocket, and with her back to the wind, she lit the candle with one match and used it to light the kindling. In no time, their fire was blazing! George smiled as he took out his hot dogs and placed them in the frying pan my mom had brought along with all kinds of stuff she had chopped up for frying. She had done all of the chopping before she came. My mom was really prepared for this cookout! With our potatoes and pork chops, Mom and George's hot dogs, and all of the other stuff, you couldn't have eaten better meals even at the Pottawattamie County fair or church pot luck!

Well, that's what I remember about the first cookout. Now we were planning another cookout. When we were finished, my mom continued to help one of the guys with his scout book while the rest of us played pirates and navy on the tables stacked one on top of the other lined up in two rows in the back of the hall. Our voices continued to rise with the pirates on top of one stack of tables and the navy on top of the other. The sea was really rough, and both ships were rocking away. Finally, my mom looked up from the other side of the room and sternly called out, "Boys, stop that! Come down from there! Those tables will fall. You are going—"

Suddenly her premonition came true. Just as she rose from her chair and started to walk toward us to show that she really meant business, one stack of tables slid right into the other stack with pirates, navy men, and ships tumbling to the bottom of the sea, or as my mom would say, the floor. We all screamed. My mom went from walking to running. George laughed. Fortunately, none of us were hurt.

Mrs. Hall (Mom) set us all down right in the middle of the mess. She didn't lecture us, which was what we were all expecting, but she did go through the safety drill we had learned in our first aid class. Then we had a discussion on "what if's." She started by asking Tommy, "Tommy, what would you have done if, after falling, Michael started to yell that his shoulder was hurting?" My mom could make a teaching moment out of just about anything.

"I would holler for you," Tommy said with half of a smile.

"Well, that's nice, but it won't help you now. What if I wasn't here? What would you do for Mike?" My mom was very persistent with her questions.

"I know! I know!" George exploded, while his hand thrashed back and forth in the air.

"No, George," my mom said very slowly as she acknowledged George but then turned back to Tommy and continued, "Tommy, the tables have fallen. Mike was hit by one of them and now lies on the floor in pain. What would you do?" Again, Mom emphasized each word gracefully as she looked toward Tommy for an answer. Then not wanting to give up on Tommy, she gave him a hint, "Remember our first aid course in August?"

"Oh, yeah, now I know!" Tommy's light bulb turned on in his brain and was shining through his eyes as his face began to beam. "I would!" And with those words, good ole "straight A" Tommy recited the first-aid manual not only by memory, but at the same time he grabbed Mike, pushed him to the floor, and quickly whispered in his ear, "Yell in pain!" Mike gleefully obliged with an ear-deafening, pain-squealing noise. Tommy took us through the procedure step by step. When he was done, we all were very quiet, including Mike, who forgot about his pretend pain and was intent on listening to Tommy's play-by-play commentary. I marveled at how good Tommy had memorized or remembered the first aid manual and wondered if anyone of the rest of us guys could do the same. I know for a fact, I sure couldn't do what he did!

"You did a great job, Tommy!" my mom said as she patted Tommy on the back when he had completed reciting and demonstrating the first aid steps. Just at that moment, Tommy added, "but there is more." He then went on to explain how he had George, who was just dying to do something, run downstairs and tell the fireman on duty that a stretcher was needed for Mike, and he would have to be taken by ambulance to the hospital in Harlan. Looking at my mother, Tommy finished by saying, "You will have to call Mike's parents, Mrs. Hall."

"Yes, I would, Tommy," my mom said with a smile as she started to clap while inviting all of us to join in. Of course, we clapped, but we also hooped and hollered in honor of Tommy's great performance. When we quieted down a bit, my mom continued. "All right, guys, we have about ten minutes left, just about enough time for all of you to put the tables and chairs in a row. I think the firemen will stack them for us." My mom was using her no-nonsense command voice again.

There were no moans or groans from any of the guys. Can you believe it? I think we all realized that we got off pretty lucky. No one actually was hurt from our ships colliding. Mom wasn't going to tell the other guys' parents, and the fire chief wasn't going to have us arrested for destroying or almost destroying fire station property. I know we will play navy and pirates again; however, next time, our ships will be closer to the floor, and our ocean not as deep.

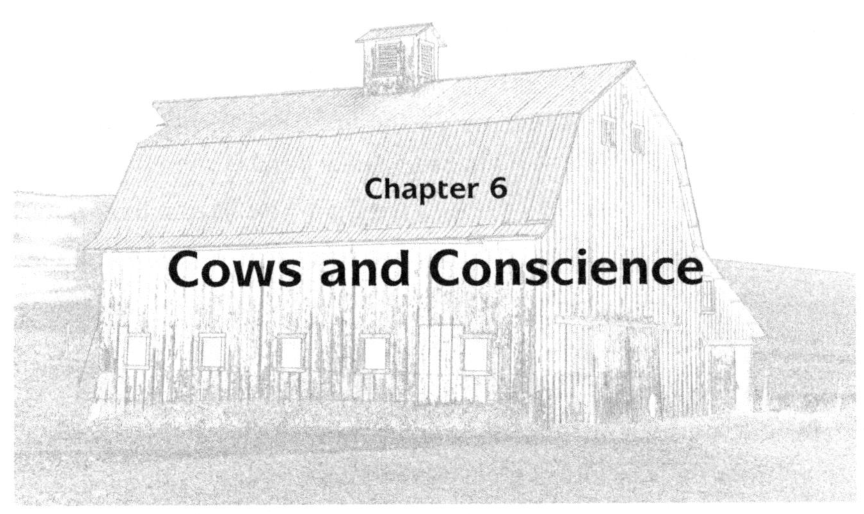

Chapter 6

Cows and Conscience

On the way home, Mom and I had a little more conversation about what had happened. It wasn't my intention to open the door to the topic, but I guess I did.

"Mom, are you going to tell Dad about what happened at the fire station?" I asked cautiously as she turned off Highway 59 onto the gravel road.

"Tell him what, Teddy?" she inquired without glancing over at me.

"Well . . . I mean the tables . . . " I was hesitant to ask her not to tell.

"Would you want me to tell your father, Theodore?"

Oops, my mom said Theodore. Maybe this whole thing was much more serious than I first thought, so I paused briefly while looking out the window. I needed to give my brain a little more thinking time. Mom knew exactly what I meant when I asked, and of course, she understood that I would not want her to tell my father. She wasn't going to tell any of the other boys' parents, so I hoped the same mercy would be applied to me. After all, my father wasn't there, but I know if he heard the story about the incident from me or the facts from my mother, he would take a very negative view of the whole thing.

I reasoned since he could not punish any of the other guys, I would be punished on behalf of all of them. I visualized a good scolding about neglecting responsibility, pictured being sent to bed without supper, having to write a letter of apology to the fire captain and to the mayor, and promising to pay for any damages. I knew if there were damages and they held me to it, I would have to give them the hay bailing money I might earn helping neighbors bale hay; but, they would have to wait until I was twelve. My father said I had to help bale the neighbor's hay for free, but when I was twelve, I might be paid for helping on my own whether my father came along to help or not.

By now, my imagination was running away with my thinking. Finally, I turned from the window and gave my mother a direct side-glance. Her eyes were clearly focused on the gravel road that had been softened by a couple days of rain. It was easier for me to speak my mind when her eyes weren't locked onto mine to catch several blinks, or an eye shift, both of which would tell her I might be speaking a half-truth or hiding information from her.

Feeling confident, I quietly expressed what had been on my mind. "No, Mom, I wouldn't want you to tell Dad. He wasn't there. He always hears things differently than if he saw what was being said. No, he'd take it all wrong, and I'd be in deep trouble." There, I gave her my full thoughts, the full page.

My mother sighed. I know she understood what I was saying. I also know she saw my father differently than I did. Of course, she did. She wasn't a kid like me. To my surprise, my mother responded immediately, "No, Theodore, I am not telling your father." We turned into our lane. Arriving home, my mother said, "Go upstairs. Change your clothes. Go do your chores. It's late. Go out and bring the cows home before you do anything else. I'm sure your father will be ready to milk soon."

I did exactly as she told me. I was relieved to hear she wouldn't be a tattletale. In a few minutes, I was scurrying through the thawing muddy cornfield awakening from winter's deep sleep.

My footsteps met the mud beneath me as I practically slid between two strands of barbwire into the pasture and started to run toward the cows. I was in a hurry even though I had been told time and again not to be in a rush when I brought the cows home. Maybe it was because my mother said, "It's late, and your father will want to start milking." Maybe it was because I had some sentences to write for English class tomorrow. Maybe the real reason was the darkness that was creeping down the hill with me and, at the same time, waiting for me across the pasture's barbwire fence. Whatever the reason, I was in a hurry.

At my age, when you are doing something your conscience says is "wrong" or "not the right way," you have to pretend you don't hear your conscience so you can convince yourself what you are doing is right. Remember, I have told you before that I have a loud conscience. So it is very hard for me to pretend that I don't hear it when it is speaking loudly to my brain, *Slow down! Quit running the cows. Your father is going to know they have been running. Boy, are you going to be in trouble—again.No!!! That is not the place to cross the creek! Go downstream and cross where you always do when you are bringing the cows home.*

But it's growing dark! I talk back to my conscience just like I sometimes hear Ryan Jones talk back to the principal when I pass by the school office. *My father wants to milk. If I'm late, supper will be late. I have homework. Sugarfoot is on TV tonight. There is nothing wrong in crossing here.* I think I won for now, but I don't know. It seems like I had to work harder than I thought I would to make the cows cross where I wanted. It was like they were daring me.

"You can't make us cross here, little boy. Who do you think you are, Moses?" it seems the whole herd was mocking me as they resisted crossing.

"I'll show you who the boss is." I said it in my head to the cows, but not out loud because that would be rather silly.

"We ain't going," they all chimed back at me with their tails waving and an occasional "moo."

"Oh, yes, you are! You can't always have things your way. You never do what I want you to do."

I reacted. What I wasn't willing to accept, at the moment, was that by instinct, the cows were smarter than I was. The place I chose for them to cross the creek was much wider because of the snowmelt and early spring rains spilling over its borders, hiding the natural boundary. It seemed like a reasonable place for crossing because it was much closer to the path heading south and to the lane leading to the barnyard.

I realized later that it would have been much easier and wiser if I had listened to the cows, and yes, my conscience, and taken the time to let them go their natural way and cross where they were in the habit of doing. But you know, I was a sergeant in the Calvary. Troops have to learn how to take orders and not talk back. Isn't that the way life is? Isn't that the way we all are brought up to believe? I was going to have my way.

You know what? I was wrong! Boy, was I ever wrong! Like most animals, cows have a certain rhythm to their routine, and they have forever been trying to demonstrate and tell me so. If you feed them, they give milk. If you have a voice they become familiar with and, in animal thinking, if they have trust in the voice they hear, they will come when you call. If you open the barn door that leads to the milking parlor, the same first five cows will step into the barn every time, not necessarily because they want to be milked, but because you have set feed out for them to eat. They are the first five just because they have a pecking order of their own. Try to replace number two and four with other cows, and you are in for a bit of a tussle.

If you are really late coming to fetch them for milking, they will walk, not run up to the barnyard gate all by themselves. They will wait and wait. If you don't come and open the gate after a while, they will turn around and start walking back down the lane toward the pasture unless, of course, it is really, really cold or snow is falling hard, and the wind is swirling the snow back up into the air. They will probably hang around a little longer because somehow again, I think by that word *instinct*, they know that only a few yards away, they will find warmth, hay, and grain in the place humans call a barn. This rhythm of life called their "instinct" enjoins with the human voice and command when there is mutual trust and benefit regardless of how it is defined.

Tonight, I wasn't thinking about the rhythm of life cows have, and this was most unfortunate because neither was I thinking about the consequences of a young boy's lack of maturity, Calvary sergeant or not. I wasn't giving much attention in the right way to my conscience either, and as I have told you before, that is a dangerous habit. Pushing your conscience into a corner or believing you can lock it in a brain closet and forget where you put it never works. Actually, I don't believe I have ever done such a thing as lock my conscience in a closet; I was just thinking about it right now. I think my conscience is much too large and tricky for me to ignore it or to allow it to be held captive. Regardless of understanding the difference this evening, I was going to have my way. After all, with or without my Cub Scout shirt on, I was still a sergeant in the Calvary, and I might be court-martialed saying what I just said, but I can be just as stubborn as my father sometimes. And so I was. As always, when stubbornness blinds your vision, you never really win anything at the end of the day.

Patsy was the first cow to step into the creek. She didn't look back. She just plodded along. I was too busy struggling to successfully maneuver the whole herd to cross over, so I did not recognize how deep Patsy was immersed when she was halfway across.

It looked like Brownie would be the last cow to start crossing. The rest of the herd was pretty much ready to start into the water, not as a group, mind you, but one at a time. Brownie has always had a mind of her own. If all the other milk cows decided to graze on the east side of the hill, Brownie would mosey down to graze on the far side of the pasture and eat alone. If it was winter and the other cows were out of the wind and snow snuggled warmly in the barn, good ole Brownie would be out in the yard with her head in the air and her tongue hanging out catching snowflakes to eat.

This late afternoon was no exception. Brownie refused to follow the trail Patsy and the others blazed through the water. Brownie took a slight turn to the left, and when she stepped into the stream, about ten feet out, she went down even deeper than Patsy and the others. She wasn't moving, and I realized I had to accept the fact that Brownie was stuck. The bottom half of her belly was probably being eaten up by alligators and stingrays which paralyze their victims so they don't feel pain. Brownie wasn't mooing. She turned her head toward me and looked as if she was saying, "All right, Big Boy, now what do I do?"

As usual, I reacted before I reasonably thought the situation through. Picking up clods of dirt, I threw them at Brownie and yelled, "Come on, Brownie! Move it!" She wiggled. Her big eyes grew wider. She wiggled harder, but she didn't move an inch. In fact, her only movement was downward, and she sank even further in the muck. I tried hard to believe that her sinking had nothing to do with my scaring her or making her nervous but was most likely caused by the alligators pulling her down farther into the water and mud. It was growing darker. I could hear my conscience from behind the door I had closed in my brain saying, *I told you! I told you!* I knew what I had to do. I had to hurry back up to the barn and tell my father.

Boy, was I in trouble—again! On my way, I started to repeat to myself the litany of possible punishments my dad might dish out. I could be sent to my room without supper and made to stay there for a hundred and one years. Worse, I probably would not be able to go on the next Cub Scout campout.

The list went on, but then another thought interrupted my litany. I thought about praying, but I reasoned, *If I had listened to my conscience, I wouldn't be in this mess.* My conscience probably told Jesus, "Don't listen to him. I told him . . ." While the other cows waddled and sloshed their way up the lane to the barnyard gate, I ran toward the barbwire fence that separated the pasture from the cornfield. Surprisingly, I crossed the fence without tearing my pants. I scurried as fast as I could through the cornfield to find my father before Brownie drowned. On the way, I still had time to wonder, *hmmm . . . who does Jesus listen to more, my conscience, who is never wrong, or a ten-year-old boy who makes a lot of mistakes but is always sorry for them and is nice to his grandmother and the older people in the church?* I decided it was the latter as I scrambled over the last fence and found myself back in the barnyard.

Without hesitating, I turned back and unlocked the gate so that the really muddy milk cows, all standing single file, could slide their way into the yard. Ahead of me, I saw the lights on in the milk parlor and heard my father whistle the familiar tune he always does when he is milking. I don't recognize the name of the tune he whistles, but I do know it is not "Jesus Loves Me."

My father was watching and counting the cows coming up to the barn door. I imagine he was also watching me because as I entered the barn just behind the first five cows, he immediately asked in a monotone voice, "Where's Brownie?"

I was both amazed and afraid that he was as calm as he was. *He's already planning your punishment,* my conscience whispered so that my father couldn't hear. *I told you,* my conscience continued uninvited, *I suspect you are really going to be laid into this time. Plead for mercy. Don't make excuses. Remember, this whole mess is your entire fault. I told you—*

Without knowing, my father interrupted my conscience and asked me again, "Where is Brownie?" He knew very well that I would not have forgotten her and left her out in the field somewhere.

Remember! No stories! Be honest! Plead for mercy! My conscience whispered as it continued to push me further into the barn.

"Well, Dad, you see," I started and then remembered my conscience saying, *be honest!* So I continued, "Dad, Brownie is in the creek. She's stuck. I made the cows cross at a different place. That's why they are so muddy. I'm sorry, Dad. I know I'm in trouble. It was getting dark. I thought

I better get them home—quickly." I paused, wondering to myself, *just how honest can I be with my father? Do I tell him the whole truth? Do I tell him why I really was in a hurry? Do I just let him know I am a fraidy cat? I am really scared of the dark, and even with the company of all of those cows, that I still have visions of being chased by wild dogs, or worse, wolves, like the ones I saw on Marlin Perkin's television show? Do I tell him that I hear strange noises that might be cattle rustlers and I don't have a horse I can ride to herd the cows better and faster to bring them home safely?* I am not sure I can tell him all of this. I really don't think he would listen to me. After pausing for what seemed like an hour, I thought I had better give the straight scoop, and like Sergeant Friday says on *Dragnet,* stick with "just the facts, ma'am."

Once again, I picked up on the truth where I had left my tongue. "Brownie didn't cross where the other cows did, Dad. She went out into a deeper part of the creek. She's stuck, Dad. She can't move. She has probably drowned by now. I'll get a job and buy you a new cow, Dad." Well, that was that. I was out of breath and cold. My feet were frozen. I was in pain, and my eyes wanted to cry, but I think the tears were frozen right under my eyelids. I am glad they didn't fall because I didn't want to cry tonight in front of my father. I just didn't want to show him my underbelly hurt. I was in real pain, though—besides my feet, my fingers were frozen. Both my shoes and my gloves had holes in them. The wind, water, and mud always seemed to find their way through those holes and eat away at my finger and toes. This wasn't pretend pain, this was real pain I was feeling, and I hadn't even been clobbered yet.

My father's face looked like the face of the character who just heard TV's star attorney Perry Mason read the character's uncle's will and last testament, stating that the uncle left all of his millions to a country Methodist Episcopal church with nothing going to him. I watched as he quietly moved up to each cow, sliding his hand across their back, as if to tell them that they were all right now, and they would be fed and warmed. When he reached each cow's head, he pulled the stanchion's wooden lock down to hold them in place during the milking. The cows didn't seem to mind. They were too busy munching down on the ground corn and oats I had laid out for them before I went out to bring them through the perils of a raging creek home for milking. When my father had finished locking the cows in, he looked up at me and said, "Come with me."

"Where are we going?" I questioned without speaking the words out loud. I decided it was wiser to stay as quiet as I could. While the first five cows stood obediently in their stanchions munching away and waiting to be milked, my father walked up to the machine shed, and I cautiously followed. Arriving at the shed, he gave the Allis Chalmers a turn with the crank handle. The tractor sputtered and coughed. It sounded much like my Uncle Harry, who my mother says, "smoked way too much when he was younger. Now he can't breathe very well, and he coughs a lot. That's why I don't want you to smoke—ever. Do you understand me?" I don't think she ever wants a real answer from me. She just wants me to listen. I think she believes hearing the coughing is enough of a scare for me.

The old AC (that's what we call the Allis Chalmers) usually sounds like that, but this evening it seemed to sound even worse. After a few more sputters and wheezes, the tractor died. My father muttered a few words to himself, but I was close enough that I heard what he was saying. I don't think he would use those words on one of the few Sundays he might go with us to church. Even though he used words I would get hot pepper on my tongue for if I ever said, I didn't try to correct him. I just watched. He put the handle in the crankcase and let 'er rip again. This time the AC sputtered a little less, started to purr, and then came alive.

"Grab the rope," my father told me as he pointed to the wall where the rope hung.

I reached up on tiptoe and was able to free the rope from its nail and climbed onto the tractor. I held tightly to the back of the tractor seat as my father backed out of the shed. I had to climb off to open and close gates twice before we reached the pasture. *That's why my father brought me,* I said again only to myself, *to open and close the gates. Maybe he will spank me out in the pasture so Brownie can see me being whipped and no one else will hear me wailing and whining.* My mind was racing with horrid thoughts, but my conscience was deaf to the words and offered no counsel or consolation.

It's not easy driving through the pasture, especially as night closes in behind you. There are a lot of ruts and gopher holes that pock the field and cause more bumps than bumper cars at the county fair. I had to hold on really tight to the bouncing tractor seat. By the time we made it to the place along the creek where I had forced the cows to cross, my father had turned on the tractor's lights. When we stopped near the water's edge, the lights shone across the water. There was no Brownie.

"She drowned, Dad," I cried out in fear and shame. "She drowned, and it's all my fault! I'm sorry, Dad!" I truly was sorry. I really was.

My father did not say anything except, "shhh . . . shhh."

When I settled down and allowed my eyes to adjust to the light, I looked across the creek, and to my surprise, I saw a very muddy Brownie standing as still as a statue. "There she is, Dad! There she is!" I eagerly pointed to Brownie with the excitement I imagined a Christopher Columbus' sailor must have had standing in the crow's nest at the time he discovered the first sighting of land in the New World.

My dad did not seem too surprised, and he showed no sign of relief or excitement that I could see in the dark of the night. As my father pulled down on the gas handle near the tractor's steering wheel, I could hear Brownie sloshing a few steps away from the stream, probably to avoid me, I decided. My father didn't dare turn the tractor off; he just looked down at me and said, "go over and take Brownie up to the crossing and bring her home. I'm going back to start milking." I knew exactly what he meant by "the crossing." It's the place where I should have allowed the cows to cross an hour or more ago. They knew the best place. The creek narrows at this place, and the cows can easily hop over and turn back on the barn side of the pasture and be on their way home. It takes a while longer, but it's a natural place to cross in contrast to the crossing I forced them to take. I was beginning to think more clearly about how the faster time or more convenient place might not always be the best course to take.

It was all I could do to hold back and not say, "It's dark, Dad! I might get lost! There might be wolves or mean dogs up a ways waiting for us." I wanted to say all of this, but it's as if my conscience turned itself on once more and clearly said, *No!* I listened this time and stepped down from the tractor and turned toward the dark with the tractor lights in back of me. As my father drove off, I walked down to the crossing and then backtracked my way to where Brownie was patiently waiting. Even though I was anxious to get back to the barnyard, I slowly herded Brownie back to the place where we could safely cross the creek, and then she and I walked quietly toward home accompanied by my conscience, my imagination, and the sky full of stars.

With Brownie sloshing in front of me, we kept our slow, steady pace. On the way, I kept singing, "Jesus Loves Me," feeling more confident now that it was a safe song for me to sing. After a bit, I tried to sing, "What a Friend We Have in Jesus." I couldn't remember all of it, so I just made up some words that sounded all right to me. Brownie seemed to be keeping time with her wet and muddy tail. As she swung her tail my way, piddles of mud would hit me in the face. I guess I deserved all she slung my way, so, even though it stung, I just continued to sing.

About halfway to the lane leading to the barnyard, I ran out of words to "What A Friend We Have in Jesus" and ended up singing Roy Rogers' "Happy Trails to You." I tried to recall words to a song we sing in church during Easter time when Jesus comes to the garden and finds Mary pulling weeds between rows of tomatoes, but all I could remember from that song was, "He walks with me and He talks with me . . . " I guess that is enough, though because Brownie didn't drown, I wasn't chased by wild dogs bringing Brownie home, and my father didn't cuss or spank me when he heard the news about Brownie. Well, at least, I hadn't been spanked yet.

I am not certain which one of us was the happier to reach the barn door, Brownie or me, but by the time we arrived, my father had the door opened and weary ole Brownie stepped into the barn to feast on a meal of ground corn and oats while the milking machine relieved her of her heavy load. After following Brownie through the door, I turned around to latch it shut, and that's when an overwhelming feeling of dread hit me.

My father had stopped whistling, and I could hear the milker humming away as it teased the milk from Brownie. I turned back toward my father and watched as he put the rag that he uses to wash off a cow's udder back into the pail. He slowly lit a non-filter cigarette, and as the smoke rushed out of his mouth and raced toward me, he finally spoke. "If you hadn't been in such a hurry, you would have never put yourself or the cows in this mess. I imagine all your yelling and clod throwing, forcing the cows to cross the creek in an unfamiliar place, scared the hell out of them. Won't you ever learn? All Brownie needed was for you to shut up, leave her alone, and wait. Dammit! Won't you ever learn?"

I know my father said a few more words that I can't repeat after this, but my ears were too full of my own conscience to hear what he said. I told you. I told you, my conscience kept prattling on sounding like a broken record, but I guess I needed to hear what it was saying. Besides, I couldn't tell if my father was scolding me or lecturing me, was angry or disappointed in me, was giving up on me, or was trying to teach me something. I don't know. He said more to me in those moments than he said to me in a long, long time. As he took another draw from his cigarette, I started, "I'm sor—"

My father quickly interrupted me, "Yes, I know you are sorry, but sorry isn't enough. You are always sorry. I am sorry too. Go to the house. I'll finish chores by myself." He turned away, trying to look busy fiddling with the milker, but it was doing just fine, and Brownie was still munching away. I wanted to do something. Something more than just walking up to the house defeated, embarrassed, and shamed. I headed toward the hay mound to throw down hay for the cows as I usually do before my chores are done. When I started to climb the ladder, I saw my father glance toward me. I expected him to yell, "I said, go up to the house!" He didn't. He just looked up at me as I disappeared into the mound.

Throwing the hay down into the west side of the barn where the cows usually hunkered down on cold or rainy nights, I thought, *He didn't yell at me to leave. He's angry with me. My conscience said I'd be in trouble. I think I have learned something tonight that I won't forget. If I am going to be responsible in the future, I need to be responsible now.*

You got it! I heard my conscience shout.

The rest of the evening wasn't the best I ever experienced. By the time I took my bath and changed my clothes, my father was done with chores. Supper, of course, was unusually late, but I didn't care. I wasn't too hungry. I wasn't much of anything that night. I had made a lot of mistakes that day. I wonder if all guys my age make mistakes like I do. I wonder how they live through them. *What do they do with their feelings? Who do they talk to? Are they sorrier than I am?* I wonder. I suppose I'll never know about other guys, I just know about myself and what I need to do, and that's probably enough for now.

I went to bed early, not to avoid everyone, but because I didn't have homework to do, so I was okay. I think I'll really be hungry in the morning.

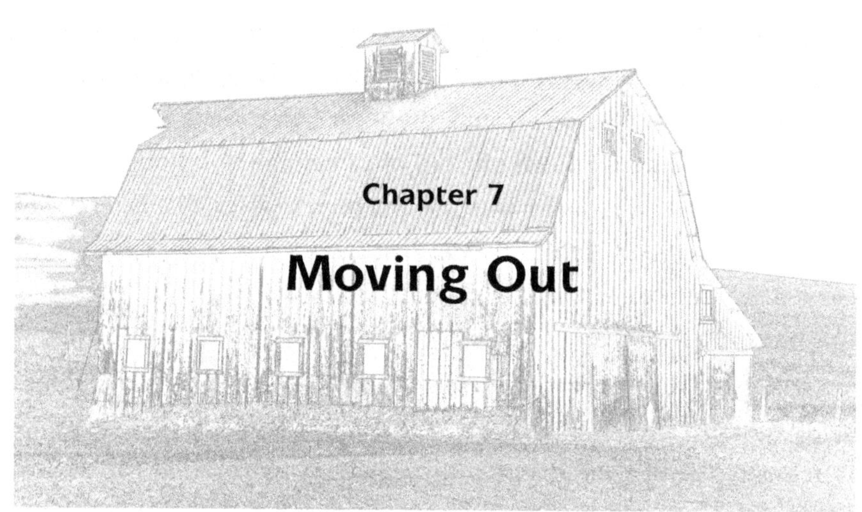

Chapter 7

Moving Out

Nothing much ever happens on Thursdays. They are dull. You might ask, "How dull are they?" They are so dull that you might go outside, dig up an earthworm or two, put them on the sidewalk, lie down beside them, and watch them crawl just for a little excitement.

In my short eleven years, as far as I can remember, nothing very major has ever happened on Thursday except maybe once a year between what is called Palm Sunday and Good Friday. It is Holy Thursday because after chores are done, we hurry and wash up really clean, eat supper with no dessert faster than usual, and go to church. There are lighted candles in the windows, and all the other lights are turned off. When it's time to sing, you can hardly see the words in the songbooks. Maybe that is why some of the men don't sing. I don't know. After some men take your money and the minister says some words about sinning and how good Jesus was to his disciples on that night, the minister says a very long prayer, and then he serves communion.

Communion is where the minister tells the adults to come up to the wooden railing. All the adults get down on their knees. After everyone stops fussing while watching Miss Mable, who insists on bending down even though Mom says she has very bad knees and it's hard for her to get up and down, the minister passes out really tiny pieces of Wonder bread cut like sugar cubes and then an eye drop or two of grape juice in tiny cups. Everyone chews the bread and then drinks the juice. Miss Mable is always in the first group, and two women are on each side of her to help her up and down. She won't let any men help her. It takes a while, but the minister just smiles and waits more patiently than I think I would.

After the first group are all up and going back to their seats, he calls the next group up. On Holy Thursday night, this all takes a while because there are usually more people in church than when we have communion on Sunday. I don't exactly know why. Maybe it's just the way Methodists do things. Oh, I almost forgot to tell you something that is very important. Before everyone gets up, the minister says some more stuff, and then very loudly he says, "Your sins are forgiven!" I think what makes this Thursday holy and different is because more men come this night than they usually do when there is communion on Sunday.

Last year on Palm Sunday, I wasn't as smart about such things as Holy Thursday as I am now. When we were in Sunday School before Miss Kate gave us our palms for the parade of palms they made us do during the church service, I asked, "Miss Kate, how do we know that Jesus really said, 'Your sins are forgiven.' And, can the minister actually forgive me of sins?"

Before she could answer, Bobby Brooks, who has horses and lives down the road from us, shouted out, "What's a sin?" Miss Kate calmly ignored Bobby. His older sister, Rachael, didn't. She rolled her eyes while calmly pinching Bobby's arm, letting her razor-sharp, painted red fingernails dig into his skin.

"Ouch! You are hurting me, Rachael! I am telling mother!" screamed Bobby.

By now, Miss Kate was used to Bobby's ruckus and Rachael's vacillating between mothering Bobby and being ornery as only a big sister can be. Quietly looking at both of them, Miss Kate said, "All right, quiet please so I can answer Teddy's question." It's amazing how Miss Kate is able to say what she does when things get out of hand in Sunday school without raising her voice or her eyebrows. I think that was not what Bobby or Rachael expected her to say or do because, in a flash, Bobby quieted down, and Rachael released her steel-tight grip on her little brother's arm. I was very curious and wanted so much to ask Bobby to roll up his sleeve so we could see if his arm was bleeding, but I knew better and kept my mouth shut tight.

Once again, Miss Kate was in charge. She turned her attention to me. Looking straight at me, she simply said, "Because the Bible tells us in red letters, those were Jesus' exact words." Miss Kate has told us before, in the King James Bible, whenever we see words written in red letters, those are Jesus' exact words. That was that. She didn't say any more about it and went on with our lesson. I guess I was expecting more. I should have waited for church and during the sermon raised my hand and asked the minister, "Reverend, did Jesus really say, 'Your sins are forgiven' and can reverends really forgive grown-ups who take communion for their sins?"

Our minister really gives long answers when you ask him a question. That is why I didn't ask him, I guess. I know I could have also asked, "Why aren't kids supposed to take communion?" On the way home from church, I told my mom and dad the questions I asked Mrs. Kate and told them the answer she gave me. I also explained why I didn't wait to ask the minister during church. I think my mom was pleased and relieved that I didn't raise my hand during church and ask those questions. Without being asked, my father commented on what I said. "I think the minister likes to hear himself talk." My mother punched him lightly on the arm and said, "Sam! That's blasphemy! You aren't supposed to talk about a minister that way. You might go to—" Mom stopped there.

Victoria and I giggled. We knew our Mom wouldn't say the "H" word. My father says it, though, and so, just to be ornery, he looked at her and said, "You mean I might go to hell?" Victoria and I put our hands over our mouths to muffle our laughs. Mom turned her head toward us and gave us a look that said, *"Don't you dare follow in your father's footsteps when it comes to swearing!"*

By now, Ruby was very confused. Her head turned from Vickie and me to Mom and then to our father. She innocently asked, "Mom, what's so funny?" Our father smiled as Vickie and I tried very hard to physically wipe the smiles from our faces and clear our throats to get rid of the giggles; however, the opposite effect occurred, and we giggled even louder until my mom, ignoring Ruby, turned back to us once more and looked at us as if she was ready to set us in the corner. We both stopped looking at each other and turned our attention to other things, which helped us to conquer our giggles. Mission accomplished; Mom gave her full attention to Ruby and softly said, "Nothing, dear." A few seconds later, we arrived home.

Look, I was talking about how dull Thursday is except for this once-a-year Thursday Night Special. So now, I want to come back to why I am telling you all of this. Are you ready? This particular Thursday was in early March. It's cold outside. I am still hauling in wood and coal to burn in the stoves. There is no sign of spring. Instead of rain, we still have snow. Instead of running water, we have ice. On most days, we are still bringing water up from the windmill pump to use for cooking, bathing, and washing. My father dumps cobs into the contraption he puts in the water tank. Then he pours a little kerosene on top of the cobs and sets them on fire. The heat keeps the water in the cow tank from freezing. The cows drink all they want, and then I have to dip my five-gallon buckets into the tank and carry water to the calves, pigs, and chickens. I guess I would have to admit that most of the time, I also water my jeans. Boy is March cold.

I need to back up a bit and tell you what happened when we arrived home from school that Thursday. As I have told you, most Thursdays in my eleven odd years have been pretty boring. So far, this Thursday has been no exception. It had been uneventful but was to end full of dreadful and yet exciting news.

My mother, father, and Cindy were gone when we had arrived home from school. There was a note on the table that read, "Victoria, you can start supper after you iron the shirts that are in the clothes basket. Teddy, you go out and do your chores. Remember, your father said, 'Don't run the cows!' Ruby, you pick up the living room and stay out of your sister's way. We should be home by suppertime. Remember, Teddy, don't run the cows!"

So here I am wearing long underwear that I definitely do not wear to school. I have my jeans on that are patched in one knee and have a brand new genuine barbed wire rip in the other knee that I haven't told my mom about yet. I have on two pairs of old socks. I wear two pairs so that one pair covers the holes the other pair has and vice versa. I put a new piece of cardboard on the bottom of one of my shoes because it's the one with the hole. I wear my cloth gloves that have the same holes in three fingers that they had the night before. Sometimes my fingers feel so cold I think they are going to break off if I hit them against something too hard. I do have a very warm, snug hat and a good winter coat that has no holes in the pockets so I can put my hands in them when my hands are frozen.

I am off to do the same old chores I have always done and that my mom instructed me to do. I knew I would have to do them. I think she wrote the note just to emphasize I am not supposed to run the cows. I know she did it so I wouldn't get in trouble.

Little did I realize, at the time, how in a wink of an eye, life could be turned upside down. Eleven-year-olds are just on the edge of thinking about life changes. While doing my boring chores, I started to think about how on Tuesday and Thursday mornings, Mrs. Schaffer, my sixth-grade teacher, makes us bring in a report from a news article that we read in the newspaper or, if you are rich, from a news magazine. She always says, "You must be prepared to talk for three minutes, and you must describe how the article changes things for those involved in the story." Then she adds, "If you or your family has something happen that changes things for your family, you can give a report on that event, but you must be able to describe how the event affects you and why. Remember, this is not show-

and-tell. It is a lesson on current events and their effects on people's lives, including your own." She calls this time of reporting Current Events.

Yes, you got it; most of us boys call it boring because we can't bring in anything about sports. This exercise is supposed to help us think about more than what is for lunch or playing basketball during gym. I am not thinking much about living on the edge tonight. I am just anxious to finish my chores without running the cows.

Now, I wish I had thought some about it. I might have been better prepared for the news my father and mother brought home with them. If I had known then what I know now, I would have also wished that it was Wednesday night because if it was, come Thursday morning when we have current events, I would really have something current to tell Mrs. Schaffer and the class!

It's not Wednesday night; however, it is a boring Thursday late afternoon. Boring! Boring! Boring! My chores went slowly because I really took my time, and I was deep in my thoughts. I didn't run the cows. I didn't carry two five-gallon buckets plumb full of water at the same time like I usually do. I spent extra time chopping ice out of the pigs' and calves' water troughs so they would hold more water, and I finished with gathering the eggs for my mom without breaking or cracking even one of them like I usually do. The hens pecking my hands and the rooster trying to scratch my legs with his spurs didn't trouble or scare me tonight. No, my thoughts kept me company and occupied.

I came onto the back porch with the egg bucket just about the same time I heard my dog, Pal, bark. When Pal barks short and loud, it usually means someone is coming up the lane. He barks whether he knows who it is or not. Sure enough, as I was taking off my chore clothes in the back room, my mom and Dad came through the front door.

Supper was pretty good even though Victoria made most of the meal. Maybe I should say, Victoria stirred up the pancake batter, fried the pork sausage, and made the hot chocolate. My mom actually made the pancakes while Victoria put the groceries away. I was surprised that my father didn't change his good clothes before supper. Instead, he smoked an unfiltered cigarette, read the paper, and drank a cup of coffee leftover from breakfast.

After supper, my mom quietly spoke. "Your father and I went to the bank today and borrowed some more money. We are buying seven more milk cows." She hesitated as if she was preparing herself to tell us some bad news. I couldn't imagine anything worse than buying seven more milk cows. Our herd would double overnight. *More trouble for me!*

"And," she started to say, then cleared her throat and started over, "And, we are moving to a farm south of here. You all will be going to a new school."

"No, Mom! I can't," Victoria yelled. "I am in band, and I want to try out for cheerleading! The spring dance is coming, and you and Daddy said I could go with Joe Larson. It's my first high school date." By now, tears were streaming down Victoria's face, but she still managed to add, "I'll be ruined! I'll just die! I know I will!"

"Yippee!" Ruby said, clapping her hands with glee. I doubt that she was excited about Victoria thinking she was going to die. While she probably didn't understand it all, I'm guessing she was just happy something new was about to happen.

"More cows . . . a new school . . . losing my best friends . . ." I muttered to myself. It didn't really matter how quiet or loud I was at the moment. While I was full of fear, sadness, and apprehension toward any change in my routine, my words were quickly drowned out by Victoria's screams, and my feelings were washed away by her tears. Anything profound or otherwise that I might say at the moment had no chance for an audience. Truth is, my parents probably never would have a hearing on this subject anyway. In our family, the decision to move or not was not for us kids to make or even discuss. The only voices to be heard or votes to be cast were my mom's and my dad's. There was nothing more to be said about it.

It is hard for an eleven-year-old boy to have a good grasp on the depth of his parent's financial struggles. I look back now and see my parent's frequent trips to the bank were probably not social calls.

My mom raised and canned all kinds of vegetables so we could have something to eat all year round. She would send me out in late summer and early fall to pick small worm and bug-infested apples from our little orchard behind the farmhouse. I would also have to trudge out to the cow pasture in the summer to pick buckets of gooseberries and wild plumbs, and from the same small orchard in the back of the house, I would have to climb the mulberry tree and pick the ripe dark berries. There wasn't much my imagination could do with the boredom that picking this or that brings; however, all of my picking was so that my mom could make jams and jellies for our table and we would have gifts we wouldn't have to buy for friends, teachers, and relatives.

My mom also raised quite a flock of chickens each year. She kept the hens for the eggs they produced until they were too old to produce. She then chopped their heads off, picked their feathers, gutted them, and then froze them so that we could enjoy roasted chickens. The roosters, except for one, were given the same treatment as the old hens, but they were for frying. My mom made very good fried chicken. She said it was her mother's secret recipe.

In his own way, my father also worked at making ends meet. He was constantly repairing his old tractors and machinery that habitually broke down. It seemed like he was always fixing fences with scraps of bailing or barbed wire instead of putting in a new fence. When he could, he would go to town on Friday afternoons and Saturdays not to have a soda but to work at the sale barn. My father was a very hard worker, and the owner of the barn was a good friend. He told my father, "Sam, you can come and work at the barn anytime you can. I will always have a place for you." Both of my parents thought that things could get better if you just work hard enough at them. They were hard workers.

This life-changing event was another attempt on their part at trying to make life come together and work for all of us. At the time, however, that's not what we kids took from the news. Victoria saw her life as ruined.

I saw more chores on the horizon and more cows that would probably hate me and never come when I called them regardless of how much I tried to imitate my father's cattle call or how nice I tried to be to the dumb things. Trailing all of these thoughts, I did not want to admit it, but there was a tinge of excitement and possible adventure a new place might hold in spite of my fear and dread.

As far as Ruby goes, I'm not sure why she seemed so happy. I can only surmise that she thought moving meant we were going somewhere across the ocean, or maybe she was going to get a pony. If I was her age, I know that's what I would be thinking.

When I went to bed that evening before I said my prayers, I thought about how, in just a few minutes, something happens, words are said, and life changes. I also began to believe there would not be any more boring Thursdays in my life, at least for a while.

Chapter 8

Saying Goodbye

"Victoria, Teddy, Ruby, time to get up! Hurry! You don't want to miss the bus." My mom was at her usual station, the bottom of the stairs, shouting out her command. Friday morning was finally here. While popping out of bed and slipping into school clothes, I vigorously rubbed the sleep out of my eyes. For a few seconds, I slipped back into the one-sided conversation around the supper table last night. *Was it a dream? Could I pretend that it was?* It was the first wonder of the day.

There is something good to be said about some routine when it seems like the world as you know it has suddenly become lopsided. With the news about our moving, the world as my sisters and I saw it had definitely become slanted, and it seemed we were slowly sliding off into an abyss. The routine that we had taken for granted for so long had become a little anchor that kept us, for the time being, from cascading off into that unknown.

I guess that's why this particular Friday morning, dressing the way I have always done since I started school at five years of age, racing down the stairs before my sisters, and pouring myself a bowl of cornflakes seemed to bring a certain comfort not only to my growling stomach but to my newly awakened daytime brain a little differently than it had last week.

Wondering how cornflakes might taste in a new house made me a little less critical of the cornflakes I was now eating. At the moment, they didn't seem to taste any better than yesterday's cornflakes, but that was okay. It had been good to find them in a familiar place in the cupboard where my mother always puts the cereal when she brings the groceries home. I also felt some satisfaction in knowing exactly where to find my bowl and spoon. *I believe familiarity and routine have a place in a kid's life,* I thought as I munched away, wanting to say goodbye to the cupboard and silverware drawer. I resisted doing so because of how silly it might sound for an eleven-year-old to do such a thing.

I didn't have to ponder the thought of saying goodbye, at least just now, because my mom came into the kitchen. She gave one look to Victoria, whom I had been ignoring, and then sighed. "You need to eat your breakfast, Victoria."

"I'm not going to," Victoria responded defiantly.

"All right, here's the deal." My mom was obviously already prepared to hear Victoria's teenage stubbornness. "If you don't eat, you cannot go to the school dance tonight."

"That's not fair, Mom." Victoria mumbled as tears once again took a very familiar path down her cheeks.

How can she cry so early in the morning? I asked myself as two cornflakes lodged between a gap in my teeth and refused to follow the crowd down my throat.

"I'm your mother. I don't have to be fair," my mother answered without a hint of being amused by the exchange of words between herself and her teenage daughter. Victoria didn't say anything more. She poured a very small portion of cornflakes, about enough to feed an earthworm, and trickled some milk on top of them and, with the spoon in hand, slowly munched away.

"I will be coming to school to meet with your teachers this morning." Having won this little struggle with Victoria, my mom was on to bigger issues. "Your father and I decided we won't have everything ready to move until next Wednesday, so next Thursday will be your last day of school. Friday, we will be moving, so you won't start your new school until next Monday."

Hmmm . . . Thursday . . . hmmm . . . I bet that won't be a boring day anymore, I thought to myself and then asked my mom, "Can we tell our teachers when we get to school this morning?"

"You can, Teddy, but I will probably be there before your bus arrives. I'm going to see your principal first, and then I'll speak to your teachers before the first bell rings for class."

"Oh," I said, wondering what my teacher might say to me when I told her we were moving even though she would have already heard it from my mother.

"Please don't come to my homeroom when I'm there, Mom. Please don't." Victoria pleaded, barely looking up from her empty cereal bowl.

"I'll try not to." My mom gave Victoria the opportunity to believe she had won a little victory, however small it was in real life. As it was, I found out at suppertime that night, my mom was able to speak to our teachers without us even knowing she was in the school building. She talked to Victoria's homeroom teacher while my older sister was at band practice.

I wouldn't have minded coming into class with my friends and finding my mom there. In fact, I would be proud. Remember I told you, the guys think my mother is really "hot," even prettier than Mrs. Schaffer, my teacher, and she is really swell-looking.

Before I tell you anything more, I want to let you know about the conversation I had with Mrs. Schaffer in the afternoon. It was right after lunch. I knew Mrs. Schaffer would be in the room if she didn't have lunchroom or hall duty, and she was there sitting at her desk as I was hoping she would be.

"Mrs. Schaffer, can I talk to you?" I asked as I walked into the room.

"Why yes, Teddy," she replied as she looked up from grading our spelling papers and quickly added, "I saw your mother this morning. She told me the news about your family moving to another farm out of our school district. I was hoping to talk to you before school was out today."

I think that was the most I have ever heard Mrs. Schaffer speak to me.

"Let's sit down," she said after taking a quick breath.

I was confused. She was already sitting, but as she pointed to Mary Jane's desk and motioned me to sit there, she rose from behind her desk and moved Tommy Duncan's desk close to me and sat down so that we were facing each other.

"What are you feeling about all of this, Teddy?" she asked softly, looking directly at me.

I have to admit that I never gave it much thought before. I mean, I haven't ever thought of what I would say to my teacher sitting so close to me and asking how I feel about something. I believe Mrs. Schaffer really cared for all of her class, and now she was giving me, and only me, a lot of attention. "I don't like it," I responded matter-of-factly.

"Oh, I see." Mrs. Schaffer responded with a note of surprise and concern in her voice. Then almost as an afterthought, she added, "Your mother expressed concern over the fact that you would be upset. She said that you didn't say a lot last night when she and your father shared the news with you and your sisters."

"I couldn't," I said. "Victoria took up all the time. She was really upset, and she cried and cried. Then she got upset and cried some more."

"Hmmm, our big sisters can do that sometimes when they hear news that sounds scary, but how about you, Teddy, what are your thoughts and feelings?"

Boy, was I surprised. I never knew Mrs. Schaffer also had a big sister. Actually, I also knew Mrs. Schaffer really didn't want to talk about big sisters. After all, she asked me, "What are you thinking and feeling,

Teddy?" No one but my mom has ever asked me directly what I thought and felt in the same sentence before.

I wonder if that's the way it is in other families. *Do kids act and react to their parent's decisions? Do parents know how to ask kids, "What do you think?" without thinking if they ask for their children's opinions, they have to do what the kids want or their kids won't like them?* I guess what could be worse is what could happen if they did—kids might begin to believe that their parents were putting them in charge to run the show because they've lost interest in being parents.

This is very heavy wondering for a kid my age. Yes, I know kids aren't in charge of the world, let alone how many cows parents buy, but just maybe some kids would like to believe what they have to say on important family decisions is heard and responded to with respect. I know I would feel better. Maybe if that happened, kids wouldn't be so temperamental about decisions that invade their view of the world and make them feel less secure.

Like I said, this thinking is heavy stuff for an eleven-year-old, so I didn't share it with Mrs. Schaffer. I just answered her with as few words as possible so as not to reveal how upset and scared I really was myself.

"That's all," I said as my head dropped and I stared at a small crack in the floor.

"Are you sure that is all, Theodore?" Mrs. Schaffer sounded like she really wasn't convinced that I didn't have more to say.

"Well," I began as I raised my head and looked straight at her, "I guess I have to say that I am just a little scared. Not scared like Victoria. You know, I wouldn't tell her this, but she is popular, and she plays in band and sings. She's good at all those things. I am not. I think it will be hard for me to fit in at a new school—"

"But Teddy," Mrs. Schaffer touched my hand as she interrupted me, "you *are* popular. Remember, the first of the year, your classmates voted you to be one of the safety patrolmen? You are always hanging around with several guys who ask you for advice, and I have heard some girls whispering about how they think you are pretty smart and cool."

"Really?" I was surprised to hear her tell me all of this and then slumped back in my chair and stared once again at the floor as I mumbled, "You're just telling me all this stuff because I'm moving."

"I could be," Mrs. Schaffer said, still smiling. "Now, class will be starting in a few seconds. You run and get a drink. Since next Thursday will be your last day, I will put some things together for you to take to your new teacher, Mrs. Warren." As Mrs. Schaffer started to stand, I scrambled to my feet but turned to her just before I left. "Thank you, Mrs. Schaffer."

I have to tell you, I was surprised that Mrs. Schaffer talked to me the way she did. It made me wish I had tried harder in math assignments and paid more attention when we were talking about one-cell animals in science class. I probably would have received better grades on my tests. You never know. I guess I will have to remember this talk when I meet Mrs. Warren because I wouldn't want her to write back to Mrs. Schaffer and tell her I was a goofball or use words that only teachers use to describe kids who are uncooperative and lazy.

I don't remember much about packing or unpacking when we moved to the farm we live on now, but I do recall this moving business was hard work.

Do you remember what I had to do on Saturday morning after chores? Of course, you don't, because I haven't told you, so I better start with supper Thursday evening after Mom had her visit with our teachers. My mom fried hamburgers. She fries a lot of food. We never have hamburger buns, just white bread bought from the grocery store.

While we were eating supper, my father said, "Teddy, tomorrow evening after your chores are done, I want you to clean out the pens where the calves are now. They'll be moved to the new place early so the pens will be empty."

Ugh, those pens are really messy. I hoped my thoughts couldn't leak out through my ear so my father could hear them. I did not want my lips to repeat what I was thinking, but I did give a heavy sigh, which my father ignored because he had more to say.

"Saturday morning after chores, I'll pull the manure spreader up to the hog house, and I want you to start cleaning that out too. The hogs will be sent to market Friday evening."

"Ahh, Dad, we are moving. Why do I have to clean out the hog house? It stinks!" This time I couldn't help myself. My thoughts left my mouth before I could stop them. At least I hope I was careful not to sound like I was whining so I wouldn't be sent to bed early or not get any dessert after supper. I held my breath.

"Moving or not moving, the hog house needs to be cleaned. You have Saturday and Sunday to get the job done." My father's voice sounded exceptionally firm, but I worked at trying to find a crack in his demands. When you are eleven and your parents are farmers who don't own their own land and have to rent, you never fully understand the stress and burden they are under and the people they have to please. There is the landlord and then the banker and then sometimes a farm manager—that's all I really know, but I bet there are more people out there who are always giving their advice like the insurance guy, the feed salesman, the tractor seller, fertilizer guy, and maybe even the weatherman. I don't know, but I know my mother and father have a lot of people telling them what to do because my mom is always baking a cake or making cookies or putting an extra pork chop in the frying pan because someone else is dropping buy to boss them around.

After a few more thoughts, a crack in my brain opened up. "What about church?" I asked. " Aren't we going to Sunday school?" My real true self wanted to add, "The Bible says we are supposed to honor the Sabbath and rest on that day." That's what I wanted to say, but my common sense self that I am learning more about told me to be quiet, so instead, I looked at my mom rather than my father. But it still didn't work. My mom was silent.

"I think God probably has something better to do than check to see if you are in church every Sunday," my father answered. "Missing a Sunday won't hurt you." I think my father was reasoning with me, but he wasn't going to give. He and God must have figured this all out before he told me what I had to do. By the way, can you believe it? My father actually used God's name in a regular conversation!

I wanted to ask him more about God but decided that might be a distraction, so I stayed on course and said, "I want to go to church." As soon as I said "want," I knew I was on a slippery slope, and we were having ice cream and Fig Newtons and wafer cookies for dessert. I was taking a lot of risks here. Lucky for me, my mom stepped in and came to the rescue, at least assuring I could have dessert.

"Teddy, we all have extra chores we will be doing until we pack up to move." Guessing my next comment, she added, "Victoria will be helping me clean out the cupboards and pack up the kitchen and bedrooms, and then we will be cleaning the stove, and I have a whole list of things we will have to do. Now, finish your hamburger or no dessert."

"Yeah, but Victoria is helping you," I objected, still feeling bold. "I'm not really helping Dad clean the hog house. I have to do it by myself." This wasn't exactly true. My father would be driving the tractor out to the field and spreading the manure. I would have gladly traded him jobs, but my legs weren't long enough to reach the pedals yet on our old AC. Sometimes, I think my father bought the tractor just so I couldn't drive it.

To my surprise, my dad didn't respond in a good or bad way about what I said. He just smoked his cigarette and read the paper until my mom gave him ice cream and three cookies!

So, unfortunately, despite my protests, my weekend was filled with work. I guess you can imagine by the end of each day, I really stunk! On Friday and Saturday late afternoons, I took a bath with a good scrubbing right after I was done with my chores. By Sunday afternoon, I had the hog house cleaned down to the cement floor. I was surprised to have finished early, and I think my father was shocked. I asked him if I could ride out to the field with him to spread the manure, and to my amazement he agreed.

It felt good to let the breeze hit my face even though it was cold. The wind was blowing toward us so we weren't drowning in the smell of manure. It was also nice to be riding on the tractor with my father even though we never spoke to each other during the trip. When evening came after a good bath and supper, no one had to tell me it was time for bed when nine p.m. came around. I even had a dream about cleaning out a hog house twice as big as ours. I was very happy to see Monday morning come!

The next three days at school were pretty normal. On several occasions, Mrs. Schaffer called on me. "Teddy, I have some things that need to go to the principal's office. Would you please take them to Mr. Cochran for me?" When she asked, Mary Jane and Susie giggled loud enough that Mrs. Schaffer heard them and had to tell them, "Shhh . . ."

I did what she asked me to do. How could I ever say "no" to Mrs. Schaffer or any teacher for that matter?

On Wednesday afternoon, right before recess, she sent me to Principal Cochran's office again with some papers. This time the door from Mr. Cochran's secretary's office into his was open. "Here are some papers Mrs. Schaffer wanted me to bring to your office," I told Mrs. Jenkins, the school secretary.

"Thank you, Teddy." Mrs. Jenkins replied with a smile. Mr. Cochran must have heard us because he called out, "Teddy, is that you? Come in here for a minute."

Oh, no! What did I do now? I cautiously entered the principal's office.

"I was hoping to see you before you moved. Sit down, Teddy." Mr. Cochran came out from behind his desk as he motioned me to sit in one of the chairs in front of his desk while he sat down in the other.

This must be really bad news. I thought. *Maybe I am going to be put back a grade in the new school because of my math papers.* "Am I in trouble?" I asked out loud.

"No, of course not. I just wanted to let you know how much I have enjoyed knowing you and Victoria. Your teachers and other teachers have said some very complimentary things about you, and I agree with them."

"Thank you," I said, still bewildered by his kindness and attention toward me.

"Are you excited about moving?" Mr. Cochran asked.

"No, not really," I answered honestly without saying anything else.

"Oh, I thought you would be, but I guess it can be quite an adjustment. I grew up in a city, Denver, Colorado. Have you heard of Denver? I went all the way through grade school and high school in the same school about three blocks from where I lived." Mr. Cochran was telling me more about himself than I ever knew before.

Thinking he had forgotten the question he had asked me, I said, "Denver is the capital of Colorado," and then continued, "It's near the mountains. I like the mountains. I'd like to have a horse and live in the mountains. Did you have a horse?"

"Hey, slow down a bit. We have a little more time." Mr. Cochran looked at his watch, "I'll tell you about the school I attended."

I wasn't sure what Mr. Cochran meant by having "a little more time" when he said it, but I was enjoying the conversation. It was only later that I learned he was stalling me from returning to class because Mrs. Schaffer and my classmates were planning a going-away party for me the following day. My friend, Jimmy, told me later that afternoon about all of the preparations that had been going on earlier, starting with Susie volunteering to bring in the cupcakes and extra napkins. "I'm helping my mother make them tonight; we're making chocolate cupcakes with fudge frosting," Jimmy mimicked Susie perfectly. "My mom says they are extra messy, so I'm bringing more napkins in case the boys make messes." We had a good laugh over that.

Jimmy went on to tell me Danny and George had volunteered to bring the white and chocolate milk up from the school's lunchroom for the party, but then George had asked if he'd have to bring extra money for the food and stuff, which sent some of the girls into fits of giggles. You can tell from one look that George likes to eat.

But Mrs. Schaffer shushed everyone and told George she'd pay for the milk.

Then Jimmy relayed the discussion Mrs. Schaffer and the class had about giving me a gift.

"We are buying a shirt," Jimmy volunteered. "It will be nice because my mom is picking it out. She always buys me and my dad shirts."

"Good, Jimmy." Mrs. Schaffer was pleased to hear that Jimmy's mother had control over the shirt buying.

"I think Teddy would rather have cowboy boots," George muttered after hearing the class was giving me a shirt.

"Yeah, cowboy boots would be better!" shouted Tommy.

The girls groaned . . . all except for Susie, who was looking a little distracted, but when the groans trickled off, she quietly said, "I think I'll miss Teddy, Mrs. Schaffer."

"Yes, I think we all will, Susie. I think we all will. Remember to let him know just that when you write a note in your cards we will all give him." Then Mrs. Schaffer asked the class, "Did you bring a quarter to help pay for Teddy's gift?"

In unison, everyone responded, "Yes, Mrs. Schaffer." Without waiting for directions, her desk was overrun with the class rushing forward with their quarters.

It must have been just about the time everyone had returned to their desks and Mrs. Schaffer had finished putting the quarters in a deposit bag to give to Jimmy at the end of the day that I returned to class and the recess bell rang.

The next day finally arrived. It was Thursday, our last day at school. My mom told us she would be picking us up after school today because we would probably have too much stuff to bring home on the bus. You know what I mean: gym clothes, papers, number two pencils, Schaffer pen and ink bottles, and other things from your desk. And that's just my stuff. I know Victoria has a whole lot more stuff because she is older and has been in school longer than me.

I gave it more thought later that night and figured out my mom picked us up so we could say goodbye to everyone and not be rushed. I guess she wanted to say goodbye to our teachers and Mr. Cochran, as well. I'm sure she wanted to do that.

Have you ever had a bushel full of goodbyes that you know you were passing out for the last time to certain people and places? This Thursday seemed to go that way. The first goodbye was to my bus driver, Mr. Jones. I knew I would possibly never see him again. "I won't be riding the bus tonight, Mr. Jones," I told him as I was getting off the bus when we arrived at school that morning.

"I know, Teddy." Mr. Jones had smiled at me. "I'm glad to have gotten to know you and your sisters. You be careful at your new school. You'll do well. I'm counting on that." Mr. Jones stuck out his hand and shook hands with me.

Well, doesn't that just beat everything! The only time Mr. Jones ever spoke to me all the times I rode the bus that year was to say, "Good morning," after I said it first or when he saw me changing seats and would holler, "Sit down Teddy!" He wasn't really picking on me. He said, "Sit down!" in a hollering voice to anyone standing up. So I felt pretty good that morning when I walked off the bus. In fact, I did something I had never done before—I turned back, and when everyone was off the bus, I waved and yelled, "Goodbye, Mr. Jones!"

Mr. Jones smiled at me again as he closed the door and drove the bus toward the bus barn.

There are thirty-three kids in my class, counting me. I know that pretty soon, I would be saying goodbye for the last time to most of them, but not at this moment. We went through our usual classwork in the morning.

When lunch came, I said goodbye to the cooks and the milk lady. One of the cooks gave me a card as she put an extra big cinnamon roll on my plate. I didn't expect a card from the cooks, but I was hoping for the cinnamon roll. I knew they had some big ones because the principal usually gets one. I read the card before I left the lunchroom. They all signed their names and then added a little note:

> Teddy, we will miss you and the ugly face you make when you see we are having tuna and noodle casserole for lunch. We hope your new school cooks don't know how to make the casserole and will always give you butter instead of gravy when they serve mashed potatoes. Come see us sometime.
>
> Your friends,
> The Kitchen Crew

If I wasn't in school, I think I would let myself cry, but I couldn't cry in front of the girls or my friends, so I just turned toward the hot lunch room and waved. Somehow, all the cooks seemed to know I was reading their card because they were all looking my way. As if on cue, they smiled and waved back in unison. There went another bunch of goodbyes that I will never give away again, but I still had quite a few left in my basket.

There might be people in the small world that I live in who have never learned to say "goodbye." Maybe it's because they have always lived their whole lives in one place. Maybe they always went to the same school without ever having to change. Maybe some of their friends or family said "goodbye" and went somewhere else, but they never did. Maybe some people just leave without going through the little ritual of goodbyes, feeling sad, a little fearful, a little excited. Maybe not saying goodbye prevents you from letting go and being open to accepting new friends, challenges, changes in your life. It's like being stuck in the mud. You're stuck. You know it, but you spin your tires anyway thinking things will change when all you do is dig yourself deeper into nowhere. I am only eleven. I don't know a whole lot about all this serious stuff and reasons why we think and feel the way we do at times like this.

I heard my Uncle Leroy once say that we all experience losses throughout life and sometimes don't recognize how deeply they have affected us until maybe later in our lives. I think I'm beginning to understand something about what he meant. As a baby, we see the world so differently when we go from crawling to walking. As we grow, we lose our total dependence on our mothers and fathers when we act on our own and are made to take the consequences for our actions like when we don't study for our Friday spelling tests. Most of us lose hair, teeth, hearing, and sight all through our lives from day one. When we are old and put into nursing homes, we lose the independence we fought so hard for in adolescence and took for granted thereafter. We even lose the ability to choose the very next steps we will take.

My Uncle Leroy told my father and me all of this after he had something called a stroke and his son flew from California to sell my Uncle's house and put him in the nursing home. My Uncle Leroy sounded really sad. I imagine he had a bushel of goodbyes to give away but never got a chance to do it. Maybe that's why he had a stroke. His heart and brain could have been really heavy. Anyway, I was just listening, so I didn't ask any questions, and they weren't paying much attention to me. After all, I was only eleven.

We had a math quiz as soon as lunch was over and we were all back in class. I ate the whole cinnamon roll the cooks gave me, all by myself. My stomach was full and I think my brain wanted to snooze, so I had to concentrate extra hard to do the math problems. I wanted a good grade so I had to work harder than I usually do because I didn't want Mrs. Warren to believe Mrs. Schaffer was a poor math teacher.

When the buzzer rang, Mrs. Schaffer announced, "All right, class, pass your paper to the person in front of you. The front row students will take their paper to the last person in your row; that way, you will be grading each other's papers. Pay attention now." Mrs. Schaffer wrote out how we would grade the papers on the blackboard so no one would be making any mistakes. Since we only had twenty problems, it didn't take us too long to do the checking and grading. I had Jimmy's paper, and he missed four problems, which meant he earned a "C." Susie had my paper. When we were done, Mrs. Schaffer told us to hand the papers back to their owners, and then she would come by and pick them up. Susie passed me my paper.

You know what? I did all the problems correctly! That cinnamon roll must have helped me think better than I realized even though my brain was a little sleepy. Susie put "100% correct! Good work!" on my paper. *Good work? Golly.* I didn't know we could write stuff on the paper besides the grade. I thought Mrs. Schaffer would do that. If I knew we could write stuff, I would have written, "Jimmy, you are my friend, but you need to study your math harder if you want to pass this year!" As for my paper, I just thought, *Wow! Susie thinks I did Good Work! Imagine that, will you?*

It took a few extra minutes to collect the papers, mostly because people were googling over their good grades and talking to each other or groaning and moaning while muttering something about the fact that the person who graded their paper must have done it wrong.

"You need to check my paper, Mrs. Schaffer!" Michael yelled out, ignoring the rule to raise your hand and be recognized before you spoke. "I know Martha did something wrong."

"Shh . . . quiet, everyone. Yes, Michael, I am going to go over everyone's papers, but I'm sure Martha did everything correctly." Mrs. Schaffer looked like she wanted to remind all of us that Martha received the math award last semester, but she didn't. Mrs. Schaffer is very good when it comes to knowing just how much needs to be said on a subject.

While everyone was settling down, I was thinking, *This is the last math quiz I will take in this school. I'm glad Susie graded my paper.*

"Goodbye," math problems. I'm glad I graded Jimmy's paper. I'll miss you, Jimmy, "goodbye." Oh yes, "goodbye, Susie." I guess there they go . . . more goodbyes gone out of my bushel. I was still deep in thought when Mrs. Schaffer's raised voice brought me back to the moment.

"All right, class, for the rest of the afternoon, we are going to have our going away party for Teddy. Everyone, please get ready. Teddy, will you come here, please?"

"Come here?" I wasn't planning on leaving my seat. I thought we'd just be eating something and drinking milk at our desks while Mrs. Schaffer read us a story, or we might play some games. I was expecting something, because of the times I was sent out of the room and Mr. Cochran's long chat with me, but not going to the front of the class.

"Teddy . . ." When I heard Mrs. Schaffer call my name again, I snapped out of my wondering thoughts and quickly answered.

"I'm coming, Mrs. Schaffer." As I meandered toward Mrs. Schaffer's desk, my classmates were busy pulling out paper and envelopes from their desks.

"Sit down here, Teddy." Mrs. Schaffer directed me to sit in her chair as she pulled it out from behind her desk and put it right in front of the blackboard. I never sat in a teacher's chair before. I hesitated thinking that if Mr. Cochran came into the room, I might be in trouble for trespassing or something like that.

I think Mrs. Schaffer was reading my mind because she took one look at me and smiled, then gently took hold of my shoulder and led me to her chair. "It's all right, Teddy. You won't be in trouble. "

As I sat down, Michael approached me and said, "Teddy, you are King for the Day . . . err . . . afternoon." Michael then proceeded to place a gold paper crown on my head. Before he walked back to his seat, he quickly added, "My mom helped me make your crown. Well, actually, she and my older sister made it. I watched."

"Thanks, Michael," I said, feeling a little embarrassed having a crown on my head. Other than King Arthur, who lived in the really olden days, the only people I knew who wore crowns were ladies on the TV show *Queen for a Day,* which comes on in the afternoon. I've only watched it with my mom when I stayed home from school sick. The queen for a day on TV is usually given a lot of stuff, and the queen always cries. I don't want to cry, especially in front of the guys or the girls for that matter, so I have to be extra careful and pay attention to my feelings. In fact, I am not sure why the queens cry. I would think they would be happy and say things like "Golly!" or "Wow!" I guess you can be happy and cry just as you can be sad and happy at the same time, too. I know that is what I am feeling right now.

"Now Teddy, saying 'goodbye' can be hard sometimes, so everyone in the class has written you a goodbye letter, and some of your classmates have volunteered to read their letters out loud. Okay, class, who will go first?"

"I will!" shouted Jimmy. "I will!" he shouted again just in case Mrs. Schaffer didn't hear him. I think she heard him the first time. Jimmy sits in the front row.

"Okay, Jimmy, you can go first!" Mrs. Schaffer smiled at Jimmy. I think she let Jimmy go first because she knew he was my best friend.

Jimmy popped up out of his seat and angled himself so he could see me and our classmates, and with paper in hand, he started to read:

To My Friend Teddy

> Dear Teddy,
>
> You are a good friend. I haven't had a friend like you, because as guys are, you are loyal. You don't always try to have your way. When I forgot my marbles last year, you gave me five marbles and one cat-eye marble. You said, "I got this from a Raisin Bran box" when you handed the cat-eye to me. After our marble game, you let me keep all of them, even the cat-eye. I know you didn't have very many marbles, but I guess that's what friends do for each other.

You like horses and are really nice to them. I like to come to your house because your mom is a good cook! You will always be my best friend forever.

Your Pal,

Jimmy

After reading his letter, Jimmy folded it quickly and then put it on my desk. Mrs. Schaffer commented as Jimmy sat down, "Thank you, Jimmy. You have a nice letter. I am sure Teddy will treasure your letter. Okay, class, anyone else want to read?"

Guess who raised her hand? It was Susie. She was the only girl with her hand raised. She didn't wave her hand like Jimmy. She just shot her hand straight up in the air.

Mrs. Schaffer looked around the room and then called out, "Okay, Susie, you can read your letter."

I could hear Jimmy whisper, "Oh, no!"

Susie promptly came to the front of the class and turned right toward me. *I am really going to get it now,* I thought. If I was not sitting where I was and Susie and Mrs. Schaffer weren't looking at me, I probably would be muttering like Jimmy, "Oh, no, what is she going to say?"

Susie took some time unfolding her letter. Then she took more time clearing her throat while looking at Mrs. Schaffer and avoiding any eye contact with me. When she looked at Mrs. Schaffer, I thought to myself, *I wish Mrs. Schaffer had read these letters first. I am sure she would have censored Susie's.*

Boy was I surprised when right before Susie started to read her letter, she turned and stared right at me, cleared her throat one more time, and began to read:

Dear Theodore,

When we first met, I didn't like you very much.

(With those words, I heard several of my guy friends moan, and I saw Mrs. Schaffer straighten up more than she already was and look like she was going to rise from her chair, but she didn't. I think she was just a little curious to hear what Susie might say next. All the while, Susie seemed to be oblivious to what was going on around her and her eyes bounced from looking at me back down to her letter. Having made a clear and unedited opening statement, Susie continued.)

You weren't very nice to me, but I wasn't very nice to you either. I think as we have been in school together, I have changed, and I think you have, too. I have changed my mind about you. You are a funny and a serious person. I like the stories you read to us in English class when Mrs. Schaffer makes us read them aloud. Sometimes I wonder, How does Teddy make up such stories? You stopped teasing me after third grade and, one time, you came to my rescue when Michael was making fun of me. Do you remember that? I am sorry to see you leave. I hope we can be friends, even though you won't be in our school.

Your friend, finally,
Susie

When Susie went to sit down, you could hear a couple of girls' "ooohhh's" and "ahhh's." Mrs. Schaffer sighed just like I hear my mother do when she is afraid I will say the wrong thing to the pastor, but it all comes out of my mouth just right. And then, just like my mom, Mrs. Schaffer let loose a big smile on her face. As for me, I was surprised! I felt a little funny when Susie walked by and put her letter on my desk, leaving a bit of a smile in the air for my eyes to catch as she turned back toward her seat.

More goodbyes, I thought, or maybe, *goodbye for now.*

"Class, that's all the time we have for letters." Mrs. Schaffer walked back up to the front of the class and looked at Jimmy. "Jimmy, it's time to present Teddy with our gift."

"Great!" Jimmy offered with much enthusiasm, and then said with gusto, "Then we get treats. Right?"

"Yes, Jimmy," Mrs. Schaffer answered, "but first the present!"

"O—kay." Jimmy opened his desktop. To everyone's surprise, Jimmy had stuffed my present in his desk. Pulling it out, it looked quite squished. The bow was dangling to the side of the package, and the paper was crackling and torn in a few places, but all in all, the package seemed to weather being held hostage in the confined space of Jimmy's desk.

"Jimmy!" Mrs. Schaffer called, looking rather shocked at what she saw when Jimmy held out the present, "I thought you put Teddy's present in the closet?"

"It's okay, Mrs. Schaffer, it's only a shirt," Jimmy innocently explained with no sense of apology.

"Oh no, Jimmy. You were supposed to . . ." Mrs. Schaffer couldn't finish her sentence. Most of the girls were laughing; the boys had rather confused looks on their faces as if they missed the punch line of a joke. Mrs. Schaffer finally let her words drift away and finished her sentence with a proper-like giggle as she and the class watched Jimmy come forward and hand me the present.

"Here, Teddy! My mom helped me pick it out for you. We all paid a quarter to buy it. Here's the card." Jimmy reached his hand into his back pocket and pulled out a folded card he had been carrying around since recess.

"Gee, thanks, everyone." I wasn't quite sure if "thank you" was enough, but no one seemed to look like they expected me to say more. As I started to unwrap my present, Tommy burst out from the back of the room, "George and I wanted to buy cowboy boots, but Mrs. Schaffer said no!"

"I asked my mom about the boots," George added, "but my mom also said no because we all would have had to give fifty cents instead of a quarter. She said some kids' parents might think that was too much."

By the time George finished explaining why I didn't get boots, the wrapping paper was falling to the floor and I was holding the shirt in my hands. "This is really a nice shirt," I said, impressed to see the shirt was all in one piece and in my favorite color. "It's blue! My favorite color is blue," I revealed to my classmates.

"My mom asked your mom, "Jimmy explained, "Your mom said you like blue. I have a blue shirt, too, but I only wear it for special things like going to my grandma's house. I wear it there because she bought it for me last Christmas and my mother—"

"I think it's time for Danny and George to go to the kitchen and bring back the milk," Mrs. Schaffer instructed. She knew that if she didn't interrupt him, Jimmy's monologue would take them on the trail of events that may never end. "Susie, your mom took the cupcakes to the hot lunchroom. Sara, you go help Susie with the cupcakes." Mrs. Schaffer seemed satisfied that the party was moving along rather smoothly and on time.

Since I have been going to school, we have had two going-away parties. One was for a girl in second grade who was only in our class for one year. I think her dad was someone's hired man. She was a nice person, and I remember she was very shy. We didn't have much of a party. We only had ice cream bars, and the teacher gave her some colors, pencils, a new writing tablet, and a red sweater. I think our teacher must have paid for it all because she didn't ask us for any quarters. The teacher passed around a card for us to sign. I remember all of this because I saw some of our classmates pass the card on without signing it. At the time, I couldn't understand why they didn't sign the card. I like to think they might have sent her a goodbye card in the mail. I don't know.

Then, in fourth grade, one of my Cub Scout friends, Tony, moved. His dad was a fireman. Tony said his dad was going out to the mountains to fight fires and they had to go with him. The day Tony left, my mom brought some cookies she made and homemade lemonade. George's mom brought us each a bag of popcorn because Tony liked popcorn. We didn't sign any cards, but our teacher had us each make Tony a card and bring it from home. I think all of the kids made cards that time. I still can't figure out why some kids didn't sign that girl's card. I wonder. I also wonder about how many goodbyes kids I know have had to give away? I don't think the girl said anything. She just smiled. Tony told us all goodbye several times.

Now it is my turn. We are seated at our desks eating cupcakes, drinking milk, and playing a remembering game Mrs. Schaffer is making us play. I'm not remembering too well because the voice in my head is going up and down the rows, telling my classmates "goodbye" one more time. My bushel is almost empty.

I was picking up crumbs from my cupcake by pinches when my mom came to the classroom door. I was both happy and sad to see her. I was happy because I like my mom. Sad because her coming meant it was time to go home.

"Hello, Mrs. Hall," Jimmy said, smiling as my mother came into our classroom.

"Hello, Jimmy," my mother returned, and as more of my classmates looked up to see our visitor, she added, "Hello, everyone! It looks like you've been having a good time."

"Hello, Mrs. Hall." Everyone echoed Jimmy. Most of my class knows my mom. She has been our homeroom mother since I was in fourth grade. The guys mostly know her because of Cub Scouts, and they really like her cookies.

I had all of my stuff in a sack Mrs. Schaffer gave me, so it was easy to just grab it and my present when my Mom said, “Teddy, it’s time to go.”

For the last time, Mrs. Schaffer told me goodbye as she and my mother stood by the door. I quickly turned toward my classmates and waved. “Goodbye, everyone. Thanks for the shirt.” I didn’t want to say anything else. The words were hurting my throat trying to come out, and they were starting to sound funny.

“Goodbye, Elaine.” Mrs. Schaffer called my mother by her first name as she gave her a hug and smiled, then added almost in a whisper, added, “Thank you for all of your help and for caring so much. I look forward to seeing you at our lodge meeting next month. You won’t stop coming, will you?”

“Oh no,” my mother said, smiling back at Mrs. Schaffer. “Lodge is one activity I do just for myself. I’ll look forward to seeing you. We can catch up then. Goodbye for now.”

“Yes, for now . . .” Mrs. Schaffer’s voice trailed off as my mother and I left the room and headed right for the school’s front door where Victoria was waiting for us with her hands full of school stuff. We didn’t say anything to each other. The three of us found our way to the car and headed for home.

“Your Aunt Rachael is watching Ruby and Cindy at home,” Mom said after a bit in the car. “She came and helped me with packing up everything this morning. When we arrive home, you two need to change your clothes. Put your school clothes in your chest of drawers and take the clothes in your closet and lay them on your bed. Teddy, after you finish, you need to go out and help your father finish chores. Tomorrow will be a busy day so just do what your father tells you to do without any fussing. Do you understand me?” My mother looked up into the rearview mirror casting her glance at me, waiting to see or hear some acceptance that I did understand and would follow her instructions.

I was quiet. I saw my mother quickly glance back at the road and then her eyes focused a little more sharply into the mirror, waiting for some type of answer from me. It's not that I didn't listen to her or understand for that matter, but I was quickly making a list in my head of all the trillions of things my father would be making me do like rolling up barbwire, picking up nails and putting them in a coffee can, cleaning out the moss from the cow tank . . . oh yeah, and going to get the cows for milking, besides doing all my other chores.

"Teddy! Are you listening to me?" My mother was still looking through the rearview mirror for the second time as she spoke.

How can she do it? I wondered to myself. Drive down the gravel road, look up through the rearview mirror for as long as she does and talk—all at the same time? "Yes, Mom, I hear you." Sometimes it's best just to leave your wonderings alone and pay attention to what or who is ahead of you. At the present, it is my mom."

You remember how I said, "Thursdays are usually boring?" Well, this Thursday certainly wasn't. *Hmmm, maybe my luck was about to change.*

Just as soon as we arrived home, I started up the stairs to change clothes. Halfway up, I heard the phone ring one long ring and three short rings. My mom answered it. "Hello, Ruth. How are you and Ed?"

My mom knew just about everyone by the tone of their voices. I bet Ruth didn't even have to say who she was. My mom knew. I stopped on the stairs to hear her say, "Oh, I was wondering what I could fix for supper. All of my pots and pans are already packed for the move . . . six o'clock? Six will be fine. Chores will be done by then. Of course, the house will be a mess . . . okay . . . I won't pick up . . . see you then . . . goodbye." Just as my mom was saying, "goodbye," I heard my father come through the back door. He said something about chores to my mom. "Ed and Ruth are coming over about six," she told him. "Ruth said they are bringing us supper. Will that be okay?"

"I guess," my father said in a monotone. I think he was very tired. After a brief pause that took my father long enough to light a non-filtered cigarette and take a long draw, I heard him ask, "Is Teddy changing clothes? We have work to do." Hearing my father say that, I scooted up the remaining stairs. I didn't want him peering up from the bottom of the stairway and catching me lingering any longer.

It was hard to explain the recent behavior of our milk cows. All the way to the barn, they would stop and stare at a tree or at the sky. I even had to tap Brownie on her behind because it looked to me that she was staring hard at a rock along the path. They weren't doing this all at the same time. They were acting like Brownie was. One stopped here. Another one stopped there. It was like they were saying, "goodbye, tree, goodbye blue sky, goodbye rock." It was either that, or the old bull told them, "Okay, ladies listen up. This is our last day in this beautiful lush pasture. Our boss is moving us. Who knows what is ahead of us? I heard him tell the kid. The kid will be in a hurry so let's play Red Light and Green Light with him just to get him wound up." I know that is probably what he told them. The bull and I never have been on good terms, and moving to a new farm won't change how we think or feel about each other. How I wish I was saying "goodbye" to this bully, but I'm not.

I guess there are a lot of things I would like to leave at this place and say goodbye to. You know my list. I'd like to leave my fear of the dark. I'd also like to leave my fear of the cows kicking me and the rooster chasing me. I would rather leave behind cleaning out a barn or hog house or chicken house, but I guess as long as animals eat, they will leave messes. It seems to me messes on the farm have always been part of my chores that never seem to go away. Talking about chores . . .

Chores and extra chores were a little bit different than what I expected. I didn't have to pick up nails or clean moss out of the cow tank, but I did have to clean out the washhouse. I remember what my mother said. "No grumbling. Your father has a lot on his mind. Be a helper, not a murmurer." I don't know what a murmurer is. The only time I have ever heard that word before was in Sunday school when Mrs. Kate read us a story about a guy named Moses that God made boss over some people called Israelites. They murmured against God because Moses made them get up early every morning for forty years. They had to walk a hundred miles or something like that each day with very few bathroom stops. God fed them only one plate of food a day with no seconds. Anyway, that's how I remember it, and that's all I know about murmurers and murmuring. I guess if you want to go to McDonalds once in a while when you are on a trip, or you want extra helpings of potatoes and corn or chicken for supper, you better be careful about murmuring too much.

I surprised myself because by five-thirty that night, even though the milk cows were dawdlers, we had all of the chores done and were all cleaned up except for my father. He was taking his bath. All we had to do was watch TV until Ruth and Ed came over with our supper. I was hungry. *I hope they bring ice cream,* I said to myself.

Victoria was playing the piano for the last time in this house. I think that's why she was playing exceptionally louder than usual. Ruby was building a house with her alphabet blocks, Cindy was trying to help her, and I was watching the second half of the *Mickey Mouse Club*. The second half is when Mickey has the "Spin and Marty" episode and a cartoon. Spin and Marty ride horses on a ranch. Every once in a while, I turn the volume up on the TV because Victoria keeps playing louder. I have to be sneaky and turn the TV up when my mother is reading and not turning pages in the newspaper. If she is turning the pages, she can see me at the same time and makes me turn the sound back down.

My dad has finished his bath and is dressed. He's reading part of the paper also, but he is sitting at the table smoking a non-filtered cigarette and drinking black coffee. Right when the *Mickey Mouse Club* gang starts to sing, "Now it's time to say goodbye . . ." we can hear Pal barking. *How can he bark so loud that we hear him over Victoria's banging her fingers on the piano?* I didn't answer my own question because my mom said, "Ed and Ruth are here. You kids behave yourselves."

I ran to look out the window and was surprised by what I saw. "Mom, there are a bunch of cars right behind Ed's car. Look! They are turning into our lane! We are having a lot of company!"

My father came and looked out the window as well. "Well, I'll be darn—" he said. My father actually said a different word than "darn," but I am not supposed to say it. As people began to pile out of their cars, I recognized most of them as our neighbors. They were all carrying stuff that ended up being food. *I won't be hungry much longer,* I thought to myself.

You guessed it. Ruth and Ed organized a going-away party for my mom and dad. I guess for us kids also. Even though it was a school night, the neighbors all brought their kids along so we had fun playing games and stuff neighborhood kids do at going-away parties. The only person in our neighborhood Victoria's age was Hubert. Victoria doesn't like Hubert very much, but she was nice to him. They just sat around and talked. The adults played cards.

Oh, supper! What a supper! There was fried chicken, ham, potato salad, potato chips, baked beans, green beans, lima beans, and about a zillion casseroles, none of which found their way to my plate since it was already full! When it came time for dessert, there was quite a spread starting with homemade ice cream that Ed and Ruth brought with pies, a cake, homemade and store-bought cookies, and a little bit of this and that.

While we ate our dessert and second helpings, Helen Sullivan and her husband Max went out to their car and returned shortly with a big box. Since Max doesn't talk much in front of people, Helen said, "Sam and Elaine, we all went in and bought you a going away gift." My father nudged my mother as they stood up, and Mom slowly opened the box Helen put alongside her chair. My father just sat there. Just like Max, my father doesn't talk very much in front of big groups that usually consist of more than four people, so my mom smiled as, together, they pulled out the brand new card table and four chairs.

I think they were both very surprised by the gift. My mother looked up after reading the card, and when she handed it to my father, she said, "I don't really know what to say." I think she really did know what to say because she immediately added, "Thank you, everyone. You shouldn't have. This must have cost a lot of money. It's beautiful." To my amazement, my father said in a much lower tone, "Thank you. Thanks to all of you."

I don't know, but it occurred to me that I have never heard anyone call a card table and four folding chairs "beautiful," but I guess that must have been how my mother felt in her heart because she sounded very genuine when she spoke the words.

After the gift was set aside and my parents repeated "thank you" several times, the grown-ups went back to playing cards, and us kids continued playing our inside games. It seemed everyone was dreading what was to come, the final "goodbyes" for some and "goodbye for now" for others. Though we all dreaded it, there were a lot of goodbyes and some tears from the women and my mom. The men didn't cry, but I noticed they shook hands longer and touched my father's shoulders. I have never seen them do that at the sale barn before, but they did it tonight. Some of the men even hugged my mom. All the ladies hugged my father. I am not sure he was actually comfortable with the hugging but he didn't say anything about it; instead, he kept saying "goodbye" and "goodbye" over and over before, during, and after the hugging.

I noticed again this evening, when some people say "goodbye" to each other, they must think the other person is hard of hearing, because they repeat it several times before they actually leave. Kids don't do all of that, and Victoria only said "goodbye" to Hubert once. Hubert tried to hug Victoria, but she politely side-stepped him and shook his hand. Victoria took dancing lessons, so she knows how to side-step.

The last "goodbye" is a strange word. It's like a period at the end of the last sentence in a chapter in a storybook or novel. You never are sure how the next chapter will start out. You might have some idea, and hints might be dropped along the way, but you never really know until you hear the first "hello." Even then, it might take a while before you once again see more clearly.

Chapter 9

Hello

Do you believe everything happens for a purpose, or do things just happen because they do? You know what I mean. Don't you? Think with me about this wondering. If you had tied your shoes earlier, would you have still tripped on the sidewalk? If you hadn't eaten three bowls of ham and bean soup, would you have still passed gas? If my Uncle Mickey hadn't been driving twenty miles over the speed limit around the curve, would he have still crashed his car? I don't know.

I do know that some people never tie their shoes and they don't trip. Some people like my Aunt Mary drive really fast everywhere they go and never crash. My mom says Aunt Mary has never been given a speeding ticket. Believe it or not, some people eat a lot of beans and, well, you understand my point, don't you? I guess I asked more than one question, but this whole business of what you do or say now seems to have consequences either down a short or long road. Since I was seven and began to think of these things, this has been one of my "wonderings."

So now I am wondering if I had never said "goodbye," could I ever say "hello" without forgetting what is now behind me? Will where I have been and what I have done influence how I am and who I am in a new place? Are there consequences in the "now" for the "then," or do I start all over, or do I do the same things that I did then, now? Does my past or my "goodbyes" influence or affect what comes after "hello?" Is it like connecting dots in a coloring book so you can see a big picture to color, or do the dots or our actions just travel on and on and on, aliens and strangers to one another? I have my wonderings about all of this, but this is not the time to tell you. Right now, I need to tell you about saying "hello."

"Victoria, Theodore, Ruby, it's time to get up!" The familiar voice rang from the bottom of the stairs, and for a split second, as my head rose from the pillow, I was thinking that I was where I had been, not where I am. Then I looked around the room. Boxes were still unpacked. My bed wasn't where it was yesterday. My room's window opened to the East, not the West.

"Hello, Hello, Hello," my mind said as I lifted my body and thoughts out of bed and jostled into a new world that until now had little expectations for the likes of me. Before I could wander too far into my wondering thoughts, they were interrupted by the voice from below. "Come on, I am driving you to school this morning," my mom called again. "I'll need to register you, and I want to meet your new teachers." The three of us came down the steps just like we had at our old house.

My mom's comments brought me some comfort. In the best way she knows how, I know my mom wants to be certain that our walk into a new school, new classroom, new everything with countless "hellos" goes as smoothly as possible. My mom is really good at trying to make things right, even in the most difficult of times. The problem is, as hard as she tries by herself, she cannot make patterns of thoughts, actions, or feelings change without the rest of us doing our parts. As hard as she will try to make our "hellos" in this new place easy for us, we will still have to struggle through our own attitudes, self-will, fears, and risks to see things just a little differently than we had before.

Breakfast was routine. Wide awake, Cindy sat in her high chair with fingers spearing small pieces of buttered toast my mom placed before her. When I came to the kitchen, I pulled the same cereal we ate at our last home out of the cupboard. The same silence was borne anew between Victoria and I while Ruby's later-than-usual arrival at the table came as a result of her insisting that she wanted to pick out her own clothes only to have a remake with Mom's help. With some defiance directed through her spoon and cereal, Ruby's crunching away drew disgusted looks from Victoria. While I was just a little annoyed by the sound, I was also amazed at how one little mouth could sound like rolling thunder across August cornfields.

We had had the weekend to clean and start putting some things away in our new home. We milked the same ole cows in a barn that looked strangely the same as the barn we had just left. Our breakfast milk tasted the same as it always has. I guess you could say, setting Ruby's stubborn and defiance aside, there was enough sameness in all of this, and we had had the weekend to make adjustments. I was ready to face the unknown at a different school.

We now live north of town across the Nishnabotna River. Our ride into town was completely on gravel roads. I told the road, "Hello." The gravel that our car tires threw up under the car clamored and clunked all the way. I imagine gravel must have its own language like Romanian or French, or maybe Russian or Missourian. As for right now, traveling along, I imagine the gravel is saying "hello" to me in English.

I wonder if my new teacher will teach our class how to learn more English. Mrs. Schaffer said, "You'll like Mrs. Warren. I know you will. I like her, and I have known her for a good while." I guess Mrs. Warren must be as smart as Mrs. Schaffer since she likes her. Mrs. Warren will know about gravel.

"Class, I'd like you to say, 'Hello' to Teddy Hall. Teddy is our new student." Mrs. Warren led me into the classroom, having already met my mom and me in the principal's office. My mom thought it best to have me settle in first since Victoria and Ruby would probably take more time, and Mom certainly did not want to be the reason for the heightened embarrassment Victoria might feel having her younger brother and sister tag along to one of her new classes or to the guidance counselor's office. Mom is wise enough to know Victoria is already put out by having her mother "escort" her.

"I don't know why you won't let me enroll in classes and take care of stuff myself, Mom," Victoria explained to my mom on the way into town. "I know what classes I am supposed to register for. We went all through this last night." It was as if my mom was singing "Yankee Doodle" in her head. She didn't really directly respond to Victoria. All she said was, "We are almost in town."

Now, back to my own class experience. After Mrs. Warren introduced me, the class shouted in unison, "Hi, Teddy!" as their heads turned to watch my mom and me. They were mostly looking at me. They knew I would be the one staying and my mom would be leaving, although after seeing my mom, I bet some of the boys wished she was staying and I was leaving.

"Your desk is right over there, Teddy." Mrs. Warren said as she pointed her finger at the third desk in the second row. She then looked toward my mom who gave her a smile and a nod of approval.

"Hmmm . . ." I said very softly as I followed Mrs. Warren's finger directing me to the desk that would soon be mine. As I sat down at the third desk in the second row, my mind was wondering if Mrs. Schaffer told her I am just a little hard of hearing. I didn't ponder that very long because when I looked up, I saw my mother starting to walk toward her two daughters that were waiting impatiently out in the hallway.

My impulse was to jump up and run after them, but I couldn't. I know the kids in the classroom would start to laugh and the guys would call me a "mamma's boy" or worse, say that I was scared. Just like my earlier wondering, my impulse was cut short by Mrs. Warren's instructions.

"All right class, take out your math book and turn to today's assignment. Teddy, your books are inside your desk." With those words, I was left with no choice but to comply and quickly lost the desire to run away with my mom and my sisters. I surprised myself by being able to understand the math problems Mrs. Warren had us go through, and when it was my turn, along with three other classmates, I went up in front of the class and wrote out the problems on the blackboard so we could all figure out the answers. Can you believe it? I was the first one to come up with the answers, and they were all correct! Now that is a "hello" I won't forget for some time!

As I went back to my seat, the girl who sat on my right side leaned over toward me and said, "Hi, Teddy! I'm Cheryl. You sure are smart!" I don't think I will tell anyone that we had these same problems last week in our homework assignment, and Mrs. Schaffer made me do two of the three over again because I had the wrong answers. I was still surprised that I was able to figure them all out and come up with the right answers the first time.

When we were all settled, Mrs. Warren congratulated us for doing so well. With a smile directed right at me, she added, "Your math problems will become much harder in a very short time, but I know all of you will do just as good as you did today." Mrs. Schaffer probably gave her a heads up on how far we were in math, reading and science, but I am not going to ask her. There are certain things you don't really want to know because they can spoil the moment, and besides, my conscience would make me tell Cheryl that I had already had this lesson. She probably wouldn't think I was very smart after that, especially if I told her I had to do two of the problems over.

Before I knew it, the lunch bell rang. "Hello, lunch bell," I whispered. My last school didn't have a lunch bell because the town noon whistle blew down at the fire hall. I guess Mr. Cochran didn't want the first graders to hear two whistles and get scared or something. I don't know. I never thought about asking him why the school didn't have a lunch bell. By now, I was hungry. My stomach told me I was hungry, so I was ready to say "hello" to the lunchroom. I hope we aren't having goulash. I hate goulash, but right now, almost anything would be better than the old stale corn flakes I had for breakfast.

The lunchroom cooks must have had the same recipe for lunch as the cooks in the school I left because I have eaten the meal they served probably a zillion times. The cooks all smiled when I came through the line, and they all told me, "hello." I recognized one of the cooks. She was Jimmy's Aunt. He told me about her, so when I saw her, I said, "Hello Mrs. Campbell." She gave me an extra big smile back and put two peanut butter sandwiches on my plate while telling the other cooks, "This is Teddy. He is my nephew Jimmy's friend. When the other cooks heard her, they all gave me another "hello" only this time they said, "Hello, Teddy. We are glad that you're here. We hope you like your new school." They served me peanut butter sandwiches, peaches, a slab of meatloaf, and a scoop of corn.

You need to know meatloaf is another food I don't like. I think I would rather have to go to bed early than eat meatloaf. Yuk! I think whoever invented meatloaf must not have known much about hamburgers or meatballs, and I suppose they didn't know you can serve old hard or stale bread to hungry chickens. The cooks in my old school never put meatloaf on my plate. They usually gave me an extra peanut butter sandwich or two peaches. I will need to teach my new cooks about leaving it off of my plate. Today it's okay. I just won't eat it. Maybe someone at the table will want to trade meatloaf for a peach half. Right now, I quit thinking about what was on my plate and started to concentrate on making new friends.

I needed to start saying more "hellos" and ignore Victoria while I am here. I saw her coming into the lunchroom with some of her new classmates. I think she spotted me also because she quietly turned the other way just in case I tried to get her attention. I noticed a group of boys who came to sit at the same table Victoria and two girls were sitting at. Victoria attracts boys like a watermelon rind attracts flies when it's left out on a sidewalk in July. I am sure no one has to tell her how to say "hello." I heard that teenagers do a lot of flirting when they meet someone they might like later on or when they want someone to pay attention to them. I guess that would be about right from what I have seen in my short life. I am not really sure what flirting means, but maybe Susie was doing just a little bit of flirting with me during my last day at my old school. Since I am not a teenager, I am pretty sure it probably wasn't actual flirting. Kids my age don't know exactly how to flirt.

During our recess, several guys asked me if I wanted to hang out and play baseball with them. Guys don't always just come out and say, "hello." They'll say something like, "Do you want to play dodge ball or baseball?" or they might say, "we're going to play baseball at recess. Do you want to play? We need a third baseman." Or, "we're going to run some races. You can join us if you want to." I think most of the time, that's how guys say "hello."

I nodded. As we were walking out onto the school playground, I said, "My name is Teddy." The tallest guy in the group said, "We know. Mrs. Warren told us. I'm Jeffery."

"I'm Hank," another of the guys said. "I was named after a western singer who my mother said was her first true love. My dad doesn't really like western singers except for the ones who ride horses and shoot bad guys."

As Hank took a breath, the third guy in the group said, "I'm Jonathan." By the time we reached the small diamond, I was calling the guys by their first names, and we were talking like we had known each other for quite a while.

I surprised myself by catching the ball when Jonathan swung and hit the first pitch that Hank threw at him. We only had one base because there were so few of us. Since Jonathan was out, we all moved up to the next spot. Each of us had a turn to bat before recess was over. I hit the ball on the third pitch, but I was put out when Jeffery caught the ball. I didn't care very much. No one booed. We all seemed to have a good time, and I was happy to have made some friends so quickly. I am not sure they're ready yet to hear that Victoria is actually a much better ballplayer than I am, even if she does act strange around boys. I'll wait until summer so they can see for themselves if they come to a Lutheran League softball game.

I forgot to tell you, even though we go, or rather went, to a Methodist country church, Victoria always rode with one of her neighborhood girlfriends to the Lutheran Church to play on their softball league. I don't think she acts like a Lutheran, though. She just plays ball with them.

By the time school was done for the day, I had given away a lot of "hellos." They were mostly to guys, but there were a few girls I dared myself to say "hello" to and ask them some questions. I felt very pleased when they answered me.

I didn't like the ride home on the bus. No one in my class rides our bus. The older boys really tried to impress Victoria. She was sitting with one of her classmates. I could tell because they had some of the same textbooks. One of the older boys was really rowdy. I tried to ignore him, but he eyed me like a chicken hawk zeroing in on a baby chick who wandered too far away from its mother.

"Hey kid, who are you?" he demanded as he reached over the aisle and poked me hard in the arm.

I didn't say anything. I learned about bullies in my last school, and I knew enough not to respond to them regardless of how loud and mean sounding they were. When he poked me again, it hurt hard enough that tears swelled up in my eyes, but I remained quiet. I was determined not to let one teardrop fall. So I kept thinking, *I am not going to cry. I am in control, not this dummy bully. I bet he has snot in his nose, and he probably doesn't even have a girlfriend.* No tears slipped out of my eyes. The bus driver looked up into his rearview mirror when the big kid poked me the second time. I know he saw what happened. The big kid ignored the mean-looking glance the bus driver gave him and shouted louder, "Hey kid, can't you hear? What's your name? Are you crying?" By now, the greasy-hair freckle-face loud-mouth was leaning out of his seat and right in my face. He could see I was holding back tears. I hope no one else was paying attention to us except for the bus driver, but I also hoped the bus driver didn't take the same course on bullies my last bus driver did. When he saw kids being picked on, he usually made them sit upfront, and that only made things worse. For some reason, that hadn't happened to me, but I didn't want to press my luck.

By now, ole Freckle Face was pulling back for another muscle packed-poke, but when he leaned forward aiming at my arm, the bus driver did something no other bus driver I know has ever done. He made the bus almost come to a surprising stop by hitting hard on the brakes, letting up on them, and moving forward. The sudden jolt really affected no one but Freckle Face who was caught off balance and lunged forward, falling to the bus floor. His turkey size stomach hit the floor first, so he wasn't really hurt. I think he was more than a little embarrassed though because he didn't say a word as he picked himself up and sat back in his seat. Most of the girls on the bus giggled, and the guys hooted.

The bus driver watched it all through the mirror, and when he saw me staring up in surprise, he gave me a smile and a wink. *Wow!* Our bus driver sure knows how to drive when a bully is on board. Someday, I am going to ask him if he learned that trick when he took his bus driver's test. For now, I'll just put it in my wonder bank and enjoy the moment.

When Freckle Face settled back in his seat, I heard the guy sitting next to him say, "Hey, you better leave him alone. He is Victoria's brother, Teddy. You know V-I-C-T-O-R-I-A, the new girl."

I doubt Freckle Face would have too much to worry about. I am learning something about Victoria's taste in boys, and I am sure he wouldn't get to first base with her even if he treated me like a superstar; however, when he heard Victoria's name, he said, "OH . . . err . . ." and then slowly leaned toward me again and said, "Sorry, Teddy."

I am not looking. I am still staring straight ahead, I said to myself, wanting this "hello" to slip out the bus window I had opened when I sat down. The rest of the trip home was in silence, but I was imagining all the possible ways ole Freckle Face would be sorry for messing with me. *Maybe he will be arrested by a Texas Ranger,* I thought, although I never heard of a Texas Ranger coming to Iowa except through television. *Maybe when Victoria really starts to date, he will have a memory lapse and ask Victoria for a date right in front of all of his friends.* She probably would say, "Absolutely not, I wouldn't date you even if you were Elvis Presley's or Frankie Avalon's brother and could sing just as good as they could. I wasn't too excited about that outcome. Freckle Face would probably take it out on me in some dark alley because he wouldn't really have anything to lose at that point.

Maybe one of those motorcycle gangs would run over him with their motorcycles. But then he might get really hurt and I don't think Mrs. Kate would like that kind of thinking from me. *Oh, I know, maybe if he has to milk cows, one of the cows would kick him so hard he'd land in a huge pile of cow manure. He would probably have to stay home from school for three days taking baths, trying to scrub off the stink because he wouldn't want to go to school and be called Stinky even by the football coach. By then, he would probably be so far behind in his schoolwork that his teachers would flunk him. The principal would most likely send him down to third grade and make him start from there.* I liked that story best of all, and a smile came to my face as my mind rehearsed how all of Freckle Face's misfortunes would come about.

When I finally did look up, the bus driver was stopping at our lane. I quickly left my seat and started toward the door, but I purposefully slowly turned my head toward greasy Freckle Face with dry eyes and confidence and gave him a smile that secretly said, "Hello, Stinky." Without further thought, I stored the greeting into my brain, and on my way out of the bus, I turned toward the bus driver and said, "Goodbye, see you tomorrow." It never hurts to gain points with a new bus driver.

You remember I told you about doing chores over the weekend at our new farm, and this Monday's "hellos" are what came after Thursday's "goodbyes?" Well, when I arrived home that first day, I had the same old chores to do only tonight, as I meandered out to the new pasture, I was giving away more "hellos."

"Hello cornfield," I said. "Hello barbwire fence," I called out, while crawling under the fence instead of trying to climb over it and risk tearing my jeans on one of the barbs. "Hello pond, hello, creek." We had a creek on our last farm and a small pond, but this pond was much larger and there were places in the creek that were deeper and wider than the other one.

When I passed by the pond, I threw a clod of mud into the water over the head of a bullfrog which immediately jumped into the water, causing a splash that was much bigger than the mud clod I had thrown. While gazing at the water circles the frog created, I enthusiastically called out, "Hello ole frog, hello all you water creatures, hello whales or big fish. This is Teddy. Good to meet you."

I didn't say "hello" to the milk cows or to the Black Angus bull. They knew me, and I knew them. They moseyed around chewing, swishing their tails, and ignoring me just like they had done at our last place. *I bet they give the same ole cow milk,* I reasoned. I threw some clods at the bull and gave a "Yip" and a "Ho" to the herd as I rounded them up for the walk home. To pass the boring time, I amused myself by thinking, *What if, when my father uses his new milking machines on the very first two cows and pours the milk into the can, it's chocolate milk? WOW! Now that would be a "hello" worth shouting. My cows would immediately go to the top of my best friend list!* Yeah, I know it is just a wild thought, and my mom calls these "wonders of the mind slips into fantasy" and my father calls them "daydreams," but you never know what might happen if you connect your wonders, thoughts, and a rolled-up-sleeve brain effort. *You never know.*

This Monday night's homework is about the same as any Monday evening homework regardless of where you are. We might live on a different farm, but I am still sitting at the same kitchen table at which I sat last Monday. Division, fraction, and multiplication problems demand the same correct answers here as they did before. As long as I live, two plus two will always be four. Cows will probably never actually milk out chocolate milk.

We did not move so far away that people speak a different language here. Maybe if we had moved to Nebraska or Arkansas, the spelling words might have been different and I would have to learn a new language, but that didn't happen. We just moved to another farm only two schools away from the old school. Homework didn't deserve a "hello!" You just do it with very little moaning because the more you moan and stall, the less TV you are allowed to watch. At least, that is the rule my mom had made in our house no matter where we lived.

Because I went right to work and had to ask for very little help, I finished my homework at 7:30. I just sat down in front of the TV and started to watch a good show while thinking of asking my mom for a snack when Pal started to bark. I popped up from the floor and went to the window to see what he might be barking at. I was hoping it wasn't a robber climbing up to my sister Victoria's window.

"We have company!" I shouted as I darted to the kitchen window to have a better view. I was just in time to see not one but several cars come up our lane. "We have a bunch of company!" I called over my shoulder to my mom as she came into the kitchen while my father, who was in the living room, put down the newspaper he was reading.

In a short time, seven adults, four kids, one baby, and a bunch of food was gathered in our kitchen. A brief glance at the kitchen table told me there were three pies, two plates of cookies, two plates of sandwiches, two bags of potato chips, a large mason jar filled with Kool-Aid, and a large urn of coffee. It's amazing. Only a few minutes ago, the table was filled with boring homework and now just look at it. It's for sure I won't need to be asking my mom for a snack tonight.

"Hello!" "Hello," "Happy to meet you." "Hi!" "Hey, Sam, didn't I see you at the sale barn last month? I think we were bidding on the same boar. I dropped out, too rich for my blood. Did you have the last bid?" So went the greetings from some of our new neighbors. Just so there is no confusion, I better introduce them.

The couple, who to me looked the oldest, was Charlie and Patricia Madisen. They even looked older than my parents and there were no kids in their car. I know because remember, I was looking out the window even though my father told me, "Stop staring out the window!" The next couple that entered the kitchen was Patti and Jerry Krelig and their baby, Toby. They lived the farthest away but were still in the neighborhood. In a flash, good ole Victoria was talking to Patti, who just so happened to ask her if she liked to babysit. "Of course," Victoria answered. "Oh, yes! I am almost always free to babysit. I can provide some references if you like."

"Oh, that won't be necessary. I will talk to your mother. I think she would be fair in telling me how well you help out in caring for your brother and sisters," Patti said, giving Victoria a smile.

Now, I can't tell you much about Patti's comments as I just met her, but listening to Victoria's pitch, I know she was already calculating how much new money she could be making babysitting for the Kreligs and how all of that money would translate into new clothes.

Mrs. Witters and her daughter and son came next. I think my mother already knew Mrs. Witters from 4-H because when my mother saw her, she exclaimed, "Hello, Mildred and Ginny, and this must be your son, Peter. Peter, this is our son, Teddy." My mom's hand clutched my shoulder, and I moved in closer to Peter as she was speaking. I was okay with my mom's introduction because I know it would have been harder to become acquainted if it had been left up to just us boys.

"Hi Pete, I think I saw you at the fair last summer showing a steer," I said as a way to tell Pete "hello."

"Yup, my steer, Renegade, made second place in his class. I don't have him anymore. My mom had to sell him after my dad died last year."

"Oh, I'm sorry. He was a good looking steer." I was surprised and sad to hear about Pete's dad dying. It was easier to think about something to say related to Renegade than to ask him further questions about his dad. The more I go to the sale barn or listen to the men talk when we bale hay together or shell corn, the more I reason it is easier for men and boys to talk about the weather, crops, livestock market, or prices of machinery than it is to talk about someone dying, especially if it is someone close.

I quickly picked up the conversation again and asked, "Pete, do you want to go outside and just mess around?" I was trying to be a good host and do some kid stuff rather than trying to act like an adult and just hang around.

"Sure, let's go!" Pete answered, and we headed toward the door.

Before I forget, I better finish my introductions. Peter's sister, Ginny, is Victoria's age. Pete and Ginny live just across the county line so they go to school in Shelby, but Ginny and Victoria are in the same 4-H club called the Wheeler Leaders. Wheelerdale used to be an old, old town with a small Presbyterian church, but the town disappeared long ago. I read about it in Iowa history. The town's gone, but the old church is still there. I know the 4-H club took its name from the town, and the girls call themselves leaders because they lead their calves, steers, sheep, or pigs around. At least that's what I think.

The other couple is Richard and Valerie Crosswaite. They have two sons, Charles and Kendal. Charles is older than Victoria and Ginny, and

Kendal is a year younger. They both are handsome. I only know that because of the way Victoria and Ginny google-eyed them and acted around them. I didn't ask Kendal and Charles to hang out with us because I could tell they were drawn to Victoria and Ginny like flies are to sour milk in the separating room, or pigs are to slop.

We had a great time that night. I found out Pete had three ponies, and he invited me over to ride with him whenever I could get away. I also found out that the Madisens really did have children, but they were all grown-up and lived on their own farms. Besides all that, Mr. Madisen told me that they had big horses called Belgians, and he wanted to know if I ever wanted to come over and help Mrs. Madisen and him ready them to show in a fair or town parade. I was so excited, I said "Yes!" even before he finished his sentence. My mom, who was listening to our conversation, laughed, but my father only grinned a little.

Oh, I probably also need to tell you, the Crosswaites have a large milking herd and so they bale a lot of hay. Even though Kendal and Charles help their dad, Mr. Crosswaite said he always needs extra help when they bale. "When your dad comes over to help us hay, would you like to come too, Teddy, if your dad says it's okay?" he asked.

"Sure I would," I told him. I know since the neighbors share work when there is corn shelling, bailing hay and sometimes even harvesting, I wouldn't be paid for helping, but that would be okay with me. I had heard from Pete that Mrs. Crosswaite made great lunches when they hayed. I reckon most of the time I'd take a good hay lunch over working for a quarter or fifty cents for haying all day anytime. Who wouldn't? Usually, a good hay lunch includes Kool-Aid and sometimes pop; baloney, roast beef, real ham, or chicken sandwiches; lots of potato chips, and plenty of dill pickles, radishes, onions, and tomatoes; pie or cake and almost always homemade cookies; and of course, potato salad. Yes, a guy can't do better than a hay lunch.

The evening ended better than I could ever imagine! New friends and new opportunities—a chance to ride horses, possibly learn how to work with big horses, and go to fairs and parades. And, I don't want to miss the chance to have a place at the table for hay lunches. Did I mention meeting new friends? I believe this evening's "hellos" were some of the best ones I have given away.

After everyone left, I went to bed. When I finished my prayers, I laid in bed wondering how this very night might look to me a year from now or maybe even in two years? Would I still have the friends I made this evening? Would the Madisens really ask me to help them with the horses, and would I do such a good job they would keep asking me? I was just wondering how everything would be. I wish I knew. No, I don't wish I knew. What would be the adventure on this journey through life for a guy like me if I already knew how the story ends?

Like I said before, sometimes my "wonderings" take a long time to unfold. I guess it is like a rocket heading off to Mars. I doubt if the rocket can be there tomorrow. Good night, "hellos." Tomorrow, you won't be the same. Tomorrow will be a new adventure. I wish it was tomorrow.

I can't tell you the time of day, nor can I even remember what day it was, but I had another "wondering." It just popped into my head when I wasn't really doing much at all. If I had to think about it, I might have been doing a geography assignment or a pre-algebra equation. It doesn't matter. Since I am not too interested in those things, when the wondering popped into my head, I paid attention.

I was wondering, *After you say "goodbye" and after you say "hello," then what do you say? The next day when you see someone you just met the day before or the day before that, do you say, "hey"? Do you say "hello"? What about if you run into someone you said "goodbye" to? Do you say "Hey!" or "Hello!" I guess it won't be the same.* So I was wondering a little deeper, *What if a person says nothing at all? What would that mean?*

I've already told you my father doesn't say very much. The most I ever hear him talk is when we are at the sale barn or have company or the feed or seed corn salesman shows up. When it is just he and I, he is mostly silent. I'm not really talking about him and me. I'm really wondering about when silence is a good thing or a bad thing when you are with other people, and maybe you should speak up.

One night on the TV show *Gunsmoke*, a tough bully beat up a cowpoke in the saloon. Miss Kitty told the bartender to run and tell Marshal Dillon to hightail it over to the Long Branch. The bully kept punchin' and kickin.' No one, not even the big guys, did anything to stop the fight, or should I say the mauling. All they did was grab their drinks and move away from their tables. When Marshall Dillon came in, he quickly grabbed the bully and pulled him off the well-beaten cowpoke. The cowpoke was really bloodied. My mom said they probably used a lot of make-up to make it look like real blood. I think they used cheap ketchup, but I don't know. It looked like real blood to me.

I told you all about this episode not to talk about Marshal Dillon coming to the rescue, but to ask, *Why didn't anyone say something? Why didn't anyone step in and rescue the cowpoke?*

Even though I'm still too young to figure it all out, I think in my case, saying nothing at all and living in the silence is really, really hard. It occurs to me the right words build bridges that connect people. Words of hope or encouragement offered by several people or even just one person who actually believes in what he or she is saying might even build a house. I know bad words can make bridges fall down and houses crumble. I know it. I also know people might reason to themselves, "If I say nothing at all, then nothing bad will happen." I wonder if they had thought about what could happen if they said instead, "I know it's a risk and some people might not like me or might laugh at me, but it is the right thing to do, so I am going to say . . ."

Now I am still just a young adolescent and I think that means I am still a kid, but I am old enough to know that our history books tell us a lot of bad things have happened to nice and decent people because too many other people were silent. At the right time, silence can be the right thing to "say," but saying nothing at all can also lead to doing nothing at all, causing a lot of hurt and pain to someone or even to a whole bunch of people.

I hope I can learn how to say nothing at all at the right time but also say something when it might make a difference or help someone who needs it. Meanwhile, I want to work on building bridges out of my "hellos" and not blowing up bridges that linger from my "goodbyes." You never know, I just might want to cross back over that bridge again with a new "hello" and an "I sure miss you."

Chapter 10

If I Should Die

I know you might roll your eyes or think me a bit stranger than I think myself to be, but sometime during the fall of my first year in junior high, I started to read the obituary page that was in the Friday paper. Why Friday? I am not sure. Ever since I first learned how to read, I read the funnies in the paper every day. Oh, you might want to know, I didn't actually jump from the funnies to the obit page; "obit" is what my sister, Victoria, said is short for obituary.

I first started to scan the headlines on the front page as an assignment in social studies class, and if something interested me, I would read more. I really liked what my social studies teacher said were "feature" stories—stories about people, animals, or things that weren't necessarily newsy or of vital political, economic information—or reports about hold-ups. My social studies teacher started to make us read the newspaper so that if we were called on in class we would be prepared to speak about current events and say what we thought about a specific article we had read. I had to read for facts. But my eyes started to wander around the paper to a thing called the "Public Pulse." To my surprise, I found the public pulse section held my attention just like obits did.

I read a lot of letters written by people who were speaking their minds about everything from poor teacher salaries to food prices at the grocery store, from farmers being cheated on by corn prices to communism and something called the Cold War (which at first, I thought must be some war in the Arctic). Boy, did I have a lot to learn.

The "Public Pulse" helped me see how people could really speak out and that what they had to say must really be important or their letters wouldn't be in the paper. It also made me think about what I had to say because writing might be just as important. I am sure glad I came up with that thought because shortly after we had to read the paper for social studies, my English teacher, Mrs. Markham, made us all write a three-paragraph paper each Friday afternoon in class about a topic that we had read in the paper the day before.

We had to describe what we read as facts, what the reporter and people interviewed thought, and the last paragraph was to be on what we thought. She said, "Okay, class, I want to see your summary of the facts, what other people were saying about the subject, and what you think. I don't want you to preach to me in the third paragraph. I want to know what you think and feel and how well you can express yourself. Bring a clipping of the article and hand it in with your assignment." Wow! That is the first time I ever heard a teacher use the word "preach" in class. When she said it, she wasn't looking at the Baptist minister's son in our class, who sits three seats ahead of me. I think she was looking at me. *I wonder why?*

Without telling my mom or father, I started to read the paper more thoroughly and I paid special attention to the public opinion along with the obits. Sometimes, I even took notes. My social studies teacher calls the page the "public pulse," and Mrs. Markham, my English teacher, calls it the "public opinion" page. I think it matters whether you are a Republican or Democrat reading the paper. I believe Republicans call it the "public pulse," and Democrats call it the "public opinion" page, and people called Independents probably don't read the page at all. It doesn't matter to me much what anyone calls it because I am finding, even though I am pretty young, that I am becoming very curious about what people think, why they do what they do, how they feel about other people, and what they strongly believe. You know—what they would give their life for, go to war for, or take a stand for—like a controversial issue.

I guess you can say I am becoming a little nosier. I am also curious as to how all of what makes a person, affects how that person sees what is happening in the world and if they care or not. Just maybe I will find some people who think like I do. On one particular Friday, the obit page was right across from the public opinion page so I didn't have to look very hard to find it. I always have found it fascinating how a person's life can be summed up in one, two, or three paragraphs and once in a while four, but rarely did you find five, six or maybe seven paragraphs about a person unless the person had lots and lots of relatives who all demanded to be listed or who had a lot of money and gave a bunch of it to the newspaper.

I do not believe the obits are articles; I believe they are stories that give us a little peek into the life of the person. Most stories I have read so far include the name, age, occupation, the date of the person's death, and a list of relatives. I know they were all dead because I don't think the paper would ever print an obituary about someone who wasn't dead yet. I don't think that would be very nice.

I wondered what difference it would make in living if a person chose to be a farmer instead of a banker or a barber instead of running a shoe store. *What does it matter what you are?* I never saw an obit talk about how many church school perfect attendance pins people accumulated or if they were nice or if a person was just a mean cuss. No obit ever told you if the person gave any money to help feed starving children. Come to think of it, there never was a mention of whether or not a person liked gravy, green peas, or broccoli.

Once I read about a baby dying, and I felt very sad. On the next day, I read about a boy my age that died in a hunting accident. My heart hurt from the reading, so I stopped for the day, but my brain began to wonder about what this boy might have become had he lived to be an adult. *What did he miss by dying so early? What would I miss if I died before bedtime? What do persons living need to do because one twelve-year-old isn't here anymore? What would my mother or father do if I died from snakebite or a rabid dog bite while I was out getting the cows?* I finally decided that this whole way of thinking could become pretty complicated for anyone and very complicated for a twelve-year-old like me. Of course, being twelve, I didn't have an answer to these questions yet.

Remember when I was eight? There were a lot of things I didn't know and I was honest to tell you that I didn't. Now that it is Friday and I am twelve, I know just a little bit more, but I am realizing there is so much more I never thought of knowing earlier in my life hitting me in the brain. I also have a new ton of questions to be asked. I don't think I'll ask my social studies teacher these questions in class because I think the other kids would laugh at me. I can tell you, though; this whole obituary business has really challenged my very, very small understanding of being mortal, which is what our youth counselor at church says we all are. It has also caused me to think about a new word, "mortality." After we had that word in a spelling test, I had to look it up in the school's library dictionary. I memorized how to spell it, but I had no clue what it meant. I read that it means "the quality or state of being mortal." Or as I see it now, the quality or state of being a human being. I guess anyone born is a human regardless of how long you live before you read about your life on the obit page.

I have come to believe, even at twelve, that the quality of being human and how you live your life matters more than how long you live. I doubt my English teacher, Mrs. Markham, would agree with me, but I am considering that a life must be like one continuous run-on sentence and the periods, question marks, exclamation marks, commas, colons, and something called semi-colons only come when we breathe our last polluted breath and stare out into the distant skies waiting for the next adventure and new chapter to begin.

I hope I get a new body too. Maybe one that is a little taller than the one I am in now. There must be a group of immortals, persons or maybe judges or angels, who have never had an obituary and who decide where all those grammatical marks belong. Then someone, probably an angel like Michael, that's who my Sunday school teacher says is God's favorite angel, reads your life story to God and Jesus with all of the correct grammatical marks, punctuations, and grammar in the right places. After hearing everything, Jesus and God probably decide if you get to go on to that next exciting adventure and chapter or just have everything about you end with a plain old period while God's council goes on to hear the next person's story. Well, that is what I have been imagining. I haven't told anyone but you about this idea, so don't go spreading gossip around about what I said.

Now, let me tell you about how I came to this thinking. It all started when I was looking for an article in the newspaper to write my Friday English paper. Since our social studies teacher didn't say that we couldn't use the same article we write on in English class, I thought the same article would be the one I would choose and be prepared to present if I was called on in class. Looking was a hard job, and because I had been thinking so much about what it meant to be mortal, life in general, and the business of dying, being dead, and thinking about people's stories on the obit page, now some of these stories seemed to be part of my life story as well.

Oh, before I begin, it is important to tell you that I have already discovered in my reading that death is no respecter of space, time, or privacy. Death doesn't care if your birthday is the day after you die or if you already bought plane tickets to go to Hawaii in January. You might care, and maybe you can do something about time, but death won't be on your side . . . *hmmm* . . . but I'm thinkin' maybe, just maybe, God is. All of this thinking reminded me of what Mrs. Schaffer once said, "Death is the end of the life cycle."

I don't think Mrs. Schaffer or my social studies teacher, Mr. Jameson, who once lectured to our class about the different cultural and religious beliefs and practices of people around the world regarding death, have actually seen much death. Well, maybe Mrs. Schaffer has. She came from a small town. Mr. Jameson came from a suburb in Chicago, and he even told us that he has only gone to one funeral in his life. I am pretty sure neither one of them has seen many dying or dead critters on a farm. Well, I have! I have seen rotten dead chickens, stomach swollen dead sows, and a few other dead critters. When there was a runt in a pig litter, my father gave it to me. It would usually die before the day was out regardless of how much praying I did or hoping my brain held. It died. I have concluded that death STINKS! Forget about it being an end in this life, and just remember it STINKS!

Well, before my brain loses its place and I ramble on, I want to come back to how I started all of this. I will probably trail off a little to tell you some other things, but I won't lose you along the way. Last night, I read a letter in the "Public Pulse" that went something like this:

> Dear Editor:
>
> On page three in Tuesday's paper, there was an article about Negro students holding a sit-in at a department store because they were not being served at the soda fountain as white people were. There was a sign that read, "Whites only." The police were called in to remove them. Some of these young people were spat upon, some hit by other customers, and the paper showed one policeman hitting a student on the side of the head because he was not getting up off the floor.
>
> Who makes up these stupid rules anyway? I don't recall reading in Genesis where God created the first humans we call Adam and Eve and that at the end of the day, God said, "Ah, this is good. I have created two white people." Nor have I ever read in Genesis a sign above the entrance

to the Garden of Eden that said, "Whites Only." While we are on the subject, when God gave this character, Moses, not Charles Hesston, the Ten Commandments, there WERE only ten, and yet some people seem to believe there were eleven and the eleventh commandment reads, "Whites are superior to all other colors of people."

Oh, and don't forget about Jesus, who Christians see as the Son of God, when he was pushed to designate the two greatest commandments, the second one was, "Love your neighbor as yourself." And when he was pushed even harder he did not define your neighbor as someone white or someone living in your neighborhood but as someone in need. For the dummies, people who had wax in their ears, or the stiff-necked people, he told them a story about a good man who helped a stranger he found alongside of the road who had been robbed and severely beaten. I think he called the man who stopped to help, while the people you thought might stop didn't, a Samaritan. Hmmm . . . I believe the stiff-necked and uptight people of Jesus' day didn't think too much of Samaritans.

So there! I've been thinking it's about time we start living what the Good Book, that's the Bible, and common sense teaches! That's all I got to say about it.

Sincerely,

A Piece of My Mind

"A Piece of My Mind" also talked about some of the students being kicked and hit by people as they were being escorted out of the store, and one student was even bitten by a police dog. What did these kids do to deserve such treatment? Now that's something to ponder over. At least, that is what I figured. Oh, I also read a short letter that simply said:

To The Public:

Did anyone besides me read the article written on page four? The article included ". . . three American non-combatant military advisors were killed in the jungle outside of Da Nang in Vietnam last Friday. This brings the total dead reported by the State Department and the military to ninety-seven."

What are we doing there in the first place? Who is the military advising? And what advice are they giving that would cause them to be killed? How many Americans will be dead there before all the advising is done? I guess I have more questions than answers. I don't know if our being there is right or wrong. Maybe for some reason, we need to be there. I don't know. Do you?

Signed,

Curious

"A Piece of My Mind's" letter really troubled me, especially because on the same day, I read on the obit page where a young Negro boy in the city had been beaten to death and left in an alley. Then to read about people being killed in a faraway place we never heard of in geography class just because they are advising, and about children and teenagers being beaten, spat on, called cuss words or bad names, and even killed because they are the wrong "color,"—all of this news reading gave me the "two-ache"—an ache in my brain and an ache in my heart. I guess I had asked for it because I wanted to be prepared for social studies class and write a B+ paper for English. I guess when you read all that I did and think hard on what happened to that young boy and everyone else I mentioned, those stories become part of you. And people in Canada, England, and maybe even Outer Mongolia, if they read the *Herald*, judge all of us through those stories. Shame on us!

I like talking in front of people because I can talk about what important people in the world are thinking and share my own thoughts.

Sometimes, I agree with people I am reporting on and sometimes, I disagree. Mrs. Markham says, "You are free to agree or disagree, but you must tell us, in a logical way, how you came to your own conclusions." The thing I like the best is that my classmates really listen to me and no one, including Mrs. Markham, ever falls asleep.

One Friday, Mrs. Markham wrote on my paper, "Good job, Teddy. Your writing is improving—good clarity in presenting your ideas in a logical order on this topic. Sometimes you are a little too preachy. Just tell us what you are thinking and avoid telling us what your reader should think." *There was that word, preachy, again. Hmmm . . .*

I remember one time Mrs. Schaffer thought one of my Friday essays was a little preachy. When I asked her, "What do you mean?" She said, "Teddy, you are giving your reader a moral lesson like a minister might do in one of his or her sermons. Your writing needs to include your thoughts, back them up with facts, and give possible solutions, and then you can challenge your readers to think on their own and so they can draw their own conclusions. Someday if you become a minister, you can be a little preachy once and a while." This is what I remember. I guess I better try and practice more what Mrs. Schaffer told me. I wouldn't want her to be disappointed if Mrs. Markham called her and told her I was still being preachy in my writing.

One time, I wrote about a little girl. Her parents said she fell down the stairs when her teacher inquired about her bruises. The next day at school, she looked worse because she had more bruises. The teacher asked her to stay behind at recess time. When the teacher asked what had happened, she started to cry and said, "My momma and daddy whipped me with their fists. The teacher called the police and someone called Social Services, which came and took the little girl. The article said the parents were charged with child abuse. I don't know what happened to the little girl, but I felt an ache in my heart and brain at the same time for her.

Shortly after my experience writing about the little girl, when Mr. Jameson, our social studies teacher, gave us the assignment to write an essay on a topic of our choosing that included information we had researched, I decided to research child abuse. He also said we would need to be prepared to do a presentation in front of the class on our topic. On the day of our presentations, I was the second person Mr. Jameson called on to present. When I got to the part telling the class that in the early 1900s people who abuse children were first charged under animal cruelty laws, my voice started to crack and my legs started to shake. I almost started to cry, but smart Mr. Jameson told me that I could sit down. The whole class was very quiet. He gave me an "A" for the day, and I gave myself a hurt. When I said my prayers that night and came to ". . . if I should die before I wake," my mind started to wander and took me to the bedroom the little girl might have had. I wondered *when she said her prayers did she ever pray, ". . . if I should die before I wake . . . ?"* I became curious to know if God was listening to her. Mrs. Kate says, "God hears everyone." *If that is true and God heard her, why didn't God stop her parents?*

Remember, I said that I didn't know what happened to the little girl? Well, I didn't until a week later when I read on the obit page that a six-year-old girl died from a fall. In my heart, I knew it was that little girl. *Why didn't Social Services keep her? Why weren't her parents put in jail for twenty years? I just know it was that little girl.* I wish I hadn't read the obit page that Friday. I don't know all the answers yet. I am only twelve. Maybe someday, God, Mrs. Kate, or the angels Michael or Gabriel will tell me, or maybe my mother will tell me. I haven't asked her about it all. I don't think my father will ever tell me. He doesn't talk to me about things like that.

I don't know how much heavy thinking a seventh grader should do or is even allowed to do. Since I am not allowed to vote, I don't know if, at twelve, I can make the president or congress change the law to make parents and mean people who beat up on or abuse children and teenagers stay in prison for a long time and eat only peas, casseroles, and bread without jelly.

I do believe that reading all of these stories on the Obit page and reading what people in the "Public Pulse" say about abuse and being prejudice toward people because of the color of their skin and other stuff is really heavy resting on a twelve-year-old's brain. It's like when my ears are stuffed because I have a cold in my head, and I can't make the cold go away. I can't hear very well, and my head feels like it is going to blow up. It hurts. Well, my bad feelings went from bad to really bad. So that you will understand why, I have to tell you about one of the death experiences I had in the spring of my twelfth year. Depending upon who you are and your own early experiences with death, you may or may not relate to my hurt and pain.

The grief I experienced was shared by all members of my family in different ways but was never talked about, so in those years, I really did not know what grief was. I cried, my mom cried, my sisters cried, but I never saw my father cry. I guess I'll talk to you more about his not crying later. The death I want to tell you about might surprise you. I remember it as if it happened yesterday.

Every spring, almost two months before school lets out for the summer, my mom orders baby chicks. Some of the chicks turn out to be hens, which lay eggs, and some turn out to be roosters. A lot of our roosters end up in our deep freeze, with all of their feathers picked off, of course, and their bodies all cut up. They rest there until my mother takes them out and fries them for Sunday dinner or when we have special company on Saturday night. This year was no exception to the chick ordering business.

My mom ordered the chicks in late March, and last week the hatchery called to say they would deliver the chicks on Monday. Saturday morning, before the chicks came to live with us, I had finished my morning chores and was heading for the house to do what I wanted to do. My dad, coming from another direction, met me at the back door porch. "Teddy, you can go in the house and have a drink of water and then meet me at the chicken house. I am bringing the manure spreader up to the south door of the chicken house. You need to clean out the west room. Remember, the hatchery is delivering the chickens on Monday, so we need to be ready. Remember, no horsing around!"

I was tempted to say . . . *but I want to have another bowl of Raisin Bran and watch some TV.* I didn't. The look on my father's face gave me a clue not to pursue my wishes or make my thoughts known. Head hanging down and slowly walking toward the house, I muttered, "Yes, Dad." I wasn't really thirsty, but that's what I told my dad I was heading for, so I let the water run for a bit so it would be really cold, and then I took my time taking my drink. Walking just as slow, I made my way back to the chicken house, grabbed the pitchfork, and began the smelly task of grunt work. So all day Saturday, I stuck a pitchfork as deep as I could into the stinky straw, ground-up corn cobs and chicken manure casserole.

I heaved and lifted it up onto my fork with all my twelve-year-old strength and carried the yuck to the edge of the door, and with a swing, let the stuff fling into the manure spreader. On my first attempt, I barely missed hitting the side of the spreader. Once in a while, I did hit the side, and the jolt pushed me backwards at the same time flinging the manure combination with a splattering affect. Some of the manure flew back into my face, a lot more fell to the ground, and a few morsels landed in the wagon. After this happened once and caught me off guard, I learned to keep my mouth closed while throwing and not be singing "The Old Rugged Cross."

Boy, those chickens sure were messy. And here we were getting more of them, which would mean more work for me! *Oh well.*

The day had also been cold and cloudy with snow threatening, so by suppertime, my mom and dad decided to put the chicks in the freshly cleaned shed and not the chicken house.

Later on that afternoon, my mom had used the tin snippers to cut strips of tin from green bean cans, and my father and I used them to nail up all the holes in the floor of the shed. We had also covered all the windows with plastic and weather stripping to keep as much cold air out as possible. Then we hung heat lamps from the ceiling in the shed to keep the chicks warm. I should have said my father did all of this, and I just did what he told me to do.

When we were finally done preparing the shed, my mom came out to inspect it.

"The two of you did a great job. I think this will be very appropriate for when—" My mom didn't finish. She just stood staring at one of the plastic-covered windows.

I wanted to say something but wasn't quite sure what to say. I didn't expect my mom not to tell us what she was thinking.

"What's wrong, Elaine?" My dad asked.

I think my mom was just waiting for my dad to ask the question so she could continue.

Before speaking, my mom pulled me and my dad over next to her. "Guys, like I said, you did a great job! I couldn't have asked for more. This shed will do just fine for the chicks after they are several weeks older, but for now, with the weather being so unpredictable and chicks, at their age, being so vulnerable, I just don't know if this will work."

I am sure my dad was probably wishing he had a better solution for the chick problem. I know I wished I could have come up with one. I remember turning and staring at the same window my mom and dad were staring at as if maybe the window would give us an answer.

It was my mother who finally came up with the next solution that almost seemed inevitable. "I guess we will have to keep them in their boxes and put them in the parlor."

"I guess so. "My father said. "It will cost too much to keep the chicks at the hatchery until this cold snap goes away or until they are older."

"I just hope it won't be for too long. The smell will be hard to get rid of unless I open up the room after we move them out."

I can remember when my mother used to bring baby chicks into the house. She would cover a washtub bottom with an old blanket and place the tub near the wood stove in the kitchen. Then she would bring chicks in that were deserted by their mother and keep them there until the weather was warm enough for them to go to the barn or until she tired from chasing them around the house when they were old enough to jump out of the tub.

But this time, we weren't talking about six or seven chicks—we were talking about more than two hundred! My mom's eyes wandered around the room while she spoke.

"It's supposed to warm up on Wednesday. Almanac says thunder and lightning storms this weekend." I guess this was my father's way of trying to assure my mom the chicks wouldn't stay inside too long—but then again, they could also be lingering longer if the storms were severe.

I just shook my head and sighed. I was simply exhausted, and by this point, I didn't care one way or another, just wanting the day to be done.

After supper, Victoria washed the dishes and Ruby dried. Cindy was in the living room, sound asleep on the couch. My mom, my father, and I went to work rearranging furniture in the parlor to provide room for the chicks.

Other than baby chicks in a tub, I don't ever recall having chickens live inside our house before, but this is the first farmhouse we have lived in that has a parlor where accommodations could be made if necessary. Once, my mother had about a dozen or two baby chickens on the back porch, but the wind must have always been blowing in the right direction because the smell never came into the rest of the house. Before bedtime, the parlor had been transformed into a temporary brooder house.

Monday after school, just as soon as my sisters and I came into the house, I could hear a "cheep, cheep, cheep," and a whiff of air told me that the aroma I smelled definitely did not come from freshly baked homemade chocolate chip cookies.

"Eeew," Victoria gasped with a disgusting look on her face.

With a gleeful voice, Cindy excitedly demanded, "Come see our babies!" as she took a hold of Victoria's hand giving it a hearty tug.

"I'd rather not. Thank you," Victoria resisted Cindy's tug and turned to go upstairs to her room.

Ruby needed no invitation. "Can I hold one?" Ruby asked as she ran to the parlor door with eager anticipation, watching the chicks rush to the opposite ends of their large delivery boxes, trying hard to flee from what they instinctually feared to be approaching danger. Desperately trying to escape, when they reached the opposite side of the boxes, chicks crowded and climbed up on the backs of their companions who managed to be first to the other side. Some of them immediately leaped right out of the box and started to scramble away. Surprised, Ruby immediately came to a halt, probably fearing that she would be scolded.

My mother simply said, "Shhh! Ruby, not so loud. You are scaring them," and placed her hand on Ruby's shoulder. Once Ruby was calm, my mother began to collect the wandering chicks. When the last one was gathered, Mom told Ruby to hold out her hands, and then she placed the chick carefully into Ruby's eager palms. "Don't squeeze him," my mother instructed as she saw Ruby's hands begin to close tightly around the chick.

"How do you know it's a boy?" Ruby inquired at the same time, loosening her grip just a little.

"Never mind," my mom answered and then instructed Ruby to put the chick back into the box.

When I saw the chicks, right away I thought, *Hmmm . . . this is a good thing, after all. The longer they stay in the parlor, the less manure I will have to clean out of the chicken house later. What a deal!* I could put up with the smell if it meant a respite from having to clean up their messes. Right now, their only mess was on the delivery box floor. I haven't ever had to clean out a delivery box.

To my misfortune, the chicks' stay in the Hall Resort was short-lived. What my father had said about the weather was correct, because by mid-week, the weather turned warm, very warm for the first of April. I remember both my mom and dad thought the chicks were now old enough to be moved to the chicken house.

By Thursday evening, the chicks were all moved out of the house into the empty side of our chicken house. I forgot to tell you, our chicken house is divided into two rooms. One side is full of chickens, the old rooster, and nests where the hens, female chickens, lay their eggs. The other side was cleaned out by my mom and dad last fall. I think they were going to use it for storage but decided not to because of the smell.

As soon as the chicks left the parlor, my mom had all of the parlor windows opened and two fans blowing in the room. It was really cold in there, but cold or not, my mom gave the room a good clean. She even scrubbed the wooden floors twice with something called ammonia with the picture of a bald-headed man with an earring in his ear on front of the bottle. My mom always used this man's stuff when she wanted the floors of the house to look and smell really clean. It's too bad we can't use the same stuff in the cow barn. Finally, she made Victoria clean all of the windows on the inside, and just for good measure, she had Victoria clean the same windows on the outside.

Friday, when we came home from school, my mom said, "Victoria, Janet's mother called and asked if you could spend the weekend with Janet. I told her you could. As soon as you change, Victoria, I have some ironing for you to do. Teddy, change your clothes and go do your chores. Don't rush through them. Ruby, you and Cindy can help me make supper.

Just as soon as we eat, we are going to town. If you behave, Teddy, and do all of your chores, you can go to the movie so let's get moving."

Movie! Wow! Peter told me a John Wayne western was playing! I was wishing I could go and now I guess I really was going! Maybe all that hard work had paid off, after all!

Later that evening, when we arrived in town, we dropped Victoria off at Janet's house. A few seconds later, we were on Main Street. My father reached over into the back seat where I was sitting, handed me some change. "Teddy, here is sixty cents, fifty cents for the movie and ten cents for popcorn. After the movie, walk over to the Busy Bee. We will be waiting there."

"Okay." I excitedly put the money in my pocket and scrambled out the car door as fast as I could just in case my father changed his mind and wanted the dime he gave me for popcorn back. Cindy was only half awake from car napping just as my dad was handing me my money. "Where's Teddy going, Mom? I want to go with Teddy."

"Cindy, you and Ruby get to go to the café with Daddy and me. Okay?" That's all I heard. My mind was already in the movie theater.

The movie was great; however, one thing I can never figure out is when John Wayne takes a shot at desperados or Indians, three or four of them always fall off their horses, but when the bad guys or Indians fire back at John Wayne or the cavalry they always seem to miss, or once in a while when they do hit someone, only one person falls off his horse. John Wayne never falls off his horse. I never complain to the high school kid who runs the projector nor have I ever written a letter to the "Public Pulse," asking why this happens.

When I left the theater, the sky was really dark, and lightning was crisscrossing the western sky. I was fortunate that it wasn't raining, so I still took my time walking to the Busy Bee. Arriving at the café, I found my mom and father sitting in a booth with friends drinking coffee. Ruby and Cindy were fast asleep, slumped up alongside of my father in the booth.

I was allowing myself to imagine that I would ask my mom for a hamburger, french fries, and a coke when a roaring crack of thunder scattered my thinking, and the Busy Bee's lights started to flicker. "We better head for home, Sam," my mom said as she nudged my father.

"Yes, I guess we should, but I think we are going to have a downpour any minute now, so I think we best wait it out here," my father answered.

"You're probably right," my mother agreed, then added, "I'm just worried about the chicks if the lights go out."

It looked like my father was going to say something when another bolt of lightning, immediately followed by a clap of thunder, came crashing down right on top of the restaurant. The lightning was so sharp it must have ripped a cloud carrying about a ton of water, causing rain to pour down so fast and thick that it looked like a wall of ice was moving right toward the Busy Bee. The Busy Bee's lights flickered one more time and then the whole place went dark. Ruby and Cindy slept through it all.

"I guess I can't have a hamburger," I said aloud, hoping someone would correct me by saying that I could.

"The grill's power went out with the electricity, Teddy," Mrs. Blanchard, the restaurant owner, explained as if she could read my mind. "Not to worry," she continued, "the ice cream freezer is on an auxiliary generator. I'll make you a two-scoop Butter Brickle ice cream cone. It's on the house." Mrs. Blanchard finished while turning her attention from me to my father.

"Is it okay?" I asked my father holding back my excitement.

"I guess so," my father replied, tossing a smile toward Mrs. Blanchard.

"Wow! Double dip! Butter Brickle! Thank you, Mrs. Blanchard!" I said as I was finding my way to the counter guided by Mrs. Blanchard's flashlight. My thoughts didn't end there because I also began to think how a Butter Brickle ice cream cone was even better than a hamburger. We have hamburgers on the farm a lot of times for supper and even sometimes at noon on Saturday, but we seldom have Butter Brickle ice cream, and when we do, the scoops are never as big as the ones Mrs. Blanchard dips out.

By the time I ate my ice cream cone in slow motion, the rain had fizzled to a trickle, and we were on our way home. I could tell my mother and father were both nervous, and I was right. As soon as my father stopped the car, my mom instructed me to wake up Ruby, who was still sleeping, and take her and Cindy to the house

Holding on to their outstretched hands, I led my sleepy sisters to the house. Without stopping to catch her breath, my mom popped out of the car and, with a desperate determination, headed toward the chicken house. In a few seconds, my father and I heard a loud scream coming from my mother. Her scream was immediately followed by, "Sam! Sam! Come here, quick!"

My father ran to the chicken house to see what was causing my mom to panic. As soon as I deposited my sisters on the living room couch, without even taking off my good clothes, I, too, went to the chicken house. By this time, the electricity had come back on, and the dark menacing clouds that had brought the downpour were broken up by stars piercing through the blackness.

Now there was plenty of light to see the carnage that had occurred in the darkness. Dead baby chicks were scattered across the brooder house floor. It looked like a war zone. There were less than one hundred chicks still alive, and even some of them had splatters of blood on their yellow fuzz that would soon become feathers if they survived that long. "What happened to the chicks?" I asked my mom with a tone of caution.

"The rats killed them," she responded, her tears falling to the floor.

"Rats? They must have been really hungry." I looked across the room and estimated that over one hundred chicks were dead.

"They weren't hungry." My father said matter-of-factly.

"But why did they . . . ?" I hesitatingly began, not sure if I should ask another question. My father seemed oblivious to my attempt, but my mom interrupted to explain. "They weren't hungry, Teddy. They kill because they smell the blood after one of them attacks one chick, and then they kill and kill and kill. They suck some blood from the chick's neck, drop it, and go after another—over and over and over. It's like they go mad. They kill for the blood. In the dark, the helpless chicks can't see them coming. Even if they did, they are pretty helpless and too small to defend themselves against several rats."

"They sure drank a lot of blood," I said, not trying to be funny. I wasn't sure if I should have said anything at all, but the silence after my mom was finished was scary to me.

"They didn't kill all of them," my mother said after she had a few seconds to compose herself. "When they started to chase the chicks, those that could ran in the opposite direction until they ended up in that far corner over there." My eyes followed her finger, pointing to the pile of dead chicks I had previously seen, figuring the rats just threw them all in a pile. My mother wasn't finished. "The chicks just piled one after another on top of each other trying to escape the rats, and the chicks on the bottom of the heap suffocated. I think the rest of them were frightened to death."

"It just doesn't seem right. They are all so helpless," I said, mostly to myself.

In a physical show of what I later came to understand as compassion, my father put his arm around my mom's shoulders and said, "Elaine, let's go change clothes. Teddy and I will come back and pick up the dead chicks. I think tomorrow we can run into town and see if the hatchery has more baby chicks or we can have them order more for us."

"I don't think we can. I don't think we can afford—I don't think we can ever afford—" my mother stopped in the middle of her sentence, but her silent tears still kept falling.

"We can't afford not to, Elaine. It will work out. Come on, let's go to the house." Without waiting for my mom to respond, my father cautiously turned her toward the door, and the three of us headed out of the barn.

As we walked away, I heard my father softly say, "Damn rats." *Boy! Was I surprised.* My father only said, "damn," when something really bad happened; he usually says a really long mess of bad words and sometimes he takes a breath and says them all again only in a different order when he's frustrated or mad. Tonight all he said was, "damn."

I didn't say any bad words. To tell the truth, I really have only said two bad words in my whole life up to this evening. I have only said, "hell" and "damn." I only said those two words when Jimmy and I were having a spitting contest behind our barn. We were trying to think of some words our fathers might say in front of the preacher and not be scolded or receive a red mark in the preacher's book, *The Sins of My Parishioners.*

My father and I returned to the brooder house in our chore clothes. Without saying a word, we picked up the dead chicks and put them in the cardboard box. The surviving chicks just stood around. They seemed to be a bit dazed, and if they were humans looking like they did, I imagined they looked like victims of a horrendous wreck or massive shooting on a highway that Broderick Crawford and his men on the TV show "Highway Patrol" were seeing for the first time as they arrived on the accident scene.

When we finished, my father carried the box out the door as I followed him. Instead of assuming I would lock the door, he abruptly put the box down, turned around, and proceeded to lock the door. I was just about to say, "I was going to lock it, Dad," when he picked up the board he brought with us and, clutching the hammer he drew from the loop on the side of his overalls, nailed the board across the bottom of the door. Afterwards, he turned to me, and I actually heard him say, "I should have done this earlier. Maybe . . ." he stopped as if he was telling me too much.

My father set the box of dead chicks on top of the garbage heap near the trash barrel and then said, "Teddy, tomorrow after you do your chores and before you change your clothes for Sunday school, I want you to pour some gasoline on the chicks and burn them."

"Burn them, Dad?" I questioned.

"Yes, we need to burn them right away, or they will draw more rats or other scavengers," my father calmly explained.

"Okay, Dad." I understood what he meant by scavengers. I've seen neighbor dogs come to visit Pal, and they all go out to the pasture or timber where they gnaw on bones from dead pigs or really old dead rabbits they have found. I don't think Pal is a scavenger. I am sure he just likes bones. I can't say the same for the all the other dogs.

If I had had more time Sunday morning when I went out to burn the chicks, I would have pretended the chicks were brave Vikings who had been killed in a war with the enemy and I was the chief setting their funeral pyre on fire as the ship carrying them was released from its mooring and cast alone on the open sea so they could travel to Jerusalem or Canada or wherever their heaven or afterlife was located. I would have watched with imaginative eyes as the ship slowly drifted away from the shore, sinking while smoke from their spirit bodies was being lifted by the wind carrying the brave warriors' spirits to that other place I am not sure of where God, or some other gods who I have read about in comic books Jimmy has, wait to honor them.

Well, I didn't have time to let my imagination go like I wanted to, so I quickly doused the dead chicks with gasoline from the fuel barrel and threw a match from the matchbook my mom gave me into the box. For a few seconds, I watched the flames leap into the air. Let me tell you, the smoke didn't smell like it was carrying any spirits; instead, the smoke carried a big stink worse than a skunk stink and I imagined it would last longer. The stink I smelled was death. Death stinks. When I went back to the house and took another bath before church, I had to really scrub hard.

There was something good that came from all of this, though. My father came to town with us and instead of going to the café to smoke a cigarette and drink coffee while we were in Sunday school and church, he came to church with us. I really didn't understand what the minister said during his sermon. He talked about something called "incarnation." I've heard of Carnation before. It's a cream my grandmother uses in her coffee. I doubt incarnation is a cream. I hope someday I learn what incarnation is. When it came time for silent prayer, I said a prayer for the baby chicks, but not for the rats. After Sunday dinner that day and before I did anything else Sunday afternoon, I wrote an obit for Fuzzy Chick:

The Life of Fuzzy Chick

Fuzzy Chick, along with most of his brothers and sisters, came to an untimely tragic death last week. Even before his birth, Fuzzy Chick's life was filled with trials. He was taken from his mother's nest only seconds after he was egg-born and was put in an adoption agency's placement home called the Hatchery, where he remained in closed confinement with little social contact until he was hatched into this life by artificial means.

His first few "beeps" were not met by a reassuring clucking sound from his mother but were joined by the "beeps" of brothers and sisters, unaware of their surroundings, afraid, and having little opportunity to spread their wings. The one consolation was a radiant light that seemed to bring them warmth and a small measure of comfort; however, this did not last very long.

In human time, not chicken time, only a week passed when, after Fuzzy Chick and his brothers and sisters were born, they were scooped away from the warm light and placed into a transport carrying them far out into a distant land. Upon arrival at their destination, Fuzzy Chick and the others were set free in a large musty smelling enclosure with three lights similar to the radiant light they had left behind at the Hatchery that cast rays of warmth upon their tender skin. Fuzzy chick now had room to spread his wings. The food and drink were new to him, but he found the drink refreshing and the food delicious. Giants tromped into their enclosure periodically to bring them more water and food. Even though the giants appeared to seem friendly, Fuzzy Chick and the others were obviously afraid of what might happen next. They would often flee to the other side of the enclosure as far away from the giants as possible whenever they would enter. In time, Fuzzy Chick came to trust the giants, but he always had his wings free, ready to spread them out and scamper away if the giants seemed to encroach upon his personal boundaries.

Just when all seemed to be working out, one evening a terrible noise rumbled across the enclosure, and streaks of light flashed across the sky as seen from the windows. To add to their fear, the warm radiant lights that always seemed to provide a source of comfort and assurance flickered once and then twice.

Without further warning, the enclosure went dark. Fuzzy Chick and his gang were terrified. Out of fear and desperation, they crowded up against each other. In a few short minutes following the blackout, small piercing lights approached the chicks. They carried a smell that was new to Fuzzy. Without warning, more piercing lights appeared, coming closer and closer to the chicks. As they approached, the smell became ever stronger, then a scream, "Beep!" cracked through the blackness, then another, and then another. In the next instance, Fuzzy felt a sharp pain on both sides of his neck. He tried to beep, but he couldn't. Feeling dizzy, he dropped to the floor and died.

The account of Fuzzy Chick's death is a sworn testimony of chicks who survived what is now called "The Night of Terror."

You just read how I imagined Fuzzy Chick's obituary would read if there had been one. I know it isn't very pleasant, but in writing the obit,

I got to thinking, *Why isn't there a page in the newspaper for obits that tell life stories of pets or helpless animals like chicks who are killed or die from the cold, floods, tornadoes, or monstrous creatures like rats?* That's when I decided I was going to write a letter to the boss of the newspaper and mail it to the "Public Pulse" and ask that question. I don't think I will ask our minister. He might think he would have to come to our house and have a long chat with me.

The other thought I had after the rats' killing spree and the reactions that our family had to it is that I believe some people have greater empathy and compassion toward the death of the more vulnerable in the world. And yet, rats still kill chicks, and parents still abuse children, and some of those children die from the abuse; wars still kill grandmas and grandpas, children and babies. *Golly, if officers of the world's armies and people they call politicians want to kill each other, why can't they just find a football field surrounded by a high fence and fight each other? I bet the politicians would talk each other to death and the officers would draw up so many plans that their number two pencils would run out of lead and they would end up having to surrender to each other.*

All of this thinking comes full circle back to what I have said before: Death Stinks! There is nothing grand about it no matter how decorative you make the Viking ship, or how expensive the casket is, or how much food you put out for the gathering after the funeral, or at the end of the day, how large of a sum a person will receive from the dead person's money and other stuff.

This is how Fridays in seventh grade usually went. One Friday in May, about three weeks before school was out for the summer and after we handed in our essays on the topic of our choice, Mrs. Markham said, "Class, next Friday, rather than have an essay on a news event; I want each of you to write a poem."

Most of the guys said, "What? Oh, no!" The girls giggled when they heard the guys. And they really laughed when Butch blurted out, "What's a poem?"

Right away, Mrs. Markham called out, "Okay, settle down now!" She then told Butch what a poem was by saying, "Butch, and anyone else who has forgotten what a poem is, read page twenty-four in your English book, and that will give you a description of a poem." Already hands were waving in the air, but before she called on anyone, Mrs. Markham added a surprise to the poem writing business, "The best poems, one written by a girl and one by a boy, will be published in the county newspaper." My ears really shot up when she said poems would be published. Mrs. Markham started to call on the hand wavers. Sharon was first.

"Can we write about clothes?" Sharon asked with a look of pretended innocence. I know why Sharon wanted to write a poem about clothes. Sharon always comes to school dressed up like she is going to Sunday school but without her bonnet.

It didn't seem to me that Mrs. Markham gave any thought to Sharon's motive for asking and simply answered, "As long as it's a poem."

Joe Winchel's hand was waving just as hard. "Yes, Joe." Mrs. Markham was obviously aware of Joe's effort to catch her attention.

"Can we write about football?" He asked enthusiastically.

"As long as it is a poem." Mrs. Markham repeated. Mrs. Markham must have had enough of repeating herself because she ignored the rest of the hand wavers and simply said, "Okay, class. I think you all know what I am expecting of you in writing a poem. Now put your things away and gather up what you are taking home. "Have a nice weekend, class, and be ready for your grammar test on Monday, and don't forget your poem for next Friday. You might want to start on it this weekend." I am not sure too many kids heard her, but I did because I sit up near the front of the room.

Chores and supper were pretty routine on this Friday, but at the supper table, when my mother passed the platter layered with pancakes, she announced that she and our father were going square dancing and Victoria would be babysitting. Even before supper, Victoria and I had known something was up because our father took a bath and put on his cowboy shirt, western jeans, and boots. Victoria must have thought we were going to have company and the grown-ups would be playing cards so her evening plans would not be ruined, but when she heard what was really happening, she was devastated. I think Victoria would rather wash all of the discs in the separator than babysit my sisters and me.

"Do I have to stay home? Why can't Teddy watch Ruby and Cindy? Clara asked me to come over this evening. I never get to do anything!" Victoria pouted, making sure she addressed her remarks toward my mother as she handed me the platter filled with pancakes at the same time.

My mother didn't answer Victoria, so I jumped in. "Can I stay up and watch Movie Masterpiece? Huh? Can I? Can I have some ice cream? Please, Mom! I won't give Victoria any trouble." Saying that I wouldn't give Victoria any trouble was always my bargaining chip. Just like Victoria, I kept my eyes fixed on my mother. I was afraid if I looked at my father he would simply say, "No," and that would be that.

With my eyes still fixed on my mother and waiting for an answer, Ruby innocently asked, "Can I go with you and Dad, Mom?"

My mother quickly prioritized her answers. She took a deep breath and started with me. "You can stay up until eleven p.m. You can have some ice cream. Victoria will scoop it out. NO, you can't do it yourself. Victoria, you can call Clara and see if she can come over here tomorrow evening."

I never asked if I could scoop out my own ice cream, but my mother knew what would happen if I did. There might not be any left in the box by the time I finished. My mom sure knows her children.

My mother took another breath, though not as deep and, smiling at Ruby, she quietly said, "Ruby, you have to stay home and help Victoria take care of Cindy. Remember, tomorrow you are going to the Girl Scout skating party so you will probably want to be in bed early." After that, there was no more bargaining from anyone. It wasn't really worth it. Pressing the issue by any one of us might mean we would lose our privileges. We kids know our mother. Ruby would usually try harder after the first two "no's," but she was old enough to know that if she tried Mom's patience or if our father stepped into the discussion, even she could lose her privileges.

After my parents left, Victoria, Ruby, and Cindy settled in to watch TV. I decided to do my English assignment earlier than I usually do—a lot earlier. With Easter just around the corner and my growing interest in the obit page, concern for children and adults being abused and treated unfairly, and people from our own country dying in far-off countries, I was led to write a poem about freedom:

Freedom

Give me freedom for all to see,
How I fled from misery,
On a wall where all could see,
I was hanging there so free.
The night was dark and very cold,
But no one noticed
I was froze.
But in the distance, I could see,
Across the meadow, across the sea,
Where my freedom waits for me.

I wanted to also write a poem about Fuzzy Chick and bloodthirsty rats, but after thinking about it, my second thought was just to let the obit for Fuzzy Chick be a tribute for all the helpless chicks and animals in the world, at least for now. Before nine p.m. that evening, I wrote twenty-three more poems on every topic that came to my mind: death, sadness, chores, sisters, ice cream, and horses, just to name a few. I also wrote four short stories. One of my stories was about a man who was kicked by a cow and what he did to the cow. I did not let on that the man was my father, and I definitely did not put any of the words I heard him say afterwards in the story. By the time I was done for the evening, I really surprised myself! And, I found out that I enjoyed writing, especially poetry.

After I was done writing, I ate my ice cream and watched a scary movie on TV and then the news came on, and I found myself so tired that I decided to go to bed. I'll tell you writing is tiring business. Writing isn't tiring in the way you feel after you have finished your chores or have cleaned out the hog house. Writing is a different kind of tired. It is a brain tired, and I think that is even more tiring than any chore I have had to do in my lifetime. My brain was still writing poems after I said my prayers.

My poem on "Freedom" won the contest for the boys. Several days after we turned in our assignment, Mrs. Markham called me to her desk before the last bell rang and told me, "Teddy, I am really surprised. You put a lot of effort into this assignment. My goodness! Twenty-four poems and four short stories! You express yourself very well, and I like your originality; plus, you have a knack for taking something common and helping the reader see it come alive in your words. I hope you continue writing, but you must learn to proofread and use the proper tense for words. In your poem on freedom, I changed the word "froze" to "frozen." I want you to look up the word in your English book and then write out why you need to use the word "frozen' in your poem. I changed the word for you so I could go ahead and submit your poem along with Carol John's poem to the newspaper. They will be published in next week's edition. Now, I want you to also take your other poems back. Proofread all of them and correct the grammar using proper tense for verbs and then hand them back to me next Monday." When she was done speaking, Mrs. Markham handed me the papers in a file she labeled, "Teddy's Poems and Stories."

I was just about ready to say, "Ah, do I have to?" but before I could, Mrs. Markham continued. "If you make the appropriate corrections, you will have a much better grade in English for this six weeks." She smiled.

Hmmm . . . a better grade . . . it might be worth it at that! So instead of complaining, I smiled politely and said, "Gee, thanks!" and returned to my desk.

Come to think of it, that was the very first time in my whole life that I ever thanked anyone for giving me extra work to do. I just wanted you to know that some good things really do happen in a person's life, and the good feeling that comes along can last a long time even through struggles and trials. Oh, even though my mom helped me by proofreading my corrections, I received an "A" when my report card came out. And even though she helped me, it made my mom really proud of me. My father smoked his cigarette, drank his coffee, read my report card, and then handed it back to my mother for her to sign. My father has never signed any of my report cards. I wonder why.

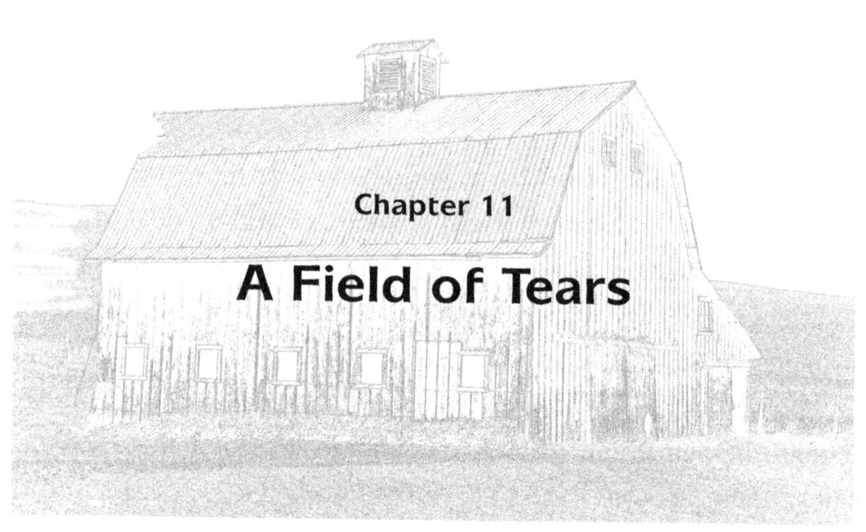

Chapter 11

A Field of Tears

The good feeling I had about my writing and the "A" lasted longer than I thought it would. The school year ended, and hay season was just around the corner, a very short corner. While I am telling you about the end of school for the summer and the good feeling that lingered longer than I expected, I want to tell you about another good thing that happened to me before the sad events that occurred in our family started again.

Without my anticipation or expectation, the surprise came right out of the blue and, if you were to ask me, "Would you have ever thought this would happen to you?" I would have said, "I have as much chance of such a thing happening as God giving the angel Michael the answers to my last math test to hand-deliver to me."

The only thing I don't like about summer is the "grunt work." I was older now and was expected to do more stuff, and my father did not hesitate to give me more chores to do even though I never asked for them. You remember that I once told you I am really short and my legs aren't very long, so I have never driven our old Allis Chalmers? Instead, I do most of the grunt work. I probably need to tell you just exactly what grunt work is. It's when you have to put more grunts or just a little more *humphs* and *hmms* into the stress and strain of heaving, lifting, pulling, and muscle power and whatever backbreaking work a job calls for you to do to accomplish the task. As far back as I can remember, which is about three years of age, I have had to do grunt work.

So on the very first Friday after school was out, I was eating icky corn flakes when my father came in from milking. He didn't sit down and have a coffee and smoke break as he usually does but instead instructed me, "Teddy, as soon as you are done with breakfast, come outside. I need you to clean out a row of fences in the cow pasture. We will bale hay this afternoon if it doesn't rain.

"Are you going to help me?" I asked, thinking I already knew the answer.

"I have other things to do, and when I am done, I will start haying. After you are done, we'll bring the load in and unload it alongside the granary. This afternoon, you can begin to pick up the bales. This is how that first Friday started. I wasn't too excited, but I knew better than to ask if I could watch TV for a while or go hiking in the pasture. Telling me what I had to do, my father left to start the old AC. After taking three more swallows of soggy corn flakes, I was out the door heading toward my father. I stopped briefly in the tool shed to pick up a hammer, spade, and wire cutters. I probably only needed the spade, but I didn't want to have to turn around and come back up the hill to collect the other tools if they were needed for me to get the job done.

Ahead of me, I heard my father cranking the AC. The putt . . . putt . . . grrr . . . sound was the AC's response to the cranking, resuscitating it to life. It was a rough ride across the cow pasture and up to the old fence, but a short one. This old fence has probably been here over a hundred years. Well, at least it's older than I am. Tearing out the old fence is not as easy as washing the milk separator or doing dinner dishes. I had to dig around the old posts, wiggle them as hard as I could, try to pry them upward, and repeat the same process over and over until they came out of the ground. There was no one around to clap for me when I pulled one up or to say, "that a boy, Teddy."

I needed the hammer to pull out the nails and staples that had been holding the barbwire in place on the posts. When the nails or staples were pounded in too deep for me to retrieve, I just cut the wire. I knew I would probably have to answer to my father later when he would unroll the wire and find that there were breaks in some of the rolls, but that would be later, so I wasn't going to fret about it in the moment. Next, I had to roll up rusty old barbwire. Have you ever rolled up barbwire without leather gloves or even cloth gloves on your hands? I have. The barbs always leave their marks. Since I wasn't wearing a watch, I wasn't sure how long it took me to tear the fence out, but by the time I heard my father coming up the hill, I was just finishing rolling the last row of barbwire into a big circle. After hitching the low boy to the tractor, I had to load the barbwire onto it and walk along beside it, stacking the posts on the bed as my father drove. Right now, you might be asking, "And this was the amazingly good thing that happened to you?" No! It definitely was not.

All morning while I was working on the fence and my dad was doing whatever fathers do to keep from having to help their sons, clouds had been building. As we were going down the hill, even before we made it to the barnyard, it started to rain. I had to hold onto the seat of the tractor tighter now. When we reached the barnyard gate, I glanced over to the hayfield and noticed there were only about a half of a dozen hay bales where there should have been dozens. Closing the gate and returning to my place with feet firmly planted on the tractor's tongue, I glanced up at my father and asked, "What happened to the bailer, Dad?"

Without glancing back at me and giving the AC more gas, he said, "It broke down. I need a new part to fix the damn thing. We can't hay this afternoon anyway, because of the rain. You'll have to start cleaning out the granary bin while I go to town."

My father said all of those words as he let his foot off the clutch. The AC lurched forward, and we were off. *I suppose he'll go to the AC Implement to buy the part and then probably have a cup of coffee with some guys before he comes home while I am cleaning out the granary bin.* These were my thoughts as we were unloading the low boy in the drizzle. When we were done, we walked to the house and were inside the back porch just as bigger drops started to hit the ground. I was happy that it was lunchtime and we did not get caught out in the big rain now falling.

My unexpected surprise of the "one more good thing happening" I was telling you about started while we were eating baloney sandwiches and potato chips and drinking grape Kool-Aid. My mom delivered it to me. "Teddy, Mrs. Madisen stopped by to see you this morning."

"To see me?" I wondered whether I might have heard my mother wrong because I have never had an adult come to our house just to see me, not even our minister.

"Yes, to see you." My mother assured me I had heard right. "She asked if it rained, could you go to her house and help her polish the brass on the harness and clean the harnesses up a bit. They are going to pull their show wagon in a parade next Saturday, and since the horses haven't been hitched all winter, the harness needed to be spruced up and the brass polished. I told her that if it rained, you could help."

My attempt at not looking too excited was met with a silent glance coming from my father, darting back and forth between my mom and me. "Is it all right, Dad?" I asked, not really wanting an answer because I was already taking my mom's word as permission.

Before my father could answer, my mom spoke up and said, "Sam, it's a good thing for Teddy to help the Madisens. It'll give him a chance to earn a little spending money."

"I suppose," was my father's answer.

Before he could say anything else, I blurted out, "Thanks, Dad." Then without hesitation, I took a long drink of grape Kool-Aid. It sure tasted good.

I told you a little about the Madisens when they came to our house-warming right after we moved in. Charlie and Patricia Madisen are the people who have the big horses called Belgians. Whenever we have driven by their place even before being their neighbors, I have wondered what it would be like to live at the Happy M Ranch, the name of their farm. I am not sure why they call it a ranch. The only ranches I have ever heard of are the ones I have seen on the Roy Roger's show.

Mrs. Madisen came to pick me up right after lunch. Since it was raining, I ran out to meet her after saying goodbye to my mom and dad. I didn't tell my sisters goodbye because they heard me tell our mom and dad, and I thought that would be enough. I didn't want it to sound like I was rubbing in the fact that I got to go to the Madisens and they didn't.

I am not sure how the afternoon went for my mom or father, but I bet I had more fun. Mrs. Madisen told me about their family and how they started raising horses. She told me about parades where their Belgians pull their show wagon carrying signs on both sides, advertising for their sponsor. A sponsor might be a feed company, insurance company, or maybe even a grocery store. I asked her if they were ever asked to carry a sign advertising a school or a church. Mrs. Madisen hesitated only a second and then said, "No, Teddy, but that would be a very good idea. I will tell Mr. Madisen that you came up with that idea." She also told me about county and state fairs where they show their horses in competition for trophies and ribbons.

It didn't take me long to learn how to polish the brass or clean the harness. About three in the afternoon, Mrs. Madisen said, "Teddy, I am going to the house to fix a little lunch for us. Charlie will be driving in shortly, and we all can have a little snack. Then we can finish our work."

"A snack! That's great! I like snacks," I said enthusiastically while thinking to myself, *I must be doing a pretty good job or Mrs. Madisen wouldn't be serving me any snack.* As if on cue, Mr. Madisen drove up the lane while we were walking to the house. I enjoyed our visit while we ate sandwiches and cookies. I asked a lot of questions about their horses. The rest of the afternoon went by quickly. Before she took me home, Mrs.

Madisen gave me five dollars. I tried to resist the money, but she said, "Teddy, you did a very good job. You deserve this."

So I took it with a big smile and said, "Thank you."

At least I had a few good things to hold onto because just a year later, some really bad things happened, and I realized how both good and bad things can sneak up on you and take you by surprise. You need not be a worrywart anticipating bad things happening or allowing your worries to steal your happiness or joy of living, but you do need to balance your life, never give up hoping for the best in people to come through when tragedy or disaster happens to you, and never, never give up on praying that Jesus will walk with you through those rough times. I was taught that in Sunday school. If you can do all of this, I believe you will never be defeated by circumstances beyond your control. I am really trying to practice what I just told you even though I am only twelve years old. Whew! That was a lot to say in one breath.

I was thirteen years old when I started eighth grade. About the only difference between eighth grade and seventh grade are the textbooks. You have the same teachers. They grade your papers the same way they did when you were in seventh grade, but now they expect more from you. Because they expect more, you have more homework in science and math, and you have to do more writing in English class. I still liked English and history the best, but because I found myself more and more curious about how people and animals came about, I was enjoying science just a little bit more. I didn't share this information with my science teacher because she would have probably called on me more in class to answer questions.

I mostly kept my curiosity to myself, but I started to discover that I was asking a lot more questions than I used to. One of the first persons to recognize what I was doing was my mother. One day out of the blue, she just said, "Teddy, you sure have been asking more questions lately. Do you ask a lot of questions in school?"

"In science, I do," I answered, but I didn't tell my mom about my surge in curiosity. To the best of my memory, I became more curious about human and animal nature when I started to read the obituaries of regular people and after the death of Fuzzy Chick and his brothers and sisters. Maybe my asking so my questions is what prompted my mother to buy an encyclopedia set from a handsome young salesman who was going through our neighborhood. If you bought a set from him, you received a current world atlas. I do know my mom had to pay for the set out of her egg money.

I didn't think the kid was handsome at all, but after he left, Victoria told me he was really handsome, and my mom told her, "Never mind, Victoria." Mom's response to Victoria after the kid left probably should have come earlier that might have kept her from asking a hundred and one questions as she and my mother listened to his sales pitch. He told my mom all the great reasons he thought she needed this set of encyclopedias that only his company sold. When he passed the A-B book to my mom to look at while he talked about some of his subjects, she went through the book with searching eyes. Then he passed the C-D book to Victoria and asked her if she had more questions. Funny, he didn't ask my mom if she had any questions. Victoria never opened the book; instead, she asked him what subject he found interesting.

Victoria never took her eyes off of the kid while he was talking. When his presentation was over, my mom said she would buy a set, and Victoria asked if he wanted some iced tea and homemade snickerdoodle cookies that she made. He smiled as he replied, "That would be heavenly." I thought I was going to throw up seeing the two of them google each other, so I left the room and ate my snickerdoodles outside. I did enjoy reading some of the articles in the books and learned my interest in human and animal behavior was all part of the worlds of psychology and sociology. I decided the book writers could name it whatever they liked. As far as I was concerned, I was just curious.

As my curiosity grew, my grades became better, but my math grade didn't change very much. I am sure having those books helped me through the year and, being only in eighth grade, broadened my scope of understanding of events that were just around the corner for our family.

In early spring of my thirteenth year, we came home from school one day and found a note on the table that read:

> Victoria, we received a call from your Aunt Velma. Grandpa was taken to the hospital. They think he had a heart attack, but Velma was not sure when she called me. Your father, Cindy, and I have gone to the hospital. We will be home late. Start fixing super and tell Teddy to bring the cows home and do all of his chores and then gather the eggs for me. If we are not home by six, go ahead and eat. Ruby, try to help Victoria.
>
> Mom

"Teddy, Mom said you are to bring in the cows, do all of your chores, and gather the eggs for her." Victoria told me all of this with a commanding voice and all the while holding her breath.

As I listened to her, she sounded to me like a general. "I know what my chores are," I informed her and then added my usual reaction to her uppity behavior. "You're not the boss of me!"

"Here, read the note yourself," Victoria whipped back at me while she threw the note in my direction.

I picked up the paper and read it out loud, substituting my own words but mimicking my mother's voice. "And Victoria, you are supposed to help Teddy bring the cows home."

"Oh sure, in your dreams!" Victoria snickered as she rolled her eyes and went off to do her own chores.

You might want to know that putting our little spats aside, I am really proud and fond of my older sister. She is an excellent musician and vocalist. She also has received straight "Ones," which are the highest score a judge can give a person at district and state speech contests. She also plays basketball and is on first team as a guard. Who wouldn't want a sister like her? She even helps me sometimes when I am being bullied at school. Don't tell her that I said all of these things even though I am sure she knows I really think she is a super sister. Just like my friends, who think Victoria is about the most beautiful and glamorous girl in our high school, most of the older guys on our bus think she is gorgeous. I wouldn't know about how pretty she is, she just looks like a sister to me.

By six o'clock I had my chores done and even brought the first five milk cows into the barn and locked them in their stanchions. I didn't put their feed down, though, because they usually eat their grain while they are being milked. I supposed that is to keep their minds off of being milked and to help them stand still. So now they are just standing there with nothing to do but swish their tails and wonder out loud to each other:

"Hey, Spotty, do you suppose the kid forgot to put our grain down?"

"I don't know, Brownie. I guess he did. I am starving. I wish someone would give his brain a twitch. Maybe he would remember to feed us." Spotty mooed to Brownie while eyeing me suspiciously.

"I don't think the kid really knows what he is supposed to do," Clara chimed in with a screeching moo and in the same breath said, "I bet if his father was here, he wouldn't be forgetting anything."

I'm pretty sure that was what all the mooing was about as I left the barn. I headed toward the house for my own supper.

Victoria had our supper on the table when I came in from choring, and as soon as supper was over, I started my homework. I was concentrating so hard on trying to solve a math problem that I didn't even hear my parents drive into the yard or my dog, Pal, welcoming them home with his friendly bark. I was surprised to see my mom, carrying Cindy, walk into the kitchen, followed by my father carrying a paper bag filled with day-old bread they picked up at a bakery in Omaha. After my mom laid Cindy down on the living room couch, she came back into the kitchen.

"How's Grandpa?" I asked as my mom and father sat down at the kitchen table.

"Grandpa is not doing very well," my mom answered. "Your Aunt Velma said the doctor is not sure, but he knows there are more things wrong with your grandpa than just his heart, so they are going to run more tests on him. Mrs. Madisen stopped by, and while we were having coffee, she volunteered to care for Cindy. She will bring her home when you kids come home from school."

"Are you going back to the city tomorrow, Mom?" I already knew the answer but just wanted to talk with my mom a little more, so I asked her another question.

"Yes, I am going back to the hospital tomorrow to talk to the doctor myself. Your grandmother also needs to go see the lawyer and go to the bank. I seem to be the only one who can take her." My mom's voice quivered as she tried to finish what she was saying, trying to sound upbeat, but no positive words seemed forthcoming from her lips, so she just stopped. Scooching her chair away from the table, she stood and went into the bathroom.

On our side of the closed door, sounds of her crying some Romanian words she repeated over and over penetrated the wooden barrier and floated right into our ears. Remember, the Romanian language is what my grandmother and grandfather like to use when they are talking to my mother and do not necessarily want us to know what they are saying, or it might be they can better explain what they want to say in Romanian. I believe my second thought is probably correct because I can't believe they wouldn't want us to know what they are actually saying.

"I put the first group of cows in the barn, Dad. They are ready to be milked. Do you want me to come out and help you?" I couldn't believe I was actually volunteering to go back to the barn and help do more chores, but talking to my father and volunteering seemed to be a lot easier than listening to my mother cry. I don't ever remember offering to do more barn chores before, but I knew that my father really liked my mom's parents and was probably feeling just as sad as my mother was even if he wasn't crying.

"No, do your homework," my father responded.

"Okay," I said, quietly feeling uncomfortable and wondering what I should be saying or doing next.

When my mom came out of the bathroom, she helped me with the math problem I was trying to solve when she and my father came home. I was grateful for the help but wished that I could take my mom's sadness away. After my homework was completed, I went into the living room, where my sisters were watching TV. Over the noise on the television, we could hear my mother bustling around in the kitchen. Soon the aroma coming from the kitchen told us she was baking a cake. When I went into the kitchen, I saw that she had a cake in the oven and the batter for another one in her mixing bowl.

"Two cakes, Mom?" I questioned, thinking that we might be having company even though it was already eight p.m.

"One is for us to eat and the other cake I am taking to your Aunt Velma's tomorrow when I go to pick up Grandma and take her to the hospital to see Grandpa, to the bank, and to see her lawyer," she explained, settling my curiosity. I knew my grandmother was staying with my Aunt Velma, and both she and my grandmother really enjoyed my mom's chocolate cake. My grandfather was in the hospital for almost a week, and my mom went into the city to see him almost every day, and sometimes even my father went. Since the hospital was right in the middle of the downtown area of Omaha, it took almost an hour to reach the hospital from our house and even a lot longer if Mom went to pick up my grandma.

Mom and Dad usually did not return home until suppertime, and Victoria would have dinner on the table when they arrived. After the first night, my father decided to do chores before he ate supper so he wouldn't be so late completing them. I guess he thought it was better to have hunger pains than cause the cows confusion regarding their milking schedule and the pigs ambushing him to get to their food. I figure routine was just as important to animals as it was to us humans. My father didn't seem to mind hunger pains, but I did! I would sneak a couple of snacks or go wander around outside after my homework was done so I wouldn't hear the mashed potatoes or pork chops yelling, "Come and find us, Teddy. Ha! Ha! Ha!"

My mom didn't cry very much after the first night, but I could tell she was very sad. The second week that my grandfather was in the hospital, when I arrived home from school on Thursday, I was surprised to see my parents were already there. "Didn't you go to the hospital today, Mom?" I asked when I came through the kitchen door.

"Yes, Teddy, we went, but Victoria has a band concert tonight and we wanted to be home in time to finish the chores and be able to go to her concert," my mom explained.

"Oh, if Dad is out doing chores already, do I have to do mine?" I'm not quite certain what prompted me to ask such a silly question. Maybe I thought since I had been on my best behavior for nearly two weeks and even did extra chores, my father might think I deserved a night off—*foolish thinking*.

My mom did not even give my question any merit. "Of course, you do, funny boy." I imagine she was even taken off guard that I would ask such a question. Then she added, "What made you think you wouldn't have to do chores?"

"I don't know," I answered, not wanting to tell her I thought my father might do them for me this one time because I had not only done all of my chores but extra stuff to help out a little more than expected lately. When I went to my room to change into chore clothes, I had a talk with myself and decided that you really aren't rewarded for doing what you are expected to do. Then, as if I was justifying my question, I thought to myself, *but I did do extra chores.*

When I came downstairs from changing clothes, my mom told me to sit at the table for a minute, and she also called Victoria, Ruby, and Cindy into the kitchen to join us. "I have something to tell the four of you," my mom started as we settled into our usual chairs around the table. My mom's tone was very serious, and I think the three of us felt it because none of us stirred.

Taking a breath and letting it out slowly, she started talking, "Okay, here's what is happening." As she began to speak, her tears began to fall, so she paused long enough to wipe her eyes with her handkerchief and then started once more. "The doctor told us there is nothing more they can do for your grandpa. His heart is responding very poorly to the medicine they have been giving him, and his other physical problems are just complicating the situation. It is hard to explain everything that is happening to Grandpa. Simply put, his body is breaking down and I am afraid to say it, but Grandpa is going to die soon."

When my mother said the word "die," her sadness opened the floodgates of her heavy heart, and tears tumbled down her cheeks once more. Seconds seemed like hours, but the four of us sat perfectly still even though it was very uncomfortable, at least for me, to watch our mother cry. Finally, the silence was too much for Cindy. She squirmed out of her chair. I thought she was going to leave the room, but instead, she crawled up on our mom's lap and pulled Mom's face over toward her as she spoke, "Please don't cry, Momma. Grandpa will be okay. Won't he, Ruby?"

Ruby heard Cindy's words as her cue and went over to Mom's side. Patting Mom's leg, she softly began to sing, "Jesus loves me."

"Shhh . . ." Victoria said to her sisters, giving Cindy a loving hug while picking her off of Mom's lap and holding Cindy herself, tightly wrapping her arms around her at the same time. Ruby stopped singing and just sat there without saying another word.

I didn't move. I also just stood at my mom's side. I knew this was serious business when I heard the word "die." I also knew this was not the time a guy should be asking his mother for a snack.

When my mom found her voice again, she surprised the four of us by saying, "Grandma doesn't want Grandpa to die in the hospital. She said that she and Grandpa have talked it over several times, and if that is what lies ahead of him, he does not want to die in the hospital either. Your aunts and uncles believe they do not have the room to take Grandpa in and provide space for Grandma, nor do they think they have the ability or know-how to take care of him.

"Your father and I decided we would rearrange the parlor and bring Grandpa and Grandma out here to be with us. We think he would rather be out in the country than anywhere else, and I know the farm would provide comfort for your grandmother also. We ordered a hospital bed, and it will be here early in the morning. Grandma will also sleep in the parlor so she can be near Grandpa. I will—no, I mean, we all will take care of Grandma and Grandpa."

"Are you a nurse, Mom?" My question really came more out of never having seen my mom in a white uniform like the kind nurses on television wear.

"I bet you are a nurse, Mom," Ruby jumped in to say and then, with a bit of youthful wisdom, added, "Sure you are because you take care of us when we are sick."

"No, I am not a nurse." Then, as if she was having second thoughts about her answer, she continued. "I was a nurse's aide during the Korean War at the hospital where you were born, Teddy, but that has been a while ago. And, yes, Ruby, I do take care of all of you when you are sick. I guess we will all be nurses and helpers when Grandpa and Grandma arrive, and we will pray that we can provide Grandpa with all the help that he might need so that he can be as comfortable as it is possible to make him." The way my mom finished her words made me realize that my grandfather was coming to our farm to die, and like it or not, we were all going to be a part of his living until he took his last breath.

My mom is really an expert in moving the conversation into action, especially when our words seem stuck or we don't know what to say next. We were in one of those situations at the moment, and once again, she came to the rescue. "Come on now, let's go to the parlor and see what needs to be done." Without another word, she led the way.

Following our mom to the parlor, Victoria was the first one to speak up. "Can we really take care of Grandpa, Mom?"

"We will do the best we can, Victoria," my mom said honestly. "We have to . . ." Once again, my mom's voice trailed off while her tears freely fell.

Looking up at Mom and tightly holding onto her hand as if to let go would mean our mother would drift away, it was Ruby's turn to plead, "Please don't cry, Mom."

Victoria did not say another word, but tears also welled in her eyes. Being the oldest, she had known Grandpa the longest. When our father was in the war, and before I was born, Grandma and Grandpa took care of Victoria while our mother worked at the hospital. She and my mom lived with our grandparents for about three years. While she vaguely remembered those years, the early memories she did have turned into stories about how Grandpa would give her horse rides on one of his workhorses, the barnyard rooster chasing after her and our cousin Patti, and "helping" our grandparents sell fresh vegetables and watermelons at their roadside stand.

Every time she told the stories, they seemed to stretch out just a little farther, especially when she told about how some customers didn't think a watermelon was ripe even though Grandpa told them they could be refunded if it wasn't. Then to prove that he knew his melons, he would take his pocketknife and make a triangle cut into the watermelon and stab the triangle in its middle, pulling out the bright red meat of the melon. Then he would give it to the customer for a taste. Ninety percent of the time, the customer commented, "Wow! You certainly know your melons. This one is delicious!" It was that ten percent who did not want to be proven wrong that always found some excuse for not buying the melon and demanding a taste of another. The rejected melons could not be sold.

Victoria told us that those were the melons they and the chickens had for a snack or with their lunch. "We always had a lot of melon to eat, and when we had a mouth full of seeds, Patti and I, and sometimes even Grandpa, would have a watermelon seed spitting contest. Patti or Grandpa would usually win," she would say without regret. I thought she wanted her story to end that way because she thought herself to be too much of a lady to be winning watermelon seed-spitting contests.

What was different now, as she told us the stories while we were working rearranging the parlor, were the tears that followed.

It didn't seem like our work in the parlor was hard. Maybe it was because we were talking to each other and remembering so much from days that we had with our grandparents. Seldom have we all together had conversations where tears and laughter were part of the mix. But our work was cut short because I had to go out and chore, and Victoria had to leave early for the band concert.

When I was walking out to fetch the milk cows, I had a talk with myself. I realized that in the past week, I have seen more tears fall from our family's eyes than I have ever seen. I haven't ever seen my mom do so much crying in front of us kids as she has done recently. The only time I have ever seen Victoria cry is when she wants to do something or go somewhere and Mom or Dad won't let her, but I saw her cry this week because she is sad. You could have scrubbed the floor with all of the tears that dropped. After a brief pause to give my brain a rest, I thought, *When you are sad and you cry, maybe you don't feel better right away, but your crying makes your spirit a little bit lighter and you start having room for healing.*

Reaching the cows, I didn't holler or throw clods at them like I usually do. I walked quietly around them, and we headed for home. My change in behavior wasn't necessarily out of respect for the cows or not wanting to spoil their milk by running them and risking a ing from my dad, it was because I wanted to have more thinking conversation before I reached the barnyard. *Tears must be a way to wash out the heaviness sadness puts on our soul,* I thought.

At that moment, I had a revelation that the tears my mom has been crying were for the pain she must be feeling that comes with her grief. The crying Victoria and I were doing were first coming from seeing our mother cry and knowing we couldn't take her sadness away and second because our grandfather is dying. I suppose his dying has a different meaning for each of us drawn from our memory and his presence, but we, too, cry because our sadness is heavy. And maybe, Ruby and Cindy cry because they, also, see Mom and Victoria and me cry. Another thing I realized was that the pain my heart felt now was not like the same pain I feel when I get a whooping or when I think my dad doesn't care for me. These tears were tears of love that had to be cried before the sadness of grief could go away. My Sunday school teacher, Mrs. Kates, told us once that the prophet, Jeremiah, said that God cries, so it must be okay for us to cry too. By the time I was done with this little talk with myself, I was home with the cows.

My mom probably knew that a lot of the moving and rearranging would have to wait until the bed arrived on Friday morning anyway. But having us help her for these few moments was probably her way of bringing us together to share our uncertainty and grief with one another while providing us some sense of strength for the days ahead. Having us pitch in to help gave us a sense of doing something for our grandparents when it seemed there was not a lot more that we, as grandchildren, could do.

It would be some years later when I would come to realize that most farm families seemed to be more comfortable having few words between them; instead, expending a lot of effort to accomplish something—like doing the neighbors' chores when they or their family members were sick, putting in their crops in the spring or taking them out in the fall, and of course, bringing a ton of food which was always a blessing and a chance for a visit in disguise.

That evening, Victoria rode to the band concert with a neighbor, and to my surprise, my father went to the concert with my mother. Going to a band concert or any of our school activities, for that matter, was something my father rarely did.

I was left babysitting with Ruby and Cindy. It was okay by me because I was given permission to scoop out ice cream for the three of us. I made sure the scoops I dished out were big! I had to sit at the table and help Cindy eat her ice cream because she is really messy. Ruby sat at the table with us, so I read them both a story while we ate. I had four scoops of butter brickle ice cream and I even treated myself to the ice cream that Cindy and Ruby left in their bowls. I ate more ice cream that night in one sitting than I have probably eaten in all of my thirteen years.

While I enjoyed my ice cream, for some reason, it didn't taste as good as it usually does. Maybe it was because when my mom scoops the ice cream, I only receive two small scoops with no chance of having seconds, so I savor each bite. Maybe it was because knowing about the changes that would soon take place in our lives, my taste buds were lost somewhere deep in my thoughts, or maybe I was just beginning to feel some of the weight of the responsibilities my parents were accepting and knew some of it would soon trickle down upon Victoria and me. I don't know why, but I know I wasn't enjoying my ice cream as much as I thought I would, regardless of how much I was allowed to eat.

The girls and I went to bed sometime before our parents and Victoria arrived home. I slept on the couch until my mother and father came home. I really don't remember finding my way upstairs to my own room that evening, so I must have been really tired. I don't even remember if I said my prayers, but I am pretty sure I did. At least, I hope so.

The hospital bed arrived on Friday while we were in school. After my mom made certain the parlor was ready and up to her standards to make our grandparents comfortable, she and my father went to the hospital to make final arrangements for my grandfather's transfer to our farm and to bring our grandmother home with them.

Our grandparents' journey took them from their farm to the hospital and then to our farm. Through it all, it never occurred to me to ask, "Who will milk grandpa's cows? Who will feed the workhorses? Who will gather the eggs or grind crack corn for the chickens?" I guess when you are thirteen, you might not think of all of these details.

I found out much later that my father and mother had taken care of it all. They had arranged for one of our grandparents' neighbors to take care of the livestock. It was further decided that my father would take care of the crops. That meant that my father would not only be farming our farm, but he would have to transport his machinery about sixty miles to our grandparents' farm to prepare the fields for planting and tending to the summer weeds that always seemed to come up in the fields before the corn plants poked their leaves out of the ground. My father would also have to harvest the fields come fall.

I know now that my father took on quite a big responsibility, but he did not seem to let it trouble him. There were very few options at the time, and the work had to be done. Again, it would be some years before I could come to appreciate what he and my mother were doing out of respect, necessity, and love for our grandparents.

By now, I was doing a lot of thinking as I did my after school Friday chores. I was slowly coming to realize an illness for humans that leaves death as its only option is a tragedy. Regardless of how much I liked Fuzzy Chick and his relatives and grieved their death by rats, being part of the audience having a front-row seat watching my grandfather's dying was to be a much more arduous journey with prayers that would not, in this lifetime, end with the miracle for which I prayed.

One of the important things I learned along the way was a new word, "priority," and its past tense, "prioritized." We had the word priority and all of its tenses for an eighth-grade spelling word this past winter, but I really didn't learn much about the word or what it meant until our rather predictable pattern of daily living was interrupted by our grandparents coming to live for the time being on our farm. I remember very clearly my mother telling us, "Our priority will be to make Grandpa as comfortable as possible and to be a support to Grandma." All of us did just as my mother said because my mom prioritized work for us, including new responsibilities for our father. My father had to really work hard at prioritizing all that he had to do, especially farming two farms that were quite a distance from one another with breakable and unreliable machinery.

When I came in from chores, Grandpa was in his hospital bed, and my grandmother was sitting next to the bed with her hands folded into his. I peeked in just to say "hi" and heard my mother softly speaking in Romanian. I knew she was praying because I have heard her speak those very same words with Grandpa when I have stayed with them for a week during summer vacation. When it was prayer time in their home, my grandfather would read the Romanian Bible and, afterward, we would kneel on the floor at our kitchen chair. Grandpa and Grandma would pray their prayers, and I would mostly listen, ready to say "Amen" when they were done. I would carefully listen to every word—which is how I recognized that my grandmother's words now were prayer words.

"Hi Grandma," I said, coming up to her side and putting my arm around her shoulders. "How is Grandpa?" I cautiously looked toward him as if my looking would cause him pain; however, I could easily see that he was sleeping, his breathing sounding like a really old truck stuck in first gear and going down a hill with half of its muffler rusted out. Hearing the sounds of his breathing made me a little afraid because I have never heard anyone breathe like that except for a guy on *Gunsmoke* who had been shot by robbers and left on the side of the road. When Matt Dillon came riding by and found the guy, the man's breathing was just like my grandpa's. The man died before he could tell Marshal Dillon who robbed and shot him. *I know, in real life, the man didn't actually die, but I can't say the same for my grandpa. I wish he could still go on living.*

My grandmother interrupted my thoughts and fears by coming up from her chair and wrapping her short, stocky arms around my waist. "Yoi, yoi, yoi, domdi, domdi," she said in a whisper, but loud enough for me to hear. Her whisper brought new tears to her eyes and to mine, as well. As our tears rolled down our cheeks, Grandma spoke to me only this time in English. "Grandpa is not good, Yohannie."

I forgot to tell you that when I was born, I was given my grandfather's first name for my middle name. My full name is really Theodore John Hall. No one but my grandmother ever calls me by my middle name except my aunt who lives in Texas, who is my grandparents' oldest daughter. When she visits, she always calls me Teddy John. She told me that everyone she knows in Texas calls each other by their first and middle names. I suspect she'll be coming for a sad visit soon. I sure hope when she comes, none of my friends hear her call me Teddy John. If they hear the name, I am sure they will stick it on me like flies on a fly strip hanging down from the ceiling in the barn room where we separate the cream from the milk.

The sudden rhythmic change in my grandpa's labored breathing startled my grandmother and me. The disturbance in his breathing seemed to be our cue that it was time for prayers. We both knelt beside his bed and prayed. My grandmother prayed out loud, but I prayed to myself. While I had my eyes still closed and finished my prayer, I listened very closely to my grandmother's sweet and tender words.

I listened, and I listened. My grandmother sometimes has very long prayers. I am sure she prays for Grandpa's soul; that is the part of your body without the flesh and blood or body organs. In fact, I am not sure if you can even see it, but I know it is there because my Sunday school teacher, Mrs. Kates, told us it was there, and just in case someone didn't believe her, she read out of the Psalms something about the soul. I can't remember what she said, but I know she was reading about the soul being part of who you are, and if the Bible says you have a soul, you know you have one.

My grandma doesn't stop her praying after she talks to God about Grandpa's soul and God blessing Grandpa; she also prays that God blesses by name all of her children and her grandchildren. I even believe she asks God to bless her cows and chickens; then, I know she says the twenty-third Psalm followed by the Lord's Prayer all in the same breath. I know she prays them because once she told them to me in English and then in Romanian so I would always know what she was saying.

My grandmother had just said "Amen" when my mother walked into the room. My mother was probably surprised to see me, especially on my knees beside Grandma. Normally, I would come off the bus and go into the kitchen and ask if I could have a snack. Next, I would go upstairs to my room and put on my chore clothes.

"Teddy, I didn't hear you come into the house with your sisters," my mom said in a surprised voice.

"I was quiet, Mom." I didn't say I was curious to see my grandpa and wanting to say "hi" to my grandmother. I really believe my mother had all of that figured out, especially since I didn't come in and ask for a snack right away. She quietly listened to my explanation and gave me one of those "understanding" mother smiles, then said, "Teddy, you can sit with your grandpa while your grandmother has a little rest after you do your chores. Now scoot."

"Okay, Mom, I'm going," I answered. To be honest, I was a little relieved that she came in and told me to go out and do my chores. I just wasn't quite sure how I could excuse myself from the room with my grandmother praying and crying and my grandfather breathing so strangely. I seemed to be held spellbound by it all.

Finally, with a smile and words of assurance, I leaned in toward my grandmother and spoke. "Grandma, I will come and sit with Grandpa after I finish my chores." My grandmother didn't say anything, but a trace of a smile came to the surface through her sadness, and her head nodded ever so reverently. I said no more and quietly made my way out of the room.

When you are waiting for a special time like summer vacation, company coming, or an evening at the county fair, the closer it comes to the event, the slower time travels, and the longer the wait becomes. It also seems the harder things like your homework, hog house cleaning, or your chores are, the longer it takes to get them done.

Don't you wish you could just close your eyes, turn yourself around three times, and make that something special happen now? I have done the eye closing, body turning, and I have even done a little praying to God asking that time go just a little faster, but it's no use. You can't hurry a chicken to lay an egg, you can't hurry Mom's chocolate cake to be done faster, and you certainly can't hurry or control time. I guess I am just a participator.

Then again, when you know something bad or really painful is going to happen like a trip to the dentist or Saturday's chicken house cleaning, or garden weed pulling, it seems those times always come just a little faster than you want them to, and they always last longer than they really should. I am only talking about all of this because I am a little confused about my grandfather's illness and his journey into dying.

When I had my week to stay with them last summer, my grandfather really didn't talk to me as much as he regularly does. My grandmother did most of the talking to me, and Grandpa listened, so I am having a hard time now remembering what his voice sounded like. Even though I wasn't expecting his dying to happen, I am probably still too young to have thought it would happen in the future. Today, I realize this is the future.

Now, I listen to him breathe, sputter, gurgle, then seem like he has no breath at all as he lies as still as a fence post until seconds later, he repeats a gasping breath, sputter, and gurgle. Seeing him now as he lies in his bed and hearing his lungs plead for a clean, smooth breath leaves me with conflicting thoughts. I have never ever prayed for someone to die; I swear by my Confirmation Bible I haven't.

I remember once I prayed for Hopalong Cassidy not to die when he was shot by a rustler. He didn't die! I know he didn't because he was in the next episode on television. He even rounded up all of the rustlers he was chasing the week before without killing a single one. I would have never prayed for him to die just because he was shot. I was only about eight years old when I prayed for Hopalong. I wouldn't pray for him now if I was watching that episode because now I realize Hopalong is just a TV star and the actor who plays Hopalong is a western hero. Heroes don't die easily, especially on TV shows; besides, the actor who plays Hopalong was a detective in a television show I saw sometime later.

So, I have prayed for someone not to die, but my grandfather wasn't shot by a rustler. He didn't fall off his horse, and he wasn't trampled by a stampede of cattle. My mom told me, "Your grandfather is just wearing out. People die when they wear out."

When I asked my father, "Why is Grandpa dying?" he didn't say anything. He just looked at me and took another drink of his coffee. I still pray for my grandpa to get up and live some more, but I am also wondering if I shouldn't tell God, "Just do what is best for Grandpa." *Would God be listening to me if I said that? I guess to settle it all in my brain, I need to ask my Sunday school teacher what she thinks would be the best for Grandpa.*

My grandpa sure has a good pair of lungs even though all the other parts of his body might be wasting away. He had that same breathing sound all through the next week. The only difference was by Friday a week later, he seemed to be holding his breath a lot longer, and when he did breathe again, it didn't seem like anything was coming out of his mouth. He quit breathing through his nose last Tuesday afternoon we when came home from school. Now, he only breathes through his mouth.

Friday, after I finished my evening chores, I was going to go into the house to talk to my grandma for a while, but my father met me at the back door and told me, "Teddy, I need you to ride out to the field with me and hook up the disk so I can do some disking after chores." In case you don't know what that is, let me explain. A disk is a tool farmers use after plowing to smooth out the ground and break up some of the clods before planting starts.

It was the first year that we had daylight savings time. The cows didn't know that we had changed the clocks, but after a while, they seemed to adjust. Actually, they adjusted a lot better than some of our neighbors did. Some of our neighbors were really defiant and refused to set their clocks ahead an hour. It didn't really seem to trouble my mom and father; unlike some of our relatives and neighbors, they did not think it was a subversive plot by the government to control our lives.

Because of daylight savings time, we had more light to do more work outside, so my father and I were off to the field. I had my old tennis shoes on, so I had to grip the back of the tractor seat really tight so I wouldn't slip off. The disk was out in what would become this year's cornfield after the seed was planted and the corn began to appear. It always amazed me how that shriveled, dried-up, dead-looking kernel of corn could actually, with a little rain, a dab of fertilizer, and rich Iowa topsoil, come alive once more in a few short weeks and sprout in the color green. From a pale looking yellow to a rich green plant, the corn seed seemed to have a transformation.

I think our Sunday school teacher told us that is what happens to our bodies when Jesus comes to takes us all to his house for a grand party that will last a long time. I have always been amazed by it all. I won't ask my father if he is amazed even though he must have some faith to go through all of this work, and he and the landlord spend all of the money to buy seed and fertilizer and then wait to see what will happen. I couldn't do any more thinking on this amazement because we arrived where the disk was resting and minding its own business.

I jumped off the tractor while my father put the old AC into reverse. For no particular reason, I started walking backwards, kicking my foot up against the back of the tractor tire, maybe out of boredom. The weather was cold, and the freshly plowed field was damp. I could smell the earth. The fragrance had an aroma that I imagined was Mother Nature's evening perfume. *She must be going out dancing with the stars later tonight,* I thought. "Kick . . . kick . . . kick . . ." The sound of my heel was drowned out by the tractor, but I felt my heel kicking the tire. "Kick . . . kick . . . kick . . ." And then there was no sound at all.

It took only a split second for me to realize my foot was no longer free because it had become caught under the tire. My heel had been grabbed by the tire wedge and was pulling my foot, and my body toward the ground as the back tire climbed up my leg.

"Dad! Help Dad! *Dad! Help! Help!*" Out of fear and desperation, I was yelling as loud as I could over and over again . . . "Dad! Help! *Help!*" The tire just kept coming. Slowly, while I was yelling, the tractor climbed past my knee, jerking me sideways and was inching up upon my thigh, dragging me further into its grip. Again, fed by fear, I heard myself yelling, "Dad! *Dad!*" I yelled over and over as fast and as loud as I could.

Somehow, my father heard my screams over the sound of the tractor's engine. For a while, the tractor's drowning sound had created a gulf between the consciousness of my father and the reality of my predicament. I'm not sure what made him turn his head. It might have been my yelling. He might have wanted to see just how much further he had to back up before I could hook the disk, or maybe—just maybe—it was God nudging him. Well, I have to do more pondering on this before I can be certain what actually caused him to turn his head. I am not sure I can ask my father what made him turn his head. He might not know himself, and then I would have even more pondering to do. I'll just have to work it out on my own, but not right now. I am in a mess.

Just as soon as he saw me, my father stopped the tractor. The soft dirt underneath me helped to ease the weight of the tractor wheel, but even more, the shock and fear I was experiencing seemed to numb any other feelings I had at the moment, especially any physical pain.

"Don't move, Teddy. Stay still," my father instructed me as he climbed down from the tractor seat. After examining how far the tractor wheel had crept up my leg with only a few short inches to go before it would have taken a bite out of my back, my father just stared at me for a second. He was obviously shaken, but when he did speak again, his words held a sense of control and command as they came out of his mouth. "Teddy, don't move. I am going to drive the tractor forward very slowly. It is very important that you hold your leg in the same position that it is in now. Hold your leg and foot perfectly still. You might feel pain, but you must not move. Do you understand?"

My voice sounded like a whisper that was coming from some distance away as I tried to answer my father. My head was starting to feel dizzy again. The dizziness wasn't like the dizzy feelings I have had before and I usually have to throw up before it goes away. This dizziness was new to me. Even though I could barely hear myself, I answered my father. "Yes, Dad, I understand."

My dad's lips began to quiver as he heard me speak. Before my father mounted the tractor, he took off his jacket, and after rolling it up, he placed it lengthwise on the side of my leg that the tractor wheel was going to roll back down upon. I closed my eyes. I was too afraid to watch as the tractor wheel moved deliberately and slowly off my leg.

I wasn't crying, nor was I feeling any pain. My mouth didn't have any words to say because my brain was too busy caught up in the whirling dizziness going on inside of my skull. I didn't notice when the tractor stopped, and I didn't notice my father dismounting from the tractor. I wasn't sure if I had passed out and took my dizzy thoughts with me or if I just had my eyes closed too tight, but I opened them to the sound of a shaky voice calling out my name. "Teddy . . . Teddy . . . Teddy . . ."

When I finally opened my eyes all the way, I could see my father. I didn't say anything, but I felt his strong right arm sliding under my shoulders as he leaned over me. Once again, my father spoke; only now, his words came out very softly and confidently. "Teddy, I am going to try to lift you up on your feet, and let's see if you can stand up on your own."

"Okay, Dad," I whispered, looking straight into his face as he leaned over. With the gentleness I imagined my mom has as she carefully picks up a baby chick that has lost his way, yet with a calm deliberateness as she delivers it back to its mother, so my father put his left arm underneath my other shoulder. Pulling up on my body, my father gingerly lifted me until my feet were both directly beneath me, and they ever so lightly touched the ground. As soon as both of my feet touched the ground, my father loosened the hold he had underneath my arms. The pain of a thousand bumble bee stings shot up the inside of my right leg, and I started to tumble to the ground only to be brought up again by the renewing of my father's strong grip securely locked beneath my armpits.

"I can't, Dad. I can't," I yelled out at the same time, trying hard not to cry, but tears broke through my thin line of attempted bravery and ran unashamedly down my face.

"That's okay, son," my father responded almost apologetically as if he had purposely caused me pain. I have never actually heard my father apologize for anything, especially to me, nor can I ever remember him referring directly to me as "son" before this accident. I must have been imagining how his voice would sound if he was actually apologizing. His calling me "son" must have really been because he was so frightened about what happened to me and maybe even afraid of what would have happened if he had not heard me screaming out to him. During all of this, thoughts were sprinting through my brain, trying to stay ahead of the dizziness and nauseated feeling that was growing stronger by the second. In a flash during one of my thinks, a picture-word came into my imagination, and I saw an image of my father reading my obituary in the paper if he hadn't heard me scream or had never turned around to see me trapped under the tractor wheel.

Before I say anything else, it is important for me to tell you that I told my mom about writing an obituary for Fuzzy Chick and the gang. I didn't tell my dad because he would have thought that I was being silly. I am not sure what my mother thought. She just said, "That's nice, Teddy." If anyone was going to write an obituary for me, besides my best friend doing the writing, it would probably be my mom. Yep, it would be my mom. She would have written the obituary, and it probably would have read:

> This is the short story version of the life of our son, Theodore John Hall. His story is short, but longer than Fuzzy Chick's life story.
>
> Theodore John Hall
>
> Theodore John Hall was born in Omaha, Nebraska. He is the son of Sam and Elaine Hall. He spent most of his growing up years on the family farm in southwest Iowa that his parents rented from some rich people who live in California, where they are spending all of the money that the Halls' made for them farming their land. Theodore was in the eighth grade. He has a very talented older sister, Victoria, a younger sister, Ruby, who is a sometimes playmate, and a much younger sister, Cindy who bugs him. Theodore is, I mean was, known to his family as Teddy, unless he was in really bad trouble and would then be called Theodore by his father or mother or even one of his school teachers. Theodore was just starting to like writing, English, and learning how and why people behave the way they do. He also liked Sunday school, and he especially enjoyed Boy Scouts because scouts went on camping trips, and when they went on a camping trip, Theodore didn't have to do his evening chores.

Theodore did not like our cows or pigs, and he was afraid of our banty rooster. People at the hatchery say the proper name for a banty is Bantam. Banty roosters are smaller than other roosters, and they can be quite ornery. Our banty rooster did not like Teddy. The rooster would sometimes chase him and spur him when he went out to gather eggs for his mother. Theodore was very fond of horses and was just beginning to help our neighbors, the Madisens. They had really big horses called Belgians.

Theodore would often talk to me about his dreams of being a cowboy or a famous writer. After a new minister came to our church, Theodore began to listen more intently to the sermons and did not fall asleep like his father does. I wasn't too surprised when one day Theodore said he was thinking about being a minister. I believe he told me that after he finished cleaning out the hog house and I just returned home from a women's meeting at the church. I told him that Pastor Jon "had been at the meeting and he asked about you."

Theodore replied, "Did he have cookies and coffee with you?"

When I responded, "Yes, but he gave our prayer first," that is when Theodore told me he was thinking about being a minister. He said, "If I become a minister, I would not have to clean out any more hog houses. I don't think ministers have hogs, and I already know how to pray. Plus, I would get to eat lots of cookies." I just smiled at him. I wish I had said more, but I didn't.

Our dreamer, Theodore, died unexpectedly when he was run over by the tractor while he was out in the field helping his father. It wasn't his father's fault. The accident just happened.

Theodore's grandfather was brought to our farm to die because the hospital said they could not help him anymore. Theodore enjoyed going to his grandparents'

> farm and helping his grandpa with his pair of workhorses, but that is another story. We will all miss Theodore very much except maybe the milk cows. I don't believe they will miss him. Goodbye Teddy. The End.

All the while my imagination was in its own fantasy writing my obituary through the pen of my mother, my father was gently laying me back down on top of the freshly turned up black soil. Through my jeans, I felt the cool, damp soil, but I didn't complain. The hurt that came alive when my father tried to help me stand on my own was sending sharp stabbing daggers of pain through my leg, up the middle of my back, and into my brain. I could really feel the pain now. I tried to say something about the pain, but I was feeling woozy once again, so I just lay there.

When he stood up, my father looked across the way toward the creek. Then looking down at me, my father asked, "Teddy, do you think you can crawl down to the creek?" Before I could answer, he continued, "I'll hurry to the house, and your mom and I will come back with the car. We will have to take you to the doctor."

My father didn't wait to hear my answer. He just climbed back up onto the tractor and took off. He had left the disk behind so he could go faster.

I started to crawl toward the creek dragging my run over leg like I saw a soldier do in a combat movie on television. I think the soldier was John Wayne or one of the men in his patrol squad. They were out on a dangerous mission. Thinking I was on a dangerous mission and had been shot, I needed to drag myself back to our side of the trenches or I would be found by the enemy.

This fantasy seemed to make the distance I had to travel in real life a little bit closer. The ground was very uneven, with lumps of earth slowing me down because my father had not run the disk over this part of the field yet. When I would hit a clod of dirt, I wanted to scream with pain; however, when I remembered if I really was a wounded soldier, I would not want to let the enemy know where I was; I endured and suffered in silence. I don't remember ever seeing John Wayne cry in a war movie, but I cried.

Finally, I could not take it any longer, and when my foot seemed to be stuck on a really big clod, I screamed through my tears as loud as I could. I guess I wasn't in a fantasy anymore, and my brain must have told my imagination to take a hike because no enemy came and discovered me. I guess it was okay for me to scream because no one was there to hear me except for two crows, and they didn't seem to care one way or another. As far as that goes, I have never heard of a crow caring about human pain or the life predicaments that we can make for ourselves. My hunch is crows have enough to do just taking care of the basic needs that animals and humans share. I doubt if they have the luxury of worrying about human beings and all of the messes humans make in life.

My thoughts about crows were interrupted by another shot of pain so I decided to concentrate on minimizing as much as possible the pain I was having. I tried to calm my pain with a mixture of mumbles from Psalm Twenty-Three, The Lord's Prayer, and Elvis Presley's "You Ain't Nothing but a Hound Dog." I would have had a better chance of God hearing me and sending an angel or two to cool my sweating brow if I had sung "Jesus Loves Me," but Elvis' song about a hound dog was the first thing that came to my mind after " . . . forgive us our debts . . ."

In a short while, I felt a little calmer so I was able to crawl a bit more. A bit more was all I could do because only a few feet away from where I was when I sang about Jesus loving me and a hound dog, my foot snagged another clod, and I let out a scream loud enough to hurt my ears. I don't know how long I was dragging, stopping, screaming, crying, and crawling more, but I was becoming quite exhausted. I closed my eyes for what I thought was only a few seconds, but I must have passed out.

Chapter 12

Pain and Suffering

I became conscious by my mom's and father's voices speaking to me.

"Teddy, Teddy, wake up!" my mom was speaking to me, but it sounded like I was hearing her through my eyes instead of my ears.

"We better carry him to the car," my father suggested while once again lifting me.

"Teddy!" The voice belonged to my mom, and now I could hear her through my ears and it sounded as if she was yelling at me.

"Mom," I answered but said no more.

"Teddy, are you awake?" I am not sure why my mom asked me if I was awake because I did answer her only seconds before.

With what sounded like a brief sigh of relief, my mom repeated my name once again, "Teddy, your father is going to take you to the car, and we are taking you into town to see the doctor. He is waiting for us at his office. The ride might be a little bumpy until we are on the road, so you might feel more pain, but your father will be careful. I will ride in the back seat with you."

I must have slipped out of consciousness again because the next thing I knew, we were driving down the road. My father had no way of driving so far into the field with the car, so he must have only driven up to the pasture fence. Later, I found out that when we reached the fence separating the plowed field from the pasture, my mother slipped under the fence and my father lifted me over into her arms. I am a fairly husky guy and heavy at that. My mother must have really strong muscular arms, or she just did what she had to for my safety. It's a miracle that she didn't drop me. Of course, it is also a miracle that my father was able to hear me and stopped the tractor before he ran over my head! I guess in spite of it all, there are miracles happening all of the time if only we humans would take the time to see them.

Putting me in the car posed another dilemma, but somehow measuring my pain reactions as a guide, my parents were able to finally settle me in the back seat, and my mom cradled my head on her lap as my dad started the car and slowly headed to town. Again, I really didn't remember going through any of this or yelling out in pain while my folks were settling me in the backseat. It seems I was not in touch with my senses until we were traveling toward town. At least, I thought I was in charge of my senses.

"Teddy, are you awake?" This time it was Dr. Jones asking me whether I was awake or not. I nodded, and looking past him, I saw his nurse with a needle in her hand. "Do you feel much pain?" Doc Jones continued.

"No, not much," I answered truthfully.

"Good," Doc Jones said and added, "I gave you a shot a little while ago. You should not be feeling as much pain as you had when you first came into my office. I don't want you to become unconscious again. Let me tell you, you are very lucky. The way your father explained how this accident happened, it could have turned out very differently. Your father also said you crawled quite a distance by the time he returned with your mom and the car. You were very brave, Teddy."

A wave of fear passed through my brain when the doctor said that it could have been much worse. It didn't take much for me to imagine what might have been. *I could have died with a smashed in foot, leg, and head, saying nothing about how squashed my brain might have been. If my brain was squashed and I was dead, my mom would have to write an obituary for me. I bet it would have been a hard thing for her to do.* "Yes, I know things could have been worse. But I prayed, so I guess that must've helped." I certainly didn't feel brave at the moment.

"You actually do not have any broken bones. It might have been better if you had; instead, several bones in your foot are crushed. You won't be able to wear a cast. I will put an elastic wrap on your foot and up part of your leg. You will have to soak your foot in hot water, as hot as you can stand it, and then cold water, as cold as you can stand it. Hot to cold, cold to hot, you will need to do this about twenty minutes four times a day," Doc Jones said.

He was telling me all of this, but when I looked up at him, I could see that his eyes were bypassing me, and he was really giving the instructions to my mother. "I am recommending that you not use the stairs for a while. You will actually have to stay in bed for a week. Your mother told me that your grandfather is at your house now. I will be checking on him in a day or two, and when I do, I will see how you are coming along. Your mom also said that there is no other bed downstairs, so you will be sleeping on the couch, Teddy, and you must use the bedpan for the first week."

"What?!" I yelled out in a tone of disgust and then echoed his words, only sarcastically. "Bedpan? Ugh, I am not going to."

"Hmm . . . well, I see, Teddy, and I respect you for your honesty, but let me tell you, if you are up and about the first couple of days or for the first week, it will be easier for you to hit your foot. Since it will only be in a wrap, you would feel a lot of pain and do more damage. Hitting your foot could also cause a blood clot to form. Then I would have to transport you to the hospital and—"

"Okay, doc. I understand," I said in a whisper.

"We will buy another bedpan at the pharmacy," my mom said without scolding me for my reaction to Doc Jones' comment.

"You won't need to, Elaine," Doc Jones said and then added, "I have a few extras. We will make sure you have one when you leave."

Doc Jones and my folks talked for a few minutes about when he was coming out and the type of pain medicine he was prescribing for me. Just before we left his office, he gave my parents his private number to call if there were complications with my situation or Grandpa's. Then he turned back to me and spoke directly. "Teddy, when you have crutches, you can use them to get up and go into the bathroom, but remember for the first week—the bedpan. Is that clear? No exceptions!"

His words sounded like a command and gave me no wiggle room to negotiate, so all I could do was nod my head in the affirmative. While my folks talked some more with Doc Jones, my mind pondered the whole bedpan business. *I have never used a bedpan before. My grandpa uses one. I think the pan stinks.* I knew I didn't like the idea, but arguing the point was useless. *I wish Doc would not have brought the bedpan up in our conversation.* I knew how the power of suggestion works sometimes, so I complied when my brain told me to leave things alone for the moment. *On our way home, I'll put my brain to work, thinking of reasons why I can't use the bedpan without actually saying the word. I will use a code word like gravy or just say "one."* By the way, I don't believe Doc Jones would ever use one unless, of course, he was unconscious, but then, how could he?

Before we left town, my parents stopped at the grocery store. My mom went into the store to pick up a few groceries while my father stayed in the car with me. There wasn't too much I could say about having to stay in the car. I was propped up by two pillows, with another pillow beneath my bummed leg. I was taken by surprise when, after sucking in a lot of smoke from his cigarette, my father turned his head toward me, and while smoke was sailing out of his mouth he asked, "How are you doing, Teddy?"

I answered truthfully, "Not too good, Dad. I am feeling nauseated again." Actually, I was becoming sick to my stomach, but it wasn't from the pain in my leg. It was from the smoke that was coming from my father's cigarette. Instead of running out through the window my father had rolled down, the smoke seemed to be sailing right toward me, burning my eyes and spiraling up my nostrils. I tried all the tricks I knew, like holding my breath, but nothing worked. Fortunately, my mom was opening the car door just about the time I was going to say, "Dad, can I stick my head out the window so I can breathe?" My mom's return to the car helped me avoid asking the breathing question.

When my mom opened the car door, a swoosh of cool air from out of nowhere came to my rescue. I took in as much of the coolness as I could before Mom shut the door. Holding the groceries on her lap, we were off toward home. Since we don't have air conditioning in the car, we always roll the windows down a little ways, and when I can get by with it, I roll my window down all the way.

If Victoria is riding in the back seat, the windows only come down a crack because she always complains about her hair messing up. I am not sure why, but when she is in the car and it's summer, she always gets her way regarding the windows. I think my mom makes my father keep his window part way down, especially when he is smoking. She knows if he doesn't roll it down some, I will make quiet gagging sounds, and Victoria will ask my mom to roll down her window just a little bit. If Victoria complains because the car smells smoky, she'll say, "Mom, my hair is going to smell like smoke." She never tells Dad that, but he hears it anyway. If there is too much wind, Victoria complains that the wind is messing up her hair. Victoria is always concerned about her hair, especially if she is going to be around some boys.

After we were on the country road, my mom turned toward my direction and said, "I bought you some Seven-Up, Teddy, just in case your stomach becomes upset, and I also bought some vanilla ice cream for you."

"I think my stomach is upset now, Mom," I said, which was partially true, but the thought of having Seven-Up to drink did have some influence on my comment.

"Let's make it home first. After you are settled in on the couch, then you can have some Seven-Up." Still looking in my direction, my mom gave me a smile, but her voice expressed a sound of caution and a clear message regarding when the Seven-Up would be served.

When our car turned into the lane leading up to our house, my dog, Pal, came running out to meet us with an enthusiastic, friendly bark greeting us with a welcome home. *Pal, you are silly,* I thought. *First, you run down the hill to say, "Hello," and then you race back up the hill, barking just as enthusiastically. Why don't you just stay up on the top of the hill and bark and not wear yourself out?* Pal never answered my thoughts, at least in any language I could understand.

It took both my father and my mother to help me out of the car, but once out, my father proceeded to lift me up and carry me into the house. Taking me into the living room, he carefully put me down on the couch. Cindy greeted us at the door with a ton of questions: "Why are you carrying Teddy, Daddy? Are you hurt, Teddy? Is Teddy going to die, Momma? Are you sad, Teddy? What did you buy me, Momma?"

No one really answered Cindy until she asked again, "What did you buy me, Mommy?" My mom simply replied, "If you are really good and eat all of your supper tonight, then maybe you can have some ice cream."

"Oh, goody!" Cindy said, clapping her hands and then she once more turned her attention back to me. "Are you hurt, Teddy?" Not waiting for an answer, Cindy continued her inquiry, "Are you sick like Grandpa? Do you want me and Grandma to pray for you like she prays for Grandpa?"

My mom listened very carefully to all of the questions Cindy was asking, and before I could even open my mouth to answer any of them, my mom spoke. "Cindy, Teddy had an accident when he and Daddy were in the field working. His leg was hurt badly, but he will be okay. Maybe when you say your prayers tonight, you can ask Jesus to heal Teddy just like you pray for Grandpa."

When I thought about how my mom answered Cindy, I realize she was very thoughtful. She didn't go into a lot of detail, and she didn't compare my accident with Grandpa's illness; instead, my mom chose to give attention to what Cindy could do. With a heart full of innocence, Cindy could pray her words for both Grandpa and me. I guess my mom must have decided the hard part would come later when my grandfather did die and she would have to answer Cindy's questions: "Momma, why didn't God make Grandpa well? Didn't he like Grandma's and my prayers?"

I am old enough to realize Cindy didn't understand it all, and any long explanation about the difference between Grandpa's illness and my accident would only confuse her, so my mom gave Cindy something that she could understand, and that was how to pray regardless of what she said, and the rest would be addressed when the time came.

After Mom gave Cindy her assignment to pray, with a willing voice, Cindy replied, "Okay, Mommy." Since no more questions followed, I am sure Mom's answer satisfied Cindy.

Can you believe it? As soon as Mom and Cindy had their conversation, it was my turn. I had to use the bedpan.

Later that evening, I just couldn't finish the Seven-Up my mom had given me earlier. There it sat on the little stand beside the couch-bed with only a few sips gone. After Ruby and Cindy went to bed, my mom returned to the living room with two pills. Handing the pills and the glass of Seven-Up to me, she said, "Teddy, for the next few days, Doc Jones wants you to take a pill to help you sleep, and this other pill is for pain. You can take one pain pill every four hours if you need it. I will be up checking on Grandpa and Grandma through the night, so I will also check on you to see if you are awake. If you are awake because of the pain and four hours have passed, I will give you another pain pill." My mom wiped my forehead with a damp cloth she had brought with her along with the pills, and then she kissed me on the forehead. I think if I wasn't tired and starting to feel the pain, I would have blushed.

"I can feel the pain now, Mom," I said, trying to ignore the kiss on my brow.

"I am sure you can. The last pain pill you took was in Doc Jones' office. I wanted to wait and give you both pills right before you were ready to sleep," As she talked, my mom handed me the two pills and my glass of Seven-Up.

"Will I burp, Mom?" I asked, thinking that Seven-Up usually made me burp. I normally wouldn't mind; in fact, I would actually try to burp as loud as I could, but right now, I didn't want to take the chance of spitting out the pills.

"I doubt you will burp, Teddy. Now take the pills and try to sleep. Victoria is staying with a friend tonight, so you should not be disturbed." My mom's words assured me it was okay to swallow the pills with Seven-Up. I was also wondering if Victoria came in late, would she wake me up. But then I remembered she wasn't coming home this evening, so I should have a good night's sleep, especially after swallowing a sleeping pill and a pain pill.

I have never taken a pain pill or sleeping pill before this evening. To me, they didn't taste any different than an aspirin. After Mom went into the parlor to check on my grandparents, I said my prayers and kept my eyes closed, hoping that would make me go to sleep faster. I slept only as long as the two pills were able to keep my foot and leg under control, but when they began to wear off, the pain in my foot and leg snuck up to my brain in a full-scale assault on my pain center. *Wake up! Wake up! How can you sleep at a time like this, Teddy? You are being attacked,* my brain yelled to my eyeballs and vocal cords. Immediately, my eyeballs told my eyelids to pop open, and my vocal cords sent out a distress signal in the sound of a moan through my mouth. Now wide awake, I took over the moaning myself and called for my mother, "Mom, Mom, ooooh, it hurts, Mom. My foot is throbbing with pain." I took a breath and then moaned again.

"Shh . . . Teddy . . . you'll wake up Grandpa," my mom softly scolded as she came out of the parlor where my grandparents were.

"I can't help it. It hurts, Mom. I am sorry. I—" Tears were pulsating out of my eyes in sync with my moans. "I hurt. It hurts, Mom." I continued to cry as my mom took hold of my hand while rubbing my brow with the washcloth she held in her other hand. My mom never said anything about me crying; she just wanted me to not be so loud.

My mom's ready-made thermometer was her right hand, so after a brief hand-holding, she felt my forehead and gave me her diagnosis. "Hmmm, Teddy, I think you might have a little fever. The doctor said that might happen. I am not surprised. Teddy, you can't have another pain pill for an hour. I'll tell you what. I will turn on television and move it out toward the couch. Maybe watching one of those really late movies will take your mind off of the pain, or maybe you might want to think about going to scout camp this summer. Won't that be fun?" My mom didn't move toward the TV but continued to sit beside me and rub my forehead.

"You mean I can go to scout camp, Mom?" I was surprised to hear her mention scout camp as a possibility. I didn't think my mom was offering scout camp as a bribe. My mother never offers bribes. I haven't even brought the idea up at the supper table even though two of my best friends have told me they are going. I am afraid my father would say I couldn't go. He would probably say it is too expensive, so I figured as long as I didn't ask, I wouldn't hear the word "no," and I could keep hoping that something would happen and I would see myself going to camp.

"Maybe you can go, Teddy. We will have to see. For now, just think about it, and it will help you take your mind off of the pain." My mom has a way with words. She didn't say directly that I could go, but she also didn't say I couldn't. Just her mentioning the possibility did help me take my mind off the pain.

"I'll try, Mom. I really will." I didn't want to worry my mom. With my grandpa in the parlor needing attention from my mother and me on the couch needing her attention also, I suspected my mom's bushel was full with all the chores she had to do taking care of us besides her normal work. I didn't want to be the cause of the bushel running over. I fell asleep. The next time I awoke, my mom was sitting beside me again, only now she wasn't in her bathrobe, she was fully dressed and the room didn't feel like nighttime anymore.

"It's time for breakfast, Teddy," my mom said as she put a tray of toast and cereal next to the couch on my little table and then continued talking. "After you eat, I will give you another pain pill, and then you must do the water exercises the doctor gave you."

I thought it was very nice of my mom to bring me some breakfast even though I wasn't very hungry, mostly because of the pain and because when I looked at the cereal, it was cornflakes. I think I told you before I don't really like cornflakes. I would rather have Frosted Flakes or Sugar Pops or Shredded Wheat. If I felt a little better and was really hungry, that is what I would have asked for. *We are probably out of the good stuff,* I said to myself and then I took a bite of toast. "Mom," I said with my speaking voice, and then I whispered because I didn't want Grandma to hear me. I knew Victoria and Ruby had already gone to school, and I thought Cindy was probably still sleeping. "Mom," I repeated slowly and then almost with words of regret, "I have to go to the toilet. Can I walk to the bathroom? I don't want anyone to see me."

"No, Teddy," my mom said matter-of-factly. "You remember what the doctor said."

"Ah, come on, Mom, he won't know," I said with an air of assurance.

"I will know," my mom quipped, "and that is that! Now, I have a urinal that Grandpa uses. You can use that, and when you have to go number two, you will have to use a bedpan."

"But Mom, I—" talking about it just made the urge to pee even greater. So I took the urinal from my mother that she had retrieved from Grandpa's room. Then she propped me up, just a little bit.

"I'll be in the kitchen, Teddy." My mom at least left me a little bit of dignity to hang onto. "Call me when you are done. Then you can finish your breakfast and take your pills. Now remember, you have to have something on your stomach, or the pills will upset your stomach and, you really don't want that to happen."

I was relieved to hear she was leaving the room, but instead of turning around and heading toward the kitchen, she continued to stand beside the couch. "Mom, I know what to do. Will you please leave." If she didn't leave soon, I knew I would have an accident.

"Okay, but holler if you need me." Her words trailed behind her as she headed toward the kitchen.

I started to do my business, but just as I started, Cindy came bumping down the stairs and into the living room. "Watcha doin' Teddy?" she innocently asked.

Oh no, I thought to myself. I didn't answer her but instead yelled out, "Mom! Come get Cindy!"

Sensing what might have happened, my mom obliged me and called out, "Cindy, dear, come in the kitchen and help me."

As she made her way to the kitchen Cindy's questioning continued. "What's Teddy doing Mommy?"

I do believe my mom should have been a diplomat because she didn't answer Cindy, but redirected her attention away from me.

"Cindy please help me fix a tray for Grandma and Grandpas' breakfast. Here, you draw Grandpa a picture, and we will put it on his tray." My mother pulled a chair out from the table and lifted Cindy into it as she was talking. Then she quickly handed her a piece of paper and colors she kept in a kitchen drawer for such times as this when she needed to occupy Cindy's mind with something different than what my little sister really had an interest in doing.

"Okay, Momma, I will draw Grandpa a horse." Cindy's independence showed through as she started to draw a horse after having asked our mom what she should be drawing. A horse was not one of the ideas Mom came up with, but drawing a horse was a lot better than asking again what I was doing, and my mom knew that.

"Drawing a horse is a good idea, Cindy. I think Grandpa will like that." I imagine my mom had a pleasant smile on her face to go along with her comment. It was hard for me to realize it at the moment, but later, I came to appreciate the conversation and situation that happened between Cindy and me and then Cindy and my mother and the fact that they offered a bit of comic relief.

On that first full day of living on my couch bed, Victoria was at an all-day track meet. I never told you that she was a fast runner. She originally went out for track because she thought running and doing warm-up exercises would be better for her than exercising. Her coach had her run something called the "440." I have never seen her run at a track meet, but she usually comes home with a blue or red ribbon. I think she runs now because she is a winner, and the coach sees her as a leader on their team.

Since Victoria wasn't home, my mom pretty much had her hands full with Grandpa in the parlor and me on the couch. Since there was no school that day, Ruby tried her best to keep a watchful eye on Cindy as she wandered back and forth between talking to Grandma and Grandpa and then coming over to my couch bed and talking to me. My grandmother was very good at helping where she could, but she mostly tried her best to tend to Grandpa's needs and do things like helping to bathe him and assisting him with the urinal and bedpan stuff. My father was out in the field, so he wasn't around to help Mom out.

Somehow, my mom seemed to manage, and at ten a.m., she came from the kitchen with a mop pail and a small bucket. The pail was filled with icy water and ice cubes, and the bucket was filled with steaming hot water. Putting both on the floor next to the couch, she announced, "Teddy, it's time for your water exercises. Don't sit up quite yet. I have to go get the towel I left on the table, and then I will help you sit up. I'll have to take the elastic wrap off of your foot, so just lean back, and I'll return shortly." Noticing something different was going to happen, Cindy stopped roaming, and she and Ruby sat in the living room recliner ready to watch me do my exercises.

Just as she said, my mom was back in the living room within ten breaths. "Okay, put your arms on my shoulders and pull up as I help you swing to the edge of the couch," my mom instructed.

"I don't think I can, Mom. I feel kind of dizzy. I—" Truthfully, I didn't want to have any more pain than I was already feeling.

"Teddy, if you want your foot to heal, you will have to do what doctor Jones told you to do. This foot therapy is part of the healing process. Now, no more foolishness, let's do this."

My weak excuse for why I couldn't do the therapy was shot to pieces, so I complied without further comment. I guess I couldn't really blame my mom. She was trying her best to take care of the whole family plus her parents. I hadn't really thought much of Grandpa being her father. He was always just Grandpa to me. My mom never knew her grandparents. They remained in Romania when my grandparents came to America, so all she had to connect her with her past were her parents, and now she was close to losing one of them through the journey of an illness that leads to what we call death. I was ruminating on this while I was exercising my foot. *We all need some way of being connected to the past or else we are just rootless flowers here today and gone tomorrow. Otherwise, when we are gone, who will be there to tell our stories about "I remember when . . ." or "my grandfather taught me . . ." or "that is what my grandmother used to say?" Who would even care? Didn't our living matter more than just drawing oxygen from this place and giving it back as carbon dioxide?*

All of these thoughts ran through my brain while my mother removed the elastic wrap and helped me lower my foot into the icy water first.

"Teddy, next time, you will have to do this by yourself. You can do it. I know you want your foot to heal properly and, besides, I am going to really need more time with Grandpa. When you are done, give me a call, and I will wrap your foot back up." My mom had a lot of confidence in me. I think she had more in me than I had in myself. The thought of taking her time away from my grandpa was enough to make me determined to do what she was asking.

"I will be able to do it by myself, Mom. In fact, you can let me do it now. I will be okay. I know I will." I wanted to show my mom that even though I squawked earlier when Cindy came bouncing into the room, I didn't want to be a burden.

"That's sweet of you, Teddy, but I want to help you this first time. Next time you can do it." My mom (aka my nurse) helped me lift my foot out of the icy water and, without hesitating, smartly tugged it under in the hot water bucket while sliding her hands upward and resting them just above the waterline.

When my foot hit the hot water, it only took a few seconds for it to suck the coolness out of my foot and, in my imagination, start roasting my foot, "Mom, that's hot! Really hot!" I yelled, and in that moment, I forgot all about being brave, not being a burden, or not even being a man about it all and bearing the pain.

"Calm down, Teddy. You will soon be used to all of this." My mom didn't scold me. She didn't "shhh" me. She just told me to calm down.

There wasn't any sympathy in her voice either. I tried to resist a little when she lifted my foot out of the hot water because I knew what was coming next. I would be standing in the Artic with one shoe on and my damaged foot naked, wrapped in the icy snow. The second time my foot went into the hot water, it actually felt really good, but soon I imagined that naked foot sinking into the hot sands of Death Valley. I counted to ten as fast as I could and then thinking to myself, "This should be long enough," I started to lift my foot out.

"Teddy, put your foot back down in the water for just a bit longer," Nurse Mom said. "No nonsense now. You can do this on your own. Remember, you said that you would. You need to do about five more minutes of this exercise. Remember hot to cold, cold to hot. Use your wristwatch to time yourself. Thirty seconds in each pail, back and forth. I have to go help Grandpa now. When you are done, I will help you lay back down," my mom's words were once again instructive yet void of any emotional pitch or expression of concern. She wasn't worried if I would do it right or not. She knew that I would. Because of her confidence in me, I wanted to please her. Besides, when she sounds very firm, I know she is saying, "Just do it." When I hear her say that, I pretty much do what she says.

Ruby and Cindy were spellbound by watching me go through the exercise. To my surprise, they just sat there. When I finished, they went back to drawing pictures. I was surprised to see every time I had to do the exercise, they were right there watching.

I went through this routine several times a day from the time I woke in the morning until just before I went to sleep at night. By the end of the day, I had the exercise down and was a little more confident that I wouldn't cause my mom too much more work in taking care of me.

I fell right to sleep after an exhausting day of foot washing. Well, not really right to sleep because I had a few thoughts wondering around in my head that I had to listen to before sleep arrived. *I probably have the cleanest right foot of any kid in my class. It's too bad there isn't a contest for foot washing. I have become an expert so I probably would win. Hot to cold, cold to hot—I sure hope this is healing those crushed bones in my foot. I am just a little tired of having to use a urinal and bedpan.* Before I had my second yawn and really started to fall asleep, I had one more thought. *It's too bad those pills cause me to sleep because here on the couch, I could be watching Movie Masterpiece after my sisters go to bed.*

When my father came in for lunch my second day on the couch, he helped my mom take care of my grandpa by turning him in his bed so he wouldn't have bed sores. The doctor told my mother that grandpa had to be turned every so often. My mom probably already knew that. She has a big medical book she reads when one of us is sick. She has been reading her book a lot more since my grandfather and grandmother came to the farm.

During lunch, my mom, father, and grandmother had a discussion. Since I was in the living room, I didn't hear everything they talked about, but what I did hear and understand was about my grandparents' farm. They decided that my father would put in my grandfather's crops and, through the summer, would somehow care for the crops through harvest time. My father said he would do this along with planting his own crops.

Listening to them, I became sad because their planning did not include Grandpa. In a way, they were also talking about life going on for the rest of us after my grandpa died. When I heard the kitchen door shut, I imagined my father with a cigarette in his mouth and an empty coffee cup on the table where he had left it before he went back to work.

Propping myself up on my elbows, I leaned as far as I could toward the door leading into the kitchen so I could hear my mom and grandmother talk. As hard as I tried, I couldn't hear much, but I did hear crying and my mom's voice gently saying, "Don't cry, Momma. Don't cry." I pictured my mother's arms wrapping around my grandma as she gently rubbed her back, trying to comfort her. Then there was silence only to be interrupted by the sounds of two people crying. They, my grandmother and my mother were both crying in Romanian. I think crying in Romanian was easier for both of them to do.

I was still propped up on my elbows when my grandmother walked into the living room. I could see tears rolling gently down her cheeks. If her tears all had names, I know they would be called Confusion, Sadness, Grief, and Loss. I believe it is possible that all of us have a reservoir of such tears somewhere in our hearts. Throughout our lives, there are times when the brain opens the flood gates and tears with names come running out across life's field. Sometimes they come very slowly, and sometimes they rush out with hardly any effort on a person's part. Some people have had more sorrow and hurt in their lives than other people have had. There comes a time for some who have experienced more pain, tragedy, and trial to drain their reservoir dry. If and when such a time comes and there is no one in their lives to cry for them, they grow a numbness to shield themselves from all feelings. From the most vulnerable to the most joyous, denying all emotions puts them on the edge of a great abyss that has no end.

Luckily, in our family, none of us has ever been close to that distant place. The only person that I know who might have ever come close to that edge might be my father, but I believe my mother's love drew him back into the present. I hope none of us ever run our reservoir so dry that Hope and Love on the road of Faith are not able to draw us back into life. It's hard for me to grasp I could have all of those thoughts jump-started by the image of my grandmother walking into the room, but I did. Looking up at my grandmother, I saw her wringing her hands in a circular motion while repeating over and over, "Yoi, yoi, yoi, domde, domde, domde."

Instead of stopping to talk to me, my grandma went into the parlor. Soon I heard her praying the prayer I have heard her and Grandpa pray when I would stay with them on their farm. Every morning and night, they would kneel at their chairs around the kitchen table and pray. Since there is no table in her parlor bedroom, I imagined her sliding her chair as close to Grandpa's bed as she could and reaching out to fold one of his hands in hers as she prayed. If Grandma's words were English words, I believe she would be praying, "Now I lay me down to sleep, I pray the Lord my soul to keep."

"If I should die before I wake . . ." It occurred to me now that my grandfather could die before tomorrow morning . . . and if he did, he would not wake up, at least not in his parlor-bedroom. I strained hard to hear my grandmother finish her prayer, but all I could hear was the sound of her tears. I knew that God could probably figure out what her tears were saying. After a minute or so, I heard no more tears, sobs, or words. I could picture my grandmother now sitting in the chair, still holding my grandpa's hand. *I bet Grandpa likes her to hold his hand,* I said to myself. *I bet he knows that he isn't alone.*

I continued thinking. *I know I would like it if I was dying that someone was holding my hand.* I shivered just a little with the thought of dying, knowing if my father hadn't heard me yelling, I could be dead right now. *If I was dead now, I would be having a lot of different thoughts than the ones I've been thinking. I now believe the pain in my leg isn't the worst thing that could happen to me.* After all my thinking, my brain quietly asked, *I wonder what will happen next?* I didn't hear an answer. I must have fallen asleep.

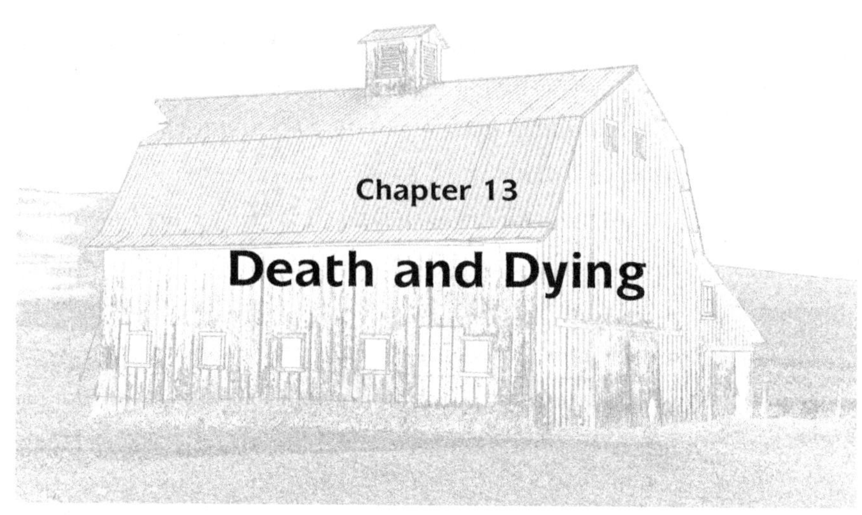

Chapter 13

Death and Dying

Grandpa didn't die that night. I was happy for him and Grandma, but I was sad that he has to do more suffering. Lying on the couch, waiting for my mom to finish sending Victoria and Ruby off to school and bring me my breakfast, I had a conversation in my head with my grandfather.

"How are you doing, Grandfather?" I asked while walking as quietly as I could into his room.

"Teddy, take these sacks of potatoes off of my chest. It's so hard, so hard for me to breathe," he replied.

"Okay, Grandpa," I respectfully answered, not understanding how he could imagine potatoes were on his chest, but then it came to me, he's breathing so hard. He must think something very heavy is on his chest.

Along with other farm produce, he and Grandma raised and sold potatoes. I often had followed behind Grandpa and picked up potatoes after he had brought them out of the ground with a pitchfork. I would pick as many as I could find in each hill and put them into a gunny sack I dragged along beside me. When the sack became too heavy for me to drag, I started another sack. Now standing by his imaginary bed listening to my grandfather's real-not-imaginary breathing, I wanted so badly to believe that by lifting these imaginary bags I could not see off of his chest, I would allow my grandfather to breathe more freely. "How do you feel now, Grandfather?"

"Better, Teddy, much better," my grandpa would answer with a smile, and then he would fall right to sleep.

"Here's your breakfast," my mother said. Her words brought me out of my imaginary conversation and back to the reality of the present. I hadn't felt like eating much since the accident, but this morning, the sight of breakfast in front of me was a good thing. I was hungry even if I did have to eat corn flakes, cow's milk, and store-bought bread with town butter and jam.

Later in the morning, my father came in to help my mom with Grandpa and have a cup of coffee. As they sat with my grandmother at the kitchen table, I heard my father say, "I haven't seen Pal all morning. He usually tags along barking when I am driving out to the field, but he didn't this morning. When I came in just now, I could see that he hasn't touched the scraps I left in his bowl from supper last night."

"Before lunch, I'll call the Madisens and Witters," I heard my mother say. "They both have dogs. Maybe Pal has been hanging out at one of their places." Then she started to speak Romanian to my grandmother. I suppose Mom was probably telling Grandma that Pal hadn't eaten any of his food since noon yesterday and that Sam hadn't seen Pal all morning.

"Yoi, yoi, yoi," was all my grandma said.

Their coffee break was interrupted by my grandfather yelling out. He wasn't calling Grandma or my mom this time. He was just saying the same Romanian words over and over in a very loud voice, and every so often, he would give out a loud groan and start all over again. Without a word, my mother immediately left the table for the parlor bedroom with my grandmother following her. Only seconds later, my mother called out, "Sam, Sam, come help me please!"

My mom's voice rushed through the living room, right by my couch bed, and met my father as he was rising up from his chair. Even before my father reached the parlor, my mom shouted, "Sam, Dad is trying to climb out of bed!" The sound of her panic trailed off as my father quickly went into the parlor. While I wasn't in there with them, I've seen this happen before with my grandfather, so I knew my father was gently restraining Grandpa while Mom and Grandma spoke to him in Romanian.

Because it is morning, regardless of my grandpa being so sick, I imagine he thought, *I have to milk the cows. I better get on with it.* Come to think of it, that probably explained why Grandpa tried his best to climb out of bed, repeating the same Romanian words over and over. In his mind, I bet he thought it was chore time, and he was calling the cows' home for milking—just like my father does. "Come boss, come boss, come boss." I am not certain why they call out "boss" when all of the cows are "bossies." I have never seen anyone try to milk a "boss."

Later, I asked my mom, "What was grandpa doing, Mom? Why is he so restless when he calls out?" With a frustrated yet sad smile, she replied, "I think your grandpa thought it was milking time, and he probably couldn't figure out why the barn door would not open up for him to let the cows in."

"Is that because his wrists are tied to the railing, Mom?" I asked.

"I suppose so, Teddy."

"I thought he was calling the cows because I remember the Romanian word he uses when he calls them. Grandpa said it means 'boss.' Dad uses the same word when he calls our cows home. When I stayed with Grandpa and Grandma on their farm, at milking time, one of them would call out that word over and over, and you know what, Mom?"

"No, what, Teddy?"

"All of the cows came right out of the pasture and up to the barn, just like they do when Dad calls them—but no cows ever come when I call them, Mom."

"It just takes time and practice, Teddy. You are always in such a hurry." My mom must have seen my disappointment, so she cut herself off. "Your grandmother told Grandpa that he had already milked the cows and that they needed to go back to the pasture. He must have accepted what she said because he quieted down and went back to sleep." There really wasn't anything left for her to say. I'm sure both she and Grandma were relieved Grandpa was able to fall back to sleep.

Because I was so busy asking Mom questions and listening to her answers, I hadn't realized my father had left the house. I can imagine he was probably already plowing one of the fields where he would plant corn. He only had a two-row plough, so it took him a lot longer than most farmers to plow up a field, and he had two more fields to plow after the first one.

Have you ever thought about how, right in the middle of a life coming to an end, somewhere on the same planet, a baby is being born, and seeds are being planted in the soil nurtured by the hope they will sprout and create life? Or how some people are celebrating life anew while others are grieving life lost? I hadn't thought much about all of this before except when it is close to Easter, and my Sunday school teacher or the preacher talked to us about Jesus dying on the cross. But now, with my grandpa dying and my near-death accident, I have been thinking about it a lot. Thinking can be hard work sometimes. When I have been thinking harder than I am used to doing, my brain sometimes walks me into a snooze.

I'm sure that's what happened to me after Mom and I had our talk about Grandpa and my father went out to plow because I went back to sleep. I was right in the middle of a dream where Roy Rogers had just lassoed a dangerous desperado and was going to take him to jail. All of a sudden, a gigantic bolt of lightning flashed from the sky, striking the earth right between Roy and his prisoner. The lightning bolt burned right through the rope freeing the desperado and causing Roy to fall to the ground. I was really surprised. I never saw Roy fall off of Trigger before, but dreams have a mind of their own. When the lightning shook the ground, I was awakened, and to my surprise, it was my mom shaking me, not a bolt of lightning.

"Teddy, Teddy, wake up, you are about to fall out of bed," my mom kept saying as she shook me.

"What, where's Roy . . . Oh, it's you, Mom. Where's Roy?" I repeated.

"I don't know where Roy is. You must have been dreaming, Teddy. You slept through the morning. Now, before I prepare lunch, I want you to exercise your foot."

Staring down at the buckets of water, I asked, "What time is it, Mom?" I still didn't believe the whole morning was gone.

"It's almost noon," my mom answered.

"Wow!" I exclaimed, finding it hard to believe I had slept so long. The last time I saw the clock, right after I did my foot exercise, it was eight-thirty a.m. I remember my mom calling out to my father to come help with Grandpa. Maybe I dreamt the conversation my mom and I had about Grandpa calling the cows just like I dreamed about Roy Rogers. When I am better, I'll ask my mom if I imagined it all or if we really did have a conversation, but I am not going to ask her now. I have my water chore to do.

"Hot water, cold water, hot water, cold water—" I had the routine down pretty good by now, and I have learned how to tolerate the change of water temperature. I am still not certain all of this is helping my foot. I will have to wait until Doc Jones comes to see me. He'll tell me if I have been doing it right. When I was done with the water exercise, I almost drifted back to sleep, but my ears perked up when I heard whispering in the kitchen, and I was straining so hard to hear what was being said that I forgot about sleeping. I recognized my father's voice. He must have not taken his lunch out to the field with him and had come in to help with Grandpa and have a sandwich. After I heard his voice, I heard a familiar sigh that I know belonged to my mom, and then I heard her starting to cry.

Why is Mom crying? I wondered. *Maybe one of the cows is in trouble or the landlord told my dad we have to move or that they were raising the rent again or . . .* I was just about ready to imagine the worst of the worse like a tornado whipping through the state of Nebraska and destroying my grandparents' farm or the newspaper saying that Roy Rogers was struck dead by a bolt of lightning when my parents came into the living room. My mom's eyes were red and she held a hankie in her hand. My grandmother joined them and they came over and stood by my couch. *Maybe Doc Jones called with bad news about my leg,* I thought, horrified. *Maybe, I have gangrene in it and he is going to have my father saw my leg off with his chain saw . . . or something really bad like that.* My father interrupted my "maybes" with news that was worse than all of my thinking. "Teddy, I found Pal. She was lying under the porch . . . Teddy . . . it is a hard thing to tell you, but Pal is dead.

"What?" I cried out, not wanting to believe what I heard. "Are you sure it's Pal?"

"Yes, Teddy," my father replied softly. "It's Pal." I guess he ought to know it was Pal. He is the one who brought him home from the sale barn. My asking was silly, but I had to hold onto my disbelief as long as I could.

"What happened, Dad?" Still not believing, I was searching for more information, anything that made sense.

"I'm not sure, Teddy. She might have eaten some poison I set out for the rats, or she might have eaten poison sown at the neighbor's barn. I know they have had problems with raccoons." My father was silent after his explanation.

My grandmother rubbed her hands and quietly said,"Yoi, yoi, yoi." My mom quietly sat beside me on the couch and took a hold of my hand. When I felt her warm hand in mine, I imagined my whole body crying for Pal when I actually wasn't crying at all.

"I suppose we won't have a funeral for Pal, huh, Mom?" I asked, wanting to do something. After all, Pal was my dog. *Something ought to be done for him,* I thought to myself.

"No, son, we probably won't, but you can say a prayer for Pal. Your dad will take Pal out to the pasture and bury her." Mom's words assured me that at least Pal wouldn't be thrown in the garbage and that it was okay to pray for your dog. God listens to any prayer, regardless of who the prayer is for.

When my father left the house, I watched out the front window as he passed by carrying Pal in his arms. I never saw Pal again. I remember my Sunday school teacher said that when Jesus comes again to take us to heaven even the dead will rise up and we will be reunited with family members we love, friends we know, and even people we have never seen before, but we will call them all by name. "Don't be surprised when you arrive in heaven who else might be coming through the gate with you," she said.

When she told us all of this stuff, it never occurred to me to ask about your favorite pet or other animals going to heaven, but Johnny did. "I loved my pony, Blackie. He was killed when a drunken deer hunter thought he was a deer and shot him. Will Blackie go to heaven?" Johnny asked her.

Our Sunday school teacher only said, "I am sorry to hear about Blackie, Johnny. I don't know if animals go to heaven or not. I guess we will have to wait and see."

I remember Johnny's face turned from looking hopeful to one of disappointment, but all he said was, "Oh." And that was that. I have to tell you again, I know what Mrs. Warren said about death not being the end, but I still don't believe it. Death stinks. I know death is a big stink especially when a chicken or pig lies dead in the summertime for several days and flies are having a picnic at the dead animal's expense. That kind of dead really does stink right up your nostrils. I don't mean that kind of stink. I mean the kind that goes against all a person can hope and pray for when you want your favorite pet or a person you know, love, or feel sorry for to be well and take a breath of life back in them. When they can't, that is the stink I am talking about.

When I am able to go to Sunday school again, I won't ask our teacher about animals going to heaven because she already said she doesn't know. I will just have to wait and ask the minister sometime. He reads the Bible more than the rest of us do. He probably knows exactly where in the Bible Jesus or God talk about animals in heaven. *Hmmm . . . come to think of it, one of those books those guys, not encyclopedia guys, but some other guys who came around selling books about the Bible sold my mom was a book with a picture of Jesus and angels standing around Him. The angels were petting a baby fawn, and a lion was sleeping right at Jesus' feet. Maybe I won't have to ask my minister about animals in heaven, after all. I will just ask my mom if I can see that book.*

When school was out, Victoria brought home my homework assignment from my English teacher, Mrs. Markham. One of the assignments was to write an essay on any subject you pick. I decided to write an obituary for Pal. I might not receive a very good grade because I have never heard of anyone writing an obituary for an essay, but I didn't care. I was going to do it. While having a think about what I would write, I finally had a good cry with tears rolling down my face, and then I wrote:

The Life Story of Pal, My Dog

> My parents say that Pal is a mixed breed dog. All I know is Pal is part Collie and part German Shepherd. Pal was friendly like a Collie, but never learned how to herd cows or pigs, so I think that part of her was growly and ornery like a German Shepherd, but she was also a great watchdog like German Shepherds can be.
>
> My father brought Pal home from the sale barn one day when she was a very tiny puppy. My sisters and I were very, very happy to have a puppy. Pal was an outside dog,

but during her first few weeks, she was allowed to stay on our back porch. One of my chores was to clean Pal's messes on the porch, play with her, and water and feed her, so we became very close. She quickly became my dog, and I told my sisters that is the way it would be, but that they could pet Pal and play with her whenever they wanted to.

Pal liked all of us. Pal never had a doghouse. I don't know where she slept at night, but during the day she often took naps on the front porch. Pal always seemed to be nearby because when I called, "Here Pal, here Pal," it never took her long to come running and jump on me and lick my face. Pal was never fed dog food from the store. She ate table scraps. I think the scraps made her fast and strong.

Pal was a very good watchdog. When someone drove up our lane, she barked and barked until one of us came outside to tell her to hush. At night, if there were strange animals prowling about, she snarled and barked extra loud. We all felt safe, and I know her snarling, showing her teeth, and then shifting from snarling to growling really mean-like kept all the burglars and monsters away.

Pal liked the neighbor's dog, Lucky. He came up to visit Pal once in awhile. Pal also liked to chase moving objects. She chased the cars coming up and down our lane. She also chased the tractor when my father was driving it, pigs when my father was trying to load them in a truck so they could go to market, and our sleighs when we went sledding down the hill in the pasture. She definitely was a chaser.

Pal could shake your hand using her paw, but she didn't want to learn any other tricks. I guess it was because she was such a good chaser. She probably figured that would be enough.

Pal was my best animal friend even though she would never go to the timber with me to bring the cows home for milking.

Pal was a scavenger. She would bring home dead rabbits from the pasture or dead chickens she found outside the chicken pen or in the garbage dump. She brought them to the back porch door and left them there. She probably thought my mom would cook them for supper, but my mom never did.

Pal was satisfied with being a farm dog and my animal best friend. She never wanted to be in the movies like Lassie or Bullet. She never wanted to move to the city or to town. She was content being on the farm with us, living a dog's life.

Pal had puppies once. There were four of them, and they were mostly black in color with a little dab of white. Two were brown and white with streaks of black, just like Pal. Funny thing, after those puppies were born, our neighbor Lucky, the dog, never came to visit Pal again.

One day, Pal died. It was an accidental death. My father said she probably ate some poison. No funeral was held for Pal, and her body is in an unmarked grave somewhere out in the pasture where she used to hunt for rabbits. No one knows in Pal's dog family who preceded her in death, but she is survived by her puppies which have all gone to other homes, and by everyone in our family. We all loved her very much.

She has probably left her grave and found her way to heaven where she is now, chasing cherubs and, in a nice way, barking at angels. I hope the angel, Michael, built her a doghouse because she never had one on earth. The End. Goodbye, Pal.

I was happy that I had all of my other homework done before I wrote my essay for English because it made me sad writing about Pal.

By the end of my second week on the couch bed, Doc Jones came out to check on my grandfather and me; he gave me permission to try the crutches he brought out. I was really clumsy walking with them, and I almost fell twice, but with the doctor and my mom walking on each side of me, I managed.

"Teddy, I want you to practice walking with your crutches twice a day. Your foot is improving, but since there wasn't a clean break and your foot has three crushed bones that are in the process of healing, it will take some time. You must continue the water exercises also. Try to stand a little hotter and colder water on your foot if you can. I know you can do it. You are tough!" Doc Jones gave me a smile when he finished.

All I could really say was, "Okay," as I laid back down on my couch-bed. I felt really tired from the walking exercise, and I didn't even walk that far. I must have fallen asleep because I didn't even hear Doc Jones leave. When I woke up from my crutch nap, I heard voices coming from the kitchen.

"Sam, Doc Jones gave Grandpa a shot to help with the pain. He also said it won't be long now before he . . ." as before, my mom's words trailed off and silence hung in the air.

Finally, I could hear my father say, "Does your mother understand it all?"

I could picture a comforting smile on my mom's face. "Yes . . . she does. She knows Dad will die." She went on to say they had talked about his dying with him before he left the hospital. Then she added, "Mama told me later that Dad seemed more ready to let go of this life than she was ready to let go of him, but they both believe heaven is where Dad will wake up." Mom's voice now sounded more like our pastor's, always filled with confidence, especially when he is reading the Bible to the congregation. Still, there was a slight hesitancy in her tone. My dad must have heard it because, in one of those rare moments of intimacy, I heard him quietly comment, "Elaine, are you ready? Are you ready to let Dad go?"

In my mind, I pictured my father putting his cigarette in the ashtray and then gently reaching out, touching my mother's folded hands resting on the table. At least, I hoped he did just that.

About the time my mind pictured the tender scene between my parents, there was a knock at the kitchen door. Seconds later, I heard my mom greet Mrs. Madisen. "Hello! Patricia! It is really nice to see you. Come in. I am just making a fresh pot of coffee."

"Hi, Elaine! Well, hello, Sam, I haven't seen you for a while." Mrs. Madisen greeted both of my parents as she stepped into the kitchen. I was just on my way home from town. I have groceries in the car so I better not stay. I promise I will come back soon and we can have that cup of coffee. I baked some cinnamon rolls this morning. Charlie is shoeing horses today, so he and the men will want a break for coffee by the time I make it home. I brought you all a batch of cinnamon rolls."

"Thank you, Patricia," my mom said, her voice full of gratitude.

"How are your parents, Elaine?" Mrs. Madisen asked with a note of compassion.

"Dad's not doing so well. Doc Jones was out to see him and Teddy. Doc said that Dad cannot last much longer. I'm surprised he has made it as long as he has. Mom is doing her best." My mother sounded tired, but her words were still spoken with love and concern.

"I know it is very difficult. I promise I will be over soon, and if you like, we can have a long talk." Mrs. Madisen sounded very sincere and, at the same time, not intrusive.

Listening to this conversation taking place only a short distance away from where I lay, I thought to myself, *Mrs. Madisen really does care about our family, and she is expressing respect for my mother's boundaries around her parents and what my mom believes is appropriate to share.*

"Oh, I almost forgot. Is Teddy near?"

I am almost certain Mrs. Madisen knew I was on my couch-bed in the living room trying to capture every word that was being said coming from the kitchen, but again, I now think her words were wrapped in the respect for boundaries my mother sets.

"Yes, he is in the living room on the couch."

"I brought him a strawberry malt from the dairy queen. May I give it to him?"

My ears strained extra hard to pick up how my mom might answer the question. "Of course you can. Come on, let's go see him. I imagine he has been listening as hard as he can to our conversation." I smiled to myself as the two of them made their way into the living room.

I was so excited about the idea of having a strawberry malt I almost jumped off the couch. *I better settle down and be a little cooler in my excitement,* I thought. In a split second, I decided I better close my eyes and try to pretend I had been dozing. So that is what I did.

"Teddy, Mrs. Madisen is here. She brought you something." My mom leaned over and gently shook me. I am almost certain the many times over the past thirteen years I've pretended to sleep, she has surely caught on to my shenanigans.

"What, oh—Hi, Mrs. Madisen," I said, trying hard to contain my excitement and not stare at the strawberry malt Mrs. Madisen held in her hand. My mom taught me long ago that it wasn't polite to stare.

"Teddy, I stopped by to bring you this malt and to see how you were doing. How are you?" As she asked me the question, Mrs. Madisen handed me the malt.

"I think I will be better now! Thank you for the malt!" Without hesitation, forgetting all my mother taught me about manners in my excitement, I inhaled a long suck on the straw until my mouth was full of the cold, creamy strawberry sensation.

"I should have given it to you right when I came in. It is probably soupy by now." Mrs. Madisen exclaimed.

"Oh, I don't mind." The words barely came out of my mouth before I took another draw from the straw.

"Oh, I also wanted to tell you, Mr. Madisen wants you to know that when you are up and about, he would like you to come up to our place and help out when we are preparing the horses to show in parades this summer. We have a lot of harness brass that will need polishing."

Mrs. Madisen ignored my bad manners, but my mom did not. "Slow down, Teddy, or you will give yourself a headache!" I actually didn't hear her words as a suggestion, but a polite reprimand.

With reluctance, retracting my lips from the straw, I took a deep swallow, and then gave a refreshing sigh, and without a pause, quickly spoke to cover up my embarrassment. "Wow! I would really like to come and help. I probably could come even before my foot is healed because I will be on crutches. Maybe if my mom says I can come, she will drive me over to your house." I only mentioned my mother because my father had excused himself even before Mrs. Madisen gave me the malt. It is a good thing he did go back outside because if he had seen my cheeks full of strawberry malt, I might not have received as polite of a scolding as I did.

"I will tell you what, Teddy, your mom has her hands full right now, but if your parents say you can come and help, your mom can give me a call, and I will come down and pick you up. How does that sound?" Mrs. Madisen glanced from me to my mother.

I saw my mom give an approving nod, and she had words ready to come out of her mouth when a sharp, disturbing groan came from my grandfather. "Excuse me, Patricia; I better go check on Dad."

"I understand, Elaine. I'll just chat with Teddy a bit more. Let me know if I can be of any help."

When my mother left the room, Mrs. Madisen once again turned to me. She asked me a lot of questions about school and what subjects I liked the best. I enjoyed talking to her because she seemed to really listen. I felt really good about our chat, and we talked until my mom returned. Only now, my grandmother came out with her.

"Patricia, this is my mother, Anna Such." As soon as my mom introduced Grandma to Mrs. Madisen, Mom looked directly at my grandmother and spoke in Romanian. She probably was introducing Mrs. Madisen to Grandma.

From my grandmother's look, I know she understood because she quickly gave Mrs. Madisen her outstretched hand. Mrs. Madisen smiled, but instead of shaking Grandma's hand, she gave Grandma a gentle hug. Grandma's eyes lit up, and a welcoming smile spread across her weary face. A brief interchange between the two ladies followed, accompanied by my mom's interpreting when Grandma seemed confused. The interpretations ended with the three of them sharing a laugh. Surprisingly, Mrs. Madisen spoke German that she learned from her grandfather. Into their conversation, Mrs. Madisen realized that a lot of words Grandma or Mom used were similar to the German words she knew. Some of Grandma's words were easy for Mrs. Madisen to understand from her German heritage, and she would ask Grandma, "Do you mean . . .?" For having their first conversation, the two ladies seemed to get along and understand each other splendidly with very little assistance or coaching from my mom. Their brief but fruitful conversation ended when another groan from my grandfather followed by my grandmother's name. With a smile, Grandma said, "goodbye," and went back into the parlor.

Mrs. Madisen returned the smile. "Goodbye, Mrs. Such. I will keep you and Mr. Such in my prayers." Mrs. Madisen then turned back to my mother. Elaine, please let me know if your father's condition changes tonight. I will bring you all supper tomorrow if you don't mind."

My mother looked a bit embarrassed upon receiving so much generosity from a neighbor. I felt good that I was within hearing distance of their conversation. In fact, I was listening so carefully, my malt was only half gone and quickly melting. The good feeling I had was from Mrs. Madisen's words of unsolicited giving. In my few years, I have become more and more aware of how my mother has been a graceful giver in every community where we have lived—to her family members, my father's family, and of course, she has made tons of sacrifices to provide for all of her children and our father. Someday, I will tell you about some of my mom's sacrifices, but not right now. It is not really necessary for her to feel embarrassed because someone wants to give and do something for her, but she does. Maybe it's because I believe she read once in the Bible or heard her Sunday school teacher read from the Bible, "It is better to give than to receive."

Right now, my foot is hurting, and it is time for my water exercises: hot, cold, hot, cold. This exercise is now followed by my crutch exercises. I wish my grandpa's pain and suffering and my grandmother's grief and tears could go away by doing some exercises. I just wish they would. After my wishing, I drank the rest of my melting strawberry malt, which made me feel a little better for a while.

I know you won't be surprised to hear that my grandfather groaned his way through another two weeks. Doc Jones came out a few times to check on Grandpa and me. Every time Doc Jones came out, he would tell my mother and Grandma, "Not much has changed with John." Doc Jones learned from my mother that John was the English translation of my grandpa's name. "I am surprised he has held on so long. He must have a strong constitution, but he is weakening, and fluid around his lungs is making it more difficult for him to breathe. You should leave his oxygen mask on. I turned it up a little. The best we can do is make him feel comfortable."

My mother quickly added, "And pray."

Hearing these words, Doc Jones gave her an empathic smile. "Yes, always pray."

Toward the end of the second week of his visits after examining Grandpa, Doc Jones followed my mother and Grandma as they walked into the living room where I laid and said, "John's breathing has become shallower and the time has extended between his breaths. I know he has been a hard-working farmer and railroad worker in Romania and America. His whole body is weak, except for his heart, which is still very strong. I could take him to the hospital and draw out some of the fluid from his lungs so his breathing isn't so labored. He's receiving more oxygen now because I turned up the flow, which should take away some of the taxing labor off of his breathing. I personally believe a move to the hospital would only add to his confusion and would be his end. The only thing the hospital move would do, besides the procedure of drawing fluid off his lungs, is maybe lighten the responsibility you all have of caring for him."

"He's my father, Tom," my mother said. I have never heard my mom call our doctor by his first name before. I don't think she ever has, at least not in our presence.

"I know, Elaine. I believe I would do the same as you and Sam are doing if it was my father," Doc replied.

Hearing those words, my mom touched Doc's shoulder as she has on all of his visits. The shoulder touch was a cue for the conversation to stop so she could interpret to my grandmother what had been said. Even though Grandma probably understood everything, my mom probably felt better repeating everything in Romanian. Very carefully, she explained the one option Doc had to offer. I only know all of this because later, when I asked my mother what they had been talking about, she told me everything. When my mom translated for my grandmother, tears accompanied her words. My grandmother's words, interpreted in English, were quick and deliberate. "No, John would not want the fuss or effort to be made. He is ready to see Jesus. It's okay. I'm ready for him to do so."

In a calm, quiet voice, my mom rubbed Grandma's shoulder. "Okay, Mama, okay."

Doc Jones seemed to understand and quietly smiled. "I understand. Nothing will be done. Call me whenever you need to. I will be here."

Walking toward the door, Doc stopped and looked at me as if he had forgotten I was there. "Oops," he said, then came over and sat in the chair beside my couch-bed. He attempted a smile that was followed by a sigh. "Now, Mr. Hall, let's see the progress you have made. Tell me how you are doing, and then I will examine your foot."

"Well . . ." I didn't go any farther because the thoughts I wanted to put into words were in the corner of my brain, covered up by all I had heard being said about my grandpa. Finally, when my thoughts were in order, I continued. "I've been practicing walking with the crutches, and my mom helps me. My mom moves the rugs out of my way. She said I could slip on them. That's all, I guess."

"Sounds good, Teddy. Are you still doing the water exercises?" Doc asked. You all need to know that my doctor really doesn't miss anything even when I try to avoid the topic. Doc goes right to the point. He doesn't chitchat like most people do.

Sometimes I've heard people say, "Well, we better be going," and then have another cup of coffee and talk some more. Our neighbors are all that way, and the men are the worst. Even on very cold winter days, when a neighbor drives into our yard, my father and he will stand outside talking and freezing. When my father says, "Would you like to go up to the house and have a cup of coffee?" Most of the time, the men will say, "Oh, I have to be going, maybe next time," and then they talk and freeze for another fifteen minutes or more. My father responds the same way when he goes to a neighbor's house. I know because I have been with him sometimes. I don't stand out in the cold though, I stay in the pickup. I have never seen my mother and a woman neighbor do this ritual, especially in the winter. They always go inside where it is nice and warm.

Sorry, I slid off the track talking about my father and the neighbors. I had to be careful how I answer Doc regarding the water exercises because I had a clear motive behind what I wanted to say. "Yes, I guess I have. Can I stop now?"

"I guess you could stop any time you want to, Teddy." Doc gave me a frustrated sigh and then added, "but do you want your foot to heal?"

What? Of course, I want my foot to heal. What kind of question is that to ask? You aren't playing fair, Doc! These words actually didn't come out of my mouth because that would be disrespectful, so I only said, "Yes, I want my foot to heal."

"Then, young man, you must do the exercise!" Doc Jones smartly answered. He had me trapped in my own "Getting By with What I Can" game.

"Ok, I will," I promised.

"Good, I knew you would want to." Doc gave my shoulder an understanding shake. "The hot and cold water exercise will help to slowly mend and strengthen your bones while they heal. Okay?"

"Okay." At the moment, I would have stuck my foot in boiling hot water, hot enough to scold the skin right off of a cow, and freezing water colder than the ice at the artic if it meant my foot would mend faster. I have barely started to walk with crutches, and already I want to walk without them. Healing, whether it be a crushed bone, a broken heart, or a breach in friendship, all takes time and has to be done in a way that makes the broken pieces come back together stronger, not weaker. At least it must be that way or Doc Jones probably would have said I didn't have to do the exercises at all. I could just lie around for a few days and then rise up and walk.

Before I said my prayers that evening, I thought over what Doc said to me about my foot, and then I clearly remembered what he and my mom and grandma talked over regarding my grandpa. My thoughts went deep into the chamber of my wonderings, and I wondered what my grandfather must be thinking now if he could be thinking at all. *What is he now aware of that can only be communicated in the language of groaning?*

Since I was so deep in wondering, once again, I wondered about dying and death. I wondered if Death has a voice. *Does Death come and talk to a human being before their last breath is drawn away from their body like a boy sucking hard on a straw to clean the bottom of a malt glass even though there is nothing more to be had?* I wonder if Jesus comes and talks to people and tells them what they hope to hear or what they really don't want to hear about their lives. I wonder if Jesus tells them all He knows about their good and bad actions—what they did out in the open and what they tried to do in secret and thought the bad was well hidden. I also wonder if angels or people who have died ahead of them come around and tell them about what might happen after they, too, are dead. If the dying people are babies, children, or maybe even teenagers, I wonder if God or Jesus sends special angels to guard their journey and care for them during the time they travel through their death sleep and wake up in God's house.

What wonders to behold. This kind of wondering brought shivers to my body, but then sleep gently came, and I slept peacefully. Right before I did fall asleep, I wondered if my grandfather's sleep was coming peacefully. I prayed that it was. Some day when I see my grandpa in heaven, I will ask him. I hope I remember to ask him.

I fell asleep on Thursday and woke up on another Friday like I have every week of my thirteenth year. When I woke up, I heard rustling in the kitchen. The clock by my couch-bed told me it was six a.m. *It must be my father because he usually is the only one up this early,* I said to myself. So I was surprised to see my mother walk past my bed and into my grandparents' room. *Mom must have been awakened by one of my grandpa's moans.*

Commotion came from my grandparents' room, and then I heard the crying. My grandmother's tears strained her voice as she repeated over and over, "Yahannie, Yahannie, yoi, yoi, yoi." I did a backward elbow crawl so I could lean forward to listen better. I could hear my grandmother and mother talking. My mother repeated in English several times and then in Romanian what I assumed to be, "Daddy's gone, Mama, Daddy's gone. He'll breathe easier now." My mother's tears followed after her words, and she and Grandma must have had a cry together. Romanians are not afraid to hug each other and express emotions. They have a hearty laugh that can be heard by clouds floating by, but when they hug and cry together, it's their tears that bend the ears of God toward the earth. My grandma and mother cried, and my grandpa said nothing.

From the kitchen, I heard the crank on the phone turning over and over. The long ring was for the operator, and I heard my father say, "Get me Doc Jones, please." There was only a slight pause, and then my father started to speak again. "Hello, Doc, this is Sam Hall. Can you come out? John must have died sometime between three a.m. when we last checked on him and six this morning, the best we can tell, anyway." My father must not have said anymore because I heard the phone click, followed by my father walking through the living room in the direction of the parlor.

For my own confirmation that I wasn't dreaming all of this, when I saw my dad walking by I quickly asked, "Dad, is Grandpa—dead?"

My father actually stopped, turning toward me without moving closer, and responded, "Yes, Teddy," and then he continued to the parlor. In a short time, I have come to accept that death cannot be sanitized, and no bathroom deodorant spray will ever mask its stink. Death's stink lingers more in the heart than in the nostrils. It takes more than people-made sanitizers to diminish and bring to demise the powerful, multi-dimensional, otherworldly, inhabiting wherever it pleases, ghost-like creature whom we cannot touch but touches so many and does not discriminate regarding gender, race, age, political party, or belief in God or something other that is a sometimes a noun, sometimes a verb, sometimes an adjective, or sometimes an adverb, we call Death.

First, it was Fuzzy Chick and company. Then it was the best animal friend in the whole world, my dog, Pal. Now it is my one and only grandpa, known to the world as Yahannie or John, but I only knew him as Grandpa. Death won again. Someday, Death will get its comeuppance, and it will lose. Whammy! It will be gone, but my believing this doesn't take the hurt, pain, or sorrow away from this hour or the hours yet to come. I just have to, no, I must believe that someday, Death's comeuppance will happen—that is my only hope. No one will ever take that hope away from me, only I can give it up, and I will never do so.

Still, Death has one more battle it has been preparing for some time and will spring on our family. The worst and the greatest losers will not be those who take up arms for or against death, but the victims on the sidelines who have no voice in the battle, the struggle, or the outcome. In the present time, there is enough grief to handle for now.

I joined my mother and grandmother in the crying, from a distance, while my father went out to chore, carrying whatever emotions disguised as grief he had in his overall pocket next to his package of cigarettes. I never knew if he cried or just milked the cows. Both needed to be done. I hope he did both.

Chapter 14

A Time for Change

There is a knack to crutch walking. If you are clumsier than the average person like I am, crutch walking is more difficult and more embarrassing than having to learn how to slow dance with a girl without stepping on her toes.

Victoria taught me how to slow dance. At first, I thought she volunteered to teach me because my mom made her, but I soon learned that she had reasons of her own. Let me tell you how these free dance lessons held exclusively at the Victoria Dance Studio came about.

Before I tell you all about this dancing business, I have to put it in the context of Saturday events at the end of my eighth-grade year and the summer that follows. The school year was coming to a fast end.

My grandma had just returned to the farm she and my grandfather had purchased years earlier upon arriving in the Midwest. Their farm was located on the west side of the Missouri River bottom in Nebraska, but she was not alone. My Uncle Pete from Texas came for Grandpa's funeral, and for reasons only known by adults in the family, he planned to stay for a couple of months. He already had a job lined up working on a pipeline that was crossing Nebraska, heading somewhere out west. Staying with my grandmother provided Uncle Pete free housing and, in turn, provided my grandmother assistance and the security the family thought she would need through the evenings and nights, at least in the weeks ahead.

I was recuperating nicely, and Doc Jones seemed to be pleased with my progress; in fact, the doctor prescribed my spending some time every day walking without my crutches. With my mother at my side to catch me if I started to fall, I faithfully began to bear a little weight on my bum foot. When I became too eager and put extra weight on my foot, a sharp pain shot up from my leg and tightly clutched my brain, causing me to yell, "Ouch!" But it wasn't too long before I learned how and when to bear down on my foot and slowly readjust to walking.

Early on this particular Saturday morning as I hobbled down the stairs, still not willing to give up my crutches, I heard my mom talking to someone on the phone. "Why yes, Jean, I would be happy to help chaperone Maribelle's party. No, she doesn't really need to send Teddy an invitation. He will be there."

I will be where? When? Hmmm . . . Maribelle, the girl who sits across from me in almost every junior high class, why is she having a party? All of these thoughts were swarming in my head as I carefully pulled a chair out at the kitchen table and sat down. When my mom hung the phone up, I was ready to fire away with my questions, but I never had time because she started to talk as the phone hit the receiver.

"Teddy, Maribelle is having a graduation dance party, and her mother asked me to help her chaperone, and I said that I would and . . ."

"I heard you say 'yes,' Mom." I interrupted her, dreading what she would be saying next.

". . . and, I told her you would be able to attend." My mom confidently finished her sentence.

"You didn't ask me, Mom," I said matter-of-factly.

"Teddy, there are some things a mother just answers for her children. She doesn't always have to ask them first. It is her right and her responsibility," she informed me.

By now, all I could do was utter, "Oh," because the whole dance thing was settled for me.

Now, are you ready for the rest of the story? Do you want to know why I think I was really invited? It probably was because Maribelle has an older sister that is in Victoria's class. To make it worse, her older sister, Lucy, is Victoria's best friend. My hunch is Lucy and Victoria planned all of this. Lucy probably told her mother to ask my mom to be a chaperone. If my mom said "yes" to the chaperone business and I had to go to the party, Lucy and Victoria could probably hang out at home and call boys or do whatever girls their age do when their parents aren't around.

So now, Victoria has set herself on a dangerous mission. Her goal is to teach me how to slow dance and do wiggles and gyrations that are part of the other kinds of dancing I have seen Victoria do in our living room. I was minding my own business in the living room and reading one of my Roy Roger's books when Victoria came in and declared, "Teddy, if you are going to Maribelle's party, you can't just sit around."

"What else am I going to do? My foot still hurts. Mom says for me to be careful. Very careful." I gazed at my older sister as angelically as I could. Honestly, I had no clue as to what thirteen-year-old guys do at a girl's dance party. As far as I knew, girls dance with each other, and guys just hang around waiting for the sandwiches and chips to arrive on the table by the punch bowl. At least that is what we did at the seventh grade Valentine Dance.

"Teddy, it is a *dance.*" Victoria emphatically added, "You *dance.* And you are going to dance with Maribelle! And you are not going to embarrass me! Do you hear that, Teddy? I am going to teach you how to dance."

"No, you aren't!" I announced defiantly.

"Mom!" Victoria yelled out from the living room to my mother who was busying herself in the kitchen, trying hard to stay neutral.

Not even knowing what the fuss was about, but assuming I was in trouble with my sister, my mom calmly called out, "Teddy . . ."

Great, Mom was already on Victoria's side.

"See Teddy, you are going to be in big trouble with Mom if you don't let me teach you how to dance," Victoria gleefully said.

Before I could counter, Victoria abruptly turned the TV station to *American Bandstand* just in time to see guys on the show walking with their partners out onto the dance floor for a slow dance. Because I didn't see a way out and still was in shock, I let go of my stubbornness and surrendered to Victoria's pull on my arm as she dragged me out to the middle of the living room. Then she put my right arm on her backside just above her waist and, without asking me for permission, she grabbed my dangling left arm and intertwined her fingers through mine, so I had no escape. With the confidence of a junior high choir director, she started to move her feet. I stood perfectly still, yanking her back. Neither Superman nor a bulldozer could have moved me until Victoria once again used her secret weapon.

"Mom, Teddy—" Victoria yelled toward the kitchen.

"Ted-dy, please don't make me come in there. I am very busy right now. Do what your sister tells you to do and, for goodness sake, learn to dance, and try not to make such a fuss about it all. Please."

A fuss? I am not the one making the fuss. The doctor never told me I had to learn how to dance. Victoria's the one making the fuss. What if she steps on my foot and causes me really bad pain, and what if she crushes my foot just as bad as the tractor did? I will probably have to go to the hospital for one hundred days. All of these words were scrambling through my brain but wouldn't exit out of my mouth because Victoria kept interrupting them with her constant yanking on my left arm, trying to get me to move. Fearing she would jerk my arm out of its shoulder socket, which would make me unable to play football next year in high school, or deliberately step on my foot with all of her weight, I relented. Not saying a word, I settled my thoughts down and stepped out with my good leg aiming toward her foot. I really wanted to step on her foot, but unfortunately, she moved at the same time I did. I missed my mark. Without further verbal resistance, I learned to dance. Well, I learned as good as any other eighth-grade guy with two clumsy feet and one of them being bummed on top of it all.

I learned the two-step while listening to Johnny Mathis and Peggy Lee's latest hits. I was also educated by Victoria on the steps and wiggles that were the signature moves of rock and roll claimed by popular teenage idols such as Ricky Nelson, Elvis Presley, and Buddy Holly. I stepped on Victoria's feet three times. Twice because of missteps and once on purpose because she was becoming too bossy, and I wanted to remind her that I wasn't in favor of this dancing business, at least for the moment.

So, in spite of my hurting but healing foot, I was prepared for Maribelle's party to celebrate our graduation from eighth grade—or in my mind, the end of our years of innocence and the setting of our sails toward the uncharted course of high school with only a short respite called summer a week away.

You could also say there was more truth to the uncharted course that went far beyond just starting high school ahead for me. I didn't know it at the moment, but some of my life was to change forever because of what was ahead, and there was very little I could do about it all.

I am not going to bore you with all of the gory details of my first dance experience at a girl's party, but I am going to let you in on how things went between Maribelle and me.

On the evening of the party, I carefully maneuvered my way up our creaky farmhouse stairs without my crutches to my bedroom, where I changed from my couch-bed clothes to my Sunday school wardrobe consisting of what was called a sports jacket my mother found at a second-hand clothing store in the city, brown slacks size Husky, a white shirt and brown tie, black socks and my Sunday school shoes.

I didn't look any different than I always do on Sunday morning but coming into the kitchen, Victoria gave me what sounded like a genuine compliment. "You look very spiffy, Teddy." And then, she smiled. More than telling me how I looked, she was probably giving herself credit for all of her effort and to show Lucy, who came out to spend the night with Victoria, how nice she can sometimes be to me. My mom, who always has a compliment, also said something about how nice I looked, and then, after giving Victoria and Lucy last-minute instructions regarding Cindy and Ruby, she and I were off for town and the dance.

If you had been there, you might have graded the evening a B+. Maribelle wore a light blue dress. She really looked sharp! As for Maribelle and me, this dance thing seemed to go a lot better than I had expected. At first, Maribelle seemed just as awkward as I was. Our mothers made us dance the first dance together. When I accidentally stepped on her toes during the first slow dance, I saw her quickly wince, but the painful look was followed quickly with a smile.

"I'm sorry, Maribelle," I apologized to her, and believing that it was very important that I confess, I continued, "This is my first dance, and you are the only girl I have ever danced with except for my sister, Victoria. She taught me how to dance, so if I don't do it right, we can blame her." I guess part of what I said was an apology and a confession, and the rest was in my defense for being taught by my sister and not one of Arthur Murray's dancers. As an afterthought, I added, "I guess my foot still hurts more than I thought it would."

"That's okay," Maribelle said shyly as she looked up just in time to see me wince a little. She knew she wasn't stepping on my foot, so she asked, "Is your foot hurting a lot, Teddy?"

I didn't want to make a big deal out of it, so I said, "just a little." Trying to hide the embarrassment I felt for Maribelle having seen me wince, I added, "but I don't care. You are easy to dance with Maribelle."

"Thank you, Teddy. Would you like to walk outside and sit on the steps for a bit? My mom said if it gets too warm in here, we can go outside for a little while. I think one of our mothers checks outside now and then to make sure everyone is behaving properly."

I never thought of doing anything else except behaving properly. I didn't want to disappoint my mother, but more importantly, I didn't want to give Maribelle the wrong impression of me. "I think that would be great, but we don't really have to go outside if you don't want to go. I mean, if you are becoming too warm—uh—I really mean . . ." I was muttering and trying to find the right words to say. I didn't want Maribelle to think I couldn't stand a little pain.

Maribelle once again gave me an angelic smile. "Uh, yes, I am a little warm, Teddy. You are very considerate. Not all the guys in our class are as considerate as you are. We can come back in and dance some more after we're both ready." Maribelle's eyes never looked anywhere else but at me as she spoke.

I was just about ready to say, "Okay, let's go," when Maribelle spoke again.

"Teddy, I didn't mean . . . maybe you'd rather dance with some of the other girls. I would under—" The only reason why she stopped talking is that I interrupted her.

"Maribelle, I would just like to dance with you, but if you want . . ." I wanted to throw any doubts away that might indicate I wanted to dance with some other girl, but I also didn't want to hog all of her time. I would if I could, though, because I didn't want to give any other guy a chance to step in and dance with her. *Golly, Maribelle is attractive,* I realized. I guess I never thought about her in such a way until tonight. I think I liked Maribelle more than I thought I would.

"I would like just dancing with you, Teddy." Maribelle gave me another one of her special smiles and quietly took a hold of my hand.

As we slowly made our way to the front entrance, I caught a glimpse from Maribelle's mother. She had nothing but a smile on her face. I was happy, very happy.

You need to know Maribelle and I held hands for the rest of the evening and my hand never became tired. We talked, and we laughed throughout the night. We talked about our older sisters and younger sisters. We wondered together about how high school would be and then we decided, right then and there, we would look out for each other all through high school regardless of what lay ahead of us. After a while, we decided to go back to the dance floor for fear our friends would start talking.

I surprised myself that evening. When we returned to the dance floor, I danced every dance with Maribelle and decided not to wince when I felt the pain in my foot. The last dance was a slow dance, a very slow one. That was a good thing because I was becoming very tired. I never told Maribelle or my mom that I was tired, though. I let go of the foot pain and tiredness and danced.

Before the last dance was over, I felt a strange feeling, something like a shiver, only it wasn't on the outside of my body. It felt like it came from my heart. Now I was the one becoming warm. Again, I didn't tell Maribelle. We just danced.

I was really quiet on our way home and my mom asked, "Did you have a good time tonight, Teddy?"

Looking straight ahead, not wanting to make eye contact with her in fear she might see more in my eyes than she could hear in my voice, I simply replied, "Yeah."

"That's nice," she said. She knew. Somehow, she knew.

The following Friday, school ended for the year. Since we live on a farm, I knew I would see very little of my friends or Maribelle over the summer and even less in days to come, but I am jumping ahead.

Instead of riding the bus on the last day, my mom picked me up at school. I had another doctor appointment, only this time I went to his office. When it was my turn to see Doc Jones, I walked into the exam room carrying my crutches with me. My mom followed behind me. After he looked at the x-ray pictures that were taken earlier, Doc examined my foot and then gave me the verdict. "Teddy, your foot is coming along nicely, but it is not healing as fast as I thought it would."

"Why?" I asked and then wondered if I was to blame for something I did to keep it from healing faster like dancing with Maribelle at the party. I didn't tell Doc Jones about the dancing; I just said, "I did everything you and my mother told me to do and . . ."

Doc Jones must have heard the defensive tone in my voice because, in his bedside manner, he explained. "Remember, you had three crushed bones. That's a little different than breaking a bone. It's not anything that you did wrong. The healing process just takes longer with crushed bone. Don't lose your patience. If you try to be in too much of a hurry, things could become worse. It's very important that you don't carry heavy loads like you would normally do when you chore. Carrying hay bales or five-gallon pails full of feed or water will put too much weight on your foot. Be careful not to make unexpected moves where you will press down on your foot to keep from losing your balance." As he spoke, Doc Jones tapped my bad foot.

"What about the fair and my calf?" I asked cautiously, wondering if I would even be ready to go to the fair and, if so, wanting to be very honest with Doc Jones. "I still need to work with my calf to be ready to show him." My words betrayed the uncertainty I had in not only accepting what Doc was saying but also questioning aloud whether or not I would have Black Iron trained to follow, stand, and not be distracted when we went into the show ring.

"Well . . ." Doc looked up at his calendar hanging on the examination room wall. It seemed to me that he was counting the days until the fair began. I wondered to myself if Doc was just a slow counter or if there was something he didn't really know how to tell me. Finally, he spoke.

"Teddy, the fair is only seven weeks away. You shouldn't work with your calf, especially if you and your father do not believe you have had enough time with him to round out his rough edges. I'll tell you what. My very first 4-H project was a steer. For a lot of reasons, I did not have much time to prepare him or myself for the fair. Not only did I show him poorly, but he broke away from me in the show ring! To be quite honest with you, I didn't even place. I was really embarrassed."

"Wow! Doc that could happen to me—I just started to work with Black Iron when this happened," I pointed to my bum foot and then was silent. There wasn't much more I could say.

My mom spoke up. "Teddy, your father and I have made some arrangements. We'll tell you about them tonight at supper time."

"What about my calf?" I could only imagine the worst. *My parents were probably going to sell Black Iron to one of our neighbors, and I would no longer even have a 4-H project. Maybe they were planning to sell him without even asking me. Or worse still, what if they were going to send him to the locker plant to be butchered?* I was a little relieved when Doc Jones' words interrupted my thoughts. It was like he could read my mind. "Teddy, it sounds to me like your mother may have a solution. Listen to what she has to say before you tie yourself up into a ball of knots. I will see you in about a month unless something happens and you need to come in earlier. Remember, easy on the foot, no heavy loads, and for goodness sake, use your crutches part of the time to give your foot a rest."

"Okay, Doc." I refused to talk on our ride home, and I used my crutches to make my way into the house. I was experiencing a lot of pain, only it wasn't coming from my foot. But crutch-walking seemed to be the easy way to draw sympathy from my mom without betraying that my real pain was on the inside.

All through supper, I refused to talk. I only ate what I had put on my plate the first time so I wouldn't have to ask for anything to be passed to me. I had no second helpings, and I was still really hungry after I cleaned up my plate, but I decided to be really obstinate, just like Victoria is when she wants something and can't have it. I was optimistic Mom and Dad would give in to me because I have never dared to try this tactic before; however, just like Victoria's antics always fell on deaf ears, my behavior didn't seem to have any effect on my parents.

As Victoria cleared the table and my mother poured my dad and her coffee, Dad took a long drawl on his non-filter cigarette while my mother began to speak. "Teddy, your father and I have decided you will go stay with your grandmother so she can have some company during the times your Uncle Pete cannot come home for the night. The pipeline has moved away from Omaha, and he is working twelve-hour days, so the pipeline company has made arrangements for the main crew to stay in a motel closer to their work. Grandma will need your help, and your aunts in Omaha will come out to the farm to check on the two of you when Uncle Pete is not able to come back to Grandma's in the evenings when his work schedule does not permit."

I quickly dismissed most of what my mother said and repeated the question I had asked Doc Jones. "But, what about the fair? What about Black Iron? I need . . ."

After another drawl from his cigarette, my father spoke up this time. "You'll be at your grandmother's about three weeks, Teddy, or maybe even less. It depends on how things go. For right now, you are wanted more at your grandmother's. I will feed Black Iron and halter him and lead him around some. When you return home, you will still have a few days left to prepare for the fair and for you and Black Iron to get reacquainted. The fair doesn't start until August first so you will have some extra time in there just in case not all goes well with your foot. By fair time, if your foot is strong enough for you to be walking on it, you'll be able to show Black Iron."

Listening to my father, I realized he had just spoken more words to me in between draws from his non-filter cigarette than I can ever remember.

The next morning, I awoke thinking that I would probably have to clean out the barn, but then rolling out of bed, the first thing I saw was my crutches. *Oh yes, that's right, I have a bummed foot.* I smile. But then my bummed foot touches the floor. Ouch. I guess I am not quite ready to go completely without my toothpicks. Toothpicks are the slang I use for crutches. I heard Doc on *Gunsmoke* use the word when Miss Kitty had a broken ankle, and she had to use crutches for the whole episode. She must have been cured by the next week because I never saw her use crutches again.

My bum foot still gives me a small shot of pain jogging up my leg. As I slowly dress, I realize that I'm still not ready to clean chicken houses or hog pens, let alone the barn. I don't even have to do evening or summer morning chores. I know this good luck will soon be over. For now, I have to practice walking and ready myself to go to my grandmother's house.

After breakfast, I cautiously make my way down to the barn where my calf Black Iron has his pen.

Leaning my toothpicks up against the wall, I quietly stand by Black Iron's side. Black Iron does not stir as I gently talk to him, telling him how much I have missed coming down to see him and feeding him. Taking everything in slow motion, which is exactly the opposite of what I did before my accident, I start to approach him. "Easy Black Iron. How are you doing, buddy? Did you miss me? Hmmm . . . as long as you were fed and watered, you probably didn't care whether I'm here or not." My voice went from quiet to louder as I talked. My father had already put a halter on Black Iron. I am tempted. The lead rope hung on its nail by the door. I continued talking to Black Iron as I took the rope from the nail and slid it back and forth in my hand. Finally, after having a tussle with my conscience, I pushed what I had promised Doc Jones about not working Black Iron to the back of my mind. I also dismissed what my father said he would do in preparing my calf for the fair. I let all of my thinking about why I should work with Black Iron crowd my reasoning.

Inch by inch, I move forward, telling Black Iron just about everything that has happened since the accident. After I clip the lead rope onto his halter, I give a tug and politely command, "Come on, Black Iron, let's go for a walk around your pen." I command, but he doesn't budge. I tug, but he is still motionless. He stands as solid and firm as a stone wall. I am becoming frustrated. What is supposed to happen is that I give a light tug and say, "Come on Black Iron," and he is supposed to oblige me; instead, he is acting as headstrong as I did when Mom drove me home after we saw Doc Jones or as Ruby behaved when she was two.

Hmmm . . . if a nice tug doesn't work, I'll just try harder, I say to myself as I tug and walk backwards, all the while trying to stare Black Iron down. The second tug progresses to a quick yank.

In a flash, Black Iron lunges forward and, I want to believe, unintentionally, knocks me over as he streaks by. Now he is tugging on me as I'm falling. By instinct, I let go of the rope while pain now shoots aggressively up my leg, screaming all the way to my brain. I feel the tears burning hot on my face, more from embarrassment than the hurt. *With the little time I have spent with Black Iron because of my accident, why should I expect any other behavior from a calf?*

Taming a calf takes time, work, and the right attitude which up until now I haven't had. Plus, neither one of us was ready.

Feeling defeated and disappointed in myself, I retrieved my crutches and took one step at a time back to the house. *I am not telling anyone what happened with Black Iron,* I told myself. *Only he and I will share this secret. We won't tell anyone. Not even Doc Jones. No sir!* My thoughts kept me from feeling the throbbing pain still running up my leg from my foot, and I put on a pretend "all is well" face when I reached the back door.

Chapter 15

To Grandmother's House

My mom took me to my grandmother's house Saturday morning. My dad stayed home, and Mom and I left right after my quick breakfast of the usual corn flakes. Saturday is my grandmother's day of worship. She doesn't work on the Sabbath after sun-up.

Actually, according to her religion, you aren't supposed to work after Friday night sundown, but when you are a farmer, you have to bend the rules a little and milk the cows and do the other chores. While the church bosses probably aren't farmers, somehow even they seem to know cows must be milked. In the summer, you have to be up pretty early to do chores before the sun slips across the Missouri River and shines on the farm. Also, no cows can be milked or other chores done in the evening until after the sun sets in the west on the Sabbath evening.

I guess when we arrived that is why we found Grandma already sitting in her rocker on the porch. She wasn't really taking it easy; instead, she was in "radio church" listening to a radio preacher talking about the end of the world and telling sinners they will be cast into the fires of "you know where" unless they repent. At least that is what the radio preacher says, and if I understand our preacher, he says the same thing though he has never really said where "you know where" is, but I know he is talking about hell.

Neither our preacher nor the radio preacher tells you what happens to you if you are one of the unlucky sinful people and are cast into the fire. I missed my chance of asking him about this when I was in Confirmation last year. Oh, I guess it must be okay for radio preachers and other preachers to say the word "hell." Their mothers probably don't mind if they just use the word in sermons to scare kids like me and their grandmothers. I know I can't use the word even when I am pretending to be a radio preacher.

After I unpacked my suitcase under my mom's supervision, my mom and grandmother talked in Romanian while my mom put together a lunch from the groceries we brought with us for Grandma. Before we ate, my grandma recited a long prayer that I recognized as the same prayer she and Grandpa always said before bedtime or when they heard bad news on the radio or when the radio preacher was talking about the end of the earth. I have come to believe her religion only knows one prayer, and she has it memorized. I thought we were going to eat right after the prayer was done, so I started to reach for the bread, but my mom and grandmother remained with heads bowed. While my arm hovered over the bread, my mom politely said, "Teddy, will you please pray our table grace? Your grandmother wants to hear you pray." If Grandma really wanted me to, how could I refuse? So, I prayed, and then we ate. My grandmother and Mom talked some more in Romanian while they cleaned up the kitchen and put the extra groceries away, so I took my crutches and walked back outside to the porch and dropped into the musty smelly couch.

When my mom and grandma finally came outside and found their way to the porch, they were still talking in Romanian, so I decided to take a walk around the farmyard. I was very careful to give the crotchety old rooster a wide berth when I saw him talking to some chickens. I also stayed clear of Grandma's gander or he would surely chase me as he had done before.

The rest of the afternoon went by very quickly. When my mom was ready to leave, she came out to the porch where I was taking a nap and gently nudged me. After I woke, my mom told me she was leaving as she needed to be home to do some chores and fix supper, and then she gave me some final instructions. "Teddy, behave, and don't cause your grandmother any problems. Uncle Pete is bringing home something for supper, so don't ask for a snack. He will be here about six. I will probably call early Wednesday evening." With those final words, Mom bent down and kissed me on the forehead. I rose from the couch and watched my mom as she drove off. Gazing down the sandy road for a long time, I thought to myself, *Now it is just Grandma, the radio, and me until my Uncle Pete comes.*

I soon came to realize that my Uncle Pete must not have much money. He arrived from Texas in a '48 Ford. He told my mom the Ford broke down two times on his way to Nebraska. It broke down in Oklahoma and then in Kansas. In Kansas, he found a garage where the owner allowed him to work on his own car and gave him the parts free of charge in exchange for a day of mechanical labor. My Uncle Pete was a good mechanic. He just didn't seem to be as good with his money as he was with a wrench.

Just like my mom said, Uncle Pete arrived from work at six o'clock carrying a grocery bag. He and I talked as Grandma took the groceries out of the bag, which contained three steaks, a half-gallon of butter brickle ice cream, a head of lettuce, and salad dressing.

I could tell there was more in the grocery bag, but somehow Uncle Pete seemed reluctant to get the rest of the items out. Grandma looked in the bag, then exclaimed, "Petro!" She said a few Romanian words I have heard her or my mom say when they were really, really mad; I think I know what they mean, but I am not going to say them in English. Then my Uncle Pete and Grandma went back and forth with more Romanian words I had never heard before. From the tone of their animated voices, I reckoned they weren't talking about the weather. Uncle Pete tried to smile as he pulled the beer and cigarettes out of the grocery bag, but try as he might, he just couldn't. *Moms always have the power to make their sons feel guilty regardless of how old they are,* I mused.

Uncle Pete quickly put the cigarettes in his pocket, nodded to Grandma as if they came to an agreement, then took the six-pack out to the cave behind the house where Grandma stored her potatoes and other items she wanted to keep cool. Summer was a good place to also store watermelon and muskmelon before they were put out in the stand for people to buy. Now its new purpose was to be a beer cooler for my Uncle.

At supper time, Grandma said her usual prayer and then, just like Mom did at lunchtime, asked me to pray. I looked up to see my Uncle Pete smiling, so I used my oldie and goodie:

> I thank you for the world so sweet,
> I thank you for the food we eat,
> I thank you, God, for everything.

Before I said, "Amen," I added, "And I thank you for the steaks Uncle Pete brings." Uncle Pete chuckled as he heard my addition to the prayer, and my grandmother gave a big grandmotherly smile as she said, only this time without any stress, "Yoi, Yoi, Yoi."

My grandma knows how to make steak one way. She fries them well done. I didn't complain. To me, steak is steak. Besides, my stomach had more serious things to be ready for, like the butter brickle ice cream Uncle Pete brought with him from the store. Neither my stomach nor my taste buds were disappointed. Right after supper, my grandma brought three bowls from the cupboard and placed them on the table, and then she scooped out the ice cream. She put three big scoops in my bowl. At first, I thought my Uncle Pete would say, "Mama, he is just a young boy. He won't eat that much and besides, leave some for me!"

I was thinking my father would have said something along those lines, but only a little more forceful, like "two scoops are enough for Theodore, Mom, no more."

Cautiously, I looked at my Uncle Pete to hear if he would say what I thought he would. All he said was, "You can have more, Teddy, if you like." I didn't need to ask for more. I was really full after eating all of my steak and three big scoops of my favorite ice cream. I had taken a walk through food heaven.

If I wasn't still partially stuck to my crutches, I would have taken another long walk around; instead, after supper Uncle Pete took Grandpa's place and read from the English Bible for Grandma and I guess for me, as well. I am not sure Grandma understood the English words as well as she would have if he could read from the Romanian Bible, but I guess she understood enough to now and then add a "yoi, yoi, yoi." Hearing Uncle Pete stumble over some of the names that even I can pronounce made me believe that it has been some time since he has read his Bible, which is strange for someone coming from Texas, but I am not going to judge him just because he has problems reading Bible names. Uncle Pete's "read" was a lot shorter than I remember my grandfather's had been. I did a very short walk after our devotion and then plopped myself back in a chair out on the porch with my Uncle Pete while Grandma did the dishes.

When it's summer and you only have kerosene lamps to light your house and the wood stove is used for cooking and baking most of the day and into the evening, your house can be very warm and dim. My grandmother's house was very warm through the summer even though she kept two fans running. Grandma didn't have air conditioning, but we didn't have air conditioning at home either, so I was used to the hot summer air and warm houses. I think my mother would like a window air conditioner for the living room, but my father doesn't say a word when she brings it up to him. His silence must mean a "No" in the language of a marriage. I doubt his silence is because he is losing his hearing. I have never heard any one of my grandmother's children, including my mother, talk to her about having a window air conditioner. I am sure my grandmother would be against it, and she would let her children know she is, but she would tell them in Romanian, not in American. I can only guess that is why we sit on the outside porch until bedtime.

We usually just listen to the radio. Once in a while, a car comes down the sandy road, and my grandmother tells us who is driving if she recognizes the car. Sometimes she tells me Bible stories. Even though I am now older, I still like to hear her tell the stories. They always seem to be a little different than the way our church school lessons tell them. She likes Noah and the Ark, and Jesus and the big catch of fish (and she carefully explains that none of the fish Jesus caught or ever ate were carp). Her best story is about Jesus' death on the cross and His resurrection.

When Grandma runs out of stories, we listen to the radio. Grandma's favorite radio show is the "Hell, fire, and damnation" sermon delivered by a radio preacher who usually asks you to send five, twelve, or one hundred dollars so he can continue to preach over the radio. If you do send money, your name will be written in a book with a golden pen, and when Jesus comes again riding to earth on a cloud, he will hand the book over to Jesus, and you will have a reserved seat on the bus, destination Heaven.

If you were to ask, my grandmother's next favorite radio show is another "Hell, fire, and damnation sermon" that is broadcast live from somewhere in California by another radio preacher, only this one calls himself an Evangelist, and his wife comes on the show with him. If you place your hand on the radio and pray with her, she tells you God will heal you of all of your illnesses. Then she says, "If you pray really hard, the Lord will bless you with the gift of tongues." I tried it once when Grandma and Uncle Pete were in the kitchen getting some lemonade. While Grandma was pouring lemonade for herself and me, Uncle Pete was drinking his "lemonade" out of one of the cans he brought home from the store.

I prayed extra hard. I know I did because my eyes were squeezed shut, and I was holding my breath. Nothing happened. I guess Jesus thought one tongue was enough for my mouth.

After praying for tongues, I was praying that my foot would be completely healed. I know nothing happened because after I had to stop praying in order to breathe, I pressed my foot against the floor. Pain was laughing all the way up my leg while shouting, "Ha, Ha, fooled you, didn't I?" When I go to church at home next time, I will ask our new pastor what he thinks the reason is that God didn't completely heal me at that moment.

I guess the news and weather reports come in third place for my grandmother. Even though my grandfather has died, when Grandma hears about world events and conflicts around the world, she still uses the same critique she gave when Grandpa was living—"Yoi, Yoi, Yoi, domde, domde, domde." Grandpa used to just listen to her and shake his head when she spoke. Now I'm doing the same thing. Uncle Pete just looks at the two of us and takes sips from his "lemonade" can.

When the weather report is over, Grandma bows her head and prays. I know she is praying because it's the same words she always uses when she prays. I bow my head and fold my hands also. I guess because she is his mother, Uncle Pete follows suit, but not until he takes another sip of his "lemonade" and a long drag from his cigarette.

This is how our evenings go after supper unless Grandma has company. Even when Uncle Pete isn't there because of his work, Grandma and I do the same thing. I suppose that is how all of our evenings will go while I am staying at Grandma's.

There isn't much change in my grandma's routine. As my foot becomes stronger, I help her feed the chickens, geese, and the three milk cows. Since my grandfather died, Grandma milks the cows. She is really good and fast. In fact, I think she is just as fast as our milking machines are. I also pick ripe apricots off of the two trees that are on the other side of the road that meanders down to the Missouri River. On the evenings Uncle Pete is here, he helps pick the watermelons and muskmelons while I pick the cucumbers.

For as long as I can remember, my grandparents have had a melon patch. Every summer, they had a fruit and vegetable stand. The stand was across the road just south of the apricot trees. The melon patch was in the middle of the cornfield, reachable by a skinny sandy road cutting the cornfield in half. The skinny sandy road would also take you all the way down to the wooded pasture that ended on the banks of the Missouri River. My grandparents were the only people that I knew who cored their melons for a prospective buyer when the buyer questioned whether the melon was ripe or not. I never saw anyone at a grocery store core a melon. In fact, I never saw anyone do it except for my grandparents.

When you core a melon, a small tringle is cut with the blade going down through the thick skin into the meat of the melon. Next, you poke your blade right into the middle of the triangle and pull upward. If you do it correctly, you will pull out a small piece of melon in the shape of a pyramid. Every time my grandparents cored a melon at the insistence of a customer, a dark red triangle rich in color and juice popped out of the melon. The potential buyer was allowed to eat the sample. There was no second helping before the melon was sold, and the sale was made about ninety-nine percent of the time. Once in a great while, persnickety customers would insist that even the ripest of melons just didn't taste sweet enough and would demand to try another melon. My grandparents always complied with their wishes but would only allow them to try one more, only one! Even when a customer insisted a third melon be cored, my grandparents would stand firm in only offering a second.

Turning to Grandma, Grandpa would have a little Romanian talk with her, all the while wearing a smile. I doubt Grandpa was telling her how nice the customer was. On her part, Grandma would usually say, "Yoi, Yoi, Yoi," and try to show a friendly face. When customers saw that my grandfather was not going to give in, they usually looked disgruntled and pulled out their wallets to pay for the melon. They were probably going to buy the melon all along, but they might have been trying to have Grandpa just give it to them. Paying for the melon, they usually returned to their cars with their purchases and tried to leave in a huff, but before they could pull away, my grandmother would usually walk over to their cars and hand them a free muskmelon through the opened windows. With a smile and in broken English, she would say, "Thank you. This is for you." I have witnessed this interaction several times. People who intend to leave with a cloud of black smoke steaming out of their ears, after recovering from my grandma's act of kindness, and with the voice of humility, would say "Thank you" back to my grandmother and drive off with smiles on their faces. People who have received the free muskmelons after their unruly behavior have become genuine regular customers trekking their way to the stand every summer and on a weekly basis. Some of them have even brought my grandparents gifts. Funny thing, the ones I recognize as having acted so nasty on their first visit seem to never ask my grandparents again to core the melon they choose.

I have been here for two Sabbath days. This Saturday marks my third Sabbath. In the summer, the vegetable and fruit stands open for business even on the Sabbath. Saturday and Sunday are usually my grandparents' busiest days for sales. God must understand that you have to make hay while the sun is shining, only in this case, you have to pick the fruit and vegetables when they are ripe and sell them as soon as you can.

As we were busy with a customer, a man in an almost new station wagon drove up and came out of the car. He was dressed in a suit and was carrying a Bible, so I guessed he wasn't there to buy a melon. I guessed correctly because the guy was my grandparents' minister. He arrived late in the afternoon. He waited patiently by his car until the customer loaded his last melon and took off. My grandmother smiled as she approached her pastor.

"Good afternoon, Anna. I wanted to stop by to see how you are doing," the minister shook hands with my grandmother.

"Let's go sit on the porch." Grandma, the minister, and I walked slowly across the road to the porch, and the minister and I sat down in the rockers. My grandmother looked at me and said, "Teddy, come help me bring out some lemonade."

"Sure, Grandma," I slowly rose from the rocker and walked with her into the house without using my crutches. I am not sure what the minister did while we were gone, but when we arrived back on the porch with Grandma carrying a pitcher of lemonade she made on Friday and me carrying three glasses and a plate of fried Romanian pastries also made on Friday, he already had his Bible opened and resting on the table next to him.

Grandma's minister drank a glass of lemonade and ate one of Grandma's pastries before I had a chance to swallow my first gulp, and Grandma hadn't even taken a drink yet. As soon as the minister's glass was empty, Grandma rose quickly and filled it again. After his second pastry, putting his half-filled glass down on the small table beside him, he smiled at Grandma. "Anna, your rolls are delicious. I will probably have to have another one before I leave. Now, would you and Teddy like me to read something out of the Bible to you?" I doubt my grandmother was going to say "no"—after all, this was her minister. I am not sure how God would look upon you if you said "no" to your minister.

My grandmother gave the minister a nod, and he quickly lifted his Bible and opened it to where he had placed his bookmarker. I guess the minister didn't own a Romanian Bible like my grandparents do, because he read from the King James Bible. The King James has a lot of words I don't really understand, but I am too polite to tell anyone. I know my grandmother has a hard time with some of the language also. The minister started to read to us about a dragon that was chasing people who did not have a mark on their forehead. The dragon had a sword in his mouth he used to cut people up, and then there was that fire again. I believe it is the same fire the radio evangelist and preacher talked about. The part about the fire brought shivers down my spine. It was really hot outside, so I know the shivers weren't because I was cold. I remember well the minister reading, ". . . and the beast grabbed the people and threw them into a lake of fire that never burned out, and people screamed and yelled, "Help!" Then the minister stopped to take a breath and another swallow of lemonade. My grandmother stopped her rocking, rubbed her hands, and cried "Yoi, Yoi, Yoi." This time there wasn't any "Domdi, Domdi, Domdi," and tears came running down her eyes.

There was a surprised look on the minister's face when he saw Grandmother's tears. He quit reading the Bible and sat in silence as my grandmother repeated several times, "Yoi, Yoi, Yoi." The minister must have been taken by surprise when Grandma started to cry. He seemed lost for words so he quit reading. Since the minister has never been to Grandma's house when she was listening to hell, fire, and brimstone sermons over the radio, he would not have known that "yoi,yoi, yoi," and "domdi, domdi, domdi" were quite natural for Grandma to utter whenever she heard sermons from the book of Revelations.

Before Grandma or I realized it, he closed his Bible and, leaving his unfinished lemonade on the orange crate that served as a small table, stood up and, after politely saying "goodbye," walked across the road to his car. The minister either forgot to pray with us or lost his prayer words after reading all of that scary stuff from ole King James. I was going to ask him to pray, but I thought maybe he was afraid he wouldn't be able to say anything that would mean much at the moment. At least he could have read Psalm Twenty-Three. Our pastor at home says that Psalm always brings comfort to people, and that is why he reads it at every funeral.

This was the first time I ever met a minister who either forgot to pray or couldn't. Even though he has only shown up at our house a very few times, our minister always prays before he leaves; however, I have never heard him read anything out of his Bible to us when he comes. Usually, our minister sits at the kitchen table with my mother and drinks coffee with her while they visit. My father never seems to be around when the minister comes to visit. He is probably out in the machine shed working on the tractor.

I enjoyed being with my grandmother and Uncle Pete, but after being here about three weeks, I was ready to go home and see Black Iron. My foot was feeling much stronger, and walking without my crutches seemed to be so good, I almost forgot that I brought them with me. I was just thinking, *I have to go home and work some more with Black Iron so he will be ready for the fair,* when my mother and my aunt and uncle from Bellevue drove up on the other side of the road.

At first, I thought they were watermelon customers. Grandma must have thought the same thing because we both rose from our porch chairs and started for the gate. I was really surprised when I realized it was my mom and aunt and uncle. The three of them met us at the gate, and after hugs and greetings, we all went into the house. I could tell my grandmother was happy to see them as well. Entering the house, Grandma drew water out of the drinking bucket into the kettle using the ladle that hung on the side of the bucket. Putting the kettle on the stove, she put a few pieces of wood in and stoked the coals with a poker. My mom pulled cups from the small cupboard, and my aunt pulled out an unopened jar of Postum from a grocery bag.

In the midst of all this activity, Grandma and her two daughters were having a very animated conversation in Romanian. Not only were they talking, but their hands were moving in all directions with the words coming out of their mouths. *This must be very serious,* I said to myself as I watched them. Every once in a while, I heard my mom say, "Lotsa ma botcha."

When my aunt and grandma went to the bedroom, I could see my grandmother's eyes swell up with tears like they did when the minister was reading to us. I didn't ask my mom if she knew why Grandma was crying because I really didn't have a chance. As soon as my aunt and grandma were out of the room, my mom turned to me and said, "Teddy, go put your things together. You are coming home." That's all she said. She probably thought I would jump right out of my chair, bum foot and all, and go collect my things, but I didn't. I wasn't moving until I understood what was happening.

"Mom, what is going on? I was expecting to return home really soon. I need to work with Black Iron, but why are Aunt Vivian and Uncle Gene here?" My Uncle Gene had not come into the house with the ladies. I believe he was outside taking a smoke and doing a walk around so he would not interfere or be pulled into the conversation.

My mom must have anticipated my wanting more information because she did not hesitate to answer. "Teddy, you are old enough to understand, so I am going to tell you what is happening with Grandma and with us at home. Uncle Pete will be heading to Oklahoma with the Oil Company and pipeline. He will be here shortly to tell us all goodbye. We have decided your grandma cannot live here alone. One of us needs to be with her, and none of us can be here with her, so the next best thing is for her to be near one of us. As you know, your Aunt Vivian and Uncle Gene have a big lot, and Gene has moved a trailer onto their property where Grandma will be living. The farm will be put up for sale. I will explain the rest to you later.

"You are needed at home," she added after a little hesitation. "You will need to learn how to run the milking machines and do the milking. You will also have to learn how to do the chores your father has always done. He and I went to see his doctor at the VA Hospital yesterday. I'm afraid the doctor didn't have very good news for your father. Your dad will have to go to the hospital for some tests and maybe an operation if they can figure it all out after the tests come back from their lab. He leaves for the hospital the day after he takes you to the fair. We have arranged with the Madisens to bring you and Black Iron home after the fair. Mr. Madisen has been kind enough to agree to do the milking so you can stay at the fair." After saying what she did, my mom took a deep breath but didn't say anything further.

Even though I felt a twinge of guilt, I tried my usual style of negotiating. "Mom, I was going to help Grandma with the melons and vegetables. What will happen now? I thought I could stay at least a few days more to help with the melons and vegetables." I was really conflicted. I needed to be ready for the fair, but I also believed I needed to help my grandmother. There was still a lot of my grandmother's melon patch just starting to take off. I was going to explain all of this to my mom, even though she probably already knew because my grandparents have been raising melons ever since they came from the old country. So I tried to justify more of why I should stay, but my mom interrupted me with a strong pronunciation of my legal first name, "T-H-E-O-D-O-R-E, your job right now is to collect your stuff. I will tell you more later this evening. Right now, Aunt Vivian and I must help your grandmother."

I knew all the changes that were coming and those that had already taken place had to be very hard on my grandmother, Aunt Vivian, and my mother. I knew the death of my grandfather was very hard on Grandma, and now she was moving away from the only place she had lived since my grandfather and she came from the old country.

Without a doubt, I also knew her faith had helped her. I had seen a glimpse of that in the past, but lately, during the past few weeks I have stayed with her, I have clearly seen how strong her faith actually is. With unwavering trust, she continues to pray, listens to her radio preachers, and lives a life of unselfish generosity through the small acts of kindness she shows to her melon and vegetables customers and her friends. More than all of these, I have seen her let go of fear, worry, and the pain of grief by believing God walks with her. My grandmother has let go of much but holds onto what really matters most. I wonder if I will be able to do the same in the days ahead.

Chapter 16

Family Ties

Since my Aunt Vivian is the oldest of my mom's siblings, I thought she would be making most of the decisions about the future for my Grandmother, and my mom would go along with whatever she said. Boy, was I wrong! The last time my Uncle Gene and Aunt Vivian came to my grandmother's, he revealed to me that Aunt Vivian told him once, "Elaine has always been the obedient and dutiful daughter. All Mama has to do is call her, and she will be there. That is why I look to her when it comes to helping Mama make decisions."

I didn't think Uncle Gene had more to say when he told me all of this, but before I could ask any questions he continued, "Why heck, she even asked your mom if she thought it would be a good thing for us to put a trailer on our lot and have Grandma live there. I am not certain your father knows this, Teddy, but I am telling you so you understand how much we have depended on your mom; she gave Vivian some money to help buy the trailer. I don't know where or how your mom got the money, but she did. We would have had to go to the bank to borrow some if she hadn't given it to us. None of her other siblings would have done such a thing. Don't you be going and telling your father or mother I told you all this. Understand?"

Golly, Uncle Gene told me a lot of stuff. Some time will pass before I really understand it all, but I knew exactly what he wanted from me in the present, so I answered, "No, Uncle Gene, I won't tell a soul, not even Victoria."

"I suspect she already knows," Uncle Gene offered.

When I started to think about my mom being the dutiful and obedient daughter, I began to realize what Uncle Gene was saying. My mom always was the one who took Grandma and Grandpa to their doctor appointments and to the bank. Her name was on their accounts, and I later found out that she was the executor of their estate, whatever that really meant. She also had Power of Attorney (someday, I will ask her what that means too). Even though my mom's brothers and sisters, all except for Uncle Pete, lived a lot closer to my grandparents, she was the one they depended on to take care of their parents. Now she had the responsibility of my father, and that would have more consequences than ever before. She was walking into the unknown with my father and all of his health issues. I wonder if it was possible for my mom to hold all of this responsibility and still take the necessary actions. I wonder what she will have to let go of when her brain is too full to take on more. I wonder what decisions, if any, she will pass on to someone else. I wonder.

When I gave my brain a respite, it traveled to another place. I often reflect on attending my cousin Patti's and her boyfriend Matt's wedding. I do this for a lot of reasons. Sometimes, I do it just to give my brain the rest I told you about. Patti looked beautiful in her wedding gown. At one point in the service, the minister told Patti and Matt to turn toward each other and take hold of each other's hands. Then she told Patti's soon-to-be husband, "Repeat after me." Matt did. At just about the end of repeating everything, she told him to say to Patti, "Until death do us part." He did exactly as she told him. Then, Patti took hold of his hand and repeated the very same thing to him.

I wondered then, and now in this moment even more seriously, how many people who married each other really did care and truly did love each other. I wonder if they truly knew what might be asked of them when they said, "until death do us part," would they actually say, "I do?" I just turned fourteen. I suspect most people wouldn't believe a fourteen-year-old would have these worries, thoughts, or wonders, but I do. People who know me would probably be surprised to know I can travel so deep in my brain. Maybe some people who have seen my poetry might believe I can, but not many others would.

Our family's model and example for caring has been and is our mother. I have seen her care so deeply, sacrifice so much, and work so hard to make sure her parents were provided for in the elder years of their lives. I have been and am the recipient, as my sisters have been and are, of our mother's care, devotion, and guidance. I see her picking up the pieces of the family's brokenness and putting things back together. When Victoria or I have had a falling out with our father, or we have been punished by my dad in a way that my mother thought was harsher than necessary, my mother has been the peacemaker. I think she always will be. Circumstances can change in a person's life, but I believe our personalities don't change very much unless, of course, something traumatic or drastic happens. But even then, people will eventually be drawn back to their core values, basic beliefs, and behaviors.

Of course, I don't know anything for sure. I might be fourteen now, but that doesn't mean I have all of life figured out, nor do I fully or maybe even partially understand my behavior sometimes. I am only saying all of this now because dramatic changes are in store for our family in the very near future that will shake all of our faiths, feelings, the way we think, and our behavior. How we come through it all is yet to be told.

My mom and I made small talk about being with my grandma and Uncle Pete. I told her about the steaks Uncle Pete brought home for supper sometimes and the ice cream we had. I even admitted that my grandma gave me extra scoops with Uncle Pete's approval. My mom didn't say much but just sighed or smiled every so often as I told my stories. Actually, she did frown a little when I told her about the ice cream.

As we turned onto the gravel road, I ran out of words to tell her, but she reflectively said, "Your Uncle Pete and I were very close playmates. We watched out for each other in our younger years when Grandma sent us outside to play, and at school, we made sure other kids weren't picking on each other. He was my defender, and I snitched and told him which girls thought he was handsome. He was a really good football player, and while Grandma and Grandpa never went to his games, he was allowed to play football and basketball but had to work at home during the spring and summer. Grandpa made all of the boys do chores in the evening. Pete had to do his chores even on nights he had football games."

"Why didn't Grandma and Grandpa go to Uncle Pete's games, Mom? Didn't they want to see him play?" I could not imagine my grandparents not supporting their children.

"They encouraged him and smiled a lot when one of us read newspaper articles about how Uncle Pete was often the star of a game. I think they didn't go because they just didn't understand the game. I remember how hard it was to put into Romanian the words they didn't understand when it came to describing sports and games like football." With her last comment, my mother also ran out of words, and her silence made me begin a new line of questioning in my head. *I wonder what happened after Mom and Uncle Pete graduated from school?* I was relieved to see that we were turning into our farmyard or I am quite certain I would have wondered out loud and asked my mother about their years after high school. Since my mom knows me pretty well, I am sure she was also happy that we were home.

I really didn't need to be told to go change into my chore clothes. Even though I had to still be careful about my foot, I knew it was time I had to pick up my responsibilities where they left off before the accident.

After carrying in the groceries and making a quick change, I made my way to the barn where my father was waiting for me.

"Hi, Dad." My words scurried sideways in front of me as I closed the barn door behind me.

"Teddy, go fill the grain bucket like you always do and then put three coffee cans full of ground corn down in front of each station." My father's instructions were his "welcome home, Teddy" greeting.

After picking up the grain bucket from where we always leave it inside the separating room door, I quickly walked to the other side of the barn where the granary was and filled my bucket with ground corn. Returning to the stanchions, I scooped out the usual portion of grain in front of each one, and then I went out to the pasture to bring the cows home.

Since I was starting chores later than usual, the cows were already walking up the path that led to the barnyard. As always, they walked in a single file with Patsy in the lead. The old Angus bull was the only one not in line; instead, he was walking alongside of Goldie, our only Guernsey. Most likely, Fred, the name I gave to the old cuss, was sweet-talking Goldie trying to weasel a date with her after milking. On Goldie's part, she just kept walking along, swishing her tail and looking straight ahead at Freckle's tail. She could have been whispering to the old cuss, "Fred, I am not really interested in you or your one night stands, buster. Go pester someone else."

Fred didn't seem to take "no" for an answer. He just plodded along beside Goldie, mumbling, "Yeah, I hear you, but one of these days, you will see me as your prince charming. Just wait and see." At least, that is what I imagined was happening between them.

I am almost certain that I told you our barn holds five stanchions, and we have thirteen milk cows. My father rarely milks all thirteen cows in a milking because the cows don't all have their babies at the same time. It would really mess things up if they did! Usually, we stop milking a cow about two weeks before they have a baby. Right now, we are milking twelve cows; the thirteenth cow, Rosie, will be having a baby any day now. Even though she isn't ready to deliver, she still comes into the barn and gets locked into her stanchion. I guess mother has to eat just like the rest of the family.

Of course, you wouldn't want a cow to forget how to come into the barn, straddle into her parking space, and stand patiently while she is being milked or just munching on her share of the evening grain. You could put names on each stanchion according to who will be the first to be milked, second, and so on, but that won't help because cows can't read English; however, they automatically park in the same place every morning and every evening, much like humans always sit at the same spot around the kitchen table when it's feeding time. Heaven forbid if you should sit in Farmer Jones' or Banker Gregory's favorite booths at the roadside diner. I once saw a man actually stand in front of "his" booth at the diner and stare until the couple occupying the booth must have felt so uncomfortable they moved to another booth, and the man sat down without even a smile or a "thank you." You know what? The same thing happens at our country church even if you are a "now and then" attender like my father. He always expects the seventh row on the right side coming into the church to be available for him.

Now back to the cows. Once I had all of the cows locked into their stanchions, I stood patiently waiting for my father's instructions.

"You might as well start from the beginning," he said. Pausing only to throw his smoked down-to-the-filter cigarette into a puddle of cow manure, he began my cow milking education. "You take the rag from the water pail and wipe off Clara's teats. Then you come back and take the milking machine up to her. Always walk on the right side of a cow."

While listening carefully, I wanted to say aloud, *Why wipe off her teats? They look clean to me.* What I wanted to say and actually did say were two different things. "Okay," was all I said. Without waiting for further instructions, I naturally proceeded to do what I saw my father do many times. I pulled the suctions cups up underneath Clara's milk bag, or more properly, her udder, and put a cup on each of her teats. Seconds later, I saw milk running through a clear plastic tube from her udder into the milk pail.

"Now take the other machine and put it on Spotty," said my father while watching me scoot up toward the next cow.

As much as I felt disappointed, I understood why my father didn't say, "Good job, Teddy" or "You already know how to do this." Giving compliments to me or to anyone else is something my father rarely does. When it comes to our relationship, I think my father reasons, "You don't compliment a person for something they are supposed to be doing or should know how to do anyway." Regardless, whether I know how to use the milking machine or not, I am quite certain my father believes I should know how. After all, I have watched him do it many times and think my father believes I was paying attention. Maybe I was, and maybe I wasn't.

When I gave this milking machine business a second "think," I guess I did know how to do it.

As the machines "swish, swish, swished" away in a rhythmic fashion, my father and I stood facing the cows alone, deep in our own thoughts. What a wonderful time it would have been had we had some conversation going on between us, but neither of us spoke a word. It was my father who finally broke the silence. "You know when the cow is finished giving milk in two ways." My father walked over to Clara and bent over. "First feel her bag. When the milking started, her bag was puffed outward and very firm. Now, her bag is soft and wrinkled. Also, if you are watching the plastic tube, very little milk is flowing through it into the pail. But the most important sign is how her bag feels. Come up here and feel her bag and then look at the tube. Tell me if she is done or not."

Without saying a word, I moved closer to Clara and felt her bag. I had never felt a cow's milk bag before. It seemed like I was invading her personal space. *Maybe I should be asking her if she minds if I am so close and personal,* I mumbled to myself, but in a split second, I reasoned, *Boy are you dumb. Cows don't share the same kind of privacy issues as humans do. Cows are in the business of giving milk, and humans are in the business of receiving milk.* When I stepped back, I said, "I don't think she is quite done yet, Dad."

"You are right." And then he said nothing more for the moment.

I guess that was okay because it gave me time to have a second think about this privacy business. *If cows don't have a personal space and try to protect it, why do they kick or move abruptly when I forget to talk to them or move up to them slowly like my father does?*

My father interrupted my "thinks' a minute or two later when he asked, "What about milk flowing through the tube now? Can you see any?"

"Oh yeah, I need to look," I turned from staring out into space to focusing back on the milker. "I don't see much milk flowing now, and it looks like the milk is moving much slower,"

"I think you are right. You can pull the tubes off, and you know how to do the rest."

He was correct. I have seen his actions before when he pulled the milker away from the cow. I followed the same routine I have seen him do. I pulled the suction cups off and hung them on the hook on the side of the machine. Next, I carefully walked away from the cow, unlocked the top of the machine, and waited for the air to seep around the lid's edges, making it loose enough for me to lift it off of the pail. Finally, I poured the milk into the cream can that we used to store the milk until all of the milking was done and we were ready to separate. All of the time, I was conscious of my father's eyes following my every move. I am quite sure if I had made a mistake, he would have taken his dangling cigarette out of his mouth and corrected me. Fortunately, I did everything correctly. The next step of instructions pained my ears, and I began to feel fear rippling from my brain down to my toes.

"Okay, Teddy, now put the kickers on Freckles. She is next." My father knew I was more than apprehensive about approaching Freckles' backside for any reason.

I lifted the kickers from their hook on the wall. Kickers in one hand and milking machine in the other, I talked to Freckles as I carefully pushed her over so I could have enough room between her and Brownie. I plugged the milker in and then scooched down beside Freckles as far as I dared. While leaning into Freckles, I reached around her legs with the kickers.

As soon as Freckles felt the first iron cuff touch her leg, she jerked back and, in a flash, kicked me. It wasn't a hard kick, but it carried enough force to cause me to fall to the barn floor. I fell backwards onto my rump with my hands behind me. Having heard my thump, Freckles did what I imagined was a victory dance as she swayed this way and that way before she settled down. I quickly moved out of the way before she stepped on me. While the milking machine stayed upright, the suction cups were spread out on the floor under Freckle's milk bag, and the kickers landed in some yuck. Regaining my composure, I realized only my pride was hurt. I picked up the suction cups and unplugged the machine. Moving out of harm's way, I reached over and picked up the kickers, holding them at arm's length.

My father watched the whole show from a short distance away. He waited until I had cleared everything out of reach of Freckle's limber back legs, and then, taking a long draw from the cigarette dangling from his mouth, he spoke. His words were coated with smoke as he exhaled. "You have to move in closer. You can't put kickers on a cow standing back as far as you were. And if you are up against Freckles and she kicks you, you won't be falling over. Go out to the pump and clean the kickers off. I will wipe out the suction cups."

Still holding the kickers at arm's length, I went out the barn door and headed toward the pump. On my way, I mumbled to myself. *Yeah, I bet I won't get hurt.* Like I said, the kick didn't hurt anything but my pride, and I was too mad to cry. I know I let my father down, and I also disappointed myself.

A few minutes later, when I arrived back in the barn, my father handed me the milking machine and said, "Here, try again." For some reason, his words sounded a little softer to me.

I think he was in a little shock when he heard me say, "No." I responded without even considering the possible consequences.

"What?" my father seemed to be caught off guard. I do not think he has ever heard me speak so defiantly.

"No," I said again, but this time added, "I don't want to be kicked again. Freckles knows I am afraid of her. She knows I am a coward. I don't care. I don't want to have anything to do with her."

My father took another very long drag from his cigarette. I could tell he wasn't going to let my pitiful defiance win the day, but I was surprised to hear what he had to say.

"Teddy, your imagination is playing tricks on you. Freckles or any other cow, for that matter, is not 'out to get you' when they kick. When we milk, we are in their personal space. When someone is behind them and they instinctually feel threatened, they kick until they are more used to what you are doing. Some cows like Freckles are more unpredictable. She even kicked me once."

"What? You mean she actually kicked you?" My voice went up a notch or two. I never thought my father would actually tell me he had been kicked by a cow.

"Yes, but only once."

Hmmm . . . She probably received a licking from you on her hind end, I thought. "What did you do?" I asked.

"Never mind." It might have been my imagination again, but I thought I saw a faint smile cross his face. "I'll tell you what, tonight go ahead and milk the last two cows and then come back to Freckles. By then, she will have settled down. I am going up to the house to check on some things. I will check on you later."

As my father left, I reflected on everything. *He is giving me responsibility to face my own fears.* I knew that most of my fears were born in my imagination, but with Freckles, I wasn't imagining. She was a force to be reckoned with.

I milked the other two cows without any incident and then approached Freckles once again. She instantly pulled back, trying to free her head from the stanchion when she felt my hand on her rump. Though my legs were betraying my anxiety, I held my hand steady as I leaned into her. I talked to her constantly as I moved the left cuff in place on her leg and then repeated the motion on her right leg. Sighing a breath of relief, I wiped off her teats and put on the milking cups. Without any words of thanks to Freckles, I stood up and took my place behind the cows while the two milking machines swish, swish, swished away. About the same time, my father came back into the barn. He took a quick glance at Freckles, and for a second, I thought I saw another smile on his face, but he didn't say anything. *I guess I only did what was expected of me, so why would there be any praise, compliment, or inquiry on how I was able to accomplish the task?* I felt my inflated pride quickly deflate again.

In a short while after the Freckle's ordeal, the cows were milked, let out into the barnyard, and the milk was separated. A pint jar was filled with cream Mom wanted for baking, and the rest of the cream went into the cream can. While my father finished separating, I threw hay down from the hay mound for the cows and the bull. By the time I climbed down from the mound, my father had already gone up to the house, so I turned off the barn lights and headed in the same direction. Since it was mid-July, there was plenty of sunshine left to follow me.

After supper, my father poured himself another cup of coffee and lit another cigarette, but before he started to read the paper, he looked at me and said, "Teddy, you have three days until the fair starts. You and I will load your calf into the pick-up Wednesday morning after chores are done, and I will take you and your calf to the fair. Mr. Madisen will bring you home like we told you." My father didn't say anything else. He didn't say that I would be doing all of the milking until the fair. He didn't ask me how my foot was doing or if my foot was hurt when Freckles kicked me. He didn't ask me if I thought Black Iron needed more work before the fair started. He didn't say anything else. I wish he had said more, but he didn't. He took another long drag from his cigarette, flicked the ashes off onto his plate, and after he put his cigarette on the plate, he just started to read the paper again.

I didn't leave the table. I just sat there waiting to see if the paper would come down, and he would talk to me some more like he did when we were in the barn. I didn't have a paper to read so I just stared down at my plate, counting the indentations that were around the edges. By now, my mother had come back into the kitchen, poured herself a cup of coffee, and sat at the table. After taking a sip of coffee, she broke the silence. "Teddy, you can wear the new western shirt your father and I bought you for your birthday when you go to the fair Wednesday. I also picked up your 4-H club tee-shirt I ordered for you. You are supposed to wear it on Thursday when you show Black Iron, so don't wear it ahead of time. Your father and I talked things over. After chores are done on Thursday morning, he is going back to the hospital. He was supposed to go earlier, but he delayed so you could be at the fair."

"I won't be there when you show Black Iron, Teddy," my father said, "but I know you will be all right and things will go okay for you. Just be sure you take care of your foot." My father stared out over my head at the kitchen cupboards, and then he added, "I'll take you to the fair and help you register and settle in. Your mother and I talked to Mr. Madisen, and he agreed to bring you home Thursday after you are done in the ring. It will be late when you come home, but you will still have to do the milking and other chores."

Listening carefully to my father, I know he repeated some of his instructions about how the next few days would play out, but I never said anything. I am not really sure how words coated with regret, compassion, or uncertainty are supposed to sound, but if I had to guess, I think my father expressed all of those emotions in the words he spoke even though his eyes never looked straight at me. It was strange to hear him speak that way. I felt happy and sad at the same time. I wish he had been talking to me and not the kitchen cupboards.

"You are a young man now, Teddy. We are giving you a big responsibility," my mom added.

"You are the one who will have to make sure all the chores are done while I am gone. You know that, don't you?" my dad asked.

Whether I was ready or not, I was given responsibility right there and then, and there wasn't any room for compromise, so I simply answered, "Yes, I guess I understand but are you sure you can wait, Dad? Don't you think you need to go to the hospital earlier?"

Neither my mother nor father gave me an answer. I felt like I was at a potluck only instead of food; my brain was dishing out a variety of emotions without my permission. I was experiencing sadness, anxiety, excitement, fear, and a deep pain extruding from my soul. Make no mistake, I did not choose any of this. I wish I could have loaded these emotions in a doggie bag and lay them away somewhere until I was ready to accept them, possibly when I was more mature than I was at the time. I also wish I could have had a voice in the conversation from the start. I wish my father could have been at the fair with me, helped me prepare Black Iron for showing, and watched me show him. I wish—but I guess my mother and fathers' conversation was an adult discussion like the ones they usually have after supper with their coffee and my father's cigarettes. Those conversations don't include me or my sisters. And for all of the wishing I did and do, I know wishing never makes what you want come true.

I am sure you know the last thing I wanted to do was milk cows, but whether I like it or not, that's what I will be doing. I will have to milk all of the cows except the ones that are dried up. I am even going to have to milk Freckles. I am not sure I am ready for the job. I am just not sure.

Chapter 17

The 4-H Fair

I was up bright and early Wednesday morning, five-thirty a.m. to be exact; of course, I had to do the milking by myself. My father thought it best that I milk by myself once before he went to the hospital. I didn't know it, but Mr. Madisen volunteered to milk for us while I was gone. I surprised myself when I was able to put the kickers on Freckles without any mishaps (or maybe Freckles was just in a good mood that morning, and she decided not to mess with me). I didn't mind having to be up so early today; after all, I was going to the fair and, not only was I going, I was actually taking a live 4-H animal. My project wasn't a rabbit or a sheep. I was taking a bull, Black Iron!

When I finished my chores, I washed up and put on my new western shirt and clean blue jeans. Next, I collected the bucket of gear I needed for grooming and cleaning Black Iron. I loaded the gear, my sleeping bag, feed for Black Iron, and my small, well-organized suitcase into the back of the pick-up, leaving space for Black Iron. By eight a.m., my father, Black Iron, and I were off to the fair. We only live about twenty-five miles from the fairgrounds, but over half of those miles are on a gravel road. You have to drive slower than the speed limit when you are in a pickup carrying a 4-H calf in the back. You don't want to have an accident.

As usual, neither my father nor I spoke very much on the way. Even though I was only staying overnight, I was really fired up, and I could hardly contain myself. The only thought that brought me down to reality was the cloud of mystery surrounding my father's trip to the hospital. I was wondering, *Why is he going? He doesn't look sick. Does he have something really bad? How long will he be gone? Will we go see him? Will Freckles behave?* I had a lot of unanswered questions, of course. *Is this the way it is in all families . . . don't kids deserve to know some things? I am fourteen now.*

Thinking about being fourteen and living, or rather growing up, on a farm stirred up some wonderings I have had before. *A lot of guys in my class have several cows or pigs. They drive tractors and help with the planting and harvesting. They tell me their fathers teach them real farming skills and they actually have conversations with their dads about farming, politics, religion, all kinds of stuff. All I ever seem to do is grunt work. I am told I am too short to drive our tractors. I have tried to hang out with my father when he is working on the tractor or other machinery, but all I do is stand around. He doesn't tell me what he is fixing or why. He doesn't have me help. I just go and try to find this or that whenever he tells me to. Oh yes, now I milk cows, but my father and I don't really share that adventure either. I am doing it out of necessity and have been told that now I have to be responsible.*

That's enough, I hear my brain say. *Ask a question or look out the window and watch the corn grow, but get out of this rambling business; you are giving me a brain-ache.*

I decide to give up on asking more questions and decide I've lost interest anyway in this whole farming business as a someday career.

Okay, I give up, I tell myself. But the next thing I know, my mouth is moving. "Dad, why are you going to the hospital? No one has really told me anything, and I think if I am old enough to milk cows, I am old enough to know what is going on." *There, I said it.*

My father shifted gears on the pickup and came to a stop right on the road, although it took me a few seconds to realize it wasn't because he had something really important to tell me and wanted to look me in the eye. When I looked up from the floorboard, I saw we had come to a stop sign. The highway was dividing our path. After looking both ways, we crossed over the highway and continued to drive on gravel. I guess I didn't really expect my father to answer my question, so I was really taken off guard when he started to talk.

"I am going to have some tests. The doctor at the VA said it will probably take several days. There are some concerns about the preliminary blood work that Doc Jones has done. The doctor at the VA wants me to have more tests. That's all I know. Victoria doesn't know, but I suspect your mother will probably tell her sometime this weekend." When my father finished, he once again slowed the pickup down for another stop sign. After more of a coasting than an actual stop, we came up on the highway that went into Brookfield, where the fairgrounds were located.

"Thanks for telling me, Dad." I wish we could have talked more about his hospital visit and milking the cows. I was left wondering, *What am I supposed to do if I can't put the kickers on Freckles?* But my wonderings came to a quick stop as I realized we had already driven through the fair's front entrance gate and were at the barn's unloading dock. I hopped out of the pickup to guide my father as he backed up to the chute. My dad hit the loading chute squarely with the pickup ready for unloading. My dad is very good at backing up. He can back up two hay wagons hooked together into the shed on the first try.

I imagine Black Iron was just as nervous coming down the chute and into the alley as I was leading him. Several times he gave a little jerk on my lead rope as he tried to have his way with me. One of those times, the jerk really threw me, and I landed on my bum foot. I felt a hurt I haven't felt for some time. I didn't want to yell "ouch" while I was in hearing range of my father, though, or he might just take Black Iron and me back home.

Black Iron settled down when my father moved up on the other side of him, and in no time, we had him locked into his pen. Our 4-H club name, River Rovers, was up on the post, but none of my friends seemed to be around at the time. After my father and I found the county extension guy, we gave him my name, Black Iron's name, and the name of the club. When we came back to the barn, I picked up my stuff from the back of the pickup and walked up to my dad's window. "Thanks, Dad. I hope everything goes okay at the hospital. Black Iron and I will be okay, and I will behave."

"Goodbye, Teddy." My father turned the engine over and pulled the clutch.

I watched as he drove away. When he turned toward the fair gate, I went back to the pen and, after giving Black Iron a brushing down, hung my bucket on a hook and sat down on a hay bale. Other than staying at my grandmother's house and going to church camp, coming to the fair is the only time I was away from home by myself. Well, I guess I really can't say "by myself" because Black Iron was here. I sat on the hay bale for about a half-hour before I heard a familiar voice.

"Hello, Teddy. Is everything all right?"

The voice sounded very familiar. I turned around, and there was Mr. Madisen standing behind me. "Hi, Mr. Madisen. Sure, everything's okay, I guess. My father just left, and no one else seems to be around, so I'm just sitting here watching Black Iron. It sure is good to see you."

"Hmmm . . . maybe some of your club members are up at the carnival or in the demonstration hall," Mr. Madisen suggested. "I just brought a couple of mares and their colts to be judged tomorrow. Jack will bring Rocky, our stud, early this afternoon. Mrs. Madisen and Joyce, our daughter, will be coming to decorate the mares before their class is judged. I just wanted to come by and make sure you arrived here okay. I'm sorry to have missed your dad."

"Thanks." All the while I was thinking, *I have aunts and uncles that live right here in town or on a farm nearby, and none of them have come by to see if I made it okay to the fair.*

"I'm going over to the café to have a cup of coffee," Mr. Madisen said. "Why don't you come along? I'll buy you a pop. We might even have a piece of pie, that is, if you think Black Iron can take care of things here for a while?"

"Pie and pop! Wow! I'd like that. I'll be back soon, Black Iron," I called and jumped up from my hay bale. And just like that, Mr. Madisen and I were off for the sale barn café. Oh, I never told you, the sale barn sits right on the fairgrounds. During the fair, the café gives all of the 4-H kids and exhibitors a discount.

In a few minutes, we were at the café sitting down. It didn't take long before the waitress came over and asked me, "What do you want, son?"

"Well," I turned to Mr. Madisen to see if he was going to interrupt me. He didn't say a word, so I continued, I'll have a seven-up and a piece of blueberry pie."

"Good choice, Teddy," Mr. Madisen smiled at our waitress. "I'll have the same thing, Sally Anne, only I want a coffee, and you will need to put a big scoop of ice cream on top of our pie."

"Will this be on the same bill?" Sally Anne asked.

"Of course," replied Mr. Madisen and then added, "You can give the bill to Teddy."

Sally Anne spoke faster than my worried thoughts could be turned into words. "In your dreams, Charlie." Then she smiled at me. "Don't let him tease you, son. He's buying. I know this fella, young man. It's good for him to shake loose some of those bills he carries in that tight wallet of his." And then, with a wink in my direction, Sally Anne walked away to put in our order.

After my third bite of pie and ice cream, I volunteered, "This is good pie. Thank you again, Mr. Madisen. When I am done showing Black Iron, I'll come over and help you with your mares and colts if you let me." I know I sounded a little pathetic, as if I was trying to push an invitation by volunteering, but helping with horses has always been a dream of mine, and besides, I would be free labor.

"Funny you should volunteer. I was going to ask you if you wouldn't mind helping when you are free. Jack has hay down, and he needs to bale it before the rain comes this afternoon, and Frank, our hired help, has to be gone this week on family business," Mr. Madisen said.

I was thrilled to hear that he was going to ask me to help. *Maybe I should have waited to let him ask me?* It didn't matter, I guess. I just wanted to make sure he knew that I would really like to help him with the horses if he asked me.

After I refused the second piece of pie Sally Anne brought over and slowly passed in front of me, Mr. Madisen paid the bill and walked me back to the 4-H barn where two of my club members, Jeff Kearns and Joe Graham, were sitting on the hay bale that I had occupied earlier.

"Hey, Teddy, we've been wondering where you were." Jeff chewed on a piece of straw.

"Hi, guys!" Happy to see them, I pointed to Mr. Madisen. "This is our neighbor, Mr. Madisen. Remember I told you Mr. Madisen raises and shows Belgian horses? He even works the horses on his ranch!"

With my introduction, Jeff and Joe stood and held out their hands. Mr. Madisen smiled as he shook them. "I'm happy to meet the two of you. Good luck when you show your calves. I know you will do well." And turning back to me, he said, "I'll check on you later, Teddy," and then was off to look after his horses.

After Mr. Madisen left, Joe asked, "Is your dad here, Teddy?"

I wasn't sure how much or exactly what I should tell them, but they were good friends of mine even outside of 4-H meetings, so I just laid out the facts. “My father was here earlier. He will be going to the hospital for a couple of days to have some tests done. Mr. Madisen told my father that he would check on me and help me if needed. He is going to take me home tomorrow after all of the livestock is judged.” My answer seemed to satisfy the two of them, and I was relieved they didn’t ask for more information, mostly because I didn’t know exactly what else I could say.

Jeff carried our conversation forward in a different direction. "Hey Teddy, I just noticed you aren’t using your crutches. Where are they?”

“They’re with my gear. Doc Jones told me I could try going without them unless my foot started to hurt.”

“Why don’t we give our calves a walk around the show ring to see if they’re going to act up?” Jeff suggested. Joe and I agreed that a walk around would be a good thing to do. In no time, the three of us were walking our calves around the arena. Only once did Black Iron give a sudden jerk on my lead rope and try to break away. There was a twinge of pain in my foot when he jerked, but I was able to hold my ground. I guess hay bailing and cleaning manure out of the hog house and barn had strengthened my muscles more than I thought.

The rest of the day went by rather quickly. I was pleased with the way Black Iron adjusted to the fair noise, people, and the show ring, which was a large circle located in a building about a city block away from the 4-H barn. It would be an easy walk.

Like my friends Jeff and Joe, I was up bright and early Thursday morning. The three of us washed our calves, and after they dried off, we gave them a good brushing. I was just putting Black Iron back in his pen when Mr. Anderson, our club leader, came looking for me. “Hi Teddy, I came by to tell you, you and Black Iron are in the second-year class for Angus bulls.”

“Uh . . . okay, but you know Black Iron has only been two for one month and . . .” I stopped because I wasn’t quite sure what difference it made what class he was in. No one ever told me there were different classes, so I guess I was just caught a little off guard.

I'm sure Mr. Anderson could see the look of concern on my face. "Oh, Teddy, Black Iron will be okay. He'll do fine in the second-year class. The classes are divided up based upon the calves' birth years. Everything will be okay; of course, he does look like he could have had a little more weight on him." Mr. Anderson's words were followed by an immediate look of regret.

"You mean he is too scrawny?"

"No, I didn't mean that, Teddy, I'm—"

I interrupted Mr. Anderson. "You're right; he is a little boney. We didn't always have enough grain, and my father said we couldn't afford any feed supplements you told us about at our meetings. I even went out and cut pasture grass to feed him to supplement the hay." It sounded to me like I was apologizing for the lack of a heftier frame on Black Iron. I really didn't know what else to say, so I was quiet after that.

"Err, Teddy, I don't really think Black Iron is boney. He is just a little leaner than most calves in his age group. Some judges like that. Some don't. I just don't want you to be disappointed if we have judges who like the fat, sluggish beef in contrast to the lean and mean machine."

I smiled when I heard Mr. Anderson's descriptions. "Thank you. I guess I haven't given much thought to Black Iron being judged. I'm just content to be here and to have the opportunity to show my calf. I guess for me, that's what really matters." What I didn't tell Mr. Anderson is that I felt lucky to have a calf even if it would only be for a short while longer. I knew we couldn't afford to keep another bull, and with what I owed the bank, Black Iron would have to be sold during the 4-H auction.

For now, I was just pleased to be at the fair with Black Iron. Being here kept my mind from focusing too much on my dad going to the hospital. I appreciated that my father and mother did what they could to make sure I would be here. I was also very thankful that Mr. Madisen had asked me to help him with his horses after I showed Black Iron. And, if I never would have been here, I would not have had blueberry pie with ice cream! What guy wouldn't be happy?

After Mr. Anderson left to go judge a class of Guernsey milk cows, I took my brush and started to brush Black Iron again. It wasn't long before Jeff and Joe came walking into the barn.

"Hey, Teddy, you're going to brush all of his hair off." Joe shook his head as he and Jeff came along beside me.

"I might," I answered.

"You were brushing him when we left. Your arm is going to be really sore if you keep it up," teased Jeff.

"Ah, come on, guys. Stop needling. Can I help it if Black Iron's hair won't lay straight? Maybe he needs another bath."

Both Joe and Jeff laughed at my last remark, knowing none of the calves had been out of their pens except when we did a walk around, and even after that, the three of us had given them a good scrubbing. When they quieted down, I asked, "Do you guys think Black Iron is too boney?"

"What?" Joe asked in a surprised tone.

"Is he boney? I mean, does he look like he needs more to eat?"

"He looks okay to me," Jeff answered.

"Well, I'm sure glad Black Iron isn't in Stubby's age group. I would really be worried." Joe eyed Black Iron carefully as if he was a judge, and then glanced toward his chubbier calf that stood in the pen next to Black Iron's. "Some judges like a leaner calf. That's what my dad said when he thought Stubby might be putting on too much weight."

"Okay, Jeff, your weight class is up next," Mr. Anderson called out, coming down the aisle. "You and your calf need to be up by the gate." He gave Joe a nod and said, "You and your calf are next so you can follow Jeff up to the ring. Don't go in with him. I'll be right up there to help you guys line up. Teddy, when you see Jeff coming back, you and your calf need to start toward the ring. Okay, guys, let's get going!" Having given his three 4-H'ers their instructions, Mr. Anderson did an about-face and started heading toward the ring himself.

"See you soon, Teddy," Jeff and Joe blurted in unison as they followed Mr. Anderson's instructions.

I watched the two of them heading toward the show ring until they were out of sight. Turning back toward Black Iron, I clipped the lead rope into his halter. Then I slipped my show number over my head and quietly brought Black Iron out into the aisle. "I guess it's just you and me, boy, just you and me." I scratched behind his ears and waited patiently for Jeff and his calf to turn the corner on their way back to the pen.

As minutes passed, Black Iron stood motionless except for his tail swishing back and forth. Starting to become a little bored with tail watching, I allowed my eyes to move up until they reached the barn's ceiling where a row of pigeons perched on a rafter. It seemed the pigeons had nothing to do but look down on me looking up at them.

"Look, Teddy! We got second place! I've never had a ribbon before!" Loaded with excitement, Jeff rushed into the barn with one hand tightly holding his lead rope and the other lifting up his ribbon to show me.

"Red Ribbon—second place, Wow! That's great stuff," I congratulated him. "I hope Black Iron can get a ribbon, any ribbon."

Jeff gave Black Iron a scratch behind his right ear and said, "Better go, Teddy. It will be your turn soon!"

I pulled lightly on Black Iron's rope, and the two of us were off.

"Good luck, Teddy!" Jeff called out.

"Thanks!" I yelled over my shoulder and then focused on heading toward the ring. When I arrived at the gate, I found myself third in line behind two guys from the Lime Grove Club. It seemed like every minute that passed was twice as long as the last. I spent some of the time talking to the guy that came up behind me in the line. When we both ran out of words, I turned back to Black Iron. While scratching behind his ears, I carried on a monologue with my captivated audience of one on the end of my lead rope. I talked about the fair and how good he had been and was now. Better than any other calf or sheep or pig, for that matter. "You are being so good, so good!" I kept telling him. On his part, Black Iron looked as if he understood every word I was saying as he nudged his head up against my side.

We received no trumpet introduction, no drum roll, no cheerleaders' encouragement nor roses thrown in the path ahead of us—the gate to the show ring simply opened, and Black Iron and I, along with the other two-year-old calves and their 4-H escorts, walked into the ring. We took our places quietly and were surprisingly composed as if we had been in the show ring many, many times before.

Please, God, please God, help Black Iron to stand still. Please help me not to be nervous. Please help us win a ribbon. Any ribbon. Amen. I had been so focused on praying I hadn't noticed the judges had approached the two of us until one said, "Son, will you have your calf step back a few steps?"

"Ah, oh, sure I will." Awakening to what was going on, I complied with the judge's instruction, and then I thought, *This is it! Black Iron is being judged! I am being judged! Wow!* More attuned now than minutes before, I started to scan the bleachers. It took me only a few seconds before I found Mr. Madisen in the second row.

In a non-expressive tone, another judge instructed, "Son, please take your calf and walk half-way around the ring and then come back in line."

"Sure," I managed, offering a smile to the judge, and then did as I was told.

When all the calves and 4-H'ers finished their walks, the judges huddled and conferred with each other. Nodding, smiling, writing, looking at the line of exhibitors and livestock, nodding, smiling, writing some more, the judges gave me the impression that they were being very thorough in their deliberations. Finally, one of the judges handed a piece of paper to the announcer.

"Folks, the rankings for two-year-old calves have been decided. First place goes to Tom Rose with his calf, Alfred. Second place winner is Cheri Matthew with her calf, Buster. Third place winner is Theodore Hall with his calf, Black Iron. Fourth place . . ." I didn't hear who the fourth-place winner was, nor did I feel my feet moving as Black Iron and I walked up to the Fair Queen, who was handing out the ribbons. It wasn't until I shook hands with the last judge and heard him say, "Congratulations, son," that I realized all that had just happened. But by the time I walked out of the show ring, clutching tightly to my ribbon and the lead rope, I was grinning with pride.

"Congratulations, Teddy, the two of you did an excellent job in there! You are a natural showman." Mr. Madisen had come down from the bleachers to greet me.

"Third place! We got third place! Thank you, Mr. Madisen." With the ring experience now behind me, I felt like I owned a grand champion.

"Great job, Teddy!" Joe and Jeff met up with me back at Black Iron's pen.

"Thanks, guys. I guess I wasn't expecting anything. I can't wait to tell my mother and father." I knew that Mom would be happy. From past experience, she always seemed to be the encourager and the distributor of praises. I wasn't quite sure how my father would respond nor what he might say. *At least I hope Dad will be happy for me,* I thought.

"You and me, Black Iron, you and me," I whispered to Black Iron after putting him back in his pen and giving him some grain to munch on for a job well done.

In a very short time, one o'clock arrived, and I arrived in the horse barn, ready to help Mr. Madisen.

"Oh, good, Teddy, I'm happy that you're here. Right now, I think Mrs. Madisen and Joyce might need your assistance. They'll need you to help them ready Patsy and Jenny for their class." As he talked, Mr. Madisen pointed to the stalls down the alley.

Walking up to the stalls, I found Mrs. Madisen on a stepladder placing artificial roses in Patsy's braided mane. "Hi, Teddy, I hear you did a great job in the show ring. Congratulations!" Mrs. Madisen complimented me as she continued her work. Charlie said you would be coming to help, and you're right on time. Would you go over and help Joyce with Jenny, please?"

"Sure," I said and then walked over to the other side of the next stall where Joyce also stood on a stepladder, braiding Jenny's mane.

I know I told you about Joyce before. She's the Madisen's daughter, and she's married to Jack. Joyce is a very sweet person. If Joyce was my age and I had never met Maribelle, I would have a crush on her. I think I do anyway. Joyce is quite an artist. She designed Mr. Madisen's show ring suit and tailored it all by herself. She also created the decorations for the horses and for their barn stables. Jenny is one of the Madisen's Belgians. Mr. Madisen told me Jenny is their prized mare and won grand champion last year at the Nebraska state fair.

"Well hi, Teddy! Boy, am I happy you're here. I'm just finishing up on Jenny's mane. Will you please go in the tack room and bring me the box of roses? You can hand them up to me. It will save me a lot of time." Joyce turned back to work on Jenny.

How does she do it? I wondered. *Her decorations are so colorful. Wow! I wish she could have decorated Black Iron for me. We probably would have won grand champion! Everyone would have been looking at how handsome he looked and would have overlooked his being lean.*

In no time at all, Jenny's mane and tail were braided with the homemade red roses. Jenny looked pretty dapper as she waited to be led into the ring. While they had been busy with Jenny, Jack had arrived with Rocky and had put him into his stall. Rocky is the Madisen's stud. Mr. Madisen told me that when Rocky is in the show ring, he can be something of a show-off. Let me tell you, though, Rocky is big and he is strong. When he wants to be cantankerous, it takes Mr. Madisen or Jack to handle him. I have seen him be a rascal out at the Madisen's when Jack tried to put him in his stall. I think Rocky wanted to be out in the pen with the mares, but Jack finally outsmarted him.

A few minutes before Jenny's class was to go in the ring, Mr. Madisen came out of the stall used for their dressing room. He looked pretty stylish himself. He had on black and gold-colored cowboy boots, a western shirt with a western tie, brown slacks, and a debonair western show jacket.

"Teddy, do you mind helping Joyce ready Rocky to show?" Mrs. Madisen asked. "I'd like to go to the ring and watch Charlie show Jenny."

"No, I don't mind. It will be fun!" I was more interested in helping Joyce than working with Rocky. *Boy was I clueless.* Remember I said Rocky can be difficult sometimes?

At the same time we were talking, a short skinny man dressed in western attire came through the alley announcing loudly, "Three-year-old mares, three-year-old mares!"

"He sounds just like the guy who told us to bring our calves to the ring," I told Joyce.

"Maybe he is the same guy, Teddy," she teased.

With his show number displayed front and back, western hat snug on his head, and lead rope in hand, Charles Madisen led Jenny down the alley to the show ring. For our part, Joyce and I stayed behind to ready Rocky for the stud class while Jack went to the ring to watch the three-year-old mares being judged.

Sprucing up Rocky was actually harder than preparing Black Iron to show. As far as standing still, Rocky was not too cooperative, so we had to be very careful not to get in the way of his heavy, hard hooves when they thundered up and down on the barn floor.

Joyce seemed to take Rocky's prancing in stride as she braided his tail.

"Aren't you a little afraid?" I asked her.

“No, not really. I am cautious, though. My eyes are watching Rocky while my hands do the busy work,” Joyce explained without turning away from her task.

“Oh, I see,” I replied, although I still wondered if maybe she should be just a little afraid.

“There, we’re done with the tail.” Joyce moved away from Rocky to give her tail braiding a once-over. What do you think, Teddy?”

I stepped back as well and observed the red and white ribbons weaved meticulously into the stud’s tail. “Wow! It’s beautiful.”

“Thanks, Teddy.” Joyce smiled.

In a short while, Mr. Madisen returned from the show ring, brandishing a blue ribbon hanging from Jenny’s halter.

“I knew Charlie and Jenny could do it!” Mrs. Madisen’s joy brought a smile to her husband’s face, and she proudly showed us a second ribbon for his winning Outstanding Showman.

“I think I only made showman because Jenny’s mane and tail were decorated so colorfully, and neither one of us pranced around when the judges came by,” Mr. Madisen said.

I gave out a whistle as I glanced once again at Jenny and her ribbon hanging from her halter, exclaiming, “Jenny’s ribbon is twice as big as Black Iron’s.”

Joyce ran up and hugged her father around the waist and planted an affectionate kiss on his cheek.

After thanking me for my help, Mr. Madisen asked, “Jack, will you be sure Teddy and Black Iron make it to the sale ring okay? I heard someone say they were ready for the sale. Good luck to you, Teddy.”

In no time at all, with Jack walking at our side, Black Iron and I were waiting our turn in the ring. “Testing one-two-three.” The auctioneer could soon be heard over the microphone which then let out a loud, shrill sound causing a few minutes of pandemonium as a couple of calves bolted and struck out for the center of the ring while others, including

Black Iron, struggled to break loose. Jack was standing by the gate to the ring, ready to come in and help me if I was having trouble. I anchored my good foot in the sawdust and clung tightly to the lead rope. Seeing I had everything under control, Jack gave me a nod and the "okay sign." Then he scurried off to meet up with Joyce and Mrs. Madisen to watch Mr. Madisen show Rocky.

After all the calves were back in their places, the auctioneer came over the mike, "Will all the 4-H'ers and calves please move to the west side of the ring? When your number is called, slowly walk your calf in front of the crowd and then come back and stand in front of the auctioneer box facing the audience."

After the instructions were given, the middle of the ring quickly cleared. By now, Jack had left to check on Rocky and Mr. Madisen. Once again, Black Iron and I stood patiently waiting to be called out to the center only now it wasn't for a ribbon; it was the beginning of what I thought would be a sad goodbye. If I had my way, Black Iron would be going home with me—but I was not allowed to have my way. Black Iron had to be sold. Like I said before, I owed the bank the money they had loaned me to buy him, and with my father in the hospital for tests, it seemed like the only option.

Waiting in the ring and holding tightly onto Black Iron's lead rope were not enough to keep my mind from wandering into doubts and fear. *What if I couldn't sell Black Iron? What if he doesn't sell for enough and I still owe the bank money? He's not heavy enough. What if he ended up in the wrong hands? What if Dad didn't make it out of the hospital? What will my mom do without Dad?* I'd already lost so much: Pal, Grandpa, and now I was losing Black Iron. I felt tears burning my eyes, but before they could slip down my face, the auctioneer's voice shook me out of my fog and back to the ring.

"Number 610, will you please come forward?" the auctioneer announced. "Folks, 610 is a two-year-old bull named Black Iron owned by Theodore Hall." To hear the auctioneer call me Theodore shook me enough to put the brakes on my free-falling for the moment.

"Come on Black Iron, they're calling us." Holding the lead rope tightly, I started out with my stronger foot leading the way.

At the same time, the auctioneer started the bidding, "Okay folks, who will give me one hundred for this fine young bull . . . Do I hear one hundred?" *Funny thing about this bidding business,* I thought. *People who go to the sale barn or to farm sales on a regular basis have their own style of bidding. Someone might scratch the right side of their head to signal a bid, another person might throw his head to one side as if he's giving a partial shrug, still another might cock his head from left to right or right to left, who knows. Honestly, I never saw people pretend they were blowing their noses or acting like they were cleaning their ears. I guess that would be a pretty funny or a gross way of signaling a bid. I don't know.*

I was quite surprised to hear the auctioneer say, "I have one hundred." I did not have a clue where the bid was coming from, but I was happy someone was bidding.

"I have one hundred, who will give me two?" cried the auctioneer.

"Two hundred, who will give me," this time the auctioneer did not wait. "Folks, I now have three hundred. Now all of you know this is a 4-H calf; you can't go wrong. Now I have four . . ."

I became deaf to the auctioneer's cries. My eyes were scanning the crowd, thinking I might be able to find the bidders. To my delight, I saw Mr. and Mrs. Madisen sitting dead center of the ring, third row. They took me by surprise because I thought they were back with the horses preparing the mares and colts for their class. Knowing they were there gave me a foundation to stand on.

"Sold!" the auctioneer cried out, "Number 14." Then in a softer voice, he instructed, "Son, you can move your calf out of the ring now and back to his pen."

While standing out in the ring with Black Iron, I wasn't paying much attention to the bidding. I couldn't understand all of it anyway because sometimes it sounded like the auctioneer was babbling; however, I did hear clearly when the auctioneer said one hundred and then two hundred, but the only thing I understood after that was when the auctioneer told me we could leave the ring. I think Black Iron heard the words also because when I turned and started toward the gate, he had no problems with complying with the command. By the time Black Iron and I reached our pen, Mr. and Mrs. Madisen were there waiting for us. "You won't need to put Black Iron in his pen, Teddy. Jack has backed the truck up to the loading dock. We need to take the two of you home," said Mr. Madisen.

Surprised by his instructions and a little confused, I looked down to the floor and then back up at him. "I can't take Black Iron. Someone just bought him. He has just been sold. Remember?"

"Teddy, didn't you see us bidding? Our bid card was Number 14. We were the ones who bought Black Iron." A gentle smile crossed Mr. Madisen's face.

I held onto Black Iron's lead rope and the tears of disbelief that threatened to fall. "You did?"

"We did, son, and we couldn't have made a better deal. He'll make a fine young bull for our herd."

"I am not even sure how much he sold for." I was still in shock over the fact the Madisens bought my calf. If anyone was going to buy him, I was glad it was the Madisens. I knew they'd give him a good home, and I would probably be able to see him sometime.

Pulling a piece of paper from his wallet, Mr. Madisen gave it to me and said, "Here's your check Teddy."

I couldn't believe my eyes. The amount was for five hundred dollars. "You are a winner, boy!" I said to Black Iron, causing everyone to laugh.

"Thank you, Mr. Madisen," I said, my voice choked with emotion. "This check will cover the loan the bank gave me to buy Black Iron and leave me two hundred dollars to put in savings. Thank you again."

"Well, we know how conscientious you were in raising Black Iron, and we know it wasn't very easy. We also know how difficult it was for your father to be able to give you much help or time. Black Iron is a good bull, and like I said, he will be a good breeder for our herd." While he was talking, Mr. Madisen looked at me, and then both of us turned our gaze toward Black Iron, who really didn't have much to say about the whole thing.

Without looking away from Black Iron, I responded to Mr. Madisen's last comment. "Yes, he will be a fine bull." Then glancing at my watch, I exclaimed, "Golly, it's getting late. Can we go? I still have chores to do."

By now, Jack and Joyce had returned with the mares and colts.

"Two more blue ribbons, Dad!" Joyce held the ribbons up and waved them in the air.

"Good job, girls." Mr. Madisen stood in between the mares giving each a gentle pat.

Having backed the truck up to the loading dock and unlatching its gate, Jack asked, "Would you like to put Black Iron in first, Teddy?"

"You bet. I think he is ready to go."

Black Iron was loaded in, and a gate was put in between him and Rocky. After the second gate stood firmly locked, the mares and colts were led up the loading dock and tied securely in place for the journey home.

I wondered if there would be room for me to ride up in the cab when Mrs. Madisen said, "Teddy, Jack, and Charles are taking the horses and Black Iron home. You can ride with me, that way you can be home earlier. Charles will come and check on you after Black Iron and the horses are unloaded."

It sounded strange for her to say they were taking Black Iron home. I thought . . . *home . . . he lives where I do,* but then I remembered, *not anymore.* “Thanks. I was just thinking about where I was going to ride. I am glad I am riding with you because it will get me home faster. I really don’t like doing chores in the dark.”“You’ll be home before dark.” Mrs. Madisen’s smile reassured me.

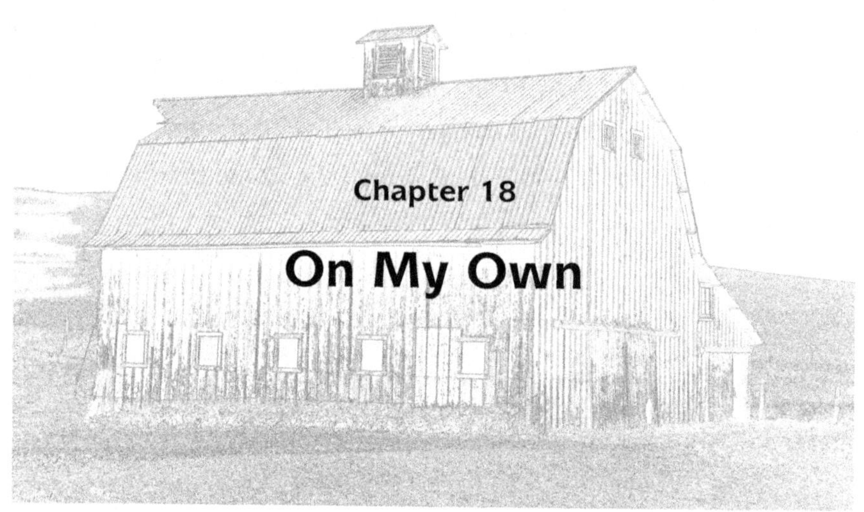

Chapter 18

On My Own

While I didn't waste any time changing clothes when I arrived home, I did manage to tell my mom about the ribbon and the 4-H sale and how surprised I was to discover that the Madisens bought Black Iron. "Here's the check, Mom. See, I have enough to pay for my loan and a little left over. Before my mother could say anything, I kept talking, "How's Dad? Will he be home soon?"

"Remember, Teddy, I told you your father has something wrong with his blood. There are several tests that must be done before the doctors know how to treat him, and before any talk about coming home can happen." My mom's eyes dropped, apparently, so she could avoid looking directly at me. "And, there's more."

"More—how can there be more? There can't be more. There just can't be!" I definitely did not want to hear anything more.

"Teddy, there is more, and you need to hear it. Remember, you said you didn't want to be shielded from anything. I told Victoria, and you need to know so that the two of you aren't left in the dark, wondering what all is going on."

"Yes, I did say I want to know, but what else can there be, Mom?" *Brace yourself,* I thought.

"The doctors say your father has been suffering from depression for a long time that's affected how he feels and thinks. They were going to describe the kind of depression they think he has, and I said, 'No, that's ok, I'll describe it.' I told them, 'He has periods of either physical or emotional withdrawal or some of both at the same time, he expresses feelings of hopelessness, and when he's only with me, he says he's a failure. He rarely talks to his children and is especially hard on our son, Teddy, when something goes wrong for him, or he doesn't do something the way his father thinks it should be done. Sam has told me growing up with his older brother and sister as "parents," they were quick to be angry with him and punish him and showed very little praise or affection, so sometimes he unintentionally acts that way toward Teddy—his anger comes out, and then he feels ashamed for his actions.'

"When I finished, one of the two doctors I was talking to only said, 'You are correct Mrs. Hall,' and then the other one said, 'We are going to recommend some couple's counseling for you and your husband, and we will give him medicine for the depression. Once that has started to take effect, we will provide group counseling with one of our staff therapists for him. After we get test results from the blood we have sent to the lab, we will know what kind of treatment to do regarding his blood disorder. We believe in telling him ahead of time what is going on.'

"Teddy, I asked them if I could be present when they tell your father all of this. They said, 'Yes, most definitely.' When I asked, 'How soon are you telling him all of this?' they said, 'Tomorrow.'"

"You're going back to the hospital tomorrow?"

"Yes." My mom said it with finality. I knew there was no room for further questioning or discussion.

"I need to go chore, Mom." I put on my boots and went out the door.

I could feel my mother watching out the kitchen window as I headed toward the pasture.

Being late August, the seasons were about to change, and it would be getting dark a little earlier, so I took a shortcut, cutting through the cornfield and climbing over the pasture fence. The sun dipped below the horizon, but I still had plenty of dull light to see the cows and head them toward home. I knew being so late, the cows had probably walked up the lane to the barnyard gate, finding it closed, lingered awhile, and then since no one came to open the gate, they slowly turned and in single file headed back to the pasture. They certainly weren't going to stay overnight in the lane. I caught up with them just before they reached the small muddy creek that divided their green haven. From past experience, I knew once they were over the creek, it would take a good amount of effort on my part to turn them around and convince them to head for home again.

"Beat ya," I mumbled aloud as I jogged up to Freckles. She led the parade, so I had to turn her around first. "Back to the barn, ladies and gentleman." My voice was not sweet nor gentle. It sounded gruff, like a platoon sergeant's voice yelling at young recruits hopping off a bus. Being second in line, Spotty took off in a trot, determined to claim her grazing spot on the other side of the creek. "Oh, no, you don't, Spotty!" I yelled as I ran in front of her, throwing dirt clods in her direction. While I was focused on Spotty, fearless Freckles had been making an about-face, but when she saw Spotty reclaiming her place in line, Freckles gave up the challenge and turned herself back around, heading in the direction I wanted her to go. A few seconds later, all the cows were retracing their steps back toward the barnyard.

Sooner than I actually expected, we made it back to the barn with the first set of cows readied to be milked. Secured in their stanchions, milking machines running and milk flowing, the cows seemed content chewing their grain. For the moment, I was allowed time to reflect on the events of the day. As I ran through all of the day's happenings in my mind, a bushel of emotions came along. I had a feeling of comradery when Jeff, Joe, and I were together. I experienced joy and pride when Black Iron won the third-place ribbon. I felt useful and enjoyed helping the Madisens with their horses. It didn't surprise me to have a mixture of emotions when Black Iron took his place on the auction block. I felt sadness, a sense of loss, and then an overwhelming elated feeling when I discovered the Madisens bought my calf, and it gave me great joy to discover how much they paid me for him. Finally, I had felt another bushel basket full of sadness, hurt, and frustration on the way home from the fair, realizing not one of my family members or relatives came to support me that day.

When I arrived home, and my mother told me about my dad and how sick he really was, I experienced a truckload of fear and shame listening to her in the kitchen as she told me my dad's sickness was both physical and mental. After she finished, I remembered my brain couldn't think of what to say. In our silence, I thought back on the conversation I had with my mom before going to the fair and how my dad took the time to take me to the fair and our talk on the way. Here I had been all the while feeling gypped growing up with a father who never praised me, never played with me, never had much to say . . . when he had had a childhood that was far worse than mine. *He probably doesn't even know how his fatherly behavior affects me or my sisters,* I thought. I felt awful.

After taking a breath and putting the milkers on different cows, I peered out the barn door toward the lot. *Something is missing,* I thought. I didn't have to search too deep for what it was. I knew. *My father is missing.* The rhythmic swish, swish of the milking machines allowed my brain to once again playback the conversation my mom and I had when I arrived home. "Your father's stay will be longer in the hospital than expected," she'd said. Her words didn't tell me much.

How much longer? The question repeated itself over and over in my brain.

The fact that my father wasn't milking the cows with me and the earlier sounds of my mother's despair caused a tremor to pulsate through me like never before. It felt like free-falling with no safety net underneath me to stop my fall. I imagined my free-falling was similar to what I saw skydivers do one time at the fair. They had jumped out of a plane and did all kinds of acrobatics and then they opened their parachutes, one at a time. But the last guy's chute didn't open when it should have. Instead, he somersaulted and did all kinds of amazing feats until he was hugging his friend for dear life. Finally, his chute opened, and the two landed with a loud bump, picked themselves up off the ground, and waved to the cheering crowd. That's what happened at the fair but, as far as I could tell, I'm still free-falling.

I didn't believe anyone would be coming to rescue me. I really couldn't say, nor did I want to guess either where I would land or how hard I would hit the ground. Turning back to the work at hand for some kind of relief, I could see very little milk flowing through the tubes, so it was time to change the machines to other cows. Moving up to Spotty and feeling her bag, I second-guessed myself and felt it again. "Hmm . . . your bag still fills like a balloon half-full of water. I think you are holding out on me. You are definitely testing my patience, aren't you, girl?"

On her part, Spotty turned her head partially toward me as if I was an intruder, then eyed me with her right eye as if to say, "What do you expect?"

Standing up, I met her eye for eye and said, "Okay, lady, I will give you a few more minutes." With that, I moved on to Goldie, felt her bag, and said loud enough for both Goldie and Spotty to hear, "Done. Aren't you, girl?" Taking the suction cups off her udder, I took the pail, unlocked the top, and poured the milk into the cream can. As I poured, the warm fresh milk filled with thick cream released a smell unpleasant to my nose into the cool air. Thinking how my grandparents would take their mugs, dip them into the milk pail and swoop out a mug full of the cream and warm milk mixture made me wrinkle my nose and mutter to my invisible audience, "Ugh! I will never understand how Grandma and Grandpa could drink this stuff."

Just before I reached for the kickers, I looked up and saw Mr. Madisen come through the door. "Hi, I'm really surprised to see you again today." I was truly happy to see him and gave him one of my best smiles.

"Well, Mrs. Madisen baked a cake for you all, and she was bringing it down, so I thought I would tag along to see how you're doing. Do you need any help?"

"Golly, I guess I really don't know. I'm going to try to put the kickers on Freckles. She has kicked me more times than I want to say. My father told me I 'wasn't close enough' and 'don't be in a hurry, talk gently, don't abruptly put the kickers on her, let your hand glide down her belly as you bend down to put on the kickers.'"

"Hmmm . . . sounds like good instructions. Did you follow them?"

The question came to my ears without any sound of scolding. "I thought I did, but I still might be too scared, and I still get kicked sometimes."

"It's possible you might have been more nervous than scared, Teddy." Taking the kickers off the peg, Mr. Madisen handed them to me. "Want to try again? Remember your dad's instructions."

Without saying a word, I cautiously took the kickers from Mr. Madisen. Still not believing I could do the job, I gave him an anxious look and finally managed, "Thank you."

"Do as your father told you, Teddy. It will be all right," Mr. Madisen encouraged.

Softly repeating the instructions, kickers in one hand while the other glided across Freckles' belly, at the same time moving myself into a kneeling position, I ran my hand down her right leg until it was about even with the middle of her milk bag. At that moment, I reached over and put on the left kicker and then the right. Still in a kneeling position and not sure I did everything right I waited to see how Freckles would react. She did not jerk. When her head turned, she did not give me a glaring look, but more of an "oh-hum" glance, and went on munching her grain. Looking back down at the milker, I saw the milk flowing freely. For the moment, it seemed I had more confidence in myself doing this milking business than I ever had before. I wanted to get up and let out a cheer. Instead, I stood up, putting on the same smile I had when I greeted Mr. Madisen earlier.

"I suppose Freckles wants to give you her milk just as bad as you want to see it running through the tube into the pail, Teddy."

"I guess so," I spoke with a voice of confidence but heard my voice betray my relief as I turned to go and check on my other machine.

"How many cows left to milk tonight, Teddy?" Mr. Madisen calmly asked.

"These two are the last of this batch, and then I have another group of five and then two more cows after that. It will take me about forty minutes before I'm done if I don't hurry. After I separate, I still have to take the separated milk and feed some to the chickens and some to the pigs."

"Well, take your time, Teddy. No rush, don't hurry. I'll go up to the house and visit with your mom and Mrs. Madisen a bit."

"Okay, I'll take my time. I won't hurry." I assured him as I went to open the barn door and let the first group of cows out. My dad was always telling me, "Don't hurry. Don't hurry." *Why did I hear those words differently when Mr. Madisen told me than when my father did?* My thoughts tagged along as I placed feed down for the next group of cows and then stepped aside so they could enter. As I had predicted, it was about forty minutes later when I turned the barn lights off, buttoned my collar button to keep out the surprising late August cool breeze, and with the mason jar full of milk, headed for the house.

"Your mom is tucking Cindy in for the night, Teddy. While you go ahead and wash up, I'll put the milk away for you." Mrs. Madisen reached out her hands, and I graciously gave her the milk accompanied by an appreciative, "Thank You."

Moments later, after washing up and changing my jeans and shirt and seeing that my supper wasn't in the oven keeping warm, I helped myself to an extra-large piece of cake sitting on the table. Just as I took my first bite, my mom returned to the kitchen. She and the Madisens continued to visit while enjoying their cake and coffee.

I was reaching for my second piece of cake when my mom" AHEMED" me and reminded me, "Teddy, we haven't had supper yet."

Mr. Madisen came to my rescue. "Elaine, may I please have another piece of cake?"

Mrs. Madisen repeated my mother's words, "Charles, we haven't had supper yet either." Mr. Madisen didn't seem bothered by her words as he continued to hold his plate in the air.

Following his lead, I held my plate up in the air also, "me too, Mom."

Mrs. Madisen gave a hopeless sigh as she looked toward my mom, and my mom smiled back at her as she placed another piece of cake on Mr. Madisen's plate. Glancing in my direction, my mom just shook her head and sliced me a much smaller piece of cake than I had cut for myself earlier, but I didn't care. I was having seconds.

After the cake passing was done, my mom turned to me. "Teddy, I told Charles and Patricia that the hospital called shortly after you went to chore. They're going to give your father a new medicine for his depression. I was telling them the same thing I told you earlier about the depression. The doctors are not sure where your father's blood poisoning came from, but they think nicotine from his cigarettes went into his system from rotten teeth he has in his mouth. Right now, that is just one of their thoughts. They believe the combination of the poisoning and depression affected your father's emotional well-being so severely he is no longer is able to cope with the low feelings he's experiencing, and that brings on his feelings of hopelessness and withdrawal. I shared with them that's why he's in counseling and that he and I are seeing a therapist also."

"Mom, you told me about the depression and the counseling earlier, but what does the poisoning mean? What's going to happen? What does all of this mean?" I couldn't even eat my last two bites of cake. I knew what my mom was saying was more important. Just like earlier, before I went out to chore, I listened very closely to all my mother had to say.

"It means that if the new medical technique works to cleanse your father's blood and the combination of medicine and talk therapy helps, your father's stay in the hospital may be shorter than we originally thought."

Mr. Madisen chimed in at that point. "Teddy, we've talked some things over with your mom, and Mrs. Madisen and I want to offer our help. I am going to the hospital tomorrow to talk with your dad. I will also come down and help with your evening chores so you can finish football season and go out for wrestling. Your mom says you like wrestling a little better than you like football."

"A little! I like it a whole lot better than football! I'm not much of a runner or catcher, but I am a pretty good takedown and escape guy." The words seemed to flow from my mouth as naturally as my hands reached out for another piece of cake.

"You know, you will still have to do early morning chores before school. Do you think you're up to it?" It felt like Mr. Madisen was becoming more like a dad than a neighbor each day, and I fought back tears of gratitude.

"Mr. Madisen, I think you know I've been really angry lately. Helping you and working with the horses was a godsend for me. I don't think I fully appreciated my father's willingness to let me help you. There's a lot of stuff I don't understand right now, like my dad's illness, the way he has treated me sometimes, and why we're so opposite from each other. I guess that's for me to figure out. Yeah, I'm up to doing those early morning chores. I have to be." A deep sigh escaped me, and all of a sudden, my face felt warm.

A few minutes of silence passed before Mom looked at me. "Teddy, how did you become so grown-up all of a sudden?"

I shrugged my shoulders but said nothing.

As if it was good timing on her part, the kitchen door opened and after yelling out "goodbye" to her friends, Victoria came into the kitchen carrying her drumsticks, music book and world history book. She looked at me. "Teddy, why is your face all red?"

"It's a little warm in here," Mom explained, rescuing me from any further embarrassment.

Victoria's eyes moved from me to our guests also sitting at the table. "Oh, hi, Mr. and Mrs. Madisen. I haven't seen you for a while. Is everything okay?"

"Hi, Vickie, we just came over to see how your father was doing." Mrs. Madisen picked up a dessert plate. "Would you like a piece of cake?"

"It looks delicious, but no thanks. I am on a diet." Victoria quickly moved her eyes from the cake toward my mom. "Mom, we have our history test tomorrow. Is it okay if I go upstairs and start studying?"

"I suppose." Mom knew history was not one of Victoria's favorite subjects, so to hear her say she wanted to study came as a surprise. She certainly wanted to encourage her.

"I don't have much homework, Mom, and I'm not on a diet," I said, holding my plate closer to the cake pan, hoping for my third piece.

"T-H-E-O-D-O-R-E, your manners!" Mom glared at me, but before she turned away to the Madisens I saw her "boys will be boys" smile.

"Oops, sorry," I said as I put my plate back down on the table, and everyone, including my mother, had a good laugh.

"My brother has a hollow leg," Victoria said as she walked away from the table and made her way to her bedroom.

"Well, no wonder Teddy's still hungry. It's past supper time." Mrs. Madisen rose from the table and started to carry dishes over to the kitchen sink.

"If you don't mind and you're not too full of cake, I could make a platter of eggs and sausage for us, and we have homemade bread for toast. It's easy and won't take long," Mom offered.

"Homemade bread! Yes!" Now it was Mr. Madisen's turn to put aside his manners.

Taking her cue from my mom, Mrs. Madisen loudly said, "Charles, your manners!" Honestly, Elaine, I think he's a bad influence on Teddy. Thank you for the dinner offer, but if I remember correctly, Charles, you said you needed to check on the mares and colts when we returned home."

"I did say that. And it's almost six pm. I guess we'd better go. We'll take you up on the supper offer another time." I remember how Mr. Madisen was still eyeing my mom's homemade bread as he was speaking and rising from the table. I giggled. *Mr. Madisen likes my mom's bread as much as I do.*

After the Madisens left, my mom sent Cindy into the living room with Ruby while she started to make our evening meal.

I was once again pondering all that my mother had said earlier, so I repeated myself and asked, "Mom, what does all of this mean? I mean, when Dad comes out of the hospital, will he still be able to farm? Will we be able to stay here? I guess I really don't want to move. I really don't. Are you happy now, Mom? Will you be happy if we have to leave the farm?" I had many more questions I wanted to ask, but before I could continue, my mother held her finger to her lips.

"About the only thing I can say right now is I don't feel as bad as I did earlier. I'm sorry you and your sisters have to go through all of this. I know you're carrying the brunt of your father's distancing behavior and what seems to be the lack of your father's care for you. I know he cares very much for you and is very proud of you. I pray and hope someday he will be able to show you. I wish I could answer all of your questions. Presently, I don't have the answers you are looking for, son. I wish I did. For now, you need to go and turn the water pump off and gather the eggs for me. I know it's getting late and dark outside, but can you do what I asked?"

"Sure, Mom, I can do that." Satisfied that my mother really couldn't give me any clear answers but had at least listened carefully to me, I retreated to the back porch. After putting on my chore boots, I picked up the egg basket, turned on the yard light, and went out the door.

The chicken house was the first outbuilding after leaving the house. By now, all the chickens were on their inside roost, and the nests were empty, so I didn't have to contend with any pecking hens. After gathering the eggs, I shut and bolted the door behind me so the chickens would not have any uninvited guests like rats or raccoons.

Leaving the egg bucket where I could easily see it on my way back to the house, I headed for the water pump. My confidence held until I reached the far edge where the yard light bumped up against the blackness of the night. At that moment, my imagination stirred up creatures of all kinds ready to devour me if I dared go any farther into the darkness. I started a slow run, sliding this way and that way in the barnyard muck, trying my best not to fall. To redirect my thoughts, I went into the first verse of "Jesus Loves Me," singing as loud as I could. Only seconds passed before I reached the pump and, after turning it off, I headed back to the security of the outer perimeter of the yard light, only now I was singing verse two of "Jesus Loves Me." Even though I knew Jesus loves me and would protect me, it wasn't until I found myself back on the porch with unbroken eggs and no body parts missing that I believed I was once again safe.

By the time I changed into my inside clothes, it was supper time. Our evening meal was very simple. We had homemade bread for toast, scrambled eggs, and sausage. I did not have seconds, and I only had one sausage. My stomach was already stuffed with cake. After supper, I sat at the kitchen table, doing my homework while my mom sat across from me, hand sewing a patch on a pair of my jeans. Looking up from my history book, I watched my mother's hand and her sewing needle moving up and down. "Mom, do you think the doctors can help Dad?"

"I hope so, Teddy."

The sound of my mom's voice when she answered me made me think, *Her words do not seem quite as hopeful or convincing as when she was talking to the Madisens earlier.*

With my homework finished, I gave my reserved and concentrated attention to the television. Competing with every word the actors were saying was Victoria sitting at the piano in the parlor with her fingers scrambling up and down the keyboard. When my mother came back into the living room after tucking Cindy into bed, I looked at her and announced, "I guess I better go to bed if I have to be up at five-thirty tomorrow morning to milk." The words reluctantly came out of my mouth as if I was waiting for some voice coming from parts unknown to say, "No, Teddy, you go ahead and watch another TV show. I'll do your chores for you." Even though I lingered longer after giving my mom a goodnight kiss, no voice came.

Eight hours of sleep does not seem quite enough when you have to rise at five-thirty a.m. There was no second-guessing my alarm clock when it went off at the right time, so I lumbered out of bed, washed the sleep out of my eyes, put on my chore clothes, and was out the door.

Don't hurry. Don't hurry. I mumbled to myself as I turned on the barn lights, put feed in front of each stanchion, and went out to gather the first five cows. On their part, the first five were not at the barn door as I hoped they would be but were congregating out in the barnyard with Fred watching over them. To my relief, neither they nor Fred gave me any resistance as I came up from behind and "shooed" them into the barn, leaving Fred to brood over his remaining harem. Whether my father or I were choring, it didn't matter. The same five cows were always first to come through the door. Fred was always hanging out with the girls. It was routine. Nothing changed except the guy putting on the milkers.

Though I had accepted the responsibility of doing the morning milking and was more than grateful that Mr. Madisen and Jack would do my evening milking, I had not changed how I went about my chores, except maybe I didn't hurry as much as I had done in the past. I don't know. When it came to putting the milker on a cow, I hadn't desired to skillfully learn the knack of having a gentle touch; however, the fact that there was feed in front of the cows seemed to hold their attention more than anything I might do differently. That's just a hunch. Unfortunately, Freckles was the exception. She made up her mind to be just as ornery as she always had been. She would not allow any gruff or careless behavior from the kid. She calls me *the kid*. Don't ask me how I know that. I just do. Either I would be gentle with her or POW! I have learned my lesson. I was gentle and slow.

As the milkers hummed away and after two or three yawns, I made the mistake of allowing my thoughts to travel down into the steep ravine of uncertainties. *My father's hospitalization, my mother's searching for off-the-farm work to make ends meet, wrestling with my own fears, hurt, and inadequacies, the unfairness of it all.* It seemed to me the entire experience was like Jacob wrestling with the angel. In Sunday school, we read out of King James that Jacob wrestled with the angel all night. He actually pinned the heavenly being, and before he let the angel free, he demanded and received a blessing.

The difference, as I saw it, was even though the Madisens came to my mother's and my rescue, they could not take away any of my hurt, anger, fear, doubt, or uncertainties. I had yet to learn how to let the anger go. I held on to the angel as tightly as I use to hold on to my teddy bear at night with the wind howling outside.

I remember lying in bed with Bear . . . I would imagine howling tree creatures breaking through my bedroom window and eating me and bear or sometimes tearing us to pieces and using us for fertilizer. Understanding the emotions that were chasing after me was something I had yet to accomplish. I wouldn't be able to accept the angel's blessing until I completed that discovery and turned to face those emotions that had become so powerful in my young life.

On my behalf, I heard my brain repeat over and over, *Stand up to your fears and all that holds you captive. Let the angel bless you. It will be worth it. You will see.* Still deep in thought, I turned again to the cows in front of me, and to my surprise, Bossy was not chewing her grain but was staring directly at me. I imagined her saying, "Stop daydreaming, kid and pay attention to real life."

When chores were done, I went through my usual routine preparing for school. I wish I could tell you something exciting happened that day at school, but there was no excitement. Well, almost no excitement. The hot lunch cooks made cinnamon rolls. They tasted delicious. I guess I will settle for that.

Coming home from school after football practice that evening, I found a letter on the kitchen table addressed to me. Since Mr. Madisen and Jack had already done my evening milking and my mother was helping Victoria finish preparing supper, I snatched the letter from the table and quickly went up to my bedroom. Sitting on my bed, I tore open the letter and read:

Dear Teddy,

I hope you're not mad at me. I should have told you by now that we are moving to the city. Actually, I am at my Aunt Sandra's in the city. Since my folks will be moving here the end of October, my mom wanted me to start the school year here so I wouldn't be so far behind my grade and would already have adjusted. I have tried to write you from the very first day I was here, but I kept tearing up the letters and throwing them away. I keep thinking you will be mad at me, and I just wouldn't be able to bear that.

My mom said you called her and asked where I was. She told you, but when you asked for my address, she thought it best not to give you my Aunt's address until after she and Dad actually move. I don't understand why. I think adults and especially parents are really hard to figure out. Oh, she told me that your father is in the hospital and she said he has been there a long time. Do you get to see him? I hope so. I know you will understand when I say I will pray for him. If I was with you, we could talk about how he is doing, but more importantly, how you are doing. Please write to me. I am sorry if I hurt you by not calling you back or letting you know about the move. I wasn't sure how to tell you. Please forgive me. Will you forgive me? You can tell your mother I wrote to you but make her promise she won't tell my mom at least until my parents move to the city.

I know your mom and my mom are really close. Maybe your mom has told you all of this. I don't know. I miss you. Do you miss me? I hope so. I promise not to like any guy in the school here. The only guy I like is the one I danced with on the night of our graduation party (you!). Please write to me. My Aunt Sandra is cool. She won't tell my mom if we write to each other before they move here. Aunt Sandra's address is Sandra Hill, 33123 Arbor Ave. Omaha, Nebraska.

LOVE,

Maribelle

I read Maribelle's letter repeatedly until my mother called up the stairs, "Teddy, supper." At first, I thought about tucking Maribelle's letter under my pillow, but giving that a second thought, I decided to put it into my King James Bible on the page where Jacob starts wrestling with the angel. *I am blessed, after all,* I thought, *angel or no angel.*

When I heard my stomach rumble, I knew it might be about time for a meal. Sure enough, as if on cue, my mom called me for supper a second time. If my mom had to call me again, Victoria would come snooping to see why I was in my room so long. After supper, I would be writing a letter, though.

Writing letters did not come naturally for me. I was not like Victoria. She wrote a letter at least once a week to someone. She bought her own stamps with money she made from babysitting. My experience in letter writing was sending a thank you note to my grandma once a year for the Christmas present I received from her, and an occasional letter to my pen pal in Montana that I had in fifth grade, but we have not written to each other for over two years now.

At first, I did not know what to write; I just let the pen I borrowed from my mother start talking. Since I was using a pen and not a pencil, I had to be careful not to make many mistakes or it would look like I wasn't sure what to say to Maribelle. I did not want her to ever think that was the case.

> Dear Maribelle,
>
> Your letter was waiting for me when I came home from school. Since Mr. Madisen, our neighbor, and Jack, the man who works for him, are doing my chores in the evening so I can go out for football, I opened your letter as soon as I could make it to my room. I was afraid I wouldn't hear from you. Golly, Maribelle, I could never be angry with you. Remember, I will only dance with you.

I have to wake up at 5:30 a.m. to go milk and be ready for school by the time the bus comes to pick us up.

My leg healed faster than Doc Jones thought it would, and I have a green light from Doc to play football. Actually, I had the green light several weeks ago to do exercises and drills as long as they are non-contact exercises. We were still in P.E. shorts until this week. Since contact drills from the playbook have started, Coach Michael makes me do running exercises in full gear and then stay on the sideline.

The coaches said we should have all the plays memorized by now. I do not think I have them all memorized. Sometimes a first-team player will goof up on a drill, and the coaches will make him run a lap and then come back and tell one of the coaches what he did wrong. I will be able to do the contact drills and plays starting Wednesday, but Coach Michael said I needed to have the okay in writing from Doc Jones. I gave it to the coach yesterday!

I thought you were going to be at your Aunt Sandra's only for the summer and then come home (I mean to Oakdale). I was surprised to learn that your folks moved to the city so I guess you will not be coming back. My mom might have known your family was moving, but I didn't. I will write you a letter every week. Will you write to me? I hope so.

I miss you. Victoria said they have a school dance on Friday after the first football game. I will probably be sitting on the bench the whole game. Even though Doc says I am "good to go," I think the coaches do not see me as a sub for a first-team player when one of them calls the player out for a huddle. I think the coaches need to see me differently, but I do not want to fool you. Even if I had a perfect leg, I probably would be on the bench unless we were ahead by fifty points.

Benchwarmer or not, the Doc says I can dance. Will you dance with me? Oops! I forgot you won't be here. You will have moved to the city by then. I am sending my letter to your Aunt Sandra's until you give me the green light. If your parents find out I have been writing to you, they might really be mad and never like me. I sure hope that does not happen.

What is the name of your new school? When I am old enough to drive, I will come see you if my parents let me use the car. I am taking Driver's Training now so I can get a driver's permit. Will you be taking Driver's Training?

My dad, is not well. I do not think he will be well for some time. Please send me your Aunt Sandra's phone number.

Love,

Teddy

P.S. Tomorrow is Sunday, so this letter will be in the mailbox with the flag up for the mail carrier to notice on Monday. We will go to church tomorrow morning after I milk the cows. Sunday being the last day of the week, as I see it, you are supposed to rest on Sunday. Mrs. Kates said God told Moses and his gang they had to rest on the Sabbath. I bet Moses and Aaron did not have cows to milk. In our neighborhood, the farmers I know, including the Madisens, don't rest. There are always chores to do. Cows don't rest. They make milk day and night, seven days a week, so I have to milk. Oops, I forgot, we do not milk cows that are pregnant. When a cow is getting ready to have a calf, we dry her up or she dries up all by herself. I do not know for sure which one it is. All I know is that we don't milk her again until after she has her calf. Dried up cows use their inside milk to feed a calf that is yet to

> be born someday. They do not have enough milk for the calf and the humans at the same time. At least, that is what I think. I bet you already knew this stuff. Chickens lay eggs on Sunday, too, so we have to gather Sunday eggs. Chickens do not dry up before they have baby chicks. They just sit on their eggs longer. We call all of those hens laying hens. A laying hen will peck your hand hard if you try to take her eggs. Roosters don't lay eggs. They just strut around. I have to feed chickens and pigs on Sunday. I do not think the pigs would be very happy if they weren't fed on Sunday. WOW! This is a long letter!
>
> P.S. I better quit writing."

I wanted to linger longer in the P.S. because of the special feelings I have for Maribelle, which came alive when we danced together at the graduation party. They're sort of like the feelings I had when Susie left her letter to me on my last day at my old school, only stronger. Now, the queasy feeling in my stomach and the light-headedness I feel on the inside of my forehead all the way to the back of my brain seemed to go much deeper. *I hope she feels the same,* I think, putting the letter in the mailbox.

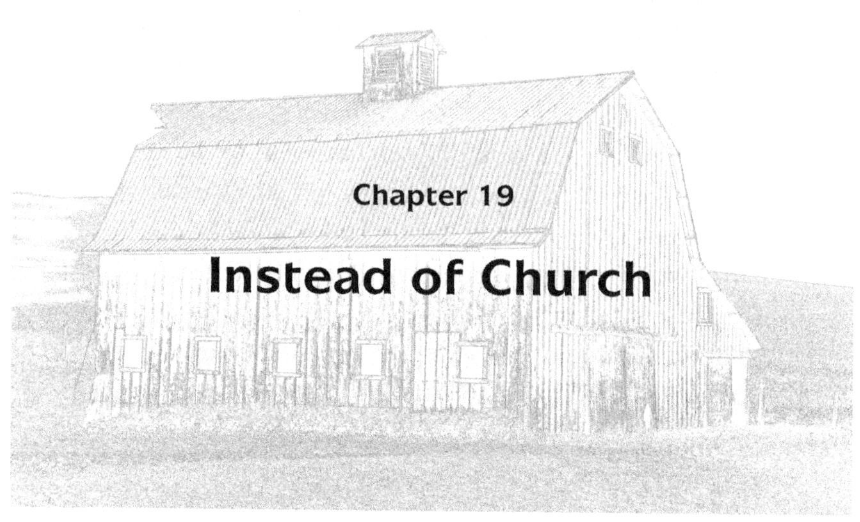

Chapter 19
Instead of Church

Sunday morning, my alarm clock came bursting through the defensive line of my brain exactly when the left guard bullied through the offensive line and tackled the quarterback before he could execute the perfect would-be-play of the year. When the victorious guard picked himself up, my dream eyes saw that it was my number on the left guard's jersey.

From experience, I had learned that I needed to jump right out of bed when the alarm went off or I might roll over and fall back to sleep. Habitually, I put on my chore clothes and tried to say the Gettysburg Address or something like that to keep my brain from being clogged by stardust cheerleaders yelling at me, "Push him back! Push him back! Way back to bed!" I also knew the quicker I jumped and the faster I dressed, stopping only long enough to put on my chore shoes before I scurried out the back-porch door, I would be ever so close to my imaginative goal post. The remaining yardage would be gained inch by inch, which in realty, were my morning chores being completed.

Every morning since my father went to the hospital, I read all of the instructions, step by step, that he posted for me next to the light switch.

"Give each cow three scoops of feed. Open barn door and step out of the way. Cows know which come in first milking, second, and final milking. If a cow is too stubborn to come in when it is her turn, lock the cows in their stanchions and go fetch the right cow. Don't hurry." I learned quickly that skipping over something would cause me embarrassment, I would become upset with myself, and receive a heavy dose of emotional pain coming from an imaginative scolding I would receive from my father.

Following my father's instructions, I took time out to think, *Wow! I have never read anything my father has written, let alone something so detailed.* I guess he knows I am apt to take shortcuts to finish my chores faster. If he were here, I just might try to finish my chores faster . . . but now, I better not. I moved out of the way for the first group of cows to enter. What once were chores my father seemed to enjoy, I reluctantly accept. I do not claim the chores, nor do I enjoy them; I just accept them. I dare not give a second "think" to the chores I inherited from my father when he went to the hospital. My not over-thinking how I feel or the responsibility I now have makes it easier for me to disown all my negative feelings before my thoughts are ground to dust.

No cows to dry up this morning. Darn. Wish Freckles would dry up. That would make things a whole lot easier, I thought to myself as I moved up to Freckles' rear.

I started talking to her. "Left hand on your right hip. I am slowly coming down with suction cups in my right. I'm bending my knees, so don't kick me, lady. Now my left hand is moving over to help my right hand while I put on your suction cups. Cups on, standing up, milk flowing, done, no kick and no glassy eye stares, and still on my own two feet . . . *good!*" I almost thought Freckles would be turning her head toward me and, with a smirk, say, "Well, if you were expecting a kick, I can give you a good one next time. Be nice to me, friend, or I will land you on your kisser! Did you hear what I said, kid? Don't cross me or else, WHAM!"

Returning to the house after my morning chores were completed, I changed out of my chore clothes on the back porch and came into the kitchen where my mother was sitting at the table.

"Are you going to the hospital after church today, Mom?" I asked.

"I am, but we won't be going to church. You and your younger sisters will be going to the hospital with me."

"Isn't Victoria going?"

"No, she won't be going. Mrs. Madisen asked if she could help her clean today."

Hmmm . . . Victoria hated cleaning. I had to think fast so maybe I could go with Victoria to the Madisens. "On Sunday . . . Victoria is working on Sunday? Mom, you know she always grumbles when you make her clean, especially on Sunday. I doubt it if Mrs. Madisen will be very happy when Victoria starts to complain, especially if she has to mop the floor. Maybe I should go with Victoria just to make sure she doesn't grumble, and she does a good job."

"I doubt she'll be grumbling very much helping Mrs. Madisen."

"I bet she will!"

Victoria slipped into the kitchen. "I heard you, Teddy! You grumble all the time when you have to go outside and work, but you never grumble when the Madisens ask you to come and help them."

"That's because they pay me," I said proudly, then I realized my mistake.

Victoria smiled, and Mom looked flustered. "Teddy, truth is, Mrs. Madisen will be paying Victoria too, so I'm sure your sister will be on her best behavior."

No wonder she isn't grumbling. My older sister had the glow of self-importance radiating from her face. I realized I had lost this battle and might as well just give it up while I was behind.

"Listen, you two, enough is enough. You both grumble whenever I tell you to do something you are not expecting to do with your time, whether it is inside or outside. And your father and I do pay you. We put clothes on your back, food on your table, provide a roof over your heads, taxi you around, and when you are sick, we nurse you back to health. Need I say more? And, Teddy, you are coming to the hospital with me." My mom's words wasted no time soaking into the depths of my brain, and the way Victoria looked, I know they had the same effect on her.

With our heads hanging down and eyes staring at the floor, in unison, we both said, "No, Mom, you don't need to say more." And that was that.

On the way to the hospital, even before we made it to the highway, Ruby and Cindy had drifted back to sleep. I felt my eyelids begging to close over my eyes as we passed by familiar countryside. I ignored their plea and started to make small talk with my mom. "What's next, Mom?"

"I am not sure what you are asking, Teddy."

"Well, Dad's been at the hospital for two weeks now. Has anything changed? Have the two of you talked to any of the doctors? When will he come home?"

"The doctors are still trying to work on the right dosage of medication for your father's depression. They have to be careful not to cause a reaction to the pain medication they'll be giving him when they pull out his teeth. They also have to very carefully monitor the procedure they're doing to clean his blood. The treatment they are using is still in an experimental period . . ."

"Oh, so they are using Dad as a guinea pig?"

"No, Teddy, your father is not a guinea pig. He is just first in line for everything they are doing for him. Your father and I are also seeing a counselor at the hospital and a social worker. A lot has happened and is happening, Teddy. We have to be patient to see how this will all end. And, at the moment, there is no definite target time for your father to come home."

"Oh," I said, and then I started to settle back into my seat, but as I did, another question popped into my head. "Will we be seeing his counselor?"

"I'm not sure Teddy, we will have to wait and see." My mom sighed, so I gave it a rest for now and actually fell asleep. "Teddy, Teddy, wake up, we're here." My mom shook me awake."Wake Ruby up and follow me. I'll take care of Cindy."

It was only a few minutes later when the elevator opened onto the hospital's fourth floor. As we walked out onto the floor, my eyes caught a look at the sign on the opposite wall, "4E Psychology." My first impression of the floor was not very favorable. One of the lights above us had burned out, and several old men with scraggly looking beards were standing at the nursing station as the nurse handed out cigarettes.

My twelve-year-old sister Ruby took a quick glance around the room and then whispered in my ear, "This is creepy." Her words were followed by a tight squeeze of my hand as we waited for our mother to take the lead.

Ruby and I continued to watch the men at the nurses' station. As they received their cigarettes, the men walked down in single file toward the end of the hall away from where we were standing. Their untied gowns revealed an array of BVDs and one bare bottom.

By now, my youngest sister was wide awake. Watching the men, her eagle eyes caught the man with the bare bottom. "Mom, that man doesn't—" Cindy's last words were stifled by Mom's outside voice.

"Okay, Cindy . . . shhh . . . let's go down the hall and see what your daddy is doing.

At first, Ruby gasped as she caught an eye full of the men parading, but then she proceeded to giggle. Her giggle ignited another and a "shhh" from my mother. Ruby immediately obeyed the command.

It's a good thing we're going in the opposite direction, I mused to myself; however, my amusement was short-lived by unpleasant aromas coming from some of the rooms. I dare not try to describe the smell other than to say it was *gross*.

Cindy was not quite as concerned about what she might say. As we passed by the second room, she freely expressed herself. "Mom, something stinks."

"Shhh . . . Cindy, people might be sleeping." My mom held a finger to her lips.

"Why do they stink, Mom?" Cindy persisted.

Before my mom could give Cindy an answer, Ruby shared her own description of the scene. "Pee-yew—ugh."

I stifled a laugh seeing my mom's anxiety and tried to help instead. "Hmmm . . . good question, Cindy, after we see Daddy, I'll tell you about the rooms. Okay?"

For some reason, Cindy was satisfied with what I said and didn't say another word, although she pinched her nose as we continued down the hall.

As for Ruby, the look my mother cast her way caused her head to drop, her eyes to gaze at the floor, and her mouth to shut; however, my ears did detect her taking smaller breaths, trying to eliminate as much of the smell she took through her nostrils her as possible.

As my mom took the lead, she passed Cindy off to me, and I took her hand. Mom led us into a long narrow room at the end of the hallway. Beds were arranged on both sides of the room, and only a thin white curtain separated them and their occupants from each other. I focused my eyes straight ahead and tried to shut my ears but couldn't escape the occasional groan or visitor asking, "How are you?"

Cindy covered her left ear with her hand when she heard, "Nurse—nurse—nurse! Why in the hell can't anyone hear me? I need a nurse! Where in the hell is the [blankety blank] nurse! " Since the speaker had a very loud voice, we all heard every word. Cindy knew what she heard were naughty words, and if she said those words, our mother would put hot pepper on her tongue.

Ruby's face showed a sign of disgust while she muttered, "Mom, do we have to?" That's all she said. My mom ignored her.

I cannot imagine how my mother must have felt when we finally stopped at the last bed in the ward and walked up to the backside of a man lying there.

"Sam, Sam, are you awake? It's me, Elaine, Sam. We have come to visit. The kids are all here too, Sam." Mom continued to shake our dad as she spoke.

It took a few seconds before Dad rolled over. His first couple of words sounded as if he had disgusting food in his mouth that his throat refused to swallow. "Elaine, I am surprised to see you. I didn't know you were here."

My father's face sent a chill down my spine. *Is this Dad? It doesn't look like my father. My father doesn't have a beard. His face is fatter than this man's face. Are there two Sams on the floor? My mom must have made a mistake.*

When I looked more closely and realized this man in the bed looking at us was my father, I was finally able to say, "Dad, it's me, Teddy."

Even though it seemed my father had first recognized us, only seconds passed before he stared at me as if to say, "Do I know you?" I know my father had heard my mom's words. Dad saw the people in front of him, but for some reason, his brain was not quite ready to acknowledge that along with his wife, his children were standing in front of him. When Dad's stare moved from my face to see Ruby standing as stiff as a statue and a half of a step away from me, he smiled and held out his arms. Dad's long arms stretched out as far as they could, almost touching Cindy's shoulder. Cindy reacted by squirming out of my grip and clutching my leg tighter than I could ever imagine a young girl her age would be able to do. She looked up toward our mother and cried, "Mommy! Mommy!"

"Don't cry, Cindy, it's Daddy. He wants to give you a hug. Come see Daddy,"

"No," Cindy said rather quickly and then nearly screamed, "No!" and squeezed my leg even tighter to the point where I thought my circulation would be cut off.

A wave of despondency slid across our father's face as his eyes moved away from Cindy toward our mother.

"Oh, Sam, Cindy's never seen you with a beard before. She just needs some time. She will warm up—won't you, sweetheart?

Cindy didn't look toward Mom and just stayed glued to my leg. Coming to my sister's rescue, Mom turned back toward Dad and said, "Sam, we passed a visiting room when we came off the elevator. Do you feel up to going down there if Teddy pushes you in a wheelchair?"

"Sure." I know Dad was relieved to have his failed attempt to gain his daughter's attention not be the focus of further conversation.

"I'll go find a wheelchair," I jumped at the opportunity to do something; I gently pulled Cindy away from my leg. Possibly to have a temporary escape, Ruby volunteered to go with me, so off we went.

When Ruby and I returned, Dad was sitting up on the side of the bed with Cindy snuggled up against his side. Mom must have luckily remembered Cindy's earlier comment when she saw the backside of the men standing in the hall lined up for their cigarettes because when Dad went to stand up, she quickly said, "Just a minute Sam, let me tie your gown for you."

"Thank you," Dad replied.

Walking down the hall, in their own way, both Cindy and Ruby seemed to become a little more comfortable with the surroundings and the man in the wheelchair. Cindy even began to talk to Dad as I wheeled him down the hall. "Hi, Daddy. Do you hurt? Where are your clothes?"

Delighted to hear her talking and especially calling him, "Daddy," Dad answered her with short sentences. "Hello, Cindy. No, I do not hurt. My clothes are in the closet."

I pulled my dad's IV pole as we walked. It seemed to me we were all adjusting the best anyone could. I'm sure Mom was glad that Ruby was not bursting to give a commentary of her own regarding what her eyes and nose took in.

For her part, Cindy seemed to disregard our current environment and looked as if she was enjoying her first wheelchair ride sitting on Dad's lap. Neither she nor my dad seemed to mind that she was probably just a little too big for a lap ride. I could tell by her facial expressions, whenever she looked at me, my mom wasn't sure how I was working through everything, but for the moment, I seemed to have convinced her I could be the young man she knew I could be when I wanted.

"You're shaking, Dad," I said as I helped my father move from the wheelchair to the lounge couch in the sitting room.

"Yes. They tell me it's the medicine, Teddy."

"Oh," I was satisfied with my father's answer. Instead of sitting, I continued to stand. Warming up to being with our father, Ruby quietly stood next to me and had one hand resting on the top of his shoulder. My mom sat across from Dad in a chair she had pulled up from the corner of the room. Cindy once again was fast asleep only now she was snuggled deep into my father's shoulder. It felt good to see our family knitted so tightly together in spite of being in a hospital with my father as the patient. While the future left a lot of uncertainty in my mind, I was content with simply being in the moment.

I didn't have to worry about speaking because my dad had more to say. His voice continued to be very soft, but now much clearer. "Are you following the instructions for milking that I tacked up for you, Teddy?"

I smiled to myself. "Yes, Dad, they help me a lot. I read them every time I milk."

"Are you still going out for football?"

"Yes, I am."

"Is Mr. Madisen still milking for you in the evening?"

"Yes, he is still helping. We have our first football game this coming Friday. I will probably be sitting on the bench."

"That's okay, Teddy. Don't be disappointed. Just do your best, and then try just a little harder. It'll pay off sooner than you think." My father looked up from his wheelchair and smiled at me.

I realized in that instant that I never remembered my father smiling at me before. He never smiled the time I brought home my best report card with a "B" in every subject except for an "A" in spelling. He didn't even smile when I was the lead character in our third grade Christmas pageant at church. *Wow! He smiled.* I gave him a broad smile of my own. "Thanks, Dad."

I knew my mom and dad had some business of their own to discuss, so it came as no surprise when Mom said, "Teddy, will you and Ruby please take Cindy back to the waiting room while your father and I talk about some things? I'll meet you there shortly."

"Okay, Mom."

Later, when my mom met us in the waiting room, we headed for the parking garage. On the way home, my mother filled me in on their conversation, while Ruby and Cindy slept.

"They're going to pull out your dad's teeth tomorrow. It takes about a month for the mouth to heal and the gums to shrink back to their normal size. After all of that, he will be fitted for his false teeth. You kids probably won't be visiting for a few days while he recuperates."

My dad has his pride, I realized. *He doesn't want any of us to see him without any teeth until he feels comfortable and accepts the circumstances for what they are.*

"The doctor said they'll continue the same procedure they've been doing with his blood if everything goes okay with the teeth pulling." Mom sighed. "And they're going to start him on speech therapy."

"Speech therapy?"

"Yes, the doctor explained it is something new. They use the same type of speech therapy for coaches, radio announcers, and people who have had throat cancer. The speech therapist wants to see if it would help improve speech for people who have had their teeth removed. Apparently, the few people they have tried it on have improved in their speaking. So, they want to try it on your father. The doctor said it strengthens your vocal cords and will help him enunciate properly."

I nodded. This was a lot to take in, so I was not fully prepared for what Mom told me next.

"Teddy, I applied for a job at the County Extension Office. I received a call from their office yesterday afternoon. I'm supposed to start Friday. I will work there part-time three days a week until maybe a full-time position opens, and I will work the evening shift Sunday and Monday at the truck stop outside of Oakdale."

"Friday? What are they going to have you do at the Extension Office?" It seemed to me that my mom had enough to do already—taking care of us kids, working on the farm, supporting my dad.

"I'm not quite sure what all I'll be doing at the Extension Office and, of course, you can guess, I will be cooking at the café." Her eyes revealed a concerned look. It's as if she was searching my eyes for a sign of acceptance. I really don't know what she found. She never told me. "Teddy, it will all be okay."

"That's a lot of work, Mom, a lot. I wish . . ." I couldn't finish my sentence. I really didn't know what I was wishing for, except I wanted all of this regarding my father being in the hospital, Mom working away from home, the money we seemed to owe everyone. I wanted it all just to go away. As soon as the car stopped in our driveway, I jumped out and called back to my mother, "I'm going to the barn to see Mr. Madisen."

Mom was trying unsuccessfully to wake my sisters. "Theodore, you come right back here and help me!"

"Ah, gee whiz, Mom." I turned back toward the car.

"Besides, you can't go to the barn in your good clothes. You have to change into your chore clothes." I already knew my mom would say what she did, which is why I tried my best to rush down to the barn.

The day had already been a long one for all of us, so I didn't want to try Mom's patience. When I came back to the car, my mom was already helping sleepy Cindy up the hill to the house. Ruby was stirring, so I simply barked, "We're home, Ruby! You gotta go help, Mom." Satisfied with myself, I grabbed the few groceries Mom stopped to buy on the way home and headed toward the house myself.

Following my mother's instructions, I left the groceries on the kitchen counter and went quickly upstairs to change. A few minutes later, racing down the stairs and hearing no other demands for assistance from my mother, I scrambled out the door. In a flash, I was at the barn. Milkers humming away, I found Mr. Madisen looking out the barn door toward the lot where other cows stood as still as statues and pigs were grunting as they roamed the lot. "Hi, Mr. Madisen, we're home!"

Mr. Madisen turned toward me and returned the greeting. "Hi, Teddy, how did you find your father?"

"Gee . . . I don't know. It's an awful place. I think he's sad. My mom says he's depressed. I don't understand it all, but I guess I will someday. They're pulling out all of his teeth tomorrow. My dad told my mom about it, and she told me on the way home." I paused, unsure what all I should tell Mr. Madisen, but then I realized he was practically family. "I guess he's had some rotten teeth for a long time. I don't ever remember my father going to the dentist. Maybe he doesn't like the dentist. We never talked about it before. Anyway, all I know is that his rotten teeth and his cigarette smoking have something to do with the poison in his blood. I sure hope he feels better when all of this is done."

I had been staring at Freckles all the time I was talking. It was my way of not looking at Mr. Madisen because I was afraid I would tear up and cry, and then I would really be embarrassed. After trying to swallow the lump in my throat that had been growing while I talked, I added, "It seems to me my father is a changed man, lying in bed with an IV hanging from a pole, speaking so softly. I have never seen him this way before, never. Before I left his room and Ruby and I took Cindy back to the waiting area, I saw him start to cry. I have never seen him cry. What causes that? Is it the medicine?"

"I really don't know, Teddy. I really don't know." I remember how surprised I was to hear Mr. Madisen say that he really didn't know. I guess there are some things even Mr. Madisen doesn't know.

The silence between the two of us after I asked if my dad's medicine made him cry was a little awkward for me, so I was actually relieved to see Freckles was ready to be milked.

"Go ahead, Teddy. I'll watch to see how you do." Mr. Madisen turned over the milking to me.

"Talk softly. Hand on hip. Slide down, bend . . ." I found myself still repeating the instructions my father left for me. They helped me focus on the task at hand rather than allowing the fear I had of being kicked dominate my thoughts. With Mr. Madisen watching me, I felt an overwhelming sense of pride in my relationship with Freckles that had been growing somewhere inside. I remember it beginning way back when I stood up to the bully in school who just happened to have freckles. Up until that moment, I realized the fear I had been allowing to control me was only as big as my imagination allowed it to be. Now I had been experiencing the same thing with the freckled cow. My father's instructions and Mr. Madisen's willingness to observe how I had progressed gave me the confidence to slow the pace of free-falling I had been feeling ever since so much had been going on in our family that I could not seem to control. For the moment, I wondered if I was experiencing the free-fall slowing down or if maybe I had been simply maturing.

Mr. Madisen interrupted my thoughts. "Perfect Teddy, you did it perfectly. I think your father would be very proud of you." A few minutes later, I took the milker off of Freckles and poured her milk into the cream can. I thought that Mr. Madisen would be heading home now that I had finished milking Freckles, but to my delight, he continued to help me with the milking. Having someone to talk to made the milking chore a lot easier, and it went so much faster. When we were ready to separate the milk, Mr. Madisen said, "Teddy, I want to go up and see your mother for a minute or two before I go home. Are you okay with finishing up on your own?"

"Sure, I can do it. Thank you again for helping me." I said.

With early morning cow milking, other daily chores, football practice, and doing odd jobs for the Madisens, I didn't have much time to allow my thoughts to do any freelancing. When I did, I wondered how my father was managing. Besides Mr. Madisen, I didn't talk to too many people at any length about how I felt but found I could freely express what I thought and felt in my letters to Maribelle.

> Dear Maribelle,
>
> How are you this week? I am okay, I guess. We went to see my father on Sunday. It has been a week since all of his teeth were pulled out. I told you we would go see him in the letter I wrote Saturday so you will be getting two letters from me this week. I hope that is okay.
>
> Golly, Maribelle, the VA hospital is awful. My father is in a long ward labeled Psychology Ward or Psych Ward. My mom said he's there because his nerves are shot. I guess I am not sure what that means. It must be hard for my mom to explain because she did not tell me much more. I guess I really do not know what the Psych Ward has to do with having your teeth pulled. The ward he is on stinks. There are only curtains separating beds from one another. You can hear moaning, angry words, and even cussing coming from men on the other side of the curtains. I did hear one man saying the Lord's Prayer when we first entered the ward. He was just at "give us

this day our . . ." but we kept going, so I did not hear the rest.

Our football game is this coming Friday. We have been in school for two weeks now. I am sorry, but as I have already explained, I probably will just be a bench warmer. I would really be embarrassed if you saw me sitting on the bench the whole game. The team is in full football gear now. When we have passing exercises, I run out and turn toward the quarterback like everyone else does, but when he throws the ball, I always seem to miss it. The ball hits me in the head or hits one of my shoulders. Sometimes, I run too far out or not enough. Some of the guys laugh at me. I think the coach groans, but he doesn't say anything when I come back in line. I am glad you do not see me. I would really be embarrassed. I am sorry I am not a good football athlete. Maybe next year when I'm fifteen I'll play better and be worth watching.

Sending you my love,

Teddy

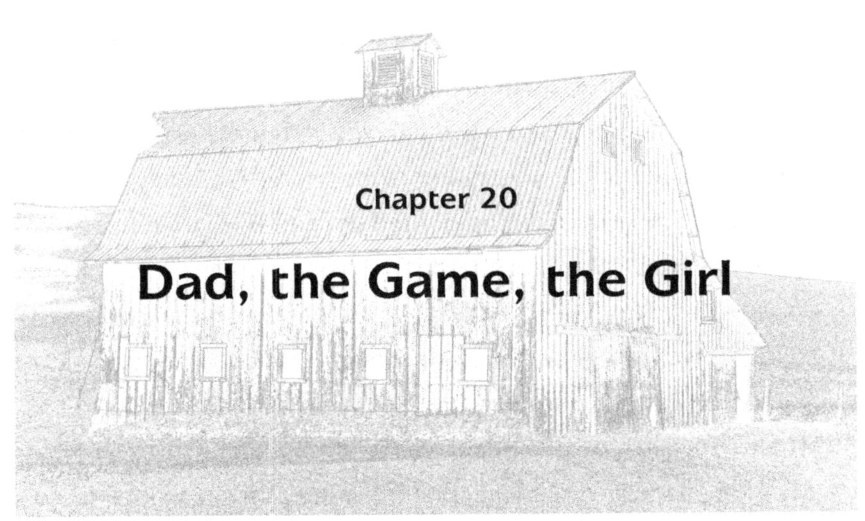

Chapter 20

Dad, the Game, the Girl

Since Thursday night's football practice was shorter because of Friday's game, I arrived home from practice earlier than usual. "Teddy, please help Cindy up to the house. I am going to check how much water is in the cistern," my mom said after she drove the car into the garage. Cindy had already opened the car door and planted her feet firmly on the ground. Reaching out to grasp my hand, the two of us headed for the house.

I apparently interrupted Victoria's phone conversation when I rushed by her with a brotherly yell, "We're home!" and then planted Cindy by her side.

"What's that noise?" the girl on the other end of the phone must have asked Victoria because I heard her answer, "Oh, it's my brother. He just came home from football practice, and wouldn't you know it, he just shoved Cindy right at me. Just a sec Lucy, I need to call my sister. 'Ruby, come and get Cindy!' Okay, now where were we . . . oh yes, I remember . . ."

Before I scurried to change my clothes and go to the barn, I stood out of sight in the hallway to eavesdrop on the rest of the conversation now that I knew Victoria was talking to Maribelle's sister Lucy.

"I don't think I'll tell Teddy that you and Maribelle are coming to the game Friday night. You know Teddy, he'll be nervous. My guy friends tell me he's not much of a ball-handler, and he seldom is able to tackle the ball-carrier when he comes through the defensive line on his right side. If he knew Maribelle was going to be there, I'm really afraid he'd be nervous and embarrassed if he goofed up, and if we aren't ahead, the coach probably won't play him anyway."

Oh my gosh! Maribelle is coming to the game? My heart started to beat so loud I was afraid that Victoria would hear it, so I had to refocus on what was being said and not what I was thinking.

When I settled down, I heard Victoria say, "Well, I had better go, Lucy. My mom just came in and is looking at me as if she wants me to do something or she wants to use the phone."

I rushed up the stairs before Victoria had a chance to see me. *There had been no letter from Maribelle telling me this. Why?* I pondered all the way down the hill to the barn. I greeted Mr. Madisen, who told me he was ready to put the milkers on Goldie and Freckles. Do you want to do one of them?"

"Sure, I'll do Freckles," I answered.

I could tell Mr. Madisen was a little surprised at my choice, but he only said, "That's good, Teddy."

When the milkers picked up their rhythm and milk was flowing, we stood side by side, staring out the barn door into the lot. "Want a piece of Spearmint?" Mr. Madisen asked me as he pulled out a pack of gum and pushed it in my direction.

"Sure," I replied, taking a piece of gum. "I think you like gum. You chew a lot of it," I said as I chewed.

"Well, I got started several years ago when I stopped smoking." Mr. Madisen confessed.

"You smoked?" I was surprised to hear that he had smoked.

"Yes, I did. I never thought it was a nasty habit until I quit."

"Why did you quit?" I asked, and then I began to wonder . . . *If my dad had quit smoking a long time ago, would he be in the hospital now?* "I wish my father had quit."

"I quit when I heard Chet Huntley give a news report on *World News* about the connection between lung cancer and smoking."

"I never heard that. Who is Chet Huntley? I wonder why my father never mentioned him? I wonder if he ever listened to him . . ." My flashing thoughts turned into question after question.

"Whoa, Teddy, not so fast. It's important to understand this business about connecting lung cancer with cigarette smoking was very early in the research. It would have been easy not to give it much thought. Chet Huntley was a newscaster on TV at 5:30 every weeknight. Your dad was probably out milking at that time. I suspect it would have been easy for him to miss what he had to say. It even took a while for articles to show up in the newspapers regarding the connection."

Seconds slipped by before I matter-of-factly announced, "My cousin and I smoked some corn stalks one time. Do you think I could get cancer?"

"I doubt it, Teddy. I really doubt it. We better check those milkers."

There was a new schedule at our house starting that Monday. By the time I finished chores and began walking up the hill to the back porch, Mom was coming out of the house, leaving for her second part-time job. After coming into the house when my chores were done, I tried to help Victoria by keeping an eye on Cindy while Ruby helped Victoria with some of the house chores Mom wrote out for them to do. Ruby and Victoria started dinner before our mom came home from the Extension Office. When it came time to prepare supper, Cindy always wanted to help her sisters. It was Victoria who came up with the idea of giving Cindy some small task like putting the silverware on the table. When she was through, she seemed content to pull up a chair near one of her sisters and supervise their tasks.

I also tried harder and harder not to moan or complain if I thought Victoria and Ruby were not doing enough or if I assumed I was working harder than they were.

After supper, I went upstairs to do some homework. My mom had told us earlier she would be leaving the Extension Office early the next day to go see my father, and Mrs. Madisen offered to go with her to keep her company. I was coming down the stairs to say goodnight when I heard her on the phone. Not wanting to interrupt, I froze on the steps and found myself eavesdropping again. I heard my mother say, "Sam, we came into this marriage for better or worse. You seem to want to be responsible for the worse. I think that is when you shut me out. It is not up to you to take that responsibility on yourself. It is ours to share. We will see this through. We will. Please have faith that we will . . ." I kept listening, unable to turn away.

"I know you still have your faith, Sam. You can't take on farming and raising a family like we have without having any. It might be more helpful, though, if you would practice sharing your faith more with the rest of us. Remember what our pastor said, you don't have to work *harder* at it, you just do it." My Mom paused, then continued. "Sam, something else we have talked about is your relationship with Teddy. He's worried about you. He prays for you, Sam. When he says the dinner prayer, right after he says, 'We thank you, God, for everything,' he adds, 'Please, make my father well. Thank you.' He has so much he wants to share with you, but I think he's afraid to. I think when he messes up or doesn't do things your way, he just really needs your direct assistance. He doesn't need to be yelled at or get the silent treatment from you."

My eyes filled with tears. I could only imagine what my father was thinking on the other end . . . *that I was a big baby.* But then again, maybe I was wrong because I heard my mom say, "I know you love him and are proud of him, Sam. It's so good to hear you say it, though. And I can't wait until you come home again to tell him all of that yourself. I'll see you tomorrow . . ."

I wiped my tears and slowly made my way up to my room. *My dad was proud of me.* In the moment, the thought of his being proud of me was enough to keep me going through everything.

The Oakdale booster club had worked all afternoon preparing a supper for our high school's football team and the cheerleaders.

"Only two, only two," Head Coach Thomas said, pointing to the Sloppy Joes on each player's plate. "I don't want you so full you can't run out on the field."

Of course, all of us players knew we didn't want to make pigs of ourselves in front of the coach or cheerleaders.

In the locker room, an hour later, with everyone suited up, Coach Thomas blew his whistle, and the first and then second team huddled around him. His eyes circled the room several times. *I wonder if he even knows I am here.* I wondered when the coach passed by me the last time.

"Okay, guys, here is the deal, this is our first game of the season, but it will be setting the bar for all the games that follow, and it will give the rest of our conference teams a peek at how tough or weak we are. Who are we?" yelled the head coach.

"We are the Hornets! Mighty, mighty Hornets! You had better run or you'll be stung! Who are we? Hornets! Hornets! That's who!" The whole team had encircled the coaches, and with arms extended over each other's shoulders, we swayed back and forth as we chanted.

After the third round of chanting, the coach held up his hand, and the room was silent once more. "Listen up, guys, the Bull Dogs' first-team is mostly made up of seniors, and all of them were first-team last year. They are tough! Don't underestimate them. They are more than experienced.

They aren't just out to shake you down for your milk money. They want your allowance, as well. You have to play smart. You understand me?"

Taking our lead from Raymond Bradly, our team captain, and quarterback, everyone yelled, "Yes, Coach!"

"Okay, I am asking you to play your best. Your very best. Tonight we set your mark for the season! Take nothing for granted." Coach Thomas's eyes circled the room again and then stopped when they reached Raymond Bradly as if the coach expected him to say something.

Raymond did not disappoint the coach. "We're ready, Coach!" Following Raymond, the team repeated the words. "We're ready, Coach!"

"Yes, yes, you are." With those words, Coach Thomas and his assistant coach motioned for a circle once more, only this time the other coaches joined us as we started to sway back and forth singing our school song. After repeating the song three times, we yelled "Hornets" so loud people outside on the bleachers probably heard us, and then we filed out the locker room door and, led by the coaches, ran out onto the field.

Since I did not hear my name called for receiving or kick-off team, after warmups, including jumping jacks and blocking exercises, I headed for the tail end of the players' bench. If I stood on the bench, I knew I would be able to see everything happening on the field. Following the national anthem, Raymond and the Bull Dogs' team captain plus both teams' coaches met with the refs out in the middle of the field for the coin toss. The opposing team won the toss-up, and they chose to receive the ball.

It took only seconds for the kick-off team to line up on the field while first-team defensive players stood near the coaches, ready for last-minute instructions before they found their places. Meanwhile, spectators, first-team players, and benchwarmers, including me, watched as our star kicker, Jason Bowen, kicked the ball.

As the ball was flying through the air destined for the ten-yard line, Joe Brady, an Oakdale all-star sprinter, and our offensive-end sprinted his way down through the Bull Dogs' front line, following the ball's lead. The Bull Dogs' linebacker had underestimated the power of Jason's kick. Only the tip of the linebacker's right-hand fingers touched the ball, putting it into a tailspin. The ball easily found its way into Joe's outstretched arm. He pulled the ball into his chest like a pro and easily trotted over the Hornets' goalpost before most of the Bull Dogs' team knew what happened. From my bench perch, I saw everything.

The Oakdale team members and crowd went wild! Cheerleaders were cartwheeling; Coach Thomas and Coach Michael smiled at one another, and then Coach Michael turned to the bench and called for the offensive linemen to take their places out on the field while Coach Thomas yelled out directions to Raymond. I can't imagine Raymond heard the coach because of the pandemonium coming from the Hornets' supporters. At the same time, we benchwarmers jumped up and down and landed slaps on our teammates' shoulder pads. When the ball was snapped, I had once again perched myself up on the bench so I could watch the action on the field.

The extra point did not go as well. After the ball was snapped, one of the Bull Dogs' guards bullied his way through the Hornets' offensive line and, with a growl, smashed the quarterback to the ground before he could raise himself up from the center's backside. Raymond lay motionless on the ground after the Bull Dogs' guard backed off. Coach Thomas yelled at the ref who blew his whistle to stop the game. Coach Thomas and Coach Michael rushed out to the field.

Kneeling down, Coach Thomas checked on Raymond and then helped the quarterback onto his feet and started to walk him to the sideline. When they came to the sideline directly in front of me, one of the refs came over and asked, "Is he going to be okay?" The ref was yelling to be heard over the crowd clapping.

"He's okay. He just had the wind knocked out of him," Coach Thomas yelled back.

Taking the opportunity to strategize, the Bull Dogs' coach called his team to the other sidelines. Before the ref blew his whistle for the game to resume, Raymond ran back out onto the field. The home crowd and visitors gave Raymond a standing ovation as the ref blew his whistle and the game resumed.

Right before half time, the Bull Dogs managed to worm their way over the goal line and make a touchdown. The Bull Dogs' offensive line held our team back while their kicker successfully made the extra point. Now the Bull Dogs were ahead by one point—seven to six.

My eyes never left the drama unfolding in front of me. I watched defensive and offensive moves as if I played both sides. I remembered, in their locker room huddle, Coach Thomas told the team the weakest side of the Bull Dogs would be their right side. I was intent on seeing every move play out.

My only distraction from the field was when I made a beeline look directly at Coach Thomas just in case he was signaling me to come and relieve a player from the field. It was then that I saw the crowd in the grandstands beyond where Coach Thomas stood and noticed the Madisens. And . . . *was that my mom and dad? WOW! My dad! How did he get here?*

And as incredible as that was, my heart almost leaped out of my chest when my eyes moved just a little bit more down the line, and I saw Maribelle Larson sitting next to her mom and dad. *My Maribelle!*

With less than two minutes to play, the Bull Dogs had the ball. Ten yards separated them from another touchdown. The only thing that stood in their way was the Hornets' defensive line. Worn, ragged, and tired, our team still held the line and gave the Bull Dogs a hard time. On the third down, when the ball snapped, what sounded like a sharp clap of thunder came from the line. The Bull Dogs made no yardage. They still had ten yards to go. The Bull Dogs' coach used his last time out and called his team over to the sideline.

Coach Thomas also called our team over. As the players came trotting over to the sideline, I could tell both coaches were watching our right defensive wide receiver, Randy Callan, who did not trot but limped his way to the sideline. "What happened, Randy?" Coach Michael asked. All of the players could hear the coach's high-pitched voice, and I strained to hear more.

"I'm not sure, Coach! I think one of their guards clipped me. Then their tackle fell on top of me." Randy grimaced even though he tried hard to hide the pain.

"Can you play?" asked Coach Thomas, walking over to join Coach Michael.

"Sure, Coach, I can play." Randy's eyes moved back and forth between the coaches hoping his positive answer would hide his pain.

"Try to take a couple of steps," Coach Michael instructed.

Randy tried to put his right foot on the ground, but as soon as it touched the grass and he applied a little pressure, he fell toward Coach Michael. While Coach Michael balanced Randy, Coach Thomas looked past his players toward the grandstand for Doc Jones. The doctor had seen Randy limping off the field and was already moving toward them. Coach Thomas could already see Doc was shaking his head, "NO!"

"Randy, go to the locker. Paul and Greg help Randy to the locker. Doctor Jones will meet you there." Randy was no longer insisting he could still play. The pain must have reached his brain and pulsated every time his big toe touched the ground.

As Randy limped away, the ref stood on the sidelines with his hands on his hips and his whistle between his lips, ready to say the time out was over. Both Coaches glanced over to us benchwarmers.

"We need someone to replace Randy," I heard Coach Thomas say as the breeze carried his voice my way. Coach Michael shook his head affirmatively as he also looked toward the bench. "We need someone," repeated Coach Thomas, "Someone." Then, he whispered something to himself.

"What are you thinking?" Coach Michael asked.

"I was wondering about Teddy," Coach Thomas said.

Did he say "Teddy?" I couldn't believe my ears, so I strained to hear more and almost fell off the bench.

"I know he's had his problems at practice," the assistant coach said. "He rarely catches the ball when it comes down on his right side, and too many ball carriers pass by him on that side, but he never lacks enthusiasm."

Yes! That's me. They did say "Teddy!"

Coach Thomas looked directly at me as he spoke. "Every time I looked over at the bench, he's always standing and looking at the teams. See? Just like he is now. Not sure why we haven't tried him before."

I had my helmet on, still standing, eyes fixed directly on Coach Thomas. If my eyes could talk, they'd be saying, "I'm ready, Coach, send me."

"Teddy!" Coach Thomas called and then turned his attention back to the field, seeing the ref with his whistle in his mouth and a look of impatience on his face.

"Yes, Coach!" I yelled as I enthusiastically darted the short distance to the coach. I would have landed on top of him had the coach not grabbed a hold of my shoulder pads.

"I want you to take Randy's position in the backfield. We need to hold them, Teddy. Stay alert! Watch their backfield! We can't let them make any more points. If we hold them and get the ball, we will have a few seconds to get into field goal range. Watch the backfield! Got it?"

"Got it, Coach!" I felt the coach's right hand give me a shove, and I ran out onto the field. Just as soon as I took Randy's place as defensive wide receiver, the ref blew his whistle.

The Hornets were well prepared, or so we thought. As soon as the front line was in position and the Bull Dogs' quarterback yelled, "Hut one—" the center snapped the ball to the quarterback. The quarterback wasted no time passing the ball off to the left wide receiver. Ball in hand, the Bull Dogs' receiver started to sidestep. At the same time, the right wide receiver raced down the field.

Our defensive front line was caught off guard by the speed of the ball passing out of the quarterback's hands. Everyone in the defensive backfield chased after the left receiver except for me. Just before he went smashing to the ground after being tackled by players from the Hornets' backfield, the receiver let the ball fly through the air.

Before telling my feet to move, my brain pulled back on the reins and demanded my eyes to follow the right receiver. *He's moving too fast away from the entanglement on the front line . . . very sneaky. Watch him, Teddy.* I started out on a run toward the right receiver. When the Bull Dogs' right receiver and I were about ten feet apart, the receiver started a sideways move. At the same time, he and I both saw the ball fly out of the left receiver's hands. With hands up high, the right receiver reached for the ball. Maybe it was the wind, maybe it was the passer's miscalculation, or maybe it was the right receiver's overreach. It didn't matter. In the blink of an eye, the ball hit and bounced sideways off the receiver's shoulder pad and landed in my outstretched hands just as I reached the Bull Dogs' side. The ball was in my hands!

I knew exactly what to do. The coaches' words were burned into my brain. *Ball in hand, pull it tight to your rib cage, bury it, run!* Since most of the Bull Dogs and Hornets were on the ground or on the right side of the field, I had a clearance to run for miles. I took off.

When Coach Thomas realized what happened, he yelled at the linemen and backfield players who were still on their feet, "Protection! Protection!"

At first, the Hornet fans were stunned by the rapid ball change. When they came to their senses, they turned their attention to the runner—me. Some even looked at their program to see who number twenty-seven was.

The Halls, Madisens, and Larsons, especially Maribelle, had no need to look at their program. They all knew it was me. "Run, Teddy! Run, Teddy!" They yelled in unison.

The Hornets' cheerleaders did summersaults and jumped up and down while shouting with the team's benchwarmers, "Run, Teddy, Run!" The Oakdale announcer, surprised by the excitement of it all, screamed over the sound system, "Well, I'll be! Who is that? Folks, it's number twenty-seven, Teddy Hall! Well, I'll be!"

Coach Thomas let out an "Unbelievable!" Then, he too started to yell, "Go, Teddy! Run Teddy! Protection! Give that man protection!"

I didn't really hear any of that. I was running ran as fast as I could, hugging the ball, knowing I was not the best runner on the team. In fact, I was far from it. I knew chances were high that I most likely would trip over my own two feet like I usually do, but not this time. My feet were landing one at a time on solid ground, step after step after step. Closer to the goal post, my good eye captured a galloping Bull Dog just yards away from me. I kept running. I passed the twenty-yard line. Once again, the Bull Dog was in my sight. I passed the ten-yard line. *Keep running. Do not look! Keep running!* my brain told my feet.

As my brain talked, Hornet Number Three came up to the same side as his adversary Bull Dog. Number Three was the number one bully on our first team. He never missed the opportunity to tease me or push me around during practices.

It was different now. As he came up between the Bull Dog and me, I heard him yell, "All the way, Teddy! All the way!"

It took me several feet past the goal post before my feet realized the run was over. I made it! The buzzer buzzed, and the game was over! The Hornets won! Number Three and the right tackle lifted me to their shoulders. The coaches and my teammates formed two lines and chanted, "Teddy, Teddy!" as I passed by. From the top of my teammates' shoulders, I could see Maribelle, my parents, the Madisens and Larsons. I waved.

Reaching the edge of the field, I slipped off my teammate's shoulders, and we all headed back to the center of the field where the Hornets and Bull Dogs coaches and players shook each other's hands.

"Good game, good game," we all said.

"Hey kid, you're a good runner!" a Bull Dog yelled at me.

"I was lucky!" I yelled back.

After congratulations and cheers from the Hornets' fans, our team was gathered back in the locker room. Having showered, we were ready to head for the after-game dance.

Before we all left, the coaches huddled our team one more time. "You played a good game tonight, guys!" Coach Thomas shouted. "The next one will be harder! The Raiders will be ready for us. But for now, you all deserve credit for a good game. No one stands above the other. Right, Teddy?"

"Absolutely, Coach! We're a team! We all land on the same ground!" I yelled.

"You did a good job tonight," Coach Thomas said, giving me credit for the touchdown play.

"We all did, Coach. We're a team." I repeated.

"Yes, we are." Coach Thomas smiled as his eyes took a broad sweep across the locker room, and then he added, "Okay guys, all of you, get to the dance!" The locker room cleared out fast, all except for me and Coach Thomas.

"Is something on your mind, Teddy?" Coach Thomas asked.

"Yeah, Coach. I . . . I am a little afraid I might never be able to do what I did tonight again. I think I caught that ball by luck. I don't want to disappoint you, my father or—"

"Teddy, wait a minute. I don't think you're giving yourself enough credit." Coach Thomas sat down on the bench along the locker room wall and motioned for me to sit down next to him. He continued, "I've seen you do this before. What I mean is, you were studying. I don't know exactly how you did it, but you studied the field before I called you out. I think that all through the game, you were watching plays and players, theirs and ours. I don't think that you moving in a direction different from your teammates was by chance. You knew what you were doing."

"But Coach—" I started to object, but the coach wouldn't let me finish.

"Listen to me, Teddy. Tonight, you did well. No, you might not always do well, but tonight you did. Sure, you have a difficult time catching the ball and seeing the opponent slip by you sometimes. I think in time you will outthink those difficulties. You did it tonight, and you'll do it again. You taught me something tonight, Teddy."

"Coach, I . . . What could I ever teach *you?*"

"You reminded me. The best ball catchers or the best tacklers are eventually more apt to take what they do for granted or to think that they're doing everything on their own. I don't think you will ever do that. All I'm asking is that you continue to try. Don't give up thinking. Who knows, Coach Michael and I might need to call on you sometime to help us analyze our plays and performance. Now, for goodness sake, get to the dance. Have some fun."

For some reason, I felt better. I knew I would continue to try, and I decided to let the rest of my worries get lost. I shook Coach's hand, thanked him, and was out the door.

When I found my way to the hall in front of the gym, my mom and dad, the Madisens, Mr. and Mrs. Larsen, Lucy and Victoria, and especially Maribelle, were waiting for me. After congratulations, hugs, and a big bear hug from my father, we kids were off to the dance while the adults headed for the diner to grab coffee and pie.

After a few dances, me and Maribelle went outside f*or a breath of fresh air.* I remembered hearing Lucy and Victoria say that when kids wanted to just talk or hold hands or maybe let the magical romance of the evening have its way, they went outside for a breath of fresh air. They had also warned, "If you don't come back into the dance by a reasonable time, a chaperone comes outside just to make sure you are breathing, and you're standing upright."

On our way out, we met Lucy and Victoria. Lucy congratulated me one more time. Before Victoria could do the same, I gave her a whopping hug and said, "Thank you!"

"What's that for, famous brother?" Victoria asked.

"I think you know," I replied. "You and Lucy are the greatest!"

Victoria returned my hug. "Right back at ya!"

Later, when we were all alone sitting on the steps outside the gym, Maribelle took a hold of my hand. "Teddy, we are moving back to Oakdale. Mom and Dad are buying the hardware store. Our Oakdale house hasn't been sold, so that's where we'll live. Everything will go back in the house right where it was before. Teddy, I mean *everything* will be back in place—it will be like we never left."

"Moving back! You are? You are! That's great! That means we can err . . ." I paused, not sure I should continue what my brain wanted to burst out and tell Maribelle and the whole world. I decided it would be now or never, "That means you'll still be my girlfriend, and I'll be your boyfriend. I mean, if—" I stopped. I didn't need to say more. I had said what I wanted to say. What my brain was urging me to say. Everything seemed so perfect up to this point. I wondered if maybe it was too perfect. *What will Maribelle say? Do I even want to hear what she might say?* I did think I stood on solid ground. *But then again . . .* I tried not to overthink it, though. I didn't want to miss the magic of it all.

"Teddy, you're silly. I have always been your girlfriend, always." Reaching up to where I sat, Maribelle gave me a kiss on the cheek.

"Golly, Maribelle, I was hoping you would be my girlfriend. Now I know you are, but when we go back into the dance, and if you want to dance with someone else, I will understand. I mean—"

"Teddy," interrupted Maribelle, "I only want to dance with you."

Saturday came sooner than expected. Maribelle and her family headed back to the city to make final arrangements for their move.

My father and I did all of the chores together. While the milkers hummed away, Dad had things to talk to me about like he had never done before. He told me about some of the good and some of the not too good experiences he had growing up. He opened his heart a little bit more and talked about what he was coming to understand better, with the help of my mother, about our relationship. He even spoke about his marriage and told me about how he met my mother and what they did when they were dating.

"Teddy, your mom and I were pretty young when we first started to date. We both graduated from Spring Brook Country School."

"You went to a country school, Dad? I never knew that."

"Yes, we did. I always thought your mom was kind of special, and I think I had a crush on her, but I never told her."

"Why not, Dad?"

"Well, as you know, sadly to say, I am rather quiet most of the time. Back then, I was even quieter. I guess you can say I was shy, very shy, but your mom wasn't." A wide smile crossed my dad's face when he told me that.

"If you were shy, how did you ever let Mom know you liked her?"

"Teddy, just like you write Maribelle letters, I wrote notes to your mom expressing my undying love, but I never signed them. When I dared look her way and saw her reading one of them, I blushed.

"Aww, Dad, I have never seen you blush. You actually blushed? WOW!"

"Remember Teddy, I was shy."

"You must have been really shy, Dad, but I guess I am shy sometimes, or at least when I'm around girls, I would say," I confessed. "What happened after you two graduated?"

"Well, we were both in 4-H, which was the only extracurricular activity my sister and brother, who lived on our family farm and raised me after our parents' died, allowed me to join.

"Oh—" before I could ask anything about my father being raised by his brother and sister, he went on. "As it was, your mom and I were in the same 4-H club. When we went to the fair, our calves were penned right next to each other. When I finished caring for my calf, I helped your mom with hers, and one thing led to another. Next thing you know, we were dating and planning our lives together.

"Hmmm . . . imagine that. I guess if you weren't allowed to have been in 4-H, you and Mom would have never been married, and . . ." I was pondering the possibilities, but my dad interrupted me.

"Teddy, I guess when you care really deeply for someone, you always find a way to make that caring come to life. When it comes to your mom, I would have found a way."

"Golly, Dad, that's quite a story. Thanks for telling me. I mean, thanks!"

"Teddy, your mom and I had a heart to heart talk over the phone the other night. I believe I really need to tell you about it."

"Okay, Dad." I could actually feel how hesitant my words were coming out of my mouth.

"Your mom says I always seem to expect the worst of things. I guess I do. We seem to have more bad than good luck lately, and I want to blame myself. She says that's when I shut her out. She also says we came into our marriage for better or worse and that it is not up to me to always take responsibility for the worse but that both are ours to share. And that we will see this through if we continue to have faith."

My father grew very quiet, so I didn't say anything either. We were so quiet, we could even hear the cows' tails swishing in rhythm with the milkers humming. I had grown used to my dad being quiet for long periods of time when we were together, but this was a different kind of quiet. It's a quiet that comes after someone has shared something very personal and you need time to think over what you heard before you say anything. Maybe you just need time to let their words find a place in your brain or heart, and you do not need to respond at all. Remember when I told you once that when two men are together and they talk about personal stuff, when there is a pause they need something to do with their hands and mouths, so they take another drink of coffee or take a puff on their cigarette, or if they are out in the newly disked field, they might kick a clod of dirt? This is one of those times.

I made the first move, so for the want of something to do, I went up and felt Spotty's milk bag. She was done. I pulled the milker off, and as I walked toward my dad and the cream can, I said, "We are ready for the next group of cows, Dad."

Smiling, my dad nodded his head in agreement. As he let the cows out, I put the feed down for the next group. It took only a few minutes for us to lock in the new batch of cows and start the milkers humming again. When we saw milk running through the tubes into the milk pails, we returned to our previous places behind the cows, where we had a good view of both machines and cows.

Then my dad surprised me by telling me about plans for our future. First, I have to say, you know how it is when you are studying for a test in a subject you think is really boring, and you don't like it much—you usually don't end up with a very good grade on the test; however, if it is a subject you really like, you study, and you receive really high marks. Well, that's how it is when I pull conversations out of my brain. The really bad stuff I bury somewhere deep in the bottom of my brain, but the really good stuff, I can recite almost word for word. What my dad told me was really good stuff, and I remember it very well. It didn't seem like my dad had much problem telling me about Mr. Madisen's visit.

"Teddy, I don't know if your mother told you or not, but Charles came to see me the other day."

"I think Mom said Mr. Madisen was going to bring you home."

"Well, actually, he came another time, as well. He came shortly after I had my teeth pulled, and I was given a pain pill, so we only had a brief time to talk, but we packed a lot in the time we had.

"Oh, I am not sure I knew that."

"Well, I think your mom and the Madisens wanted to keep it a secret until I told you directly."

"Okay, Dad, what is it?" I didn't know if I should prepare to feel happy or sad.

"First, he told me that Jack had false teeth."

"I couldn't tell. Huh, I didn't know that." I really didn't know, but I wasn't sure what that had to do with my dad, except he would be having false teeth also. I guess in retrospect, it was what people would call an "ice-breaker."

"Charles told me Jack's experience wasn't any picnic, so he was really surprised I was doing so well. But Teddy, what I really want to tell you is this—Mr. and Mrs. Madisen are considering buying the sale barn on F Avenue in Council Bluffs, but they won't if things don't fall into place. When I asked him what needed to happen, I was stunned to hear his answer."

"Well, Dad, what did he say?" My dad's telling me this was something like a suspense story I might be watching on TV and a commercial comes on. I wanted to get right back to the story.

"Teddy, Charles told me Jack is going to auctioneering school in Kansas City, and if I apply for a rehab scholarship, I could attend at the same time. Charles thought we both have an excellent eye for livestock and could run the auction. We would also sell some of our own livestock we buy direct from cattle raisers or buy at the sale barn if the price is right, and proceeds would go into the dividends we all would share. Jack and I would be paid a salary, and eventually, we could buy Charles out. We would hire Joyce to be our clerk, and Patricia was going to talk to your mom to see if she agreed they could run the café together. Teddy, this means we could stay on the farm."

"What did you and Mom say, Dad?"

My dad gave me a mischievous smile, the kind I use to see on his face years ago. "What do you think we said, son?"

"I hope you said 'YES,' Dad." I held my breath waiting for his answer.

"That we did, Teddy! That we did!"

"Look, Dad, it's time to change the milkers." And so we did. The rest of our chores went by without any problems and all, it was a very good and surprising evening.

Time goes by rather quickly when you are at peace with yourself, the world seems right side up, and your heart is filled with joy. That afternoon over pie and coffee, the Madisens, Jack, and my family, including me, discussed how the partnership in the sale barn would actually work. Everyone agreed with the plan regarding Dad and Jack attending auctioneering school in Kansas City. I was surprised and pleased to know they agreed I could attend the junior course. Another good thing was that no one said a word to me when I put a second piece of pie on my plate.

"Working with us will be a good way for you to earn money to help pay for your college," my dad told me.

College! I thought, *WOW!* Lately, I hadn't been thinking that far in the future, but it sounded pretty good to me.

"We will have horse sales on Monday evenings, on Saturdays the regular livestock sales, and then you can help us in the summer with the horses when you can. We'll keep you busy, Teddy!" Mr. Madisen said.

"That is if you don't fall behind in your schoolwork, son," my father added.

"What do you say, Teddy. Are you up to the challenge? Mr. Madisen asked.

"Wow! Yes, of course! I like all of what you said. I promise to keep up with school, Dad." I suddenly felt like the luckiest kid on the planet. "Thank you all. I feel really blessed."

"Yes, we all are blessed!" my mom said.

"Amen to that," Mrs. Madisen echoed.

"AMEN!" I shouted.

When the last day of the week, Sunday, came around after milking and cleaning up, all of us Halls headed for church. After taking Cindy to junior church, Mom and Dad went to the adult Bible study, Ruby joined her friends in the junior high class, and Victoria and I went to the high school class where we found Mrs. Kates waiting for us.

When we all settled into our seats and the gossip had taken its course, Mrs. Kates explained, "Mrs. Marcel wanted to take a break and go to the adult class, so I'm going to be your teacher. Some of you may have had these lessons in the junior high class, but now we will look at them just a little differently. I do not think it will hurt any of us to repeat a lesson when it comes to the Bible and how to apply it today. Okay, class, turn to Genesis: 32:22-32. Will someone read the verses for us?"

After what seemed like a prolonged silence, my sister said, "I will."

"Good. Go ahead, Victoria," Mrs. Kates said.

Victoria read with the eloquence of someone doing a reading at a speech contest. When she came to verse twenty-six, where Jacob asks to receive a blessing, Mrs. Kates said, "Stop there, Victoria. Before Victoria reads any further, I want to ask, have any of you received a blessing this week?"

As usual, no hands went up. Like everyone else, it seemed I was sitting on my hands, but my brain was very busy, nonetheless. *Blessings, hmmm . . . blessings . . . yes! Boy, have I ever! Touchdown Friday night; Number Three lifting me up on his shoulders; Mom and Dad's partnership with the Madisens and Jack; Dad and me going to auctioneering school; mention of college; working with the horses; Maribelle moving back to Oakdale! Boy, I am lucky! I have a bushel full of blessings!*

Since no hand was rising, Mrs. Kates turned to my sister. "Victoria, what blessings have you received this week?"

"Yes, well, ahem . . . okay, I will start. I received blessings this week. First, my best friend, Lucy, is moving back to Oakdale, and my little err . . . I mean my famous brother won the game for us Friday night with his touchdown." The class did not wait to hear whether she had any more blessings or not. The word "touchdown" created a release of hooting, cheering, and clapping from the usual tongue-tied and lips-sealed class.

From the mirror in my mind, I saw my face turn red, and a wide grin came along for the ride. Mrs. Kates allowed for a few minutes of pandemonium. When the class had it all out of their system, she continued to go around the circle asking for blessings. Mary Beth came after Victoria.

"My Aunt may come to visit us this week. She is my favorite Aunt," said Mary.

Greg was next. "I received a new bike. It wasn't my birthday or a late Christmas present, and the tooth fairy didn't leave it for me. My folks just bought it for me."

Then came my turn. I would not have any problems reciting the litany of blessings I had received. Before my lips could move, though, I had a second "think." I remembered my thoughts and feelings when it felt like I was free-falling and did not know what would happen next. The free-falling and all that it included did not feel like a blessing at the time, but now I could look back and see how it had been, after all. So I wrapped all of my blessings in one. "I've landed on my own two feet with God's help and everyone who God sent to help me."

Before I fell asleep that evening, I said my nighttime prayer that included the review of all my blessings. Then I ended with something simple but heartfelt. "God, I don't know what tomorrow may bring. I may have joy or sorrow, success or failure, trial or jubilation, but I am going to keep my trust in You. I am blessed. Amen."

I used to believe that Sunday was the last day of the week but, as I gave the whole week business another "think," I figured maybe Mrs. Kates was right all along. With all of my blessings and landing my two feet on solid ground, I have come to understand that Sunday truly is a new beginning and indeed is the first day of the week. *Just thinking.*

Meet the Author

Wayne Clark is a retired United Methodist minister. He has been a member of the Iowa conference UMC under appointment for forty-two years. Wayne has had a dual career in parish ministry and as a therapist. He has served congregations in Iowa as a pastor and as a District Superintendent and appointments beyond the local church.

Wayne has a Doctor of Ministry focusing on Pastoral Psychotherapy with special interest in the impact genetics has on couples and families. He also has certification in Pastoral Counseling from Care and Counseling, St. Louis, Missouri. Before retiring full-time, Wayne was an approved supervisor in the American Association for Marriage and Family, a Diplomate in the American Association of Pastoral Counselors, and a licensed Marriage and Family Therapist. Wayne has been published in professional journals and magazines. He has given presentations at national and regional conferences for AAMFT and AAPC, Hospice, and the United Methodist Board of Ministry.

Since retirement, Wayne has volunteered in numerous ways but particularly enjoyed his work with a local therapeutic horse riding program designed for children and adults.

Wayne wrote his first Christmas Storybook in 1977 followed by stories every year since. He folds messages for both children and adults into each story.

Wayne's wife, Susan, is a retired nurse. They have two children: Nathan and Nicole Jones. Nicole's husband, Andrew, is also an important part of their lives. Wayne and Susan live in Ankeny, Iowa, where Wayne maintains a small counseling practice and continues to write.

Wayne's Christmas Books

Christmas in Stories is collection of Wayne's stories, written for those who yearn to be drawn back into the deeper meaning of the season. Each story is poised to greet readers (young and old) who will turn these pages throughout the Christmas season. The stories are heard best if read aloud by a grandparent to a child or by a child reading to a parent who sets aside the busyness of the season and listens with an open heart.

It is his fondest hope that you find your place in one or all of the stories. Maybe it will be through a character, a theme, the narrative, or dialogue that draws you into its pages and allows you to become part of the story. Whatever resonates, may you experience the transforming power and love that the miracle of Christmas has for you. Get ready for *Christmas in Stories* to shine a light upon your heart through imagination.

Potato Christmas is a most unusual story. The setting is a rural community in Ireland at the tail end of the Potato Famine (1845-1851) and a few years following the famine. While the famine affected the total population, those who suffered the most were the poor. Many were tenant farmers and farm laborers; however, sorrow and grief and the pain of loss were suffered by all classes.

Since the beginning of time, stories have revealed core beliefs, cultural values, trials, struggles, successes, and what the heart treasures. From generation to generation, stories have given us a glimpse into the lives of those who came before us. Stories deep within Christian tradition help us to better understand our own personal journeys as we walk by the light of faith.

In the broken places of our spirit, we find our strength. In the darkest of nights, a light shines to guide us to a new day, but only through the eyes of faith can the light be seen. Natural or human-made forces bent on destroying the human spirit can never defeat those who truly believe that on a distant night in the small town of Bethlehem a child was born. This child, Christ our Lord and Savior, is the greatest gift and act of love ever given. All we have to do is accept it and live out a life that practices giving to those we know, those we meet, and the stranger who comes our way. Potato Christmas will set the tone for your holiday season to be especially meaningful.

Order Info

Available from amazon.com
or your favorite bookstore

For autographed books
or to schedule speaking engagements, contact

M. Wayne Clark
suespruce@aol.com
515.964.5119

For bulk orders, contact
Candy Abbott
Fruitbearer Publishing, LLC
302.856.6649 • FAX 302.856.7742
info@fruitbearer.com
www.fruitbearer.com
P.O. Box 777, Georgetown, DE 19947

Made in the USA
Columbia, SC
18 January 2021